AEON LEGION

LABYRINTH

BOOK 1 IN THE AEON LEGION SERIES

BY J.P. F

D1502135

©2016 by Joseph Beaubien

1st Edition

Published by Steel Hoplite Publishing

v1.5

CONTENTS

MAP OF TIME

WEST
INDUST
REVOLU

1600 AD

THET.
1300 AD   1600 AD
THETA

ZETA
RECONQUISTA

1200 AD

THE EDGE

600 AD   600 AD   600 AD

ALPHA
PERSIAN REBIR

BETA

THE BEGINNING
OF TIME

0 AD   800 AD
12 BILLION BC   0 AD

100 MILLION BC   0 AD

ZETA   DELTA
THE
12000 BC   PUNIC
WARS

4000 BC   DELTA
265 BC

150 BC
ALEXANDER'S
CONQUESTS   PI

ALPHA   CHINESE VOYAGES
OF EXPLORATION
NU   200 BC
PI   RH

500 AD
NU
THE EDGE

1300-1500 AD
ISLAMIC INVASION
OF INDIA

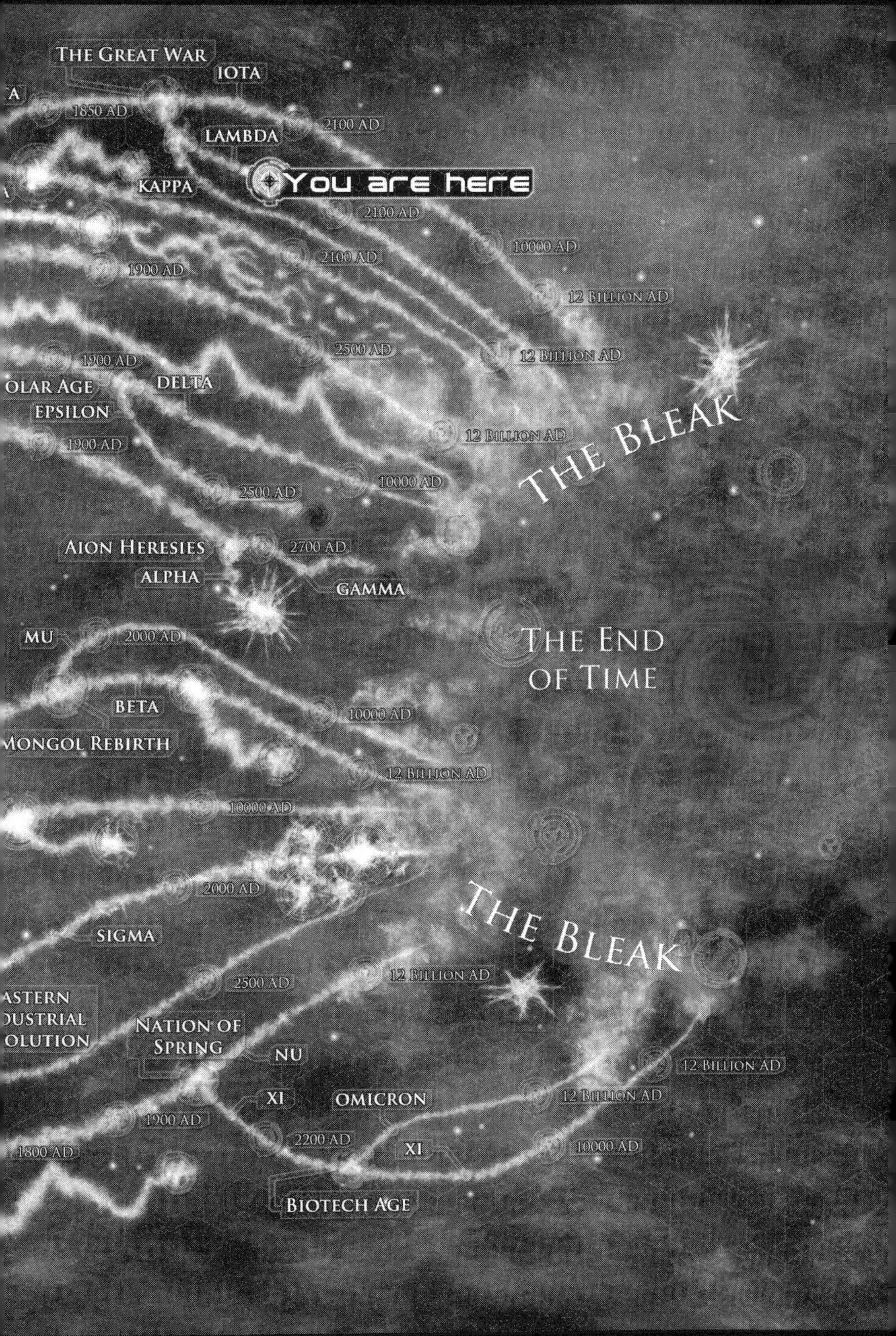
The Great War
IOTA
1850 AD
LAMBDA
2100 AD
KAPPA
You are here
2100 AD
10000 AD
2100 AD
1900 AD
12 Billion AD
2500 AD
12 Billion AD
1900 AD
DELTA
EPSILON
12 Billion AD
1900 AD
The Bleak
10000 AD
2500 AD
Aion Heresies
2700 AD
ALPHA
GAMMA
MU
2000 AD
The End
of Time
BETA
10000 AD
Mongol Rebirth
12 Billion AD
10000 AD
2000 AD
The Bleak
SIGMA
2500 AD
12 Billion AD
Nation of
Spring
NU
12 Billion AD
XI
OMICRON
12 Billion AD
1900 AD
2200 AD
10000 AD
1800 AD
XI
Biotech Age

ΌΣΟΝ ΖΗΙΣ, ΦΑΊΝΟΥ,
"While you live, shine,
ΜΗΔΕΝ ΌΛΩΣ ΣΥ ΛΥΠΟΥ
have no grief at all;
ΠΡΌΣ ΌΛΊΓΟΝ ΈΣΤΙ ΤΌ ΖΗΝ,
life exists only for a short while,
ΤΌ ΤΈΛΟΣ Ό ΧΡΌΝΟΣ ΆΠΑΙΤΕΊ.
and time demands its toll."

-The Epitaph of Seikilos.

CHAPTER I
UNEXPECTED VILLAIN

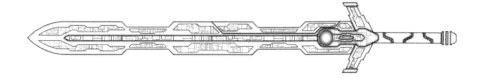

A quiet day of surfing the internet at the local library was interrupted when Nazis kicked in the front door.

Terra Mason frowned, glancing up from her seat at a computer next to the geology section she saw several armed men wearing Nazi uniforms storm into the library. She froze as her mind tried to comprehend what she was seeing.

The librarian marched up to the soldiers. She faced one of the taller Nazis and pointed a finger at his face. "Not funny, young man. Go somewhere else for your little reenactment. This is a public library, not a theater."

The soldier gestured to behind the counter and said something Terra did not understand. She assumed he spoke German, but was not really sure. While she could not understand his words, Terra did study the man. He didn't seem like a reenactor to her. The only World War II reenactors she had seen were at the neighboring town's history festival and most were Middle aged, pot-bellied Americans with bad postures and fake accents. These lean and fit young men moved with a soldier's precise discipline.

"Oh very funny," the librarian said. She pulled out her cell phone. "I'm calling the police."

A nearby soldier regarded the librarian's phone with wide eyes as she dialed. He pointed at the phone and barked an order in German.

The tall soldier in front of the librarian snatched the phone from the librarian's hands, dropped it on the floor and crushed it under his boot. He pointed, again, behind the counter and spoke. His words were harsher this time.

The librarian scowled. "My cell phone!"

The soldier shot her a dark glare. Unable to get his point across, the Nazi chose the universal language of violence. He aimed his rifle in the air and fired, shattering a section of the glass skylight.

The library patrons fell silent as the clink of the bullet casing echoed on the hard floor. Again, he pointed to behind the library counter then put a finger to his lips.

A new order of implied violence settled over the library. Confronted with a real gun, the pale faced librarian made no further protests and the library patrons offered no further resistance as the Nazis herded them behind the checkout counter.

Terra slid from her seat and hid behind a nearby marble pillar, taking care not to draw attention to herself while trying to keep her panic in check. This wasn't how her day was supposed to go. At the urging of her favorite teacher, Mr. Alden Smith, Terra had volunteered to help shelve books at the library after school. In truth, she hoped to avoid her parents' endless pestering about finding a good college in the face of her looming graduation. Now she was trapped with a bunch of armed lunatics.

She peeked from behind the pillar to count at least a dozen soldiers, with two more entering from the front and moving into the open reading area at the library's heart.

More soldiers moved around a large sunlit statue of the Greek goddess Nike that stood under a wide glass skylight. They searched between the labyrinth of bookshelves for stray patrons. A pair moved between the large marble pillars near the perimeter of the library while others deployed a machine gun nest in one corner.

Terra felt her heart race. They had guns, real guns! She forced herself to keep calm in spite of a rising panic. Then she remembered her cell phone. She hadn't even started dialing when she head a soft click behind her; the noise a rifle made when chambering a round. Her sudden turn caused the soldier to aim his rifle right at her face. She stood as motionless as stone.

While keeping his gaze on Terra he called to the other soldiers in German.

The Nazi looked Terra over, his posture tense and his weapon still pointed at her. Worn jeans and a stained jacket marked her as much a civilian as her nonathletic pear shaped body and slightly hunched posture. Terra's youthful sunburned face had a dusting of freckles across her nose while her hair was deep brown, messy and cut short just above her shoulders.

Terra's frightened expression put the solider at ease. He lowered his rifle after taking her cell phone away.

The Nazi motioned with his rifle, pointing to the crowd of patrons gathered behind the checkout desk. Terra put her hands up and began walking.

She eyed the Nazi intruders as the soldier escorted her to the checkout counter. Their gear appeared used, well maintained, and functional. She noted the R shaped runic insignia on the collar of their steel-gray uniforms. Most carried rifles. One was armed with a flame thrower while another wore a sword at his belt. Each soldier wore a strange device on his belt; a flat and round metal plate shaped device with a convex glass light. Its glass face glowed a bright green. The device reminded Terra of an oversized pocket watch.

The soldier escorted Terra to the other patrons. Those gathered were the usual library goers. Terra looked around to observe what the intruders were doing.

A soldier set up a tall antenna like device on a tripod base. A green glowing light on the top hummed in unison with a luminous, rhythmic pulse that grew faster as the soldier backed away. It glowed bright green before a flash of light filled the library.

From where the antenna had stood a sphere of green light burst, its edges crackling with electrical bolts. The sphere grew to fifteen paces in diameter before a pair of German soldiers wearing pitch black goggles emerged from the glowing portal. They dragged a wheeled anti-tank cannon behind them. As they left the light, the soldiers discarded their goggles before loading the cannon. They wheeled it to one side before turning over book shelves to set up a makeshift fortification.

The patrons gasped while Terra stared with awe, the afterimage still flashing in her eyes. *What is that?* she wondered. *Fireworks? Projectors? CGI?* She couldn't deny the strange sight. These Nazis had appeared from nowhere.

Another half dozen soldiers swarmed from the glowing sphere. As the last group emerged, one stood out. Terra recognized him by the twin lightning bolt symbol on the collar of his black uniform. A soldier of the

SS. He carried some kind of long, heavy weapon with a grenade at the tip. Terra guessed it was a launcher of some kind?

The soldiers then made way and stood at attention. One more Nazi emerged before the sphere dissipated with a loud, screeching crack. The carpet edges were singed where it had met the sphere and a faint smell of smoke now hung the air.

The Nazis saluted the newcomer. Terra felt surprised to see a traditional military salute, rather than the Nazi salute she often saw on documentaries.

This newcomer appeared to be in his thirties with a rectangular, clean shaven face. He removed his officer's peaked cap to reveal his neatly parted, dark brown hair. He wore a blue-gray officer's long coat with a rank insignia Terra didn't recognize. An even pattern of polished medals and insignias hung on his well pressed uniform with an "R" runic insignia on the collar. His belt holstered a pistol and in his left hand he carried a large pocket watch with a green glowing face. He hung the watch at his belt and surveyed the area. The sincere smile would have made him charming, even handsome in spite of his precise military bearing, if not for the red Nazi armband he wore.

There was a brief exchange between the soldiers and the officer. The officer spoke in a calm, inquisitive tone while the soldiers explained.

A young child among the patrons started sobbing and unfortunately drew the officer's attention. He smile and pointed to the child before uttering something in German.

The soldier nearest to the child put his hand on a holstered pistol. Terra and the other patrons gasped. She didn't even have time to react as the soldier thumbed his weapon. Then to her surprise the soldier reached past his gun to pull out a small package. He unwrapped it to reveal a candy bar.

"Chocolate?" the soldier asked with a heavy accent. He smiled as he offered it to the child.

The patrons stared silently at the soldiers, their expressions a mixture of shock and horror.

The soldier with the chocolate leaned back, his brow furrowed. He looked to the officer, expectant. The officer issued orders in a soft, confident tone before the soldiers guarding the patrons dispersed. He said something to the SS soldier. The SS soldier glared for a moment then stalked away.

The officer turned to the patrons and approached with hands clasped behind his back. His smile appeared genuine. "I apologize," he said. His English had only a faint German accent. "I do not intend to keep you here long, but we must ask you to remain here to avoid further complications. Rest assured, we have no intention of harming you and we will be out of your way soon."

The patrons exchanged nervous glances while the child trembled. Terra wondered when the nice guy act would disappear.

Another silent moment passed. The officer's smile lessened. After a moment he cleared his throat. "My apologies again. I should introduce myself. I am Hanns Joachim Speer, commander of the German Zeit-macht and I am from your past. I have come from the year 1940 by way of time travel."

Hanns smiled again as if waiting for questions. None came.

Terra raised an eyebrow. *Time travel?* she thought. *What kind of trick is this?*

Hanns cleared his throat again and muttered something under his breath. His gaze searched the crowd. "If I may ask a favor, could someone tell me the current year and location? Given the language, I believe this to be the United States."

The patrons answered Hanns's question with blank stares as room's oppressive silence filled the pauses between his questions. Footsteps made by patrolling soldiers and the occasional soft click of weapons stood out all the more in the awkward quiet.

"Anyone?" Hanns asked as his gaze searched the gathered patrons. "Anyone at all?"

Terra wondered if, perhaps, Hanns felt accustomed to people being more friendly with him. His charm did little to set them at ease when he dressed like a villain from an old war movie.

Hanns frowned again after another moment of silence. "Why do you stare at me like I'm a monster?"

"How can you not know?" Terra whispered, thinking out loud.

Hanns heard and his gaze snapped straight to her. "Excuse me?" he said, forcing a smile. Hanns looked relieved to find someone who would talk.

Terra tensed before forcing herself still. "I guess you couldn't know," she said, having to force out the words.

A soldier approached Hanns and stood at attention and reported.

Hanns listened to the report. He then nodded, dismissing the soldier and looking at his watch again. "So it would seem our enemy has not shown yet," He said before looking back up to Terra and smiling. "Young lady, would you mind accompanying me?" Hanns asked, gesturing to the library shelves.

Hanns gave Terra a reassuring smile and stood with hand outstretched, like a gentleman offering a dance to a lady. She frowned before following Hanns.

They walked to a stack of bookshelves while Terra observed the soldiers' activities. They had set up a machine gun in one corner and a wheeled cannon near the bathrooms. The rest of the soldiers patrolled the outer perimeter of the library.

The soldiers ignored the patrons. Their wary sight darted around the room and they often looked up as if scanning for an unseen aerial foe. They exchanged dark looks with the SS soldier, but kept their distance.

"Are you a student of history?" Hanns asked in a conversational tone as he inspected the first book shelf.

Terra's eyes snapped back to Hanns. "History? I haven't even graduated high school yet."

Hanns shook his head. "Just like the young, ignorant of the past. Admittedly, my university focus was more on science and engineering. I love ancient poems though. *The Odyssey* and *The Iliad* are my personal favorites."

Terra, again, forced herself calm. She had to focus, to figure out why Nazis were here in a library and if they really were time travelers. Hanns didn't seem like the Nazis portrayed in movies and video games. He didn't even wear a monocle and, so far, hadn't let out a mad cackle. Terra wondered if she should encourage him to talk more since he didn't seem hostile yet. "Um. I actually prefer geology," Terra said in a shaky voice.

He smiled. "Geology? Wonderful. The study of the intersection of earth and time." He turned to the shelf and ran an index finger across the row of books, stopping on one called *Understanding Spacetime*. He thumbed through a few pages before putting the book back. They made their way to the next section.

Terra looked up at the shelves, wondering what Hanns was after, assuming he was a time traveler. They stood in the science section one row down from literature. The row after that was history. Her eyes went wide as she stopped. "History," she whispered.

Hanns grinned while he continued to trace his finger across the books. "A single history book could change everything. The Waffen SS wants to confirm their glorious future," Hanns said, rolling his eyes. "But I need it to save lives."

"Save lives?"

"If we know our enemies movements and strategies, we can end this war with minimum loss of life. After Poland and France fell so quickly, I doubt the rest will last. Victory is assured, but why prolong the conflict? With a simple book, we can soundly defeat our enemies and end this war with minimal bloodshed."

Terra stared at Hanns with wide eyes.

Hanns looked over his shoulder at Terra. "However, I am curious why you Americans appear fearful of us? It's not like we will declare war against your country. The United States is neutral. I suppose we will have gained a fearsome reputation by the end of the war, but I assure you, we are not your enemies."

Terra grimaced. "You talk like you are the good guys?"

Hanns faced Terra and regarded her with a piercing stare. "We took a failing nation and turned it into a superpower. We avenged our soiled honor after that *venomous* treaty in Versailles. You can't tell me that treaty was fair, laying the blame for the sins of the Great War solely upon us! We stood up for ourselves against the entire world. How are we not the heroes?"

Terra raised her hands before stepping back. "Sorry! Please calm down."

Hanns's expression softened. "I apologize. I didn't intend to frighten you. I went through difficult times after the Great War. We all struggled during the Depression." He grimaced as though recalling a bad memory before he shook his head and smiled. "Now exciting things are happening. The new Nazi Party looks only to the future, unlike the old Republic. They even supported my time travel project despite the strange premise. For the first time in years, we have hope for the future."

"I don't understand. Why all the soldiers if you're after a history book?

Why not disguise yourself as a normal person or just grab a book and run?"

Hanns frowned, tapping a book with his finger. "You think I didn't try that?" Hanns said under his breath. He took a book titled *Escalation of the Vietnam War*. Hanns thumbed through a few pages before putting it back. "Why would the Americans attack a French colony?" he said, more to himself than Terra. "In answer to your question, we ran into... complications."

"Complications?" Terra asked before glancing at the books ahead of Hanns. They stood only a few steps away from the World War II books. She felt her heart begin to pound as she pondered the implications of Nazis finding a history book. Just before Hanns's finger brushed over a book titled *D-Day: A Narrow Victory*, a blue light illuminated the area.

Above the skylight a small glowing blue ring formed over the library. It moved down at a steady pace growing bigger. Soon the glowing ring encircled the building. Between the ring, a translucent grid of light beams passed through the walls. The grid passed right through her before it continued downward until disappearing into the floor.

Hanns glared at the passing ring while his hand tightened around his pistol. "The gods are hard to handle when they come blazing forth in their true power." He stood, silent for a moment. "She's here!" he said through gritted teeth. He drew his pistol before pointing to a nearby marble pillar. "Young lady! Hide behind that pillar and stay down."

Before she hid behind the pillar, she saw a sudden flurry of activity from the invaders. Their rifles clicked, the machine gun's ammunition belt clinked, the cannon gave a mechanical growl as the crew adjusted its firing angle. Even the SS soldier took cover.

A stillness settled over the library broken only by the sound of a rising wind outside the building. Terra knelt on the ground behind the pillar, covering her ears with her hands.

Nothing happened.

Terra lifted her hands to hear light footsteps on the roof. The soldiers noticed too and raised the aim of their weapons.

A soundless moment passed. Terra let down her guard just before the glass skylight shattered, raining shards over the library. A figure descended through the broken skylight. A woman dressed in white armor landed gracefully on top of the statue of Nike, her long silver hair streaming behind her in the wind.

CHAPTER II
SILVERWIND

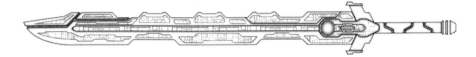

Continuum: Lambda.

Continuum Time: 4:23pm, February 10th, 2000 AD (local calender).

Location: Continental United States.

Enemy Forces: Approximately 1 platoon, early 1940s heavy weapons.

Lethal force is not authorized.

Warning: Recommend full strike team for this engagement. At least tw—

Warning overridden.

Warning: Civilians in area. Advise that on—

Warning overridden.

Attention Centurion Silverwind. Strategos Orion left the following message for you.

"You know, Alya, just because you can match an army by yourself doesn't mean that—"

Message skipped.

-Combat log of Centurion Silverwind

Terra ducked as Hanns regarded the newcomer. "Silverwind," he said in a low tone. He then pointed at the woman. "Feuer Frei!" Hanns yelled.

The guns roared as rounds pelted the statue where Silverwind stood, but she moved so fast that Terra saw only a blur. The woman jumped down into the maze of bookshelves as the statue shattered under the gunfire.

The gunfire stopped as Nazis scanned for Silverwind's location. They moved forward, searching between bookshelves. Four of them stalked around the corner, rifles raised and ready to fire. They stopped before one motioned to proceed forward into the maze out of Terra's sight.

An alarmed shout sounded from one of the soldiers. Gunfire rang through the library, forcing Terra to cover her ears again. When the shooting stopped, a helmet rolled across the floor into Terra's view. Seconds later, a soldier flew over the shelves. He grunted as he struck the ground and rolled into a nearby wall. He did not get back up.

The remaining soldiers pointed their weapons toward the disturbance, waiting for Silverwind to show herself while Hanns dug through books nearby. Terra then understood. This woman, this Silverwind, somehow knew about this temporal intrusion. Hanns's soldiers were trying to buy him time to find a book.

Six more soldiers moved to the center of the room toward Silverwind's last location. They stood close by one another with bayonets attached to their rifles while one soldier drew a sword.

Silverwind stepped out to face them, drawing a silver sword unlike any blade Terra had ever seen. Its translucent edge glowed a faint blue and took on a static grainy appearance. Above the cross guard, a small orb burned bright blue.

She stood straight backed with feet together and lifted the blade in her left hand. Silverwind then placed her right hand behind her back and raised the edge of the blade a few inches in front of her face with the guard just below her chin. She held this pose for a few seconds as though saluting her foes. Her confident smile showed no hint of fear as she faced a heavily armed group of the greatest villains in all of history. In fact, she seemed impressed they were trying to attack her at all. Then she swung her sword out at an angle to her side as though to signal her salute finished and that she was about to attack. She did.

It lasted seconds. Silverwind moved too fast for Terra's eyes. Like a whirlwind, she moved in a blur of motion. She seemed to strike each soldier simultaneously, dancing around them as though they were statues. All Terra could see was the woman's long, shimmering hair trailing behind her as though she were a silver wind.

The soldiers all fell at once in a heap of broken bones and bleeding faces while their weapons lay cut in half upon the ground. Only the Nazi wielding a sword remained. He slashed at the woman as she raised her own sword to block. Blades met, yet there was no ring of metal meeting metal. Instead, the woman's blade sliced through the Nazi's sword with his own momentum. He stared at his clean cut blade with wide eyes before the woman struck his neck and he fell.

Silverwind faced the remaining soldiers. "All combatants, you are in violation of the Temporal Accords! You are ordered to return to your home time immediately! Fail to do so and the Aeon Legion will consider this a crime against Time and you will be dealt with accordingly!" she said in perfect English.

A hail of gunfire sounded from the room as the machine gun fired. More fire came from the anti-tank cannon shooting at a steady, but slow rhythm as its rounds punched through walls. Silverwind braced herself, raising her right hand to reveal a small device with a glowing orb that was attached to her forearm. She held it in front of her like a shield. Armor piercing rounds froze in place just as they struck a translucent field that emanated from Silverwind's forearm device. Each impact sent a ring of energy rippling across a force field that extended from the orb of the device. The energy field was shaped like a buckler and Terra guessed it had the same function as a shield from antiquity, only more powerful and able to stop bullets. When Silverwind lowered her shield, the bullets remained frozen in mid air.

"Infinite!" Silverwind said, smiling. "I hate boring missions!"

The machine gun and cannon kept firing, sending tracer rounds streaking towards her. The woman's afterimages flashed between bullets before she jumped over several bookshelves in an impossibly high leap. Soldier's manning the machine gun tried to shift their aim, but the woman attacked too fast. A silver blade sliced through the machine gun's steel without effort. The soldiers didn't even have time to yell as she grabbed one and flipped him into the other.

The cannon fired again, but she dodged the shells with impossible speed before jumping onto a vertical wall. She then ran on the wall as though it were a floor. The soldiers angled the cannon upward and fired. Shots hit around her as she weaved between the rounds with inhuman reflexes.

Stray hits sent large chunks of marble downward towards Terra. She scrambled out of the way as debris rained around her.

Silverwind jumped on the top of the cannon. The gun's two crew members tried to draw their pistols, but were too slow. The woman crouched and kicked one on the side of the face while jabbing the other in the throat with her hand. She jumped down, slashing at the cannon with her blade. A bright light flared from the edge of her sword as it hit the cannon. The cannon exploded and Terra fell to the ground, hands covering her head as small bits of smoking debris fell around her.

After a smoldering wheel rolled by her, Terra opened her eyes to find Hanns who stood next to the SS soldier. He held a book in one hand titled *World War II: The Turning Point* and his glowing watch device in the other. Hanns pointed at Silverwind before uttering something to the SS soldier. The SS soldier snarled and pointed his rocket propelled grenade launcher at the woman, but shifted his aim to the cowering library patrons.

Hanns eyes widened when he saw where the SS soldier had aimed. He tensed and yelled before he tried to grab the weapon away from the SS soldier. The weapon fired, missing the civilians and instead exploded above them.

A heap of debris fell toward the library patrons. Terra closed her eyes, cringing at the inevitable outcome. The screams suddenly stopped. She opened her eyes enough to see Silverwind standing in front of the patrons. The debris now drifted down slowly, like settling dust.

"Hurry! Take cover around the corner over there and don't move!" Silverwind shouted.

The SS soldier fired with a submachine gun while Hanns retreated into the maze of shelves. Shots impacted on her shield as she covered the retreating patrons. When the last patron cleared, she charged the SS officer so fast it seemed as though she appeared in front of him in an instant.

Their hand to hand fight was as short as it was brutal. Within a single heartbeat, the elite and feared SS soldier lay on the floor in a heap of broken bones. He groaned, unable to move.

When the remaining Nazis began throwing grenades, Terra crawled behind a large chunk of marble while keeping her head down. She noticed Hanns hiding behind a shelf. He wiped the sweat off his brow as he worked with his pocket watch device. The gunfire fell silent.

A flamethrower armed soldier approached Silverwind. He aimed and shot a stream of fire at her. The fire froze in midair on Silverwind's shield. She struck him and he fell incapacitated. With the final soldier beaten,

Silverwind searched between bookshelves for Hanns. "This is your third infraction Hanns. One more time and they'll authorize lethal force."

Terra's eyes widened. *She's holding back?* Terra thought.

Hanns activated his hand held device, forming another green glowing sphere in the center of the library. He shouted more orders in German and the remaining soldiers dragged the unconscious bodies of their fallen comrades into the portal. Hanns then grabbed a nearby book, tearing out a clump of pages before hiding out of Terra's view.

Silverwind patrolled between book shelves at a slow, but steady pace, searching for Hanns. When she neared the end of the aisle, Hanns darted in front of her a few paces away. He drew his pistol with his right hand while keeping his left hand behind his back. He fired.

With her usual blindingly fast reflexes, Silverwind brought up her arm to shield herself. As her shield activated, Hanns threw a wad of torn pages at her that he had kept hidden in his other hand. The pages froze in midair, obscuring Silverwind's view.

Hidden behind the frozen papers, Hanns fired several shots. The shots impacted the woman's shield. She charged, grabbing Hanns's right arm and breaking it. Hanns had switched the pistol to his left hand during the distraction. He aimed point blank at a gap in the armor on her abdomen beyond the woman's shield. A shot rang out.

Blood seeped out of Silverwind's mouth as she swayed.

Hanns wasted no time and kicked the woman to the floor. He holstered his pistol and used his unbroken left arm to pick up the history book he had dropped amid the scuffle. Victorious, Hanns limped towards the portal in the center of the room as his broken right arm dangled to his side. His men had already retreated into the portal.

Terra sank behind the marble debris, trembling as her thoughts raced. Hanns had won. He held the history book in his hand. If he made it back into his own time, history might be forever altered.

Hanns took another step closer to the portal.

Terra slid down further onto the floor, trying to control her rising panic. Maybe another sword wielding time traveler would stop Hanns? She could stay behind her happy little rock until this insanity ended.

Hanns took another step closer to the portal, standing a few paces away from Terra now.

Terra gritted her teeth to stop herself from trembling. She had always been like a stone; trod upon, ignored and beneath the notice of everyone, even Hanns as he limped past her.

Being like a stone wasn't so bad though. Most left her in peace but she never did anything brave. Stones didn't need to be brave unlike the heroes and heroines of history she admired. Those heroes and heroines would have urged her to act right now.

Hanns took a step away from Terra, walking past her.

Sweat beaded on her brow. She knew it was suicidal to try to stop him. Hanns was a trained soldier and armed. Terra was a nearly graduated high school student without a direction in life. He was from an age of warfare and strife. She was from an age of sitcoms and video games.

Hanns took another step. He now stood a few paces away from the portal.

Terra sat alone with only her thoughts. She could just sit there, close her eyes, and wait for it to be over. It would be easier to be like a stone and do nothing. But she was the only one who could do something now.

Then she felt anger sink into her stomach. *How dare Hanns!* she thought. *How dare he wreck my safe library, putting everyone at risk for his own ambition!* It was just like the bullies at school. No one ever stopped them just as no one was left to stop Hanns.

Terra then realized that right now, she was time's only defender. No one was going to help her. No one was going to save her. Evil was about to win and only she could stop it. It was her chance to be a heroine.

Terra set her jaw and stood to search for something, anything to use against Hanns. She grabbed a loose fist size chunk of marble before she charged. In spite of spraining her ankle, she caught up to the limping Hanns just before he took the final step to the portal. She raised the rock as high as she could before smashing Hanns on the back of the head. He crashed to the ground, book falling out of his hand onto the floor a few steps away while his gun fell into the portal.

Terra smiled, dumbfounded, not at the Nazi soldier in modern day America, the time travel portal, or the silver haired soldier with strange powers, but at her own hands. "I... I did it! I stopped him!"

Terra's smile vanished as Hanns groaned before standing and rubbing his head. She paled, hesitating as an angry Hanns turned to her. He clenched his left fist, but instead of striking Terra, looked to the book.

Terra yelled, shaking herself out of her panicked state and dove after the book. Hanns ran as they both grabbed the history book at the same time and pulled at opposite ends. Terra was thankful for Hanns's numerous injuries as he was still strong enough to match her with just one arm. The tug of war went on seconds longer before Hanns dragged both Terra and the book towards the portal.

Before Hanns gave the final tug, a light breeze blew around Terra. Hanns's eyes went wide at something behind her. Silverwind descended towards Hanns, her blade pointed at his chest. He let go of the book, falling back into the portal before the blade could stab him.

The portal dissipated, leaving a small crater at its epicenter. Terra gazed at Silverwind with wide eyes. She searched for a bullet wound on the woman but no trace of damage remained. After surveying the room for stragglers, the woman sheathed her sword.

As the silence returned, other survivors emerged. Terra appraised the damage; marble pillars not smashed to pieces appeared riddled with bullet holes and chunks of marble and burned books lay strewn across the floor mixed with empty bullet casings and scorch marks. A fire remained frozen in midair while the debris from the grenade blast still fell in slow motion. No one seemed hurt. The Nazis had recovered all their fallen comrades before disappearing through the portal.

The woman scanned the room. "No deaths on either side. Good," she said before touching the convex glass face on her forearm device. "Mission accomplished. Minerva, *Restore* this area."

For the first time, Terra looked at the woman in detail. She appeared in her mid twenties, with silver hair that reached halfway down her back. The tanned hue of her skin contrasted with bright, sky blue eyes.

Terra couldn't help but feel envious. Not of Silverwind's beauty, but her power. This woman stood without a single scratch amid smoking ruins, a breeze flowing through her silver hair. An immortal with power over time itself who used that power to stop villains and save the innocent. A real heroine.

Terra wondered, just for a moment, what it would be like to have such power. What would she do with that power? If she had that power, she wanted to be like this heroine.

"Who are you?" Terra asked at last.

"Me? Don't worry. You won't remember I was here," she said. "What is your name?"

Terra observed the blue light overhead again. The same ring descended over the library, however this time it restored the building to its previous state as it fell, erasing all the damage caused by the battle. Terra shook her head and looked at the woman again. "Name... Yes! My name. It's Terra. Terra Mason."

"Well Terra," the woman said as she looked Terra up and down, "You should know that your tactics were awful. A direct charge against an armed foe? You should have at least tried a flanking maneuver or engaged in a ranged attack using commandeered weapons."

"Um. What?" Terra asked, her brow furrowed.

The woman turned to walk away from Terra as she touched the glass face on her forearm device. "Minerva, access Saturn City Archives for a person named Terra Mason, age late teens, reference year two thousand on Continuum Lambda, eastern continental United States."

Terra raised a finger to ask another question when the ring passed over her, erasing her memories of the library invasion and returning everything back to normal. At least for now.

CHAPTER III
CROSSROADS

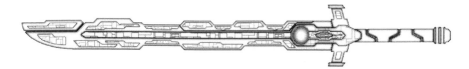

"Alya Silverwind, we need to talk about this report. It just says 'Bad guys defeated.'"

"Right. That sums it up rather nicely."

"Crashing End, Alya! Have you ever considered filling these out properly?"

"You know Orion, that's the thing I like most about you. You are adorable when you try to give me orders. Although I suppose I should have noted how that girl saved the mission. I think her name was Terra."

"Who?"

"It was rather odd. Her tactics were awful."

"Well whoever it was, have you considered that she might be just a civilian?"

"Oh. You may be right. I spend too much time around Legendary Blades. I tend to forget that even civilians can be brave. You know, I think I may actually look into that."

"The Hanns case?"

"The girl. Yes. I think I will. Orion, I will send you the rest of the data on Hanns. Have Minerva issue a formal warrant. Meanwhile, I am going to take some personal time. I will talk to you later."

"Wait what? Alya? Crashing End. No one ever listens to me!"

-Conversation log appended to case file for Hanns Speer, full report still pending

"These memories we will cherish forever..." the girl trailed off, her speech paused as she rubbed tears from her eyes.

Terra rolled her eyes. The graduation robes made the

crowded gymnasium even more hot and stuffy. Graduation had dragged on long enough without every student giving a speech breaking into tears. Why did they care so much? She had no happy memories of this place. Almost all the classes were boring and most of the students didn't even acknowledge her existence, except for the ones that annoyed her.

Hannah, the class valedictorian, dabbed her eyes with a handkerchief before continuing her speech. "These memories we will cherish forever, even though we go into a larger world. Now we, the graduating class of 2000, stand at a crossroads. We shall keep the past in our hearts while we go forward into the future."

She walked off the stage as the history teacher, Mr. Smith, approached the podium. "Congratulations class of 2000! Go forth into a new world!"

A cheer went up from the students as applause thundered through the gymnasium. Terra allowed herself a brief sigh. High school was done.

Terra made her way through the crowd, searching for her parents. She just wanted to go home. Now a slow, packed crowd stood in her way.

She grimaced when someone stepped on her foot again. Such things happened often to her as people never noticed her presence until they stumbled into her. When she looked down, she saw a graduation card at her feet dropped by the person who had just walked by her. Terra looked over to see Ray who walked to meet his family.

One of the football team's stars, Ray was built like a bulldozer and was about as perceptive as one. How he convinced the ever growing gaggle of admiring girls to do his homework for him remained a mystery to Terra.

Terra picked up the card, opening it to read the words*Congratulations Ray. Love Grandma!*. Three one hundred dollar bills lay in the fold. Terra closed the card, leaving the money untouched and followed Ray.

"Such a smart young man and so sharp," an older lady said to Ray. "What are you going to do after graduation?"

Ray grinned and saluted. "I'm joining the Marines."

"Why?" she asked.

Ray smiled. "Because I want to be a badass!"

Terra cleared her throat and Ray turned. She presented the card to him.

Ray checked the card. "Hey thanks! See. I have everything covered."

Terra rolled her eyes as she walked away. She rejoined the crowd, trying to push through to find her parents.

"Well if it isn't Terra the Terror, herself?" came a voice from behind her.

Terra turned to see Hannah with her arm outstretched towards Terra's face. Hannah's graduation gown sleeve concealed her hand.

"What?" Terra asked, crossing her arms. She knew Hannah plotted something as usual.

Hannah smiled as she shot her hidden diploma out of her sleeve, stopping right in front of Terra's nose.

Terra stared at Hannah, unblinking.

Hannah shook her head. "Didn't even flinch. Do you know why I'll miss you?"

Terra pursed her lips. She would not miss Hannah's strange mind games. "No."

Hannah grinned. "Because I'm better than you in almost every way. I'm prettier, smarter, have better grades and I'm more motivated. Despite all that, you are better than me in one way."

"I don't stroke my own ego every five seconds?"

"You never flinch. In a way, I'm really glad you didn't try hard in class. Otherwise, I would have had to actually work to be valedictorian. Though I am also kind of sad that you didn't compete with me. I feel cheated, like I never got to see Terra Mason at her best."

Terra scowled. "Are you done?"

Hannah stared at Terra for a moment before tearing up. She then embraced Terra. "I will miss my rival!"

Terra rolled her eyes while she patted Hannah awkwardly on the back.

After a moment Hannah let go and wiped her eyes. "Now if you will excuse me I have to go gloat some more before I accept all my scholarships. A PhD won't earn itself! Good luck and I hope you find a decent rival to replace me."

Terra almost asked Hannah what her plans were after graduation, but decided not to give Hannah the pleasure. No doubt she had already planned her future unlike Terra, who spent most of her time reading about the past.

"Miss Mason," someone called.

Terra turned to see her history teacher, Mr. Alden Smith. "Mr. Smith."

Smith nodded as he approached before cracking a slight smile that always preceded his usual criticism. "Well, it seems you have graduated despite your lack of effort."

"Hey! I made an A plus in your class after you gave me extra assignments, like that report on FDR."

"I did that to push you into doing better. Why didn't you try to get all As in your other classes? I know you are capable."

"Why should I? This place is stupid."

Smith shook his head. "Honesty isn't always tactful, young lady. To you this place seems stupid, and yes much of school is foolish, but you still owe it to yourself to try harder. You are tougher than you look. I can only imagine what you could accomplish if you turned all that stubbornness into determination. So what will you do now?"

Terra gazed down. "I'm not sure. I want to go into geology but I'm still undecided. Everyone else already seems to have a career choice."

Smith smiled. "Well just remember, Terra, that you have a choice. I think the hardest thing for you is realizing that you have choices. You are always so busy holding still that you forget to move forward."

Terra looked at Smith. "What should I do then?"

Smith gestured to the other graduates. "You see these youths? They all think they know what they want. Wealth and fame. Others have already planned their futures unaware of just how much the future doesn't care about their plans. What should you do then?"

He locked eyes with Terra.

"While you live, shine," he said with a smile. "Be the best person you can be. That is all anyone should ever do with their life. Don't squander your time staying still, Terra Mason. Grab opportunity when it drifts by on the wind. Make the most of your life because time demands its toll from us all."

∞

The next three months flew by as summer began to fade into fall. Days passed quickly while Terra read and spent time in her quarry. Today, she returned home after visiting the library for the first time all summer. She had avoided the library. She no longer felt safe there for some reason.

That missing afternoon at the library bothered her at first, along with her sudden fixation on World War II books. By the time of graduation though, she had dismissed the whole missing day affair. Instead, her mother's relentless college campaign became Terra's primary concern. She worried as the final battle over college with her mother drew close.

Terra approached the door to her home and opened it with care to avoid the creaking sound it made when opened too fast. She peeked into the hallway, making sure it was clear. With the hallway vacant, Terra crept with soft footsteps around the boards that squeaked. In the living room, she could hear the television playing while her mother, Bethany Mason, sat facing the computer with her back to the hallway.

Terra made her way to the stairs. When she was out of sight of the living room, she sighed in relief.

"Terra. Come here please," Beth said from the living room.

Terra grimaced as she let out a low growl. How did her mother do that? She sighed in frustration before walking back towards the living room.

"I think you may like this one," Beth said, still sitting, as she turned to face Terra. Bethany Mason was still in her business dress. Terra almost never saw her out of formal business attire or without an unimpressed frown. "They have a really good finance and accounting program. I think your high math scores can get you admittance."

Terra looked at the computer screen, pretending to read. "Do they have a geology major?" Terra asked in a bored tone, already knowing the answer.

"Well no."

"Don't care."

Beth sighed. "No wonder you have so much difficulty making friends."

"Sorry, Mom. I have no interest in finance, accounting, business, nursing, law, or medicine," Terra said, counting each with her fingers.

"Well you should. Those are all good, high paying fields. Geology is just a hobby. I want you to be successful."

"I know," Terra said, turning to escape while praying this conversation was finished.

"Young lady," Beth said as she stood with hands on her hips. She was slightly taller than Terra. "I did not say we were finished."

Terra slouched, stopped, and sighed before turning around again.

Beth shook her head. "Terra, would it kill you to do something difficult every once in a while? You drifted through school without ever pushing yourself. You have done nothing all summer long but read World War II history books and dig up rocks in that pit behind the house. Now it's fall semester and soon it will be too late to enroll in a good college."

Terra crossed her arms and glared at Beth.

Beth frowned before pointing at Terra. "When your father and I still struggled—"

"Yes I know," Terra said, trying not to roll her eyes at hearing the same story for the thousandth time. "Our family went through hard times before you were promoted. Dad had to work double shifts. You don't want me to have to go through the same thing."

Terra hoped that would end it. She turned to leave again only to find her father, Fredrick Mason, blocking her escape.

"Good news!" Fred said. He was slightly shorter than Terra and as poorly dressed. He wore a stained T-shirt and worn bluejeans. She often wondered what her mother saw in him until Fred smiled, which was always difficult to not return. "I talked to my friend Jeff today. He says he could use a part timer for his garage. Basic stuff; answering the phone, a bit of cleaning. That sort of thing. Interested?"

Terra shook her head. "No, not really, Dad."

Fred winked as he nudged Terra. "Come on. It will get your mother off your back."

Beth glared at him.

Fred shrugged. "I know you want her to go to college, but maybe she just needs to work a little to find her calling?"

"Look," Terra said, trying to hide the irritation in her tone. "I just want to take it easy for a while."

"Easy?" Beth said as she crossed her arms, a habit she often criticized Terra for. "Very little of anything easy is worthwhile. This family prospered because of my determination and your father's self-sacrifice. Besides, I know you are capable of working hard. There isn't much that can stop you once you make up your mind. God knows we could never do anything with that bullheadedness of yours."

Terra clenched her jaw as she glared at Beth, unblinking.

Fred sighed. "Oh great. She just went into stubborn mode."

Beth's eyes narrowed. "Oh I know that look. Now you will just stand there until we give up. Fine! I didn't want to do this, but here is your ultimatum. You have until the end of this week to enroll in a college."

Terra wanted to say "Or what?" but decided against it since it would prolong the fight.

Fred put a hand on both Terra's and Beth's shoulders. "Okay. Why don't you both stop trying to out stubborn one another. Families fight, but families love too."

Beth scowled at Fred who simply smiled back. After a moment, Beth's scowl faded. "Oh all right, but the ultimatum still stands. If she can find a job, then that is acceptable as well," she said before leaving the room.

Terra let out a long sigh.

Fred turned to Terra. "I know she's pestering you, but it's only because she lo—"

"I know. Because she loves me," Terra said as she returned Fred's warm smile, "but I need time to figure things out."

Fred nodded. "You just need to do *something*. Sometimes we have to follow the wind."

∞

After dinner, Terra went upstairs to her room. The floor remained clear of any clothes or other items. A dusty television and old game system sat on the dresser in the corner. Her open closet contained untouched dresses, worn jeans, and stained tee-shirts.

A sizable, overcrowded bookshelf took up much of the room. The top of the bookshelf, dresser and window seal hosted an impressive collection of rocks, minerals, ores and geodes. Diorite, gabbro, basalt, pumice, marble, quartzite and obsidian all decorated the room. Some she had found herself while others she bought. Terra had arranged them in groups according to the layers in which they are naturally found.

Vestiges remained of Terra's younger teenage years. A dusty make up kit lay on the dresser though a large lump of rock crystal rested on top of it. The edges of a poster featuring a long forgotten boy band protruded slightly under another poster of Franklin D. Roosevelt. The poster read *Men are not prisoners of fate, but only prisoners of their own minds.*

Terra gathered her worn rock hammer, chisel and a small spade, placing them in her tool bag before leaving. "I'm going to the quarry again.

Be back in a bit!" Terra said before she left the house, not waiting for a response.

The colors of fall painted the trees as Terra walked through the backyard. Patches of yellow dotted the mountains in the distance while red leaves floated in the creek she crossed. Knee high golden grass swayed in the fall winds as Terra passed through the fields.

The quarry lay near her house a short walk away. The couple who had lived here before had considered the pit an eyesore so they had planted a row of trees to block the view. In fact, her family had gotten a good deal for the property because of it. Although it devalued the property, for Terra it was a boon. She had often played there during her childhood. As she grew older, she used it to find a few of the ores and minerals for her rock collection.

The terraced pit descended five tiers, each six feet deep. A small dark pool was at the bottom. Moss grew in patches on the flats while tree roots grew into the top tier. Dark veins of ore marbled the walls. Over the years, Terra had chipped away at the walls, sometimes finding new pockets of ore like a gardener cultivating crops. After all, this place was like her garden. A place of sanctuary for her.

She climbed carefully onto the first tier. Terra took each step with care which she had learned years ago when she still rock climbed. When she reached the bottom of the first tier, her heart was racing from exertion while she wheezed. After resting for a moment, she started working.

Taking out her small, worn rock chisel, Terra chipped away at a patch of dolomite. Last week, she had found traces of magnetite ore and now hoped to hit a larger vein. She dug around a large chunk of rock before trying to pull it out with her bare hands.

Terra grunted and strained as she pulled at the loosened chunk of dolomite stone. "Stubborn stone!" she said through gritted teeth as she pulled harder. The stone did not give and Terra slipped, falling down to the ground in a hard thump.

She lay on the ground, gasping at the exertion. Terra's mind wandered to the future as she gazed at the sky. The clouds moved at a steady pace, swept along by the wind. She closed her eyes as a gentle breeze washed over her.

Terra sighed. "Do something. Follow the wind. Yeah, right. That's not how it works. The future never comes to the present."

When she opened her eyes to the sky, they seemed to be playing tricks on her. It looked as though someone stood in the tree above her, balancing on a large branch. After a moment, her eyes focused. She then realized someone really was in the tree, watching her. A woman with silver hair.

CHAPTER IV
UNCERTAINTIES

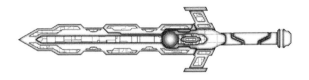

The Squire System, while antiquated, works well for Aeon Legion recruitment. Given stagnant Saturn City demographics, recruits must be drawn from various historical periods instead. Naturally those with military backgrounds are preferable but talent comes in many forms and the Aeon Legion's mission encompasses so much more than warfare. However, it is highly advised that all legionaries vet their potential squires before enrolling them into the Academy's training program. If a legionnaire does not put the effort into recruiting a squire, then why would the recruit put effort into the training? Choosing a potential squire has nothing to do with luck.

-Introduction to the Aeon Legion's *Squire Recruitment Manual* by Praetor Lycus Cerberus

Terra Gasped as she searched for her rock hammer. She grabbed it and held it close to her chest. The stranger jumped from the tree before landing next to Terra with the grace of a falling feather.

"Good ages Terra," the silver haired woman said with a voice that carried on the wind. Her wavy silver hair reached down her back and curled at the tips. Sky blue eyes contrasted with the tanned tone of her skin. Her slender, athletic build and youthful narrow face made Terra guess the woman's age in her late twenties. The woman smiled, grabbing Terra's arm and pulling her up without even a grunt. "Infinite apologies about my sudden appearance. I didn't mean to frighten you."

Terra steadied herself before stepping away from the intruder. "Who are you?"

The silver haired woman stared at Terra as though expecting to be recognized.

Terra looked at the woman's uniform, feeling a strange sense of deja-vu. The woman's sleek, pearl white armor was segmented with metal seams and decorated with glass orbs. A thin stripe of blue decorated the edges of each plate. Underneath her armor, she wore a form fitting white suit. Her armor, along with the sheathed sword she carried at her belt, made the woman's overall appearance look like a futuristic rendering of an ancient knight.

"Crash. I keep forgetting that," she said after a moment. She looked down to a long and narrow device worn on her right forearm that covered from her wrist to nearly her elbow. The complex instrument had a convex, glowing glass orb above her wrist, like the face of a wristwatch. When her left hand drew near it, a series of holographic translucent blue buttons appeared over and around the edge of its glass face. She touched a button. "Minerva, Restore Terra Mason's memories."

Terra raised an eyebrow when a glowing blue ring formed around her center. It moved counterclockwise around her. She tried to escape it but it encircled her within seconds before vanishing.

The moment the ring dissipated, Terra's missing memories flooded back into her mind. She remembered Hanns, the soldiers, the battle at the library and the silver haired woman who fought them by herself. Finally, Terra remembered her own struggle with Hanns over a history book. She remembered everything.

Forcing herself calm, Terra turned to the woman. "Who are you? What did you do to me?"

The woman assumed a military posture before putting her right fist over her heart while snapping her feet together in a strange salute. "Centurion Alya Silverwind of the Aeon Legion. I am the wielder of the aeon edge Silverwind which is also my alias. I am a citizen of Saturn City and twelfth member of the Legendary Blades."

Terra gazed at the woman with a blank expression. She looked over Alya's strange uniform again and noticed the word *Invictum* which was displayed below a golden infinity emblem on her upper arm. Below the infinity emblem was a patch that depicted twelve swords arranged in a circle and pointed inwards. Terra did not recognize any of the other insignias.

"Oh! I'm also a time traveler," Alya added, as though it were a minor detail.

Terra's eyes narrowed. "I find that hard to believe."

"Let me show you," Alya said as she snatched Terra's rock hammer. Before Terra could protest, Alya held it in her right hand, the same hand with the strange watch like device. The glass orb in the watch began glowing before the hammer started to levitate in the air. Terra's eyes widened as the worn edges and dents faded from the hammer's surface. Alya handed it back to Terra, who inspected the hammer. It looked new, like the day she had first bought it.

Terra stared at Alya. "How?"

Alya pointed to the watch like device on her right forearm. "It's called a *shieldwatch*. It's singularity technology that controls time. Everything I did in the library was all singularity technology. Well, also a lot of training and experience."

"So time travel is real? Those were real Nazis?"

"Making a time machine is easy. People have built time machines as far back as 1895 AD in your continuum's dating system. Most are scientists and explorers who want nothing more than to witness history, but others like Hanns cause trouble by changing things."

Terra's mouth hung open for a moment. She then put the hammer in her bag before turning back to Alya. "Um. Silverwind is it?"

Alya glided closer. "You may address me as Alya if you wish."

Terra leaned back when Alya drew close. "Well then, Alya... Um... So why are you here, exactly?"

Alya again moved closer to Terra. "I wanted to thank you in person for helping me stop Hanns. If not for you, Hanns would have gotten away with the book and things would have escalated."

"Um. You're welcome?" Terra said, raising her hands in front of her and stepping back.

Fortunately, Alya backed off before studying Terra with narrowed eyes. She put her hand under her chin while regarding Terra. "I suppose I need to do a brief physical examination and check a few other things. I'll be back in a few hours."

"What?" Terra asked before another glowing ring formed around Alya, moving clockwise. The ring left a trail of light which formed a sphere around Alya that dissipated, leaving no trace of the silver haired woman.

Terra stood for a long moment and stared where Alya had stood.

"I'm still not sure," came Alya's voice from above.

Terra looked up to see Alya pacing on the top tier of the quarry. "That wasn't a few hours."

Alya ignored Terra and continued speaking while staring at the glass face of her shieldwatch. A small holographic disc glowed above the glass face. Alya's finger traced the surface of the disc as though it were a touch screen. "No medical conditions a shieldwatch can't fix. Good vision too. Still, she is physically unfit and will need to work hard to catch up in that area. Her grades are good. Could have been better, I think. Excellent history score. Slightly above average sciences and math. I will have to ask her teacher about that. Minerva, give me a list of good times to interview her teacher and parents. Also, will removing her from the continuum affect its integrity?"

"No," came a female voice from Alya's shieldwatch. "No significant changes will occur if she is removed from this continuum."

Terra tried to see what the small holographic disc said, but she didn't recognize the text. Instead, Terra tried to regain her composure. What did this strange woman want? Terra knew Alya had wiped out a platoon of trained soldiers by herself. If she wanted Terra dead, it would take little effort on Alya's part. Terra knew Alya wasn't evil. An evil person would have let the hostages die in the library. This woman put herself in danger to save them. "What are you after?"

Alya looked at Terra as though she had forgotten about her. She then smiled and jumped down in front of Terra. "Oh. Apologies again. I wanted to ask a few questions."

Terra scowled. "You want to ask questions? You interrupt my day, invade my quarry, violate my personal space, tell me you are a time traveler and then you want to ask questions?"

Alya smiled and nodded.

"Fine!" Terra said before crossing her arms.

"First: Who in Aion's origin were those people at the library, the soldiers with silly red armbands? I asked Minerva, but she lectured, at length, about the history of Continuum Lambda."

Terra's brow raised. "You don't know who the Nazi's are?"

"Nazis? What an awkward name."

"Haven't you ever heard of World War Two?" Terra asked, putting a hand on her forehead.

"You mean the Great War? Continuum Alpha doesn't have another one of those."

Terra stared while her brow lowered.

"Well your continuum is rather strange. It's one the few where European civilizations become dominant. It's like... how would your culture put it?"

"Backwater," came a female voice from Alya's shieldwatch.

"Thank you, Minerva. Yes. The Legacy Library is the only interesting thing from this continuum. The Time cartographers from the Eighth Cohort haven't mapped this part of Time well. This makes it rather difficult for me to find and arrest Hanns."

"So are you some kind of time police force?"

"Let's see. What is a good way to describe it from within your culture's context? What are those people called in those colorful picture books? They don capes and masks to fight crime for justice."

"Superheroes?"

"That's it! That's what we are. We are good guys and we stop bad guys from destroying history."

"Why not tell everyone this? Wouldn't it be easier to tell everyone about the dangers of time travel rather than charging into libraries and beating people up?"

Alya frowned while waving dismissively. "Oh, yes. That worked *really* crashing well! After the First Temporal War, we decided to use a different approach. Keeping time travel somewhat secret makes temporal traffic manageable. Less traffic, fewer fools who try to change history and cause Temporal Crashes by accident. I already explained all this to Hanns and he is still trying to abuse time travel."

"Why tell me any of this?"

Alya smiled, leaning closer. "In truth, you caught my attention. I made a mistake when I underestimated Hanns. If it weren't for you, then Hanns would have escaped with the book. However, Hanns made a mistake as well. He underestimated you. Now I wish to know why. Why did you try to stop Hanns?"

Terra felt a spike of fear. Had she done something wrong? What if she had damaged history by accident?

Alya stood, expectant.

Terra clenched her fists and faced Alya, deciding that she had done nothing wrong. She wouldn't flinch in the face of a time traveler or whatever this strange delusion was. "I don't know why I did that. It's not like a wanted to. I was really scared but at the moment I was the only one who could stop him. For a moment, I thought I could be a heroine."

Alya's eyes narrowed in a piercing stare for a long moment. Then she smiled. "Infinite! That is exactly the answer I was looking for. I still need a little more information but I can get that elsewhere."

Terra tensed, waiting to see what Alya did next. To her surprise, Alya turned and jumped onto the top of the quarry as though gravity were more a suggestion than a force.

Alya looked over her shoulder at Terra. "Okay, Terra. I will return in a couple of months, once I take care of a few details," she said, silver hair streaming in the wind. A ring formed around her, moving clockwise to form a glowing sphere. She vanished with the sphere of light.

Terra stood alone in the quarry for a long moment. The breeze faded, leaving her surrounded by silent stone.

"Huh, that was kind of weird," Terra said, her tone calm. Then her heart jumped when the ring formed at the top tier of the quarry, dissipating to reveal Alya once again.

"Ages, Terra!" Alya said, smiling. "Sorry it took longer than I expected. I meant to be back last week, but I got sidetracked."

Terra scowled. "You were just here!"

"Oh. Right. I am accustomed to Edge time. I keep forgetting you are in the continuum's time flow. Regardless, I have wonderful news! After much consideration, interviews with your parents, and high praise from your history teacher, I have decided to extend you a formal invitation to join the Aeon Legion as my squire! Isn't that infinite!"

Terra's brow furrowed. "When did you talk with my... wait! What was that last part?"

Alya moved closer, once again getting too close for Terra's comfort. "Your single brave act in the Library was enough to get my attention. After that, it was a simple matter of checking to see if you meet a few other minor additional qualifications. Congratulations! You meet all of them! Now all we need to do is get you a shieldwatch and registered in the Aevum Academy."

Terra stepped back. "The what Academy?"

"The Aevum Academy. It's where the Legion trains new squires. They perform basic training. After that, I finish up advanced training. Simple."

Terra stared at Alya with a blank expression.

Alya squinted. "I seemed to have confused you at one point?"

"At the part about time travel," Terra said before taking a deep breath. "Okay. Excuse me if I seem slow. Still trying to process this. To be clear, I hit a guy on the head with a rock because he tried to borrow a book and this makes me qualified to join the time police?"

"Aeon Legion," Alya corrected. "Also, we do a lot more than police time travel. Besides you don't just join the Aeon Legion, you have to pass the training program at the Academy first."

Terra was about to say no when another ring formed around Alya, again instantly shifting her pose.

As the ring faded, Alya's expression changed. Her smile vanished and Alya now stood stoically. "Let's try this again. Before you say no, consider this."

Terra glowered, but listened.

"Joining the Aeon Legion grants many perks," Alya explained. "The biggest is that the shieldwatch makes you immortal."

Terra raised an eyebrow.

"Well biologically immortal, technically speaking. The shieldwatch gives you eternal youth."

Terra opened her mouth to speak again when the ring formed around Alya a second time.

Now Alya frowned slightly and had taken off the shoulder pads of her armor. "You also get to see historical events in person."

Terra grimaced, raising a finger to interrupt when the ring formed around Alya a third time, again shifting her pose. Now Alya stood without her torso plate and her hair was more frayed at the edges.

Alya glared back at her. "You get a device that controls time! What more could you crashing want?"

Terra clinched her jaw, preparing to argue back when the ring formed around Alya a fourth time. Now she wore only the form fitting suit under the armor while her hair had become untamed.

Alya scowled, pinching her upper nose with her eyes closed. "Really crashing brilliant Alya," she said as though to herself, "bringing up the training's fatality statistics."

Terra's eyebrows raised. "What?"

"Never mind," Alya said, shaking her head. "Do you have any idea how *stubborn* you are? At first I liked the challenge, but now you are just being obstinate. Smith said you were willful, but good Aion! I've met Manticores more agreeable."

Terra scowled. "Stubborn? You haven't let me get a word in!"

Alya sighed, pacing in front of Terra. She then faced Terra. "Did I mistake your courage? Are you not a heroine?"

Terra perked up. "A heroine?"

Alya's slight smile returned. "Yes. That's what I'm offering you. That's what I'm looking for."

Terra stared at Alya, confused. "But I'm not a heroine."

"Oh really? So anyone would charge a trained soldier armed with only a rock?"

"But I'm just an average person. I don't have crazy time powers or anything."

"So average people can't become heroes and heroines then?"

"Well yes, but..." Terra trailed off as the ring formed around Alya again.

Alya's smile was wider this time and her hair better kept. "Now we are making progress!"

Terra frowned. "Stop time traveling to win arguments against me!"

Alya leaned closer. "Which, by the way, is another perk of time travel."

"Why are you trying so hard to recruit me?"

Alya's smile widened as if she expected Terra to ask that very question. "Because, Terra, I like you. While you have just met me, I have spent a lot of time getting to know you. You are honest, direct, loyal, much more clever than you appear and most importantly, courageous when it counts."

Terra was going to say something about flattery not working on her when the ring formed around Alya again.

"What's holding you back is fear," Alya said, her expression neutral again. "It's why you hide in this quarry. Why you avoid your mother's insistence on finding a college or your father's attempts to find you employment. It is the main reason you never tried hard in school or competed with Hannah."

Terra remained silent, wondering how Alya knew all this even with time travel.

Alya's expression turned hard as the wind picked up around the quarry. She spoke with a quiet intensity. "But I have seen the steel in you. When everything else has failed, the real Terra steels herself and fights! I want to take that Terra from this quarry and purify her, turn her into steel. That Terra could be amazing. That Terra could be a great heroine!"

"But I can't do any of those things you did in the library."

"Training and technology, Terra. Exercise isn't exactly singularity science. The rest is simply the shieldwatch. This is the power I offer; power over time itself. That power should be wielded only by the worthy, by those who desire to be a hero or heroine. You are worthy, Terra Mason."

Terra hesitated while she considered Alya's words when another ring formed over Alya and again changed her pose.

Alya's smiled had returned in full. "How about I show you time travel?"

Terra recoiled. "I don't know..."

"Trust me. You will love this! Don't worry. We will be completely safe. The Sybil have precogged no temporal storms. You will be fine."

Terra narrowed her gaze as she thought. If Alya had ill intent, then she could have simply abducted Terra many times over by now. "Will I be gone long?"

Alya laughed. "It's time travel."

"Oh... Right."

"Infinite!" Alya said as she grabbed Terra, pulling her close. "Let's go!"

Terra was about to push away from Alya when a glowing ring formed around both of them, moving clockwise around them. As the ring passed, it wiped away the quarry and replaced the landscape with a strange grainy storm of blue energy.

Terra's eyes went wide as she looked at the surreal landscape. The distorted world around her was now a shade of translucent blue with a static grainy appearance. The plants and animals around the quarry became ghostlike, surrounded by moving after images that bled into one another. Everything seemed in flux, moving in an azure shadow that stretched into a line on the horizon. A pale light illuminated the surroundings and when Terra looked up she could see the stars as though it was night. Somehow the sky looked strange filled with so many stars, more than she had ever seen before in her life.

Alya grabbed Terra's arm. "Hold on to me," she said in a calm tone that echoed in the blue haze.

"What is this?" Terra asked, her grip tight on Alya's arm.

"This is the Edge of Time. Don't worry. This trip will not take long. Our destination is close in Time."

Alya walked forward as the surroundings blew away, like a hurricane had suddenly swept through. Terra could feel the wind blow against her, trying to force her back. However, Alya didn't seem to notice the strange energy storm, acting as though this were normal.

After a few moments, the current died down and Alya stopped. She then looked at her shieldwatch for a long moment. Alya searched through a menu before pressing a holographic button. A ring formed around her, changing her appearance in an instant. No longer did she wear her armor, but an ankle length navy blue dress. Her long, silver hair was now curly, short, and dark brown. Terra thought Alya looked like someone from the 1930s. "How did you do that?"

"Shieldwatch," Alya said as she checked her appearance. She then looked at Terra. "I suppose you will not be too obvious."

"What time are we going to?"

Alya grinned. "You'll see," she said before pulling Terra a little closer. A ring passed over them both, erasing the strange grainy blue haze and replacing it with an alleyway. The air was cold. Partly cloudy skies loomed overhead.

Terra turned, trying to gauge her surroundings. While Terra gawked, Alya put a hat on Terra's head and handed her a jacket. Terra then faced Alya who now also wore a hat and had hid her sword in a large bag she carried at her side. "Where did you get that?"

Alya sighed. "Listen, Terra. Don't ask questions. Right now, just follow me."

Terra followed Alya into an open area out of the alley. She immediately recognized the Capital Building ahead. A small crowd gathered there.

"Washington D.C.?" Terra asked.

Alya nodded. They walked to a spot near the East Portico and waited. Others gathered. Their clothes appeared dated to Terra. However,

Terra felt out of place in her jeans and tee shirt. The only period clothing she wore was the jacket Alya had given her.

Alya pulled Terra close again before their surroundings accelerated, like the world was on fast forward. When the crowd grew large, time returned to normal.

"Did you just speed up time?"

Alya grinned. "Yet another perk. I wish it worked in Saturn City. Crashing Timeport crowds!"

Terra was about to ask what they were waiting for when a procession arrived. She gasped when she saw Franklin Delano Roosevelt arrive at the podium.

Terra couldn't believe it. She was watching the presidential inauguration of her favorite president! He was right there. Terra stood in a historical moment, in person. It all felt so surreal, yet his words were clear and Terra could see him with her own eyes.

After he took the oath of office, Franklin D. Roosevelt started his famous inaugural address. "I am certain that my fellow Americans expect that on my induction into the Presidency I will address them with a candor and a decision which the present situation of our people impel."

Cheers and applause erupted from the crowd. Terra had heard the recordings but this was without the audible sharpness of the old broadcasts.

"This is preeminently the time to speak the truth, the whole truth, frankly and boldly. Nor need we shrink from honestly facing conditions in our country today. This great Nation will endure as it has endured, will revive and will prosper."

More applause came.

"So, first of all, let me assert my firm belief that the only thing we have to fear is fear itself—nameless, unreasoning, unjustified terror which paralyzes needed efforts to convert retreat into advance."

Terra listened to the rest of the speech in awe. When the speech drew to a close, Alya leaned in closer. "Was it everything you had imagined?"

Terra shook her head. "So this is history?"

Alya looked back to the podium while the crowd cheered. "This is Time. This is what we protect. This is what you can be a part of. To protect the history you love. In this world, history is more than just words on a page. It lives and breathes. But if you are not careful, it dies too. You can protect it, Terra."

Terra looked away. "I don't know. This is wonderful, but I don't think I am brave enough to join this Legion."

Alya smiled, gesturing to Roosevelt as he turned to go. "Even after his words?"

Terra hesitated.

"Fear holds you back, Terra. Courage drives you forward. One cannot exist without the other. In most, courage and fear exist in a shifting equilibrium. Not you though. Your brave actions shattered that balance within you. Fear is the only thing stopping you from getting what you want. But, courage will get the better of you eventually. That courage needs to be shaped, hardened, and polished."

Terra looked away.

Alya then pointed to the shadows behind the podium. "Terra, look to the darkness there."

Terra did, but saw nothing.

"Now imagine Hanns stepping out of the shadows and pointing a gun at your favorite president."

Terra scowled before turning to Alya. "He couldn't! Could he?"

Alya shrugged. "Maybe. Time travelers have assassinated leaders before. The Forgotten Guns were particularly good at it. The Legion could stop Hanns though. Even if Hanns succeeded, history would likely turn out the same. Still, more dead bodies have never made history a better place. These are all uncertainties though. The one thing that is certain is that you can face your fear." Alya smiled. "Terra, you have already protected history once against all odds. Now I offer you the power of time itself to protect something you love. Yes there is danger on the way ahead, but I wouldn't extend this offer if I thought you incapable of enduring it. However, if you wish to let nameless, unreasoning, unjustified terror paralyze you, then go back to your little quarry and hide. I can even erase your memory again if you wish, but you need to make your decision knowing what you gave up."

Terra bit her lower lip. "I just don't know. This is so sudden."

"I won't lie to you. If you choose to come with me, then it will be the hardest thing you have ever done in your life. If you choose not to come with me, understand that you are giving up both history and the power to defend it. Everything I did in the library, the abilities, the sword, time travel, all this could be yours. But you have to choose it."

"Right now?"

Alya sighed. "You have no idea how long I have been trying to recruit you. However, I would be willing to give you a week if you really need that long."

"What if I change my mind after reaching this Academy?"

Alya burst out in laughter which drew the attention of several people nearby. "That will not happen. Trust me. If you change your mind after seeing Saturn City and getting a taste of the shieldwatch's power, then you will be making history."

After leaving the crowds, Alya brought Terra back through time to the quarry.

Terra checked the sun overhead, noting that it had not moved at all since she left. She then looked around the quarry. "So I won't meet myself will I?"

Alya changed back to her original armored form with silver hair. "No. It's impossible to meet yourself using time travel. I don't remember the technical details but once you time travel, then that instance of yourself will erase any doubles to times you travel to."

Terra turned to Alya. "So what now?"

"As promised, I will give you until the end of this week to make your choice. Not that I consider it much of a choice but I can understand if you feel it's sudden. Just remember, Terra, Hanns is still out there. While you spend your time deciding, he spends *his* working towards victory."

The ring formed around Alya a final time and she vanished. Terra waited for Alya to come back again just as she had before but she heard only the sound of a fading breeze.

Terra sat in the quarry for the rest of the afternoon, thinking. Alya had offered Terra almost everything she wanted. In truth, Terra had wanted that power in the library. Knowing that history was more than just words on a page now made the offer irresistible. What Alya had offered Terra was the power to touch history.

She looked at the quarry wall and used her small pick to dislodge a bit of magnetite ore. Terra tossed the ore in her hands as she looked up at the darkening sky. This was her choice.

When the first stars appeared in the sky, Terra climbed out of her quarry. She reached the top tier before stopping to look at the quarry. In that moment, Terra realized that she was about to leave everything behind. After a long moment of solace, Terra turned and walked back to her parents' home.

"There you are," Beth said, looking at Terra's feet to make sure she didn't track mud into the house again. "How many opportunities did you find in your quarry?"

Terra sighed. "Actually, one found me."

Beth raised an eyebrow while Terra sat at the kitchen table.

Fred walked over to the refrigerator to get himself a drink. "So you think about that job offer any?"

"Sorry Dad," Terra said as her shoulders drooped. "It seems I have another offer."

They both stared at Terra.

"What offer?" Beth finally asked.

Terra spoke in a whining tone while laying her head on the table. "I'm joining the time police."

CHAPTER V
THE EDGE OF TIME

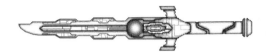

It is highly advised that one discuss what to expect from time travel with the potential squire. The worst thing any legionnaire can do is to send a new squire into the Edge with no explanation of what is going on. All squires must be brought through the timeport and this process can be simplified if they are prepared for the shock of seeing Saturn City for the first time.

-Chapter Two from the Aeon Legion's *Squire Recruitment Manual* by Praetor Lycus Cerberus

High winds gusted around her parents' home the day Terra was to leave. Terra grabbed her bag from her room before saying goodbye to her parents. After promising to call them once she arrived at the Academy Alya had spoke of, Terra walked to the quarry. She stood and looked at it for a long moment.

Alya appeared as she had before with the strange glowing ring dissipating around her. She looked at Terra's bag and smiled before moving to stand next to Terra. "I have made a lot of mistakes. My last squire, I really didn't give her much say in the matter." Alya faced Terra. "I don't want a conscript this time. I want a volunteer. This is your choice now. If you turn back, I won't blame you. Are you ready?"

Terra met Alya's eyes. "I've made up my mind. I'm done hiding in this quarry and wasting time. Let's go."

Alya smiled before touching the glass face of her shieldwatch. A ring formed around them and the world transformed.

"What is this place?" Terra asked as they entered the blue haze again.

Alya consulted her shieldwatch. "This is the Edge of Time, a place where all time blends together. Follow. We have to find a *salient.*"

Terra walked closely behind Alya, clinging to the woman's forearm at all times. "What's a salient?"

Alya frowned. "Some piece of singularity technology. Don't worry about it."

Like last time, the wind picked up when they moved. Terra struggled to stand but Alya seemed unaffected.

"So," Terra said after noticing the strange echo this place had, "How exactly does time travel work?"

Alya shrugged. "I have no idea. All I care is that it works."

Terra looked up to see the stars tinted blue. They lit up the sky, unnumbered. Terra knew little about astronomy, but felt sure there were not *that* many stars in the sky. However, when Terra turned to face Alya, she saw a bright burning light that dwarfed every star in the heavens.

The bright blue light was massive enough to make the sun look small. Circular tendrils swirled from it, dancing like oil in water. A large tendril fed away from it, like a flowing river branching at different points. Terra traced the stream and discovered she stood upon one of its many branches. She pointed to the bright blue light. "What's that?"

Alya sighed. "Haven't you heard of the Big Bang? That's similar. It's the Beginning of Time. Nothing special."

Terra's eyes were still wide as she wondered. *Nothing special?* she thought. She only gazed upon the origin of all time and Alya considered it nothing special?

Alya pointed the other direction. "It lies opposite the End of Time."

Terra turned, looking at the large dark shape on the horizon behind her. The End of Time was as colossal as the Beginning. It hung in the sky like a shadowy maw. Unlike the Beginning with its chaotic tendrils, the End twirled in a spiral. It was like a black hole surrounded by a blood red light in contrast with the Beginning's blue glow. Branches, like the one Terra now stood on, all converged at the End and bled into the red haze as though the End were devouring it. Looking at the looming, dark shape made Terra feel uneasy as the wind and glowing haze around her seemed to pull in that direction.

"Don't worry about that," Alya said, pointing to something in between the Beginning and End of Time. "That's where we are going."

In the distance, Terra saw a pearl white object drifting in the star filled void.

"There it is," Alya said, gazing at the structure in the distance. "Saturn City."

Terra saw a blue light burning bright like a beacon in the distance. However, it was too far away for Terra to see in any detail. Alya moved forward again and Terra followed. She approached a ring shaped structure.

Around the structure's outer wall stood twelve tall metal spires, all equally spaced. A small diameter ring hovered above the structure. It had a low wall with a ramp up the side. As Terra drew close, she saw it was constructed of a pearl white metal that appeared similar to the material of Alya's armor. The whole structure was the size of her quarry. Unlike the misty, ethereal world around them, the solid structure stood out.

Alya walked to the center of the metal structure, what Terra assumed was a salient, and touched the glass face of her shieldwatch. A glowing ring of energy ran around the inner edge of the salient and Terra watched the haze around the device shift as the ring passed. When Terra looked up, she saw the ring structure had transported them nearer to the city.

Terra got a closer look at Saturn City. The monolithic scale of the structure stretched hundreds of miles in diameter. The outer ring edge of the structure shimmered pearl white. A convex energy field formed a dome in the center, covering both the top and bottom of the structure. Its outer design reminded Terra of a pocket watch.

The blue grainy energy field was transparent enough to see a city that sat upon a large disc made of mountains, forests, plains, and lakes. Terra could barely see the tall white buildings that stood clustered in certain areas on the disc. She counted twelve sections, each occupying a slice of the disc.

Terra felt dizzy as she took in the sight of the pearl city floating in time. After a moment, Alya touched the orb on her shieldwatch and the salient transported them again. This time, the haze and city faded to reveal a circular room around them.

Another glowing ring formed and passed around them in a clockwise direction. "Biological hazards sweep clear," came a female voice over the speakers in the room.

Alya shook her hand, trying to get a clinging, pale faced Terra to let go. After a moment, Alya took her free hand and pried off Terra's iron grip. "It's okay, Terra. We're here."

Terra swayed as she tried to regain her footing. The world still seemed to spin and her stomach churned from the strange experience.

Alya put her hands on her hips, waiting for Terra to recover. "Don't worry. You get used to it."

Terra's vertigo passed after a moment and her stomach settled as she heard noise from a nearby crowd. She looked up, expecting to see the stars, but instead found clear blue skies overhead with the beaming sun above her. Terra wondered why the outside of the city looked like a night sky, while the city's interior looked to be midday.

"Come on," Alya said, walking forward.

Terra shook her head, trying to focus before following Alya. Her vertigo returned once she walked out of the room, though not because of motion sickness.

It started when a man with silver hair passed by, pushing a large metal disk. It hovered off the ground surrounded by a glowing translucent field. Atop the disk, a saber-toothed tiger paced the inside, looking as confused as Terra. He pushed the hovering bubble as though it and the predator within weighed nothing.

Alya turned to Terra and put two small devices in Terra's ears. "For translations until you get a shieldwatch," Alya said.

The murmurs changed when the devices in Terra's ears activated. She could now understand the hum of conversation around her.

Alya looked both ways before stepping out. "Let's try not to draw attention. I just want to get through timeport processing without being noticed."

Alya set out through the timeport and Terra followed closely behind.

Terra glanced to another entryway near them. A man with insect eyes and chitin shells on his arms and legs stepped out.

"An alien?" Terra asked.

The bug-man whirled, searching with his insect eyes. "Where?"

Alya tugged at Terra. "Not an alien. He is probably from Continuum Xi. They have a lot of biomorphic technology."

Terra wondered what biomorphic technology was as she continued to gawk at the sizable crowd. They made their way down an open area, moving towards a large pearl white structure ahead. Others entered and exited chambers like the one Terra had arrived in. Many stood on the sidelines, either sitting on benches or chatting with others.

"Stay close," Alya said, surveying the crowd with a wary gaze.

Terra followed while gawking at the colorful mob. Those with silver hair wore similar dress to Alya. They directed and assisted others. They all carried shieldwatches even if they didn't always wear armor.

Those without silver hair or a shieldwatch were more varied. One man in an American Civil War Confederate uniform argued with a silver haired man. The Confederate soldier held an automatic assault rifle in his hand.

"No. For the last time, you can't take it back with you!" the silver haired man said as Terra passed. It was the only part of the conversation she caught.

A few paces away, a silver haired woman yelled at a man dressed in fine silk robes. He had an old wooden cart full of strange caged animals. Terra saw a Dodo bird along with many animals she didn't recognize.

The woman scowled as she pointed at the animals. "Most of these animals are extinct or haven't evolved yet in your time. These are temporal invasive species! You can't take them back or they will devastate that time's ecosystem."

The man raised an eyebrow. "What's an ecosystem?"

"This place is busy," Terra said as they passed by the argument.

"I hate the timeport during busy hours," Alya said as they passed what looked like a dockyard to Terra. Several docked ships hovered in the air, looming over them like metal titans. "Time travelers must check in here before returning to their home time. We check them for cross-time diseases or illegal items. Timeships dock here as well."

Ahead, a metal building stood blocked off by a series of gates, each engraved with a Roman numeral. A long, slow line of people stretched from each gate. Alya grimaced as her gaze searched the gates ahead while shying away from anyone else with silver hair. She led Terra off to the side to get a better look. They stopped at a small overlook. While Alya searched for a gate with a short line, Terra looked up as a wide shadow passed overhead.

A massive metal structure passed overhead like a boot might pass over an ant. It was miles long, stretching into the distance. When she looked out from the balcony, she paused, taking in the sight.

A huge mechanical pillar stood in the center of the city. In the middle of the pillar hovered a bright blue orb of burning light. Above the orb moved three huge hands that Terra guessed were miles long by themselves. One thick hand moved slowly while another shorter one held still. A third hand projected a row of blue light beams that shot over the city. This one moved the fastest and was the one that had just passed over them.

Around the pillar and between the ring edges lay the buildings of the city itself. Terra had seen a city before during school trips though she had never seen a city where buildings floated in the sky. Many buildings possessed a glass orb embedded in sides that looked like the glass face of a shieldwatch.

In another part of the city, distant forested mountains stood. In the skies hovered saucer shaped aircraft that flew at a steady pace. "That explains so much," Terra said as her eyes followed the strange aircraft.

Alya tugged at Terra and pointed to a gate with a shorter line. Terra followed after stealing another glance at the city glimmering in the light.

They waited at the back of a lengthy line. Terra took her eyes off the flying saucer in the sky to listen in on the conversation ahead. An old man stood at the gate. His leather clothing was in tatters and his hair unkempt as he spoke in a desperate tone to the gatekeeper.

The young gatekeeper had a full head of sliver haired and a legion uniform like Alya's. He sat at a desk in front of the gateway. The silver haired man at the gate kept his eyes on a holographic disc projected above his shieldwatch face. His bored expression remained constant while the old man begged.

"Please," the old man said, his voice hoarse. "Give me citizenship. I'll be a good citizen! I swear. I have never broken any laws of the Temporal Accords! I need to become a citizen. I need immortality!"

"I am sorry, sir," the silver haired gatekeeper said in monotone. He did not look at the old man while he spoke, keeping his attention on the hologram. "The only way you can earn citizenship is if you join the Aeon Legion."

"Please!" the old man begged.

"I am sorry, sir," the gatekeeper replied, his tone still neutral. "You cannot enter the city nor can you become a citizen."

The old man looked down before walking off, dejected.

The gatekeeper shook his head. "Crashing dustrunners," he said, under his breath.

The next man stepped up. He wore a white button up shirt with a dark jacket and trousers. "Excuse me but I was told by the Aeon Legion that I am not allowed to visit my continuum's future."

The gatekeeper spoke in a bored tone. "If you had read the Temporal Accords when you registered your time travel device, you would have discovered that acquiring knowledge of the future is not allowed. You may inquire at the timeport office for permission."

"I did," the man said, frowning. "They rejected my request. Instead, I want access to the Archives at the Aveum Academy."

"No," the gatekeeper said flatly. "You don't have permission to enter the city, much less visit the Archives. If they won't let you time travel to your continuum's future, then they are not going to let you into the Archives."

The man rubbed his chin before he smiled. "I understand." He turned to leave.

"And don't try to time travel there yourself," the gatekeeper added. "The Sybil will precog your attempt and you will find yourself thrown into a dark cell in Tartarus."

The man frowned, but walked off without protest.

Another man approached. This one wore strange bright yellow garb with edges of gold. He had several others with him dressed in less impressive clothes. Each carried an ornate box. Terra assumed these were servants.

One of the servants approached "All hail Emperor Seres of the golden lands," he said in a lofty voice. "He has come to this pearl city to purchase a shieldwatch."

The gatekeeper continued to read without reaction, save for a yawn.

The servant frowned but the Emperor did not react to the slight.

"Where must we go to purchase a shieldwatch?" the servant asked.

"We don't sell shieldwatches," the gatekeeper said.

The servant scowled and was about to speak when the Emperor stepped forward. He had a servant open one of the cases. Gold and jewels filled the box to the brim. "Perhaps the guard needs a gift so we may pass?" Emperor Seres said in a deep voice.

The gatekeeper regarded the gold and then the Emperor with a flat look. He sighed. "You don't get it do you?"

Emperor Seres frowned. "I am bribing you to do your job."

The gatekeeper scowled. "My job is to keep people like you out. Besides, no amount of gold or any other treasure is worth a shieldwatch."

Alya rubbed her forehead as the exchange continued to go nowhere. "I always get in the shortest but slowest line. Now how am I going to get through without too many questions being asked? A mask? No. They would check under it. Cut my hair? No. That didn't work last time."

Several silver haired soldiers passed. Unlike Alya, their uniforms were a dark gray color with a crescent moon patch on their upper arms. All carried aeon edges.

Alya snarled, gripping the hilt of her aeon edge as the soldiers passed.

Terra tensed but the soldiers ignored them.

One soldier approached the gatekeeper. "Got another delivery for Time King Endymion. Private collection this time," He then touched the face of his shieldwatch before dragging the small holographic disc to the gatekeeper.

The gatekeeper glanced at the holo before nodding. He then returned to reading his own hologram. "Go ahead."

Emperor Seres gestured to the armed entourage. "You let them through!"

The gatekeeper sighed. "They work for Endymion. You don't."

One soldier stopped and stared at Alya.

Alya kept her hand on the hilt of her aeon edge while regarding the soldier with narrowed eyes.

The soldier then shook his head. "No. Can't be her. She'd never wait in line."

Another soldier looked to his gawking comrade. "See something?"

"No," he said, turning to go. "Just a Silverwind lookalike."

Once the soldiers passed, Alya relaxed.

Terra felt her tension return. She worried Alya may have lied to her, assuming this person was Alya.

The Emperor straightened his garb. "I will bring my armies to this city if I am not allowed through."

"Now I'm scared," the gatekeeper said in monotone. He sighed after seeing the lengthening line. When he saw Alya, his eyes went wide. He shot up before standing at attention. "Centurion Silverwind! I am so sorry, I didn't see you there!"

Seres frowned as he looked over the line, trying to see who the gate-keeper had spotted.

Alya pinched the upper part of her nose and sighed. "Well. I suppose it can't be helped," she said before motioning for Terra to follow.

"How may I assist you?" the gatekeeper said, still saluting with a fist over his chest.

"At ease," Alya said. "No need to be so formal."

"It's my honor," the gatekeeper said as he relaxed. "Centurion, you may go right on through. No need to bother yourself with checking in."

"I know, but I have a guest," Alya said as she gestured to Terra. "I need someone to grant her clearance to enter the city. Also she needs a shieldwatch."

The gatekeeper looked to Terra and nodded. "Right away, Centurion Silverwind. Is she a new squi–"

"Just a friend," Alya interrupted. She leaned in close and spoke in a hushed tone. "I want my presence here off the record. Understand?"

The gatekeeper nodded, keeping his own voice low. "Understood. Legendary Blade business no doubt. You have my full discretion," he said before turning to Terra. "Bag please."

She handed the gatekeeper her bag.

The gatekeeper froze the bag in midair. It hung there encased in a glowing translucent sphere. "You may retrieve it in a few hours at processing. Hand please."

Terra held out her hand. The gatekeeper grabbed one of her fingers and touched it to a device he drew from his belt.

"DNA cataloged," came a female voice from the gatekeeper's shield-watch. "Welcome to Saturn City, Terra Mason."

"Go ahead and bring her to processing," the gatekeeper said, smiling. "You're clear to enter."

"Thank you," Terra said as she followed Alya while trying to ignore the glares of those who had been rejected from entering the city.

As soon as Alya walked past the gate, the gatekeeper shouted, "That was so infinite! I got to meet the famous Silverwind. It's not everyday you meet a Legendary Blade!"

Alya groaned as she rubbed her forehead.

Emperor Seres pointed to Alya. "Oh? Why does that cur get special treatment? Is it because she has your silver–"

The gatekeeper whirled, grabbing the Emperor by the lapels of his imperial robe and lifting him off his feet. His face twisted into a snarl as he spoke in a low tone. "Listen here you worthless dustrunner. That woman, Alya Silverwind, is one of the greatest heroines of this city. She has saved Time a hundred fold. You owe her your life many times over and you will show her your respect."

Terra gawked until Alya drew her away. She followed Alya past the gateway and into Saturn City. *At least I know that's the real Alya,* Terra thought.

Once they were clear of the gate, Alya sighed. "Good thing we got through before a mob formed."

Terra was going to ask Alya a question when a man came running around the corner. He wore the same armor as Alya and stopped in front of her, out of breath. He then looked up at her. "It's true! You are here! Silverwind the Legendary Blade!"

Alya's gaze darted around, looking for a quick exit.

"Please make me your squire!" The man said while he struggled to draw himself up after what Terra guessed was a lengthy run.

Alya pursed her lips while still searching for a way to exit with grace.

"I have passed the Labyrinth with good marks," the man said with a desperate edge to his voice. "I can secure recommendations from my instructors if needed."

Alya gritted her teeth. "Listen, I am sure you are re–"

"Please!" the man begged. "I would do anything you requested! I know everyone wants to be your squire, but I would be exceptionally dedicated."

"You're famous?" Terra asked, staring at Alya with a wide gaze.

"At attention," came a man's voice.

The legionnaire who petitioned Alya stood at attention as another man approached.

Alya grimaced as she turned but smiled when she saw the man walking towards her. The man wore the same armor as Alya though it had a good many more emblems and medals. He stood a bit taller than either Terra or Alya. While he shared Alya's tanned skin tone and silver hair, his dark eyes contrasted with Alya's eyes of sky blue. Terra noted he had a handsome face with a genuine smile. His rigid stance made him appear more professional when contrasted with Alya's graceful motions and playful demeanor.

The petitioner gasped. "Strategos Orion. Two Legendary Blades in the same place!"

"Orion," Alya said as she smiled. "I am surprised to find you out. Prometheus finally let you out of the office?"

"I wish," Orion said as he stood in front of her. "I'm on an errand, as usual."

Terra wondered why neither saluted the other. It didn't seem very military to her.

Orion turned to the petitioner. "Young man, would you do me a favor?"

"Anything for a Legendary Blade!" the petitioner said with eagerness.

Orion smiled. "I need a team to focus on analysis of sensory data from the Edge. They require a few more members and I think you will work as a last minute addition."

"Yes, sir! I won't disappoint you!" he said, smiling before turning to Alya. "Silverwind, I have sent you my contact information. Please consider taking me on as a squire."

Orion turned to Alya as the petitioner departed. "Rather odd, Alya. Usually you escape such petitioners."

Alya smiled. "Thanks, Orion. I'm grounded at the moment. I will take care of that soon enough. Why are you here?"

"A temporal anomaly drew me out of the office," he said. "Did you see anything odd while out in the Edge? I know you were returning from a personal trip."

Alya shrugged. "Nothing strange. Why?"

Orion held up his shieldwatch before reading a holo projected over the glass face. "We had an energy spike that seemed to..." he trailed off when he noticed Terra. His smile vanished.

Terra raised an eyebrow.

"Who is that?" Orion asked.

"Oh. Well. Um..." Alya said, looking off to the side.

"Did you find another squire? How did the Sybil not precog another Qadar?"

"Not so loud, Orion," Alya said in a soft tone. "I don't want another riot."

Orion frowned, gesturing for them to follow. "Come with me."

Alya scowled but followed and Terra trailed behind wondering if she had done something wrong. Orion entered a nearby building before leading them down a hallway. It ended in a dead end with a metal archway built into a wall. The wall then faded away, leaving the archway open. Terra stared in amazement as they entered an empty room that, to Terra, looked like an interrogation chamber.

"Don't start with me, Orion," Alya said as soon as the wall faded back.

Orion shook his head. "Good Aion! You could have at least warned me."

Terra poked the solid wall or rather what she assumed was a door. It remained solid.

Alya sighed. "...and you're starting!"

Terra stood to the side. She raised a finger. "Um. Excuse me?"

Orion crossed his arms, still staring at Alya. "How many years has it been since Kairos? Nearly a century?"

Terra's arm fell to her side. "A century? You're that old?"

Alya turned her back to Orion. "Don't speak of Kairos like she's dead."

Orion's expression softened. "I'm sorry, Alya. But she's been missing for over a century. You need to accept she's gone. Regardless, you need to give me warning when you chose another squire."

Terra raised a hand. "Excuse me. I have a question."

Alya turned her side to Orion. "If I want another squire then what business is it of yours? I don't need your permission. Regulations allow it."

Orion raised his arms in frustration. "Crashing End, Alya! Last time you found a squire, a month later we were overrun by Faceless."

Alya faced Orion, stamping her foot on the ground. "You talk like it's my fault the Faceless tried to kill everyone!"

Terra sighed. "And I'll guess I will just stand here and talk to myself."

Orion raised a finger. "And the one before that, we were drowning in Manticores!"

Alya shrugged. "Coincidence?"

Orion's eyes narrowed. "Name me one squire you found that didn't precede some huge crisis."

Alya rubbed her chin with her left hand. "Um. Maybe Tahir?"

Orion sighed. "We were already in the middle of the First Temporal War, remember?"

"Oh right," Alya said as though she had forgotten this detail. She shook her head. "Well if the Sybil have foreseen nothing then we shouldn't worry. Don't be so superstitious, Orion."

Terra's gaze darted from Alya to Orion as she waited for a point to break into the conversation.

Orion gestured to Alya. "I'm not being superstitious, I'm being practical. If I had known you were getting another squire, I would have put the Second Cohort on alert."

Alya grinned. "I'll prove you a fool. Care to make a wager?"

Orion raised an eyebrow.

Alya gestured with one hand. "I'll bet you five hundred years that nothing happens."

Terra tilted her head, wondering how one gambled time.

Orion shook his head. "Oh come on, Alya. You know that's nothing to us. We both have more years than we know what to do with. How about this. If I'm right you'll wear that dress I like."

Alya smiled. "An acceptable wager. But if I win then you'll take a week off work and we can go somewhere nice for a while."

Orion hesitated as though a week off work was worth far more than five hundred years. "Fine," he said at last.

"Hey!" Terra shouted, waving her arms during the brief lull in the conversation. Orion and Alya turned their attention to her. She cleared her throat before counting with her fingers. "Question one. How old are you both? Question two. Who's Aion? Question three. Who's Kairos? Question four. How do you gamble time? Question five ho–"

Orion looked at Alya. "Well. I see you have briefed her about as well as the rest of your squires. Have you ever considered actually explaining things to the people you drag through the Edge?"

Alya shrugged. "That's what the Academy is for. Besides, I only like to show them the interesting things, like how the shieldwatch works."

Orion rubbed his brow. "Let me guess. You were just going to dump her at the Academy and leave?"

"So? Why does it matter? It's their job to train squires in the basics. Besides, I hate explaining things everyone should already know and I have no interest spending the next few months supervising her exercise."

"Just like you. You blow through like a storm and leave someone else to clean up the mess."

Terra's brow lowered. It was just like when her parents argued. She never got a word in with them either.

Alya glanced at Terra. "You're being awfully quiet."

Terra shot Alya a baleful glare.

Alya raised an eyebrow. "What?"

Orion looked at his shieldwatch. "Well I'll go ahead and inform the others about the new squire."

"No!" Alya said, turning to Orion. "I mean no. That's a bad idea."

Orion paused.

Alya looked away. "I sometimes wonder if that's what drove Kairos away. People treated her like a savior figure."

"But she was," Orion said. "She saved this city, not to mention the rest of Time. There is a reason they call her the greatest of the Legendary Blades."

"And the price she paid for that was loneliness and isolation," Alya said, staring forlornly to the side. "You can't be friends with someone you worship."

Orion regarded Terra while rubbing his chin. "Well I guess it would make things more complicated if everyone knew. Not to mention the endless *Trial of Blades* challengers she'd have to endure. Very well. I'll keep this between us and Consul Prometheus for now. Just be sure she knows that."

Alya smiled. "Thanks, Orion."

Orion turned to Terra. "What is your name?"

"Terra Mason, sir," Terra said.

"Well, Terra Mason," Orion said. "Just be sure to keep the identity of who you are squiring for a secret. If people knew you were Alya's squire, it would create a terrible commotion."

Terra grimaced. "I paid attention to the conversation even if you two ignored me."

Orion grinned. "Blunt. Very different from Kairos."

"How did you know I was Alya's squire?" Terra asked.

"You look a little like her," Orion said.

"Alya?" Terra asked.

"No. Kairos," he said as he turned to leave. He looked over his shoulder before he exited. "I look forward to working with you, Tiro Mason, when the next calamity hits. And, Alya. I look forward to seeing you in that dress."

After Alya's argument with Orion, she brought Terra to customs to retrieve her bag and finish timeport processing before disappearing. Processing turned into a lengthy ordeal. Terra finished a physical exam before calling her parents on a terminal. After that, she endured a lengthy interview with a psychologist which Terra thought an odd requirement. The interviewer said that these tests had something to do with the training at the Academy. With her exams and interviews done, they instructed her to pick up a shieldwatch.

Terra found the shieldwatch station guarded by a man in a similar uniform to Alya. After he checked with Minerva, he handed Terra a shieldwatch. She then thanked the man before leaving and wondered where to go next.

Terra turned the shieldwatch in her hands. A length of metal shorter than the forearm made up most of the shieldwatch with the glass face on one end while the other held an embossed infinity symbol. Its glass face glowed a faint blue color and functioned as a display screen. Two padded clamps under the device allowed it to attach to the top of the forearm. It was not as thick as Alya's shieldwatch who likely had a tougher, military model.

"Clamp it on your off hand like a shield. It works better that way," came Alya's voice from behind Terra.

Terra suppressed her instinct to jump and instead glared at Alya. "Do you always come and go as you please?"

Alya grinned. "If someone wants to buy that shieldwatch, don't sell it for anything. That device is far more valuable than any amount of gold, gems, money or anything else they try to trade it for."

After struggling, Terra clamped it on her left forearm.

Alya tapped her chin with her index finger. "There was something I was supposed to tell you. Now what was it? Something about an accident?"

Terra raised an eyebrow as Alya thought.

After a moment, Alya shrugged. "I suppose it's not important. Forward unto eternity, Terra. I will see you in a few weeks."

Terra's eyes widened. "Wait! What about lodging? What about food? How do I get to this Academy?"

Alya rolled her eyes. "I will not count the seconds for you. You made the choice to come here, so work through these problems yourself. As for the Academy, just be your usual stubborn self and they should let you in eventually."

With that, Alya turned and walked away, leaving Terra in an empty hallway of the timeport.

Terra scowled. Orion was right. Alya had just abandoned her.

After a long sigh, Terra made her way out of the timeport to get her bearings. The city lights flickered on as darkness fell and already a few of the brighter stars shone in the sky.

Terra walked to an overlook that showed a view of the city in the distance. She could see why they built the main gate here. The first thing that any newcomer to the city saw after stepping through the gate was a full view of the city center. With darkness settling in, Terra could see the lights of the city in the distance.

Darkness had cloaked the pearl colors while blue lights lit up the city like a glowing sapphire. Buildings in the distance shone like jewels in the night that reflected on the waters of the more scenic areas. The sight took Terra's breath away. Terra almost didn't hear the person approaching behind her.

Chapter VI
Saturn City

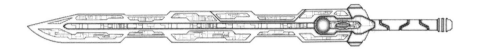

Saturn City is the greatest civilization in history. We say this without boasting. It is the closest humanity will ever get to a utopia. The city's only flaw is that life here is near perfect enough to remove all desire for change.
-Consul Prometheus

Terra turned to see a young woman. She was taller than Terra by a few inches with tan skin similar in tone to Alya's and the other city natives.

"Would you perpend," She said in an airy tone, "relocation to an adjacent space?"

"What?" Terra asked, raising an eyebrow. Terra inspected the woman. Her straight sleek hair was a lighter shade of brown and reached below her shoulders. Terra couldn't help but feel jealous of the woman's slender body, long legs, and flawless skin. The glow of youth made Terra guess the girl's age a few years older than her, though Terra didn't want to make assumptions about age here.

"As I am a cartographer of the crepuscular sky, this has made me seek vantages such as this to give me a vista," she said, continuing in her ethereal tone. In her ears were the same device Alya had given Terra when she had arrived at the timeport, though Terra wondered if it was working properly. Over one shoulder the woman wore a white shawl with silver edging and embroidered in intricate sinuous designs. A silver broach with a sapphire center held the shawl in place near her neck. The shawl dipped down below her waist to the top of a knee length white dress.

Terra's brow furrowed. "What are you talking about?"

"In shadows, the stars can—"

"Get to the point!" Terra said, scowling.

The woman cringed at Terra's outburst. "I just wanted you to move," she said, her eyes watery.

Terra's expression softened. Perhaps her mother was right and she needed to be less blunt. "Sorry. I didn't mean to snap at you. I'm just lost right now."

The woman relaxed her pose. "Do you need directions? Minerva can provide those."

Terra sighed. "I feel so out of place here. I don't even know what Minerva is. This is the first time I have time traveled."

"What is your home time?"

"Twenty first century United States."

"Oh. You must be here to join the Aeon Legion."

"How did you guess?"

"If I remember correctly, the Americans were a warrior culture. They loved war so much that they declared it against concepts like poverty, drugs and terror when there was no one else to fight."

"Why do you want to go to that overlook so badly?"

"I came to observe the movements of the astral bodies in the evening skies," she said as her airy tone returned.

"I think you just said that you were stargazing but I'm not sure. Why are you so indirect?"

The woman maintained an aloof air while looking at Terra. "That is a direct, untactful question. In answer to your query, my statements are indirect by necessity. Others here take apart my words so I must spend them carefully. Why are you so direct?"

"I don't mean to be blunt. People never seem to take me seriously so I'm direct. I'm frustrated right now since I just got to the city today and I'm tired, hungry and without a place to stay," Terra said, sighing. "My name is Terra. What's your name?"

She looked at Terra again while her expression remained unreadable. "I am Delphia, a native to the city."

"Oh," Terra said, looking at Delphia's hair. "Then why isn't your hair sil–"

"Silver is the color of condescension!" Delphia said as she crossed her arms and looked away.

Terra's brow furrowed.

Delphia turned to Terra and moved closer. "Well I hope you have

not judged our city based on a few cruel citizens. They delight in criti-
cizing those younger than them but I assure you we are not all like that.
To prove it, allow me to help you."

"You don't have to."

A slight smile curled Delphia's lips. She moved closer, standing right
next to Terra. "To use my knowledge to aid others is something I seldom
experience. Are you hungry?"

Terra nodded while taking a step back. She hadn't eaten since she
arrived. "Actually do you know a cheap place to rent a room for the
night?"

Delphia tilted her head. "Cheap?"

"You know. A place that won't cost a lot of money?"

Delphia raised an eyebrow. "Money? What's that?"

Terra sighed. "Never mind. Is there a place where I can spend the
night?"

"You could ask my mother if you can stay at my home. She loves to
have guests over and she would probably allow you to stay in the guest
room until the Academy training starts."

"Really?"

"Oh yes. Saturnians are rather fond of new companionship. They are
very amaranthine so they like to have new guests to converse with."

Terra wondered what amaranthine meant while Delphia gazed at her
shieldwatch before typing on a holographic disc projected above the face.
A moment later, Delphia turned to Terra. "She is interested in meeting
you. Let's go to the Convivium to meet my mother."

"The what?" Terra asked, now wondering what a Convivium was.

"Delphia," came a voice behind her.

Terra turned to see a handsome man approach. He had a well toned
body with beautiful eyes and could have been a model if he wished.

Delphia turned to Terra. "I apologize. Let me address this small
detail."

"My friends are waiting for us," he said with a grin.

Delphia looked away from the man. "I am sorry but I have committed to another engagement."

"What?" the man asked.

Delphia spoke in her usual ethereal tone without a hint of emotion.
"I am afraid I must terminate our romantic involvement for now on

account of numerous minor details too superfluous to warrant citation."
She then turned to lead Terra away from the confused young man.

"Wait," Terra said after they were out of sight of the young man. "Did
you just dump him?"

Delphia shrugged. "He stuttered a little and his eyes were a rather
off shade of blue."

Terra wondered how Delphia could be so casual about leaving such
an attractive man.

Delphia smiled and grabbed Terra's hand.

Terra shook her hand loose. "Delphia, no offense but I am not into
that."

Delphia tilted her head. "Into what?"

Terra rubbed her forehead while trying to think of a graceful way to
explain it Delphia.

"Minerva," Delphia said. "Explain please."

Minerva spoke from Delphia's shieldwatch. "The act of holding
hands in Terra's culture is a symbol of romantic involvement. In addition,
same sex romantic relationships are considered taboo in her culture."

Delphia faced Terra. "Well in Saturn City, Terra Mason, holding
hands is a sign of friendship. Since you are in Saturn City, you should
do as we Saturnians do."

Delphia grabbed Terra's hand and led her to a large sidewalk sized
glowing line on the ground. When they stepped on the line their surroundings faded out before fading into a new view.

"What is going on?" Terra asked as the surroundings faded again only
to be replaced again.

Delphia pointed to the tall city buildings in the background. Terra
watched it fade out to be replaced by a similar view of the city except
closer. She then pointed to the glowing line they stood on like a neon
sidewalk. "It is called a *fadeline*. This allows the people of the city to
move from zone to zone quickly. Faster than horses. Safer than vehicles."

As the center of the city drew closer, she learned that bigger fadelines
took one further away than smaller fadelines, which faded into shorter
distances. Delphia grabbed Terra's hand again and led her off the fadeline when she spotted an icon on the ground labeled *VI*.

"Where are we now?" Terra asked as Delphia walked off the fadeline.

The smell of food filled the air along with the rumblings of a large gathering of people and music.

"This is the Convivium in zone six."

"What's the Convivium?" Terra asked.

"It's the recreational zone. Many gather here every night to celebrate."

"Celebrate what?" Terra asked, looking at a sizable crowd of people both leaving and entering the area, all with silver hair. These people wore more varied dress than the uniformed staff at the timeport. They all appeared in their mid twenties with no children or elderly in sight.

Delphia considered for a moment before leading Terra again. "I guess they are celebrating being in Saturn City. Festivities are held here every night."

Terra continued to gaze as Delphia led her through the crowd. They passed many buildings with some hosting foods belonging to specific cultures and time periods though Terra did not recognize them all. Other buildings were bars or what she assumed to be night clubs.

There were other attractions. She passed several bands playing in open areas or on stages. Other places hosted numerous crafts and hobbies, too many for Terra to count. Many things she only barely recognized; a group playing a kind of sport, a couple dueling with strange holographic creatures like a video game, onlookers watching a holographic play and a person on stage reciting poetry.

"How many zones are there?"

"Twelve in total. Four residential zones, a park, a preserve, the timeport, the prison facility Tartarus and a few other areas. This is the most popular zone."

After leaving a large crowd, Delphia found a quiet spot next to a lake that reflected the lights of the city. They sat at an empty table. After Terra sat, Delphia scooted closer which caused Terra to shift back. Terra looked around to see that most Saturnians stood or sat close to one another.

"Mother said she would meet us here," Delphia said while holding her shieldwatch hand out, palm facing up. She touched the glass face of her shieldwatch with her other hand and a ring formed above her open palm. As it circled, it left a dish of steaming hot food in its wake.

Terra narrowed her gaze, staring at the plate. "How did you do that?"

"Were you not instructed on how to use the shieldwatch before entering the city?"

"No. I was pretty much deserted here with no explanation about anything."

Delphia grabbed Terra's shieldwatch arm and moved it in front of her. She then touched its face and dragged a holographic disc from it. "This is called a holoface." she said while sliding it in front of Terra. The disc shaped holoface had a thin border on the edge with twelve small buttons arranged like numerals on a clock. The center of the disc displayed a list of food categories.

Terra touched the holoface which made the tip of her finger tingle. "Huh," she said after seeing one of the categories expand to show her even more choices. Terra then touched one of the buttons on the edge and found she could drag the holoface around to wherever she wished. Then she touched the opposite edges with both her hands and discovered she could scale the holoface's size.

After a moment of shifting through menus, Terra touched one of the options. A holographic image of a dish of food appeared in front of the holoface vertical to Terra. She touched it again and a ring appeared. It circled around the holoface, forming the dish exactly as the hologram had appeared. But, the plate dropped to the table and shattered after forming.

Terra cringed. "Is there a trashcan here?"

"Trashcan?"

Terra gestured to the broken plate. "To clean that up."

Delphia moved her shieldwatch hand above the plate. A small transparent sphere flickered briefly around the plate as it reformed.

"How did you do that?"

"The shieldwatch is singularity technology. I just moved the plate back in time before it broke. Don't worry about discarding refuse here. The City's hands erase unwanted items from the city every hour."

"How does food appear out of nowhere though?"

"A shieldwatch can take a single instance of time and save it in a state. It can then recall that state whenever needed. In more simple terms, the shieldwatch rolls back time until when the food was near it. This allows a shieldwatch to replicate most things using time. Your shieldwatch has many such items saved into its states directory."

Terra stared at the plate, thinking. No wonder they had no concept of money here.

Delphia pointed to the large metal structure overhead that passed over them. "This is the minute hand. It passes over the entire city once every hour, cleaning as it goes. The second hand moves over the city once every minute and sends information back to the other hands. The hour hand passes over the city twice a day and makes any major changes to the city to return it to normal such as Restoring a collapsed building."

Terra stared at the titanic metal structure that moved over the city. She pointed to the bright orb in the center of the city that glowed blue in the distance. "What's that?"

Delphia looked at the light. "That is the Temporal Singularity. It powers the city and its technology."

Terra scratched her head. "I... have no idea what any of that is."

"You should ask Minerva, the Saturn City's artificial intelligence, about it. She would have more technical and historic details. Though I doubt you would find such a thing interesting. Temporal immigrants seldom care for long, boring histories or science," Delphia said, averting her eyes.

Terra shook her head. "Oh no! I love boring history. Hard to bore someone who digs up rocks for a hobby."

Delphia turned to Terra with a slight smile.

"Why are you smiling?"

Delphia still spoke in an aloof tone, "It's just, I rarely find those who genuinely listen to what I have to say. For someone to take me seriously is an uncommon enjoyment for me."

Terra smiled. Had she made a friend? "So where is the Academy?"

"The Aevum Academy is in zone eleven. Many citizens and time travelers take classes at the Academy. I start classes there soon myself since my boring hobby is astronomy."

"Astronomy?"

"I love the stars and the sun. Light in the dark. Things of beauty and power."

A young silver haired woman approached them. She waved at Delphia.

Delphia waved back. "Mother!"

She smiled and sat with them. She wore a shawl in similar coloring and style to Delphia, though hers was far more revealing. The shawl fit over a short, form fitting dress that showed off much of her well toned body. A gold flower ornament held a loose bun of silver hair in place with a single lock falling to the left side of her face.

"Terra," Delphia said, gesturing to the woman. "This is Vita, my mother. Vita, this is Terra. She's trying to join the Legion."

"Good ages, Dhimmi Terra," Vita said in a friendly tone. Like other silver haired Saturnians Terra had met, she appeared youthful. In fact Terra could have mistaken this woman for Delphia's sister.

"Hi," Terra said, feeling awkward at her own ignorance of what the proper greeting was in the city.

Vita looked Terra over. "Apologies, but you certainly look like a new-timer if ever I have seen one."

"I just got here today, actually," Terra said, trying to appear natural.

Vita looked at Delphia. "And you didn't even offer to get her new clothes? Manners Delphia. How could you let the poor lady wander our city without at least offering her the option of trying our fashions?"

Delphia glared at Vita. "Crashing End Mother! I did tr—"

Vita waved a finger at Delphia. "Watch your language, child."

Delphia stiffened, glaring at Vita. Her normal aloof tone changed into a low growl. "I am not a child. I am twenty one—"

Vita sighed. "I doubt you even offered to help this poor girl."

Delphia's face turned red as she stomped off, tears forming in her eyes.

Terra raised an eyebrow as Delphia left. *She cries too easily*, Terra thought. Terra would never run away from arguing with her mother.

Vita sighed. "Youth. Much like the Oracles of Yakarl, they take everything too seriously."

"Actually," Terra said. "She offered to help. She said I could ask you if I could stay in your guest room. I was abandoned at the timeport so I am in a bind."

Vita nodded. "Not many legionnaires take a direct interest in their squires now. They know we Saturnians will take care of them. If you wish, you may stay at my home until the training starts at the Academy. We haven't used the guest room in some time and you wouldn't impose for very long since recruits are required to move into the Academy's dorms for the training.

"Thank you so much!" Terra said, grateful that she solved at least one problem today.

Vita smiled before sitting at the table. She then slid close to Terra. "Well then. If this is your first time to the city, then let me be the first Saturnian to offer you a drink. What do you wish?" Vita said looking at a holoface she called up with her shieldwatch. It had a lengthy list of drinks displayed on it. "Do you like wine, mixed drinks, or liquor?"

"What? No! I'm not even twenty one yet."

Vita stared, expressionless, at Terra for a moment before laughing. "We don't have a legal drinking age here. Go ahead and pick something. Anything you desire."

Terra shook her head. "No thanks."

"You sure? Don't worry about a hangover. Just use your shieldwatch to *Restore* yourself in the morning."

Terra scratched her head, wondering what a Restore was.

"Well just tell me if you change your mind," Vita said before replicating herself a drink.

Terra narrowed her gaze at Vita. "Is everyone always so friendly to time travelers here?"

"Of course! The Sybil would have you arrested before you caused trouble. Besides, I have had the same company for nearly a thousand years. It would be nice to converse with someone new for a change."

Terra blinked. "A thousand years? You're that old?"

Vita sighed. "Why do they always find that surprising?"

Terra knew the Saturnians were older than they appeared but she had no idea they were *that* old.

Vita pointed to her shieldwatch. "We can restore our bodies with a shieldwatch indefinitely. A fountain of youth on our wrists." She paused. "Sorry. I doubt you understand that reference."

"No. I got that one," she said before looking at her own shieldwatch. "How many centuries old is Delphia?"

"Delphia? She's only twenty one. That's why her hair isn't silver. I was lucky to win the baby lottery and have her."

"What's with the silver hair?"

"It's a tradition. For every lifetime a citizen of the city lives, they dye a lock of their hair silver."

Terra scanned the crowd. Almost everyone had a full head of silver hair. "What's to stop someone from just dying their hair even if they are young?"

Vita chuckled. "We would know. Youth is like a nostalgic aroma. We can smell it on you. Even if you dyed your hair, your actions give you away," Vita said as she drew out a small container. She opened it to reveal several colorful pills. "Want one?"

Terra stared at the small colorful spheres. "Candy?"

Vita grinned. "Oh nothing *that* dull. Take a green one if you want to feel good, red gives you a lot of energy, blue calms your nerves, yellow gives you visions and the purple ones make sex amazing."

Terra blushed at the mention of the last one. "Um. No thanks. I don't want to get addicted to drugs."

"Addicted?" Vita said, rolling her eyes. "You are as bad as the Trivian Purifiers. Just use a Restore on the shieldwatch. You temporal immigrants. Always so obsessed with consequences."

"I am still getting used to the city. I feel like Alice down the rabbit hole."

"Lewis Carroll, 1865 Continuum Iota. Though I think he used a pen name. It has been a while since I read it."

"You've read that?"

"You read a lot when you're immortal. Regardless, I wouldn't worry about being new to the city. You are welcome to stay in my home until the training starts. Poor thing. You must still be reeling from future shock," she said as her shieldwatch beeped. Vita then typed on a holographic keypad, responding to a message she had received. "Oh. I better add you to my friends' circle on the shieldwatch contact list."

Terra narrowed her gaze, watching many of the natives stare at their shieldwatch faces. "Actually, a few things here seem rather familiar."

As Vita finished typing on a holoface, a silver haired man approached. He had the same tan skin as the others Terra had seen though he wore no shirt over his muscular chest which the shawl only partially covered. He slid close to Vita.

"Vita," he said in a conspiratorial tone, "Be wary."

"What is it, Adel?" Vita asked in an excited tone.

Adel glanced behind him before turning back to Vita. "Varius spoke to me a moment ago."

Vita titled her head. "The high timeborn running for city council again?"

"He talked about reform," Adel said, rolling his eyes.

"Again?" Vita asked in an indignant tone.

Adel shook his head. "I know. Such a brazen show of ambition. One could almost forget that he is a first generation Saturnian and mistake him for a dustrunner."

Vita tensed, turning to Terra with a wide gaze.

Terra just looked confused.

Adel then turned to Terra and paled. "Dhimmi!" he said in an awkward, surprised tone. "Infinite apologies! I should really watch my language around mixed company."

Terra raised an eyebrow. "I'm confused."

Vita relaxed. "I don't think she understands that term yet."

Adel sighed. "Infinite apologies again, dhimmi. You see, dustrunner is an offensive slang term for well... you."

Terra frowned. She didn't like being so ignorant that others had to explain to her when she was supposed to be offended. "Exactly what does dhimmi mean?"

Vita smiled. "That is an honorific for a time traveler. That one is not offensive."

Adel stood. "Well regardless, may we go now? I am quite eager tonight."

Vita faced Terra. "Delphia should be along shortly. She can show you the way back home."

Adel narrowed his gaze on another man nearby. He chatted with a couple, talking about ways to improve the city.

"Shameful," Adel said, shaking his head, "showing such ambition. It's important that we maintain traditional Saturnian values."

Vita nodded. She took Adel's arm and they strolled off into the crowd.

Moments later, Delphia returned with another young man in tow. "Where is my mother?"

Terra gestured to the crowd. "She went off with some guy."

Delphia sat next to Terra. "She is bad for that. So did mother give her approval?"

Terra nodded.

Delphia smiled. "Good. It will be nice to have the company."

Terra glanced to the young man. He was like the last one, gorgeous and looking good in a uniform. She wondered if she should even bother to remember his name.

Delphia's usual aloof air vanished as she leaned forward, smiling. "I just heard an interesting rumor! Alya Silverwind was spotted at the time-port today."

The handsome man leaned forward. "I heard she discovers the best squires."

Delphia nodded. "They say she had someone with her. A youth about the right age for a squire."

He nodded. "How interesting. I may train alongside Silverwind's Squire. What an honor! I wonder what he's like?"

Terra sighed. "Assuming she even makes it in."

The young man rolled his eyes. "He will be accepted. I'd guess he would be admitted without delay. I mean he is Silverwind's squire after all and she's a Legendary Blade."

Terra looked at Delphia. "Okay. I have got to ask. Who are these Legendary Blades I keep hearing about?"

"They are the greatest heroes and heroines of the Aeon Legion," Delphia said. "The most skilled of the Legion become Legendary Blades and only twelve of them exist at one time. The only way to become a Legendary Blade is the defeat a current member in a Trial of Blades."

Terra's brow lowered as she struggled to understand all these new terms. "So they are the leaders of the Legion?"

Delphia shook her head. "No. Not really. They are the best *soldiers* of the Legion. Some have a high rank like Consul Prometheus. Silverwind is a centurion though. A middle rank."

Terra thought about Alya. She certainly wouldn't be a good leader given what Terra knew of her flippant attitude.

Delphia and her boyfriend finished a few more drinks before heading back. Once they left the Convivium, she dumped the man like the last one. Terra grimaced. Delphia discarded two boyfriends in one day while Terra had yet to experience her first kiss.

They traveled to a place called Dār al-salām labeled with the numeral *V* which Delphia explained was a tier two residential area. Spotless pearl white towers crowded this zone. These tall, flat skyscrapers stood straight save for small angular sections cut out of the sides and each reached hundreds of stories into the air. Large glowing glass orbs dotted the structure while wide open seams ran horizontal along the sides. Vegetation grew in the seams which were wide enough to allow a person to walk on. Some of the towers were divided into sections that floated above one another connected by blue beams of light.

Terra followed Delphia to a tower that hovered above, seemingly connected only by a beam of light that shot up to it.

Delphia walked into a beam of light. She floated upward at a steady pace while Terra followed. Terra glanced down to her feet while she felt herself lighten. She felt as though she were swimming in light. They floated through a translucent field before drifting down on top of the field like it was a floor.

Terra followed Delphia down a long hallway with a row of arches on the walls, each inscribed with a numeral. Delphia approached one arch as the wall behind it faded and they entered.

"Do you not have normal doors? What about a key to get in?" Terra asked.

Delphia shrugged. "You mean the *fadedoors*? They just fade when you near them. Why would it need a key?"

"To lock it?"

Delphia raised an eyebrow while taking Terra's bag. "Why would you lock a door to a home? Locks are for prisons, not homes. Here. Let me show you to the guest room."

Terra followed Delphia into her immaculately clean home. Holofaces glowed a faint blue on the walls which took the place of pictures. Many of the holofaces showed pictures of Delphia and Vita. Others depicted great works of art that faded into a new picture or painting after a few moments. Delphia gestured to an empty room. "What's your favorite color?" Delphia asked.

"Um. Blue I guess," Terra said, wondering where she would sleep.

Delphia touched a holoface on her Shieldwatch. A grid of light beams passed from the ceiling to the floor, changing the room into a full guest room complete with a bed and furnishings all with a blue tint.

Terra might had been more surprised if she hadn't spent the rest of the day being surprised. She looked at a holoface projected on the wall. The poster sized holoface showed a picture of a young woman. Terra noted that the girl looked a little like her, though thinner with a well toned body. Still the girl's hair and eyes matched Terra's as did her height. The girl wore Legion armor like Alya's and led several other legionnaires.

Terra pointed to the picture. "Who's that?"

"Oh that girl?" Delphia said, looking at the picture. "That's Kairos. She is Silverwind's most famous squire. Well she was until she vanished."

"Oh," Terra said, still staring at the picture. She then sat down, taking off her shoes to rub her aching feet. In a single day, she had walked more than she had all year.

Delphia gestured for Terra to follow. Terra followed Delphia onto the patio garden. She stepped out and sighed at being able to tread on the grass and dirt again. Standing grounded on the soil felt good on her feet. When Terra looked to Delphia, she saw Delphia staring at the sky. Terra looked up to the stars. Just like when she had first time traveled, the stars seemed beyond number. Even the city lights were not enough to blot them out.

"All of the stars," Terra said. She knew little about stellar formations in the night sky but she knew there were not *this* many stars in the sky. At least not in her time.

"They say there are as many stars as pages in Saturn City's history," Delphia said in an airy, aloof tone. She pointed. "Taurus, Canis Major, Canis Minor, Orion, Gemini."

"Why are there so many stars? I have never seen the night sky so full."

Delphia's slight smile returned. "Light travels at a set speed. Here in the Edge, the light from every star has had time to reach us. You are looking at every star to ever exist in the universe."

"It's beautiful."

Delphia glanced at Terra and smiled. "Thank you."

Terra turned to her. "For what?"

"For sharing this with me. Most don't care about my strange hobby."

Terra grinned. "That's okay. One day I'll force you to go to a quarry with me. Then you can be bored with my hobby."

Delphia turned back to the stars. "I guess you'll be busy soon. I hear just getting into the Legion training is hard."

Terra frowned. She didn't want to think about her task ahead. She had little information on the subject. How would she gain admittance? Alya had told Terra to be her usual stubborn self.

Delphia looked back into the room at the poster of Kairos. "At least you are not Silverwind's squire. If it's true that Silverwind has a new squire then I pity whoever it is."

"Why is that? Isn't Alya's squire supposed to be the best?"

"Because," Delphia said, facing Terra. "All Alya's Squires. They all did great things. All of them became Legendary Blades. They all had amazing accomplishments, but after they accomplished them. Well..."

"Well what?"

Delphia became still as she met Terra's eyes. "Well. They died."

CHAPTER VII
ODYSSEUS

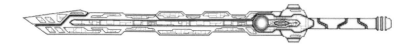

Without a sign, his sword the brave man draws, and asks no omen, but his country's cause.
-From Homer's *The Iliad*, translation by Alexander Pope

Hann's right arm still hurt while it healed in a cast. Thankfully the broken arm did not impair his work as much as he had feared given he was left handed. It did make work slow. Keeping the microscope view centered proved time consuming. The slightest shift would ruin the view and take time to reset back on the part.

"One more," he said as he attached the power source to the device with a small pair of tweezers.

The door opened. "Sir," came a voice from behind Hanns.

"I am busy," Hanns said in an irritated tone. He had told his men he was not to be disturbed.

The soldier saluted. "Sorry Sir. The Brigadeführer wishes to see you immediately."

Hanns groaned, wondering who had arrived. "Tell him I will see him in a moment."

The soldier cleared his throat and shifted. "Sir. You realize he out-ranks you?"

Hanns grinned as he gazed back into the microscope. "Yes. I also realize that I am the only one who can make the calculations for the time machine. He can wait."

The soldier saluted and left.

Hanns finished placing the last piece into the device under the microscope. It was a glass sphere with a metal ring around it the size of a pea. Hanns picked up the device with tweezers and dropped it into his right hand that stuck out of his cast. Holding onto the sphere, he stepped outside into his fortification and frowned at what he saw.

A convoy had pulled into the base and hundreds of SS troops had arrived. *Too many,* Hanns thought. "What is this?"

"Progress," came a voice nearby.

Hanns turned to see a pudgy man in a sharply tailored SS officer's uniform. He stood half a head shorter than Hanns and had a disapproving scowl that made others around him uncomfortable.

The SS soldiers around him didn't seem to mind and all grinned as though they enjoyed the fact they were displacing Hanns's Zeitmacht troops. The regular Zeitmacht troops regarded the SS invaders with wary expressions as the interlopers unloaded the trucks.

The edge of Hanns's lip curled, but he still gave a traditional Wehrmacht salute to the man. "Brigadeführer Emmerich Klein."

Emmerich smirked. "You may address me as Emmerich. I know how you hate formalities, Hanns, and I wish to move this transition along quickly. Are you busy right now?"

Hanns narrowed his gaze. "I am on my way to the labs to deliverer the key to—"

"Good," Emmerich interrupted, gesturing for Hanns to follow.

Hanns scowled when they reached his office. A pile of boxes stood outside that contained his furnishings and items. Two SS soldiers carried out the remaining boxes and dropped them on the floor. They kicked Hanns's box of notes and laughed before leaving.

Hanns walked into what had been his office, now newly furnished, as Emmerich sat down in a fine leather chair. Emmerich smiled as he settled into the chair. "Not much of an office, Hanns, but I guess it will suffice for now. I can't believe you worked in this... cell."

Hanns pulled up a rickety metal chair and sat. "Well some of us, Emmerich, are far too busy to worry about comfort."

"Really, Hanns? I would hardly guess you were busy based on your results."

"We had setbacks."

"Yes I read a few of the reports," Emmerich said, his tone dismissive. "Some kind of sword wielding goddess with golden hair."

"Silver."

"Whatever. Regardless, you and your men failed to beat a single woman with a sword. You call that a setback. I call it pathetic but that's not why I'm here to take command."

Hanns expression hardened. "I was told I would have complete control of this project. You have no jurisdiction here."

Emmerich smiled and pulled out a letter before handing it to Hanns. "You have new Orders."

Hanns took the letter with his unbroken arm and unfolded it. He read the letter, grimacing.

"Signed by Himmler himself," Emmerich said with a smirk. "Your Zeitmacht is under the Waffen SS now."

Hanns folded the letter. "Very well. What are your orders?"

"I want your machine activated immediately. I want to conduct some trials before our major expedition."

Hanns frowned. He didn't need Emmerich drawing Silverwind here. "I don't think that is wise. We do not want to cross paths with Silverwind again. Especially not here."

"You mean the gold haired woman?"

"Silver haired, and yes. She claimed she was from a city in the future that policed time travel. There was something about a treaty called the Temporal Accords and she told us we had to register our time travel device."

"Did you register then?"

Hanns scoffed. "No. Why should we bow to imperialists regardless of what time they come from? Those Temporal Accords are probably little better than the Treaty of Versailles. If only I could have gotten my hands on that book."

Emmerich shook his head. "A book, Hanns? What good is that?"

"A history book could change everything. Specifically a history book from the future. It would tell us everything we need to know to win this war. The first time, I went alone and sneaked into a local library. Silverwind, however, found me before I could get back. She gave me a warning. After that we went in force."

This was a half truth. The book was only part of his objective. He had needed a limited skirmish to ascertain the Legion's strength and response time. The Legion intervened each time he touched a book that might let him change history. They somehow knew. He needed to find out how they were intercepting his attempts to alter time and neutralize it. He needed to get to their base of operations.

Emmerich stared at Hanns. "A history book? A history book! You wasted a time machine on trying to get a history book? You could have at least have tried to steal weapons from the future."

Hanns rolled his eyes. "We can't use stolen future technology. We have no way to maintain it or even the infrastructure to build more. By the time we finished figuring out how it works, the war would be over."

Emmerich shook his head. "Even still, taking a book seems like an awful waste of the time machine's potential. It's a good thing I'm here to take charge. You may be a brilliant scientist, Hanns, but you lack practicality."

"Then what would you use it for?"

Emmerich stroked his chin. "Well I wouldn't waste it on finding a book that tells us what we already know. We will win this war. Everyone knows this. I have something more important in mind. Something that will allow our nation to prosper for centuries to come."

"And what would that be?"

"Why the discovery of our origins, Hanns. I plan to visit the ancient Aryans themselves."

Hanns regarded Emmerich with a flat look. "What? You can't be serious?"

Emmerich beamed. "Yes. We will see the glorious civilization of the Aryans at their height. The scientific secrets we will gain from them will likely be invaluable for our future. We can even take breeding stock back with us to help strengthen the bloodlines."

Hanns had to stop himself from crumpling up the letter in his hand. "You can't tell me you believe in that eugenics pseudo science?"

Emmerich raised an eyebrow. "Hanns, I would think you of all people would appreciate our eugenics program."

"I have read numerous books on the subject. It has no real scientific basis. Eugenics is garbage science."

Emmerich's face went red as he stood. "Are you claiming that the entire scientific basis of the Nazi party is wrong?"

Hanns rubbed his forehead with his good hand. "Emmerich, you and the SS do not solely define the Nazi party. There are those of us who choose not to build a political platform on hate and garbage science. Some of us want to build the party on more solid foundations."

Emmerich curled his fists. "Wake up, Hanns! This is the party and you stand alone in your fringe beliefs. Now I know you are loyal to our cause so I will forgive this one transgression. Get your time machine up and running. I want you to send us to ancient Germany."

"It will take a few months to accomplish this," Hanns said with a straight face. It was a lie, but he needed more time before they faced Silverwind again.

"And why is that?"

Hanns looked away. "Calibrations and fine tuning. I am still working on the latest model. It's larger and more accurate than the others. We can send a few platoons through with the new model and it charges faster, but it needs a lot more work before it's ready."

Emmerich narrowed his gaze on Hanns. "You are most fortunate that you are the only one who understands how that infernal thing works. You have two months, Hanns. Dismissed!"

Hanns stood and left the room. Finally he could get to the labs. As he walked across the fortress grounds, his second in command, Alban, joined him.

"Sir," Alban said as he walked beside Hanns. He glanced to the SS soldiers in the distance. "Will this be a problem?"

Hanns grinned and checked to make sure no SS were in earshot. "No. Emmerich is a fool. I met him a long time ago at the university. He failed his classes. He got his position because he knows who to flatter. Our plans will go forward, albeit with a few minor modifications."

Alban nodded.

Hanns opened the doors to the lab but stopped and turned to Alban. "Alban, keep an eye on the SS. When we face Silverwind again, make sure they are on the front lines. No need for our troops to suffer."

Alban snorted. "They would barely slow her. They are brutes, not real soldiers."

Hanns nodded. "If my gamble pays off, we will be rid of them soon enough."

As the door shut, sounds of metal bangs and the bright flashes of welders at work greeted Hanns. The building's interior held a large open space. Metal catwalks hung on the interior edge while a massive machine dominated the center of the room. It stood hoisted by metal scaffolding and girders. He walked past the huge time machine as the metal groaned like a beast.

It was spacious enough to send through an entire platoon of panzer tanks. Large concentric rings lined the outer shell of the machine. The rings alternated between turning clockwise and counter clockwise, forming a long tube at least three hundred paces in length. Gear teeth lined the interior of the rings, like the maw of a monster. A neon green glow emanated from the hollowed center of the machine with a ramp that led up to it.

Hanns entered a side door into a smaller lab where his assistant, Lenz, worked. Lenz wore a lab coat while he operated a machine that put glowing green bullets into their casings. There, a large collection of glowing tipped bullets in a variety of calibers lay in neat rows.

"Lenz," Hanns said as entered the room. "How is our project progressing?"

Lenz stood. "Has Emmerich taken command? Has he terminated the project yet?"

Hanns crumpled the letter in his hand and tossed it in the trash as he entered. "Yes, he is technically in command, but the Zeitmacht soldiers are still loyal to me. Emmerich will not be a threat to our operations for now. More importantly, have you made progress here?"

Lenz gestured to the large stockpile of green glowing tipped bullets. "Do we need so many?"

Hanns smiled. "As many as we can make. We will need them for my gamble. Just be sure to hide them after you are done. I don't need Emmerich asking too many questions."

Lenz gestured to Hanns. "Did you finish your part?"

Hanns smile widened as he opened his right hand, revealing the tiny sphere.

Lenz's eyes went wide. "What is it?"

Hanns picked up the tiny sphere with his left hand, holding it as it radiated a green light. "This, Lenz, is our key to victory. For the war and our future."

Lenz frowned as he stared at the small glowing sphere. "But I heard what the other soldiers said. Didn't that silver haired woman wipe out your platoon by herself? This is folly. I worry this plan will doom you Hanns."

Hanns smiled as he looked to Lenz. "Ah, but everything is more beautiful because we're doomed. No one can hurry me down to Hades before my time but if a man's hour is come, be he brave or be he coward, there is no escape for him when he has once been born."

Lenz stared at Hanns with a raised brow.

Hanns frowned. "I see you must have slept through mythological studies, Lenz."

Lenz shook his head. "Are you sure about this, Hanns?"

Hanns grinned and held the small sphere high between his thumb and index finger. The sphere's glow cast a green light on his face. "No man or woman born, coward or brave, can shun his destiny. For now, my part is to play Odysseus."

CHAPTER VIII
AEVUM ACADEMY

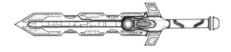

There are three kinds of recruits that commonly appear at the Aevum Academy. The first are the truly talented. A few of these arrive each year and they rarely make it past the training. Talent often becomes a crutch for the talented and they cannot cope with true adversity since, in some situations, talent cannot substitute for hard work.

-Excerpt from Chapter Three of the Aeon Legion's *Squire Recruitment Manual* by Praetor Lycus Cerberus

The academy wasn't what Terra had expected. As she walked through the hallways she noticed how clean and polished everything appeared. In fact, the entire area looked new as though recently constructed. It didn't meet with her original notion of an aged Academy complete with the musty smell of old books.

She also noted the heavy security. Legionnaires stood guard in every corridor with aeon edged swords at their belts. They watched the other potential recruits with wary gazes.

The potential recruits wore varied clothing, though Terra paid little attention to them. She kept her focus on gaining admittance to the training program and had awakened early this morning to do so.

She asked several staff there where to enroll in the Legion training program. Most tried to direct her to academic enrollment. When she corrected them, insisting it was the training program, they gave her confused stares before shrugging and pointing her in the right direction.

Terra found the registration office where a sizable crowd had gathered near the office fadedoors. She guessed it was the right place since most of them did not have silver hair nor wear white like the natives. Those in the crowd chatted while they waited near the fadedoors. Others sat on nearby benches next to a shallow indoor channel. A large fountain she had seen near the entrance fed the channels which branched out in sharp angles throughout the Academy.

Finally the doors faded and the hum of conversation hushed. Terra shifted, trying to see ahead. A silver haired man stepped out of the faded doors and cupped his hands over his mouth to project his voice. "First time applicants please form a line to the left of me! Returning applicants to the right!"

Terra assumed she should go to the left. She felt awkward when she noticed she stood alone while the line on the right stretched well past a bend in the hallway.

The silver haired man turned to Terra. "Well it looks like you're first today. Good luck."

"Thanks," Terra said before entering the room while trying to appear confident.

The room was dim save for a single spot in the center of the floor. A curved balcony overlooked the room. Seated in a semicircle on the balcony was a group of individuals each dressed in the same uniform as Alya though without the armor. Only one had a full head of silver hair. He sat at the back of the group, shadows obscuring most of him. The rest sat at the front with numerous holofaces gathered around them. No one looked at her as she entered.

A lean man with a long beard and scarred face gestured to the light in the center of the room. "Please step into the center light." He had four locks of silver in his hair.

Terra did so while standing as straight as she could manage. The light made it hard to see.

A young woman with dark hair dyed with three locks of silver and tan skin looked up at Terra. When she looked at Terra she smiled, shaking her head. "Oh sorry dear. You seemed to be lost. Academic registration is down the hall to the left."

The bearded man looked up as well. "You are definitely in the wrong place."

"Do you need someone to show you the way?" the woman said with a smile.

"Oh no," Terra said, still holding firm. "I'm here to join the Legion."

They exchanged glances with each other. After a moment of silence, they all laughed. All except the silver haired man in the back. His gaze narrowed on Terra.

Terra glared at them as they continued to laugh. The bearded man almost fell out of his chair as he shook with laughter. After a few moments, the laughter subsided.

"I haven't laughed that hard since I saw an Athenian try to use a sword," the bearded man said. When he looked back to Terra, his brow lowered. "Oh. You're still here?"

Terra clinched her fists. "Yes I am. I said I want to join the Legion."

Another woman leaned forward and glared at Terra, She had more silver hair than not. "We only accept recruits who are selected as squires. Now leave."

They all turned back to their holofaces as though that ended the discussion.

"Someone did choose me as a squire," Terra said in an even tone.

The first woman glared at Terra like a parent at a fibbing child before she typed something on a nearby holoface.

Minerva's voice sounded from her shieldwatch. "I am sorry, Centurion Shani. That information is restricted."

"What!" Shani said standing. "Restricted! I am a centurion for Aion's sake!"

The silver haired man who sat obscured in the back spoke. "Calm down, Centurion Shani. Orion's second cohort probably picked her up on some black ops mission. I'll access it."

"Greetings, Praetor Lycus Cerberus," Minerva said from the silver haired man's shieldwatch. "Authorization granted."

"Give me a holoface Minerva," Lycus said. "Also can you show me who locked this information?"

A series of holofaces appeared around Lycus's shieldwatch.

"Continue," Lycus said before he began reading. "I'll read the restricted information while I send you her stats and psych exam."

The group exchanged looks before arranging their holofaces. They read for several moments, occasionally shaking their heads.

Lycus read for a moment before grimacing. He regarded Terra with an intense stare.

"Is this the entire file?" Shani asked. She turned to the bearded man. "Centurion Nikias. Am I missing something?"

Nikias shook his head. "No combat experience. No service record. Zero high honors or significant academic achievements. I don't think she's even killed anyone yet."

Shani's expression hardened as she glared at Terra. "Look at her. She's so... out of shape. Definitely a softtimer. She probably couldn't even kill a Manticore mite. What crashing fool made her a squire?"

The other woman spoke. "She's an American from the United States."

Nikias turned to her. "Refresh my memory, Centurion Isra."

Isra spoke in a calm voice. "Americans. Loud, rude, rebellious, and warlike. This one is from the height of their empire though, when they spent most of their time being entertained. Softtimer for sure."

Terra's fists turned white. She felt tempted to tell them that Alya had chosen her, but remained silent, remembering her promise. She would endure this verbal beating.

Terra could just see Lycus's sneer through the shadows. "I know exactly why she is here, but it doesn't matter. Hurry. We have a long line of rejects today."

Shani glowered. "Fine. On the record though, I've seen corpses more qualified than her."

Nikias leaned forward. "Why do you want to be a soldier? I see no indication in your records that you want to fight?"

Terra considered her next words. "I don't want to fight, but I will defend myself if I have to. I was told that the Legion was not an army, but a group heroes and heroines. That's what I want to be."

Shani narrowed her gaze. "That may be true, but that means we have even higher standards than most militaries. We normally look for hard-timers, those from eras of strife and conflict. You are from the wealthiest nation on Continuum Lambda during a time of relative peace. You are a softtimer. While the program accounts for those without formal military training, I see no other special talents in your record to compensate."

Terra stared at Shani. "A bunch of records don't define me. Besides isn't courage and determination worth more?"

Shani glared as though Terra had just said something stupid. "No. No it's not."

Nikias rolled his eyes at that as though he disagreed, but did not argue.

Isra eyes narrowed. "She also hasn't taken a life yet. She is untested."

Terra frowned. "Why is that so important?"

Isra leaned back, still focused on Terra. "The Sons of Oblivion will kill. The Forgotten Guns will kill. A Manticore would eat you whole. And the Faceless..." she shivered when she mentioned the Faceless. "Well let's just say that killing you would be the kindest thing a Faceless could do to you. A killing instinct is necessary and we cannot be sure you have it."

"But I–"

Nikias shook his head. "Look, child. You are not ready for this. You need to get a few things in order first."

"Like what?"

"First, you need to hone your athleticism. How many pushups can you do right now?"

"Um..."

"That's what I thought. That probably wouldn't take too long. Maybe a month and a half at most with the acceleration gyms. That could be done before the training even started. More is needed though. Right now you would be dusted in five seconds if we let you into the training program."

Lycus sighed. "Just hurry and reject her so we can move on."

Terra felt her heart sink. Rejected so out of hand? They hadn't even given her a chance.

Shani shook her head. "If only I could get another recruit like Kairos. She had talent! When will Silverwind find a new squire?"

Nikias closed the holoface. "Try again next year."

Terra narrowed her gaze at the group while her fists clinched and teeth gritted. Alya said be determined and they would admit her. "No. I am not moving from this spot until you accept me into the program. You will have to throw me out kicking and screaming."

Lycus jumped down in front of Terra.

Terra froze, her face paled as Lycus Cerberus glared down at her. Like Alya his skin was tanned and his short, swept back, silver hair stood like raised fur. He towered over Terra with a lean, but muscular physique and looked at Terra like a wolf might stare at a weak animal.

With strong arms, he grabbed her around the waist and lifted her as though she weighed no more than an empty trashcan. He carried her out into the hall in front of the rest of the waiting recruits while Terra tried to kick him from the awkward angle he held her.

"Put me down!" Terra screamed.

Lycus did just that and dumped her into the fountain. Terra landed with a splash on the hard marble of the fountain while Lycus dusted off his hands as though he had just taken out the garbage.

Lycus turned to the potential recruits. "Next!"

"Well that could have gone better," Terra said after a moment as she sat drenched in the fountain. She rubbed her elbows. The cold water came up to her knees and was too shallow to absorb much of the fall.

A few of the waiting recruits laughed at her and some pointed. Most ignored the disturbance as though an instructor tossing out a potential recruit was a common sight.

Terra continued to sit in the fountain, her gaze downcast. They had laughed at, humiliated, confused, belittled, and ignored her. Most of all she wanted to return home to her nice little quarry under the warm sun. At least no one there would tell her she wasn't good enough. Perhaps she had made a huge mistake in coming here?

Terra stood and shook her arms dry. The dripping slowed when another splash of water drenched her again. She looked up to see Lycus dusting off his hands in dismissal again.

"Next!" he yelled before walking back into the exam room.

The person, thrown next to Terra, stood. He wore camouflaged fatigues with an insignia she didn't recognize. The man shook off the water and walked straight to the back of the line for his next attempt.

For the first time, Terra noted the other recruits. Now that she took the time to stare at them, she realized that they were a scary crowd. They possessed scarred faces, lean builds, athletic physiques, grim expressions, shields, scabbards, and armor, lots of armor and uniforms; armor and uniforms from every time period. They all stared ahead with intense focus and discipline; the kind a soldier would have.

After climbing out of the water, Terra walked outside to collect herself. She saw more soldiers on her way out. Along the way Terra recognized a Roman legionnaire, a Mongolian warrior, a samurai, several soldiers in modern fatigues, and what she thought was an American Civil War cavalryman. A rare few wore training uniforms under their original clothes.

Terra wandered onto the Academy grounds. A large creek ran near a stone patio. Several potential recruits ate and chatted there. Smaller groups were scattered over the area. Legionnaires watched with hands resting on their swords. Terra noticed that most recruits did not wear training uniforms yet, as they wore their original, period clothing.

"So how did you get in so fast?" someone asked not far away from Terra.

Terra stopped and searched for the source of the comment. She saw a crowd of potentials standing on a small stone bridge that crossed the creek. They all stood around a young man who wore a white tunic with a red cross over a chain mail shirt. A training uniform was slung over his shoulder. He sat barefooted, for his boots and an iron helmet lay next to the creek on top of a shield with a red cross on it. Terra recognized the tools of a knight. The young man appeared little older than her. He smiled at the others. "Ah. You see that is an interesting story I ought to share, but I am far more intrigued by your story my friend."

Another man across from the knight spoke. He wore a Roman legionnaire's armor over his own training uniform. "There is not much to say," he said in a gruff voice. "This is my third attempt at the training. The early parts are familiar to me. However, most newtimers like yourself seldom get in so easily the second day of admissions."

Terra stepped in closer, joining the group at the back. She recognized the Roman Legionnaire as the voice she had heard earlier.

The knight smiled again, speaking in a smooth, disarming tone. "Now Tacitus, please share with me your knowledge, for you see this is my first time here. I arrived only a few days ago. Surely not myself alone, but the others present could find your experience useful. After all I am very interested in keeping my immortality."

The other potential recruits nodded in agreement.

Tacitus frowned after being put on the spot. "I am forbidden to tell you. I mean no offense, sir. That is the proper address for you correct?

The knight nodded. "Yes. Sir Roland Delmare is my name with title, but I have many other titles that are rather unimportant. I am not as proper with rules and titles as others so fear not of offending me. Though I would be rather disappointed if you choose to forgo sharing information with me and the others that could be of use on the morrow."

Tacitus pursed his lips. "I told you I can't te–"

The knight named Roland raised a finger. "How about a gamble then? If I lose, then I will tell you how I came to be here in this city of pearl knights. Should victory favor me though, you can tell me a little about the training. If the instructors find out, then you may blame me for forcing you to keep your honor."

Tacitus narrowed his gaze at Roland. "Agreed, but I insist on using my dice."

Roland smiled and nodded. Tacitus brought out a pair of dice and they each agreed on the rules. Each rolled three times in a game that Terra didn't recognize. However, during the third roll Roland moved one hand in a smooth motion that drew everyone's eye. However, Terra didn't flinch. She saw that during Roland's slight of hand he reached out his other shieldwatch hand. She caught the faintest hint of a shieldwatch field. The spherical grainy field flashed just for a moment before the dice rolled back once. When Tacitus looked back he frowned.

"God smiles upon me yet again," Roland said in a cheery tone.

Tacitus nodded.

Terra watched the others who remained neutral in their expressions. No one else had caught it.

Tacitus sighed. "Indeed. But I won't reveal too much. They listen using our shieldwatches. All I can say is that most of the training and tests have hidden meanings. Little is as it appears. I can't really be too specific since they change each year. Most dust out during the survival test on the fourth week. I've never made it beyond that. People say the final test in the Labyrinth is even worse."

Roland nodded and continued to smile, but did not press Tacitus.

Tacitus gathered his dice. "It takes most a few weeks just to get into the training unless they are attempting it again like me. I only know of one other this year who got in with one try."

"Who's that?" asked one of other potentials.

Tacitus glanced to the recruit. "Some girl named Hikari. I think she is from an island warrior culture. She's on my list when I start building my strike team."

Roland lounged on the side of the bridge. "Really? How did she get in?"

Tacitus shrugged. "She impressed an instructor. That's how most get in. She apparently fought a sparring match with Centurion Nikias.

Almost defeated him I hear. He had to use a shieldwatch to win. Pretty rare when that happens. Especially since he's a Spartan."

Terra's eyes widened. Nikias was a Spartan? No wonder he was so unimpressed with her.

One other hopeful nodded. "I tried Nikias already. You have to be bold and skilled in combat to impress him. He won't take anyone who hasn't seen combat already. A few people have had luck with Centurion Shani."

"She only cares if you are talented," another of the hopefuls scoffed. "I hear it takes forever and you don't even have a chance unless you already have a bunch of medals or achievements."

"Centurion Isra takes people sometimes," another said who stood towards the back of the group.

Tacitus shook his head. "She only likes survivors. I will say who you can't go to. Praetor Lycus Cerberus."

"The silver haired man?" said another hopeful towards the front. "What's so bad about him? I hear he's a Legendary Blade."

Tacitus shot the hopeful a dark glare. "Lycus Cerberus rarely lets people in and those he does... well let's just say that if he allows you in, then he has something nasty planned. I pity anyone chosen by him. While he is a Legendary Blade, that only means it's near impossible to best him in any contest."

Everyone hushed for a moment.

Tacitus faced Roland. "I still wish to know how you got in."

Others inched forward as all eyes turned to Roland.

Roland smiled and shrugged before standing up from his lazy lounge. "Very well. I hate to give away valuable secrets, but I am a generous soul."

The others grew silent, waiting for Roland's story.

"You see," Roland began. "I saved an instructor from a wrathful recruit who, in anger of rejection, had attacked him. Naturally this is a result of putting so many soldiers in one place. What do they expect to happen? Most soldiers here would never turn down a fight or a meal."

Everyone laughed except Terra.

"It was a treacherous Saracen of course. He waited until the instructor's back had turned before drawing a dagger. One of the strange oracles of the city had foreseen the attack, but the others found distraction from a different fight that occurred at the same time. I saw the Saracen raise the dagger to strike," he said, building the suspense.

The others' breath seem to catch while Terra raised an eyebrow.

"Thinking quickly," Roland said. "I took off my shieldwatch and flung it at the Saracen, striking him in the face. The instructor turned in time to see the attack. Grateful for his rescue, he accepted my petition to enter the training."

Terra just rolled her eyes. *What lies*, she thought and wondered how Roland really got into the training.

Roland finished his story. "That is how I was chosen for the training. Now if you excuse me. On the morrow, I plan to begin my own preparations."

The crowd dispersed, seemingly inspired by Roland's fabricated story.

"I like him," one hopeful said as they walked away.

Tacitus gave Roland a salute. "If you make it past the first day, I may try to get you for my strike team. Until then, good luck sir knight."

Terra regarded Roland with narrowed eyes as Tacitus left. When he was alone, he walked down to the creek and dipped his feet into the water. There was something about him that Terra didn't like. He had hidden how he had really gotten into the training. She would find out just how he did it. Terra followed him to the stoney creek below the bridge.

"How did you really get in?" Terra asked, hands on hips as she stood on a large stone that bordered the creek.

Roland smiled and sat down on the grassy bank of the creek, his feet still in the water. "Ah. So you didn't like my story?"

Terra crossed her arms. "Or your little cheat with the dice. I saw you use your shieldwatch to alter the number."

Terra got a closer look at Roland now. His oval face was handsome with smooth youthful features. However, messy dark hair gave a slight rough edge to his appearance along with his casual lounge. Roland's wry smile that put others at ease appeared arrogant to Terra.

Roland looked Terra over with his ocean blue eyes. "Is this what warriors look like in your time?"

Terra blushed and looked away. She then clenched her fist and turned her focus back to Roland. "That's not important. Are you a knight?"

Roland shrugged, still lounging. "Unless someone has wrested that title away while I slept. Why should that matter?"

Terra narrowed her gaze. "Knights are supposed to be chivalrous, not cheat and deceive others."

Roland raised an eyebrow. "Chivalrous?"

"You know. Protect the weak? Give aid to those in trouble? Fight fairly and with honor? Don't lie or steal?"

Roland's eyes narrowed. "That sounds completely foolish. What naïve child thought of that?"

"I don't understand. How did a jerk like you get into the training?"

"Jerk? I am unfamiliar with this expression. Does it mean incredibly handsome, smart, and wealthy?"

Terra clenched her jaw and glared at Roland.

Roland chuckled. "Well you don't need a translator for that look. As your insults have so thoroughly amused me, I will grace you with the true story of how I made it into the training. I cheated. Again. You see, I witnessed an instructor telling a legionnaire to add a recruit to the accepted list. This was after the legionnaire had seen me chatting with that instructor earlier. I approached the same legionnaire a short time later. I explained that the instructor had sent me on his behalf as he had forgotten to tell him that my name should be scribed on the list. After some persuasion, they accepted me."

"You smooth talked your way in! I should turn you in to the instructors."

Roland's smile faded. "You remind me of someone I don't like. He had a bad habit of tempting me into honesty as well. Regardless, I doubt they would take your word over mine if your shock at me being a dishonest knight is genuine."

Terra ground her teeth. How had Roland gotten her so angry?

Roland's smile returned. "Besides, I refuse to spend the next few weeks bowing before the instructors' whim to gain a slim chance of acceptance. After getting thrown into a fountain the first time, I went down the easier path. As you have no doubt seen, I don't rely on luck," he said before collecting his things and turning to go.

Terra's hateful gaze followed him until he disappeared into the Academy. She let out a long sigh. It all seemed so unfair.

∞

"I can't help you. They don't let us decide who gets into the program. Try talking to one of the centurions," the silver haired man said, his tone cold as he walked past Terra. He was one of the staff members of the program, most of whom held the rank of optio. She had almost begged him to be let in, but he turned her away like all the rest.

Terra bowed her head low and sighed. This was the last of the optios she hadn't talked to. Others had given the same response. Centurions now recognized her on sight and refused to even speak with her. This was after she had spent the last couple of weeks pestering them. She had tried everyone now. Everyone, but one. The one she wanted to avoid. The one who had thrown her out first. Praetor Lycus Cerberus, head of the training program.

Lycus terrified her. That wolfish grin seemed so unnatural. Even the optios shied away from him and she found it difficult enough to face the centurions. However, her options grew thin.

It had been three weeks since her first day at the Academy and training started tomorrow. She stopped exercise early today so she could have more time to find someone who would let her into the training program. The past weeks she had split between trying to gain admittance and exercising with Delphia who had enthusiastically agreed to help her.

Terra found exercising much less stressful than trying to get into the training. At least in the acceleration gyms she made progress. Delphia had shown her that the gyms on Saturn City used time to accelerate regrowth of muscle and to alleviate fatigue. A week in an Acceleration Gym was equal to almost two months of normal exercise. She could exercise all day if she wished, stopping only to sleep and eat. Even the food at the gym accelerated the body's absorption of nutrients, though it tasted foul and made her sick for a few moments.

Terra did feel frustrated that her appearance remained mostly the same. She did lose some weight as she found her old clothes fit a bit too loose for her now. Now Terra wore Saturnian clothes. It took a while for her to find something that was modest enough to suit her tastes. Terra never felt comfortable showing much of her skin.

Despite her progress in exercise, her time at the Academy proved wasted. She wandered the halls of the Academy thinking. Should she confront Lycus? He had already rejected her the first day. Perhaps she should wait like Nikias had suggested? Maybe if she could find Alya? No.

She hadn't even seen Alya since the timeport and couldn't depend on her. Why had she come here at all? Maybe she should just go home back to her nice quarry. What did this place offer her anyway?

She stopped as she spotted a familiar sight. In a large open room to her side was several bookshelves. A holoface hanging over the entryway changed to English as she drew near. It read *Aevum Academy Library.* Terra stepped inside.

The library was the size of a large stadium. It was circular in design with book shelves arranged in semicircles around several large open areas in the center. To the sides were smaller circular plates that projected holographic images above them. When the library patrons stepped on these plates, the holographic images appeared and Minerva's voice could be heard when one drew close to them.

Terra walked amongst the bookshelves. She found most books were written in various foreign languages, all originals. Soon she came to a pair of large metal fadedoors decorated with golden text she couldn't read, but two guards in Legion armor stopped her.

"Sorry dhimmi," one said, holding up a hand. "This area is forbidden without special permission from the Aeon Legion."

Terra looked at the fadedoors. "What's behind these doors?"

"The Saturn City Historical Archives," the other guard said.

Terra glanced back to the guards. "If it's just history, why is it forbidden?"

"Time travelers have a bad habit of trying to change history after they learn about it," the first guard said. "So now we only let those in who can be trusted. Those who are accepted into the Aeon Legion training are given limited access."

The second guard pointed to a disc shaped platform nearby. "The holo readers give you limited access through Minerva though."

Leaving the fadedoors, she made her way over to a disc shaped plate. She stepped onto it and it lifted, hovering off the ground a few paces as a holographic image appeared. It read *Saturn City Archive Holo Reader.*

"Welcome, Terra Mason, to the Archives holo reader," came Minerva's voice from the platform. "What do you wish to know?"

Terra thought for a moment. What didn't she want to know? After a moment she thought of something she wanted to see. "FDR's first inaugural address?"

The graphic changed. A map appeared, showing the Edge and its many branching continua. A dot raced along, moving to Continuum Lambda and stopped at 1933 AD. The graphic changed again. This time, the area on the plate transformed into a full color scene with Franklin D. Roosevelt standing on his podium.

The graphic projection seemed to extend far beyond the bounds of the plate, though the graphic became translucent beyond the edges, revealing the library. Franklin D. Roosevelt, however, was in its center in perfect focus. Although Terra had already heard the speech in person, the quality still impressed her.

"Gettysburg Address?" Terra asked.

The graphic changed again. While the quality was impressive, Terra couldn't help but wish she was there in person especially since she knew this was possible.

"Can you show me the future of the United States?" Terra asked after a moment.

The holographic image disappeared before the plate lowered to the floor, going dark. "I am sorry, Terra Mason. I am not authorized to give you that information or show you those events."

Terra sighed. "The one time I want spoilers," she said as she thought. This was all interesting enough, but it didn't help her current predicament. "Minerva, I don't suppose you could show me something that could help me get into the training?"

"That is a broad context. If you could narrow your inquiry, I may be able to help you."

Terra thought for a moment. "What about something relevant to recruit quality?"

The graphic changed again, revealing an Academy classroom filled with military officers, though they wore different uniforms than the Legion. A commanding woman stood in the center of the class. She wore a silver crown that complemented her beautifully designed and ornate dress appearing as a cross between royal attire and a sharp military uniform. She stood tall with a regal bearing.

"That is a good question," she said to one officer. "If I had to choose a single most important quality in a soldier, it would be courage. Superior training and equipment are certainly not disadvantages, but a well trained, equipped, and experienced soldier is still worthless when fleeing battle. Every force takes the most casualties when retreating. This is as true of the battlefields of Time as it is in the battles of history."

"Who is this?" Terra asked.

"This was Time Queen Ananke," Minerva said. "During the reign of the Kings and Queens of Time, she administered this Academy and used it for her officer training program. She is considered the foremost expert on post time warfare."

"How do you identify courage then?" asked an officer.

The holo projection of Ananke paced the room. "I would accept a recruit who hesitated in front of the wolf's den, knowing the danger over the recruit who charges without hesitation. One denotes acknowledgment of their fear and the other overconfidence in their talent. Only those who acknowledge fear have any chance of overcoming it. Cultivating budding courage is far easier than overcoming narcissism and hubris."

Terra's eyes went wide when she realized. Courage. It was so simple. She had no other qualities. One girl had got in by fighting with a Spartan. Roland had got in with his silver tongue which, while unfair, was still a skill. Both were talents Terra did not have. All she had to show for was her one brave act in the library. She had to showcase that quality and there was only one way she could think of to do that. To move forward, she had to face Praetor Lycus Cerberus.Hanns finished placing the last piece into the device under the microscope. It was a glass sphere with a metal ring around it the size of a pea. Hanns picked up the device with tweezers and dropped it into his right hand that stuck out of his cast. Holding onto the sphere, he stepped outside into his fortification and frowned at what he saw.

CHAPTER IX
GUARDIAN OF THE GATES

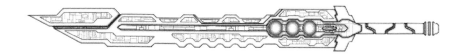

The second are the vultures. These are brutes who take from those weaker than themselves. Vultures never make it through the training. They are only useful as examples of what not to do.

-Excerpt from Chapter Three of the Aeon Legion's *Squire Recruitment Manual* by Praetor Lycus Cerberus

Terra gathered her courage as she stared ahead at the office of Praetor Lycus Cerberus. Before she could knock, the door faded and a tall dark haired man walked out with a self satisfied smirk on his face. The man didn't so much walk as saunter out of Lycus's office. She wondered if his dark blue futuristic armor gave him his confidence.

"Yes. Vand, you will be an excellent example to the other recruits," came Lycus's voice from the office.

Terra peeked in to see Lycus half obscured in shadows. A wolfish grin drew across his face as though he was about to jump the man walking out of his office and tear his throat out. That grin made Terra shiver while the man named Vand seemed oblivious.

Terra struggled to rebuild the courage that Lycus had undone with one terrible grin. After a moment to gather her nerves, she entered.

It was dark with seamed black and gray metal walls, more like a den or dungeon than an office. There was no exterior window and a blue glow from a nearby holoface cast an eerie, otherworldly light in the office. It was as though Terra stood before the gates of the underworld.

To her right was a shelf with a collection of odd objects, memorabilia, and what she guessed were war trophies. A black smooth oval mask lay on the top shelf with a red wing emblem painted on it. It lay next to an old, stained photo of a man in a strange uniform with his family. Nearby, a stationary holoface displayed a full color group picture of twelve individuals. They stood in two rows, each dressed in full legion armor and holding aeon edges. Terra recognized Alya, Orion, and Lycus in the holoface display though none had silver hair.

Lycus sat at his desk, the blue light illuminating his sharp featured face. Terra was thankful he no longer grinned, but now he instead stared intently as though seeing right through her. It was as if he had a different face now. Not the predatory, grinning monster, but a cold emotionless face.

Terra stood straighter as she approached. She planned for this encounter the best she could. He likely wouldn't recognize her. "Sir. I am Terr–"

"I know who you are, Terra Mason," he said, his cold gaze unwavering. "Some of the instructors complained of your persistence."

Terra hesitated. "Well then I–"

"I know who made you a squire so don't bother with that tactic. Silverwind may have chosen you, but that means little to me. If anything, it puts you at a disadvantage. You certainly don't measure up to Kairos who got in on her own merit."

Terra glared at Lycus.

"I am not letting you in," he said plainly.

Terra clinched her fists. "Let me guess. It's because I'm not a soldier, or maybe I just have no talent. More than one said it was because I hadn't killed in combat yet. The rest just said I wouldn't make it. So what's your excuse?"

Lycus's expression remained cold. "You talk a lot about wanting to join, but you ignore the warnings others are giving you. We are doing you a favor. You will not endure this training even after your little bit of exercise at the acceleration gyms."

"Alya believes in me."

Lycus sneered. "What do you think this training is? Do you think you are some kind of superhero who gains and masters her powers in an instant?"

Terra raised an eyebrow.

Lycus grinned, a hint of the snarl he showed Vand flashed in that grin. "I am familiar with American culture from your time." His tone turned cold. "It is a culture steeped in entertainment and luxury. You see yourself as the protagonist of a story who follows a mythic arc. You are not. You are a spoiled child from a middle class home. Now you come here to my Academy without knowing what truly awaits you here. This training isn't a montage. Mastering a shieldwatch takes months in addition to all of the other skills you must learn. Nothing will be given. Everything must be earned. Now you dare to come into this office and ask to be admitted to the training. What ignorance. What audacity. No wonder you hesitate at the door after seeing your first real obstacle. Such a fearful heart has no place here."

Terra paused. She had heard of Lycus's brutality, but she hadn't expected him to be so knowledgeable. Terra studied Lycus. His hostile tone did not match his cold expression. He searched for something, testing her. She wondered what he was looking for. Then she answered. "Only those who acknowledge fear have any chance of overcoming it."

Lycus paused. "Time Queen Ananke. Lectures on Post Time Warfare." He looked to the shelf full of memorabilia, his expression became distant.

Terra observed Lycus's demeanor again. He had changed. She watched as his gaze locked on one of the objects on the shelf, his face betraying a hint of remorse.

"Still, more is needed than a sharp mind," he said before looking back to Terra. "Why are you so unyielding in your pursuit of this?"

Terra thought for a moment. "I became a squire when I st—"

"Yes. I read the report. Impressive," Lycus said, his tone mocking. "You stopped a time traveler from stealing a library book. Dumb luck does not make you a soldier."

"I don't want to be a soldier! I want to be a heroine! Although I'm no soldier, I still faced one head-on without any crazy time powers." Terra looked away while speaking in a low tone. "My whole life I've done nothing but hide." She then looked straight into Lycus's eyes. "Then someone told me I was a heroine and I could be a better one. If someone told you that, then wouldn't you make the most of that opportunity? I don't want to hide anymore."

Lycus's bestial grin returned. The grin became more terrible as the shadows crept over him when he leaned back. "Oh that was almost good."

A cold chill shot through Terra's spine as her instincts told her to run. Lycus looked like a different person. His face, his terrible snarl, looked so different from the remorseful man she had just spoken to or the cold one before that. She held firm, refusing to move even after seeing this third face of his.

Lycus snarled as his hand went to the hilt of his aeon edge. "Those are bold words, Terra Mason. Will you stand by them?"

Terra stared at the terrifying man, his teeth bared in a horrible smile. Jaw clenched, she stood straight and met his predatory glare. "I won't hide or run. Once I decide to do something, I don't back down!"

It happened in a flash.

Lycus drew his aeon edge and slashed downward. The blade descended towards her with incredible force, the edge aimed right between her eyes. Panic shot through her, but there was a part of her that told herself to hold. Her panic fought with her wisdom that knew this was a test of resolve. She wouldn't back down even if Lycus smashed her head in with his blade. She wouldn't let him win. Terra didn't flinch.

The aeon edge stopped inches above her head as the wind from the swing flowed over her. Terra's breath and heart beat caught up with her seconds later.

Lycus's grin faded and after a moment he withdrew the blade before sheathing it. His expression became blank before he sat and touched a nearby holoface.

Terra blinked. The panic bled away as the color returned to her face. She scowled, clenching her fists. "Hey! That was rea—"

"You're in," Lycus interrupted without even glancing at Terra as he finished typing on a holoface.

"What?"

"I have registered you in the program. Training starts tomorrow at 0:600 hours. Be sure to pick up your uniform at the armory then find your assigned dormitory room," Lycus said as he turned to Terra. His expression and voice remained cold. "Tiro Terra Mason, you have proven you have more than words. Now I want to see the steel in you."

Terra arrived for the first day of training wearing her Academy uniform. Form fitting, but comfortable, the design was similar to a wetsuit. Like everything else in the city it was a matte white with blue edges. Blue hex patterned patches on the sides of the torso extended all the way down to the ankles. A thin blue strip outlined the slightly thicker shoulders. The upper arms displayed an embossed golden infinity symbol above the words *Novus*. While the uniform lacked pockets, it came with a belt that had several pouches. Thick white combat boots didn't match the sleek suit, but fit well.

Terra stopped at the gate, looking out into the courtyard. Other recruits gathered there. Terra passed through the gate into the main training courtyard. She found it surprising that no one had yelled at her in the morning like boot camp. Instead she woke early and got herself ready.

A stage stood towards the back while a metal wall encircled the courtyard with several buildings built into it. At the center of the courtyard was a tall, carved stone pillar. The optios herded recruits in a line for inspection. When the recruits reached the end of the line, an optio assigned them to one of several groups who stood in formation. Each formation consisted of twenty five recruits arranged in five rows of five.

Terra got in line with the rest. The first optio used his shieldwatch to generate a glowing ring that passed over Terra clockwise before disappearing.

"State saved. Move along," he said.

Terra walked up to the next one.

"Name?" the woman asked.

"Terra Mason," Terra said.

The optio touched a holoface on her shieldwatch and a ring formed over Terra again. It swept around, changing her uniform. Her name now appeared on the sides of her uniform's upper arms while the word *tiro* was on the front of it. The last optio pointed to a group of recruits near the end who stood in a square formation.

"You are in Decennary twelve," he said.

Terra walked over to the group. They stood on a square labeled with the numeral *XII*. She stood on the back corner.

Moments later, Nikias walked over to the formation while chatting with an optio. Nikias wasn't as tall as Terra had expected. Terra thought his lean build and scars combined to give him a savage look. He wore a uniform with the same design as the training uniform save for the emblem on his upper arm. Over the formfitting uniform, he wore armor pads of the same design as Alya's. Terra thought that now Nikias looked like a Spartan.

"These are your groups, centurion," the optio said, gesturing to several poorly formed squares of recruits.

Nikias sighed after looking at the group. "I swear they get worse every year. All right. Form ranks!"

The recruits shuffled around while Nikias shoved those who were out of place into formation. Terra settled into her corner with little trouble. She got a closer look at Nikias as he passed. His scar looked different up close. It was an x shaped scar on his cheek. She could have sworn it was different the first time she saw him.

One recruit saluted Nikias. "Sir. My name is Th—"

"I'll learn your name if you last more than a month," Nikias interrupted. "Now stand at attention and remain silent."

After a moment, Nikias stiffened to stand at attention. Terra glanced at the other centurions who also visibly tensed. Terra looked to the distant stage. Lycus walked up on the stage overlooking the courtyard. He surveyed the recruits with a cold, expressionless face.

After a moment, Lycus grinned his feral snarl. Like Nikias, he wore armor over his uniform though Terra couldn't make out the details at this distance. The armor did not make him look any less intimidating. He paced back and forth on the stage with a slow, methodical step like a beast before a lunge. When he spoke, his tone was calm but carried a savage edge as it echoed. "As of this moment I am your enemy. You are all now accepted into the program at the rank of tiro so you must observe saluting protocol. Keep in mind, though, that you are not a legionnaire yet and my goal is to make sure you do not become one. You are unworthy of this highest of all honors."

Lycus turned, pacing the other way with soft, controlled footsteps. "During this training I will find a reason to eliminate each and every one of you. However, if you perform well, you will receive points. Points may be exchanged for gear and other perks. You need one point each week or you will be dismissed from the program. You will need a great number of points to get into the Labyrinth, the final exam for every tiro."

He paused for a moment while his eyes searched the crowd "Any of your instructors can also take away points if they wish, including me. Spend them wisely."

After a moment Lycus moved to the center of the stage again. "Every day your numbers will dwindle whether through voluntarily resignation or failure. You may give up at any time by discarding your shieldwatch at the base of the pillar in the central courtyard. Then we will let everyone know you gave up."

As if on cue, a holoface appeared near Terra's shieldwatch. She looked to see a picture and name of another recruit. There was a fair amount of text detailing his age, sex, height, weight, and biographical information. A flashing red line above his name caught Terra's attention. It read *Terminated from program due to tardiness. Arrived twelve seconds late to training.*

More holofaces appeared with each saying the same.

Lycus pointed to several tirones who the optios escorted to the pillar. There they discarded their shieldwatches in front of everyone. Those who hesitated drew glares from the optios who gripped their own aeon edges. None challenged the optios.

Lycus then closed the holoface. "Yes. We will eliminate you from the program if you are even a second late in any part of the training. We are not like a normal army. They enforce discipline. Here you must already have it. Now if by some miracle you make it to the end of the program, you will undergo the twelve trials of the Labyrinth. This is the final test of the Aeon Legion. Amongst those standing next to you, only a handful will make it to the Labyrinth. Of those, one in twelve will die there."

There was a moment of silence.

He grinned. "We don't train soldiers here. We forge heroes! Now, let's begin the eliminations."

They followed Nikias to an open area. It had a circular concrete floor encircled by a wall with twelve spires like an arena. It reminded Terra of the structure she and Alya had used to enter the city. Above them hovered a large ring half the diameter of the wall. A metal catwalk circled around the edge with ramps at every spire that led down to the concrete floor. The open area could fit a large building inside of it.

Nikias touched a holoface and a glowing ring descended from the metal halo floating above. As it descended it transformed the flat concrete floor into a shallow pool still slick with large clumps of thick mud. Foul smelling sludge bubbled to the surface and Terra could see things moving in it. Oil slicks floated in patches, discoloring the water in many areas.

The tirones stared in awe of the transformation. Terra put her hand in the air, feeling a light breeze from the edge of the arena. Terra wondered how a salient could even simulate weather within a localized area.

Nikias replicated a handful of silver coins and scattered them. They sank into the noxious mud. "Welcome to the salient, an arena that can recall any area in Time. This first day has three trials. Every trial is optional. You must pass one test. The first trial starts now. All you have to do is to try to find one of these," he said as he held up a silver coin before flipping it into the mud.

The tirones exchanged glances. Terra noted they were a varied group that stood in a semi circle around Nikias. Although each wore the Legion's training uniform, most also had armor or clothing from what Terra guessed was their native time. She assumed it wasn't forbidden so long as a recruit wore their training uniform underneath their native garb. One tall and muscled, dark skinned man held a patched hide shield in one hand and a short spear in the other. She thought he was a Zulu Impi warrior, but wasn't sure.

Terra found herself surprised to find as many women here as men. One girl who Terra guessed was a Native America wore a red bandanna on her head with a leather vest and a knife on her belt. Another fair skinned Celtic girl stood out with intricate blue tattoos on her face and arms while her hair was bleached white and styled into spikes. An Asian girl, who wore the training uniform with no other weapons or armor, stood out. This made Terra feel a little better about not having a weapon for herself. When Terra visited the armory, they had said she could only bring weapons with her into the training she had already trained with, which for her was nothing.

A tall tiro stepped forward. Terra recognized him as the young man named Vand who had walked out of Lycus's office a day before. He took one look at the mud and shook his head. "I will not wallow in filth and anyone who does is an idiot. I'll pass."

Many nodded in agreement.

Vand looked to Nikias. "We can just do the next one if we want right?"

Nikias shrugged. "I said they are optional."

Terra's gaze narrowed. Had she missed something? Lycus had said the training would be brutal. Why was this test optional? Still, that pool of muck smelled awful and she would hate to think what lived in it. Perhaps she should skip this one and wait for the next test?

Nikias glanced at the tirones before checking his shieldwatch. "Well I better go get the other groups started. I'll be back soon."

Terra gathered her courage and stepped into the mud. After all, Nikias hadn't said she needed to find a coin, only try. Years spent in a dusty quarry made her not mind getting dirty. She sank knee deep after a few steps. Laughter and a few chuckles came from behind as she waded waste deep. It reeked much worse when up close and she could see worms and other small creatures wiggling in the cesspool.

Vand laughed, pointing at Terra. "Look at the piggy wallow in the mud!"

Terra ignored him. Instead she focused on the center most point of the pool. That's where most of the coins had landed. However, when she drew close to the middle, the pool deepened, coming up to her neck. She would have to do this the unpleasant way. Holding her breath, she sank down into the water.

She reached down with her hands, probing along the bottom for metal. Her fingers brushed against something hard and smooth before grabbing it. She gasped when breaking the surface. After coughing out the foul tasting water and almost vomiting, she held up the shiny silver coin.

By the time she drew near the shore, others now waded into the muddy, viscous water. Most went waste deep, trying to avoid dunking their heads under and hoping to get lucky.

Terra walked onto the metal ramp, the weight of the mud slowing her pace. She then stood to the side, letting the mud drip off of her while examining the coin. When Terra looked up, panic shot through her upon seeing Vand stare at her coin with hungry eyes.

Vand looked over his shoulder for Nikias and smirked when he realized they were alone. He shifted his attention to Terra and walked over while cracking his knuckles. "I want that coin, piggy. You will give it to me now."

Terra squeezed her grip around the coin, glaring at Vand. "Why would I do that jerk?"

Vand towered over Terra. "Because I can kill you without much effort. Besides, I'm doing you a favor. Everyone here can see you don't belong. You'll be dusted in a day."

"Dusted?"

Vand gestured as though throwing a handful of dust in the air. "Dusted. Done. Washed out. Failed. You will fail, losing your chance at immortality and die of old age. Die and turn to dust. These people are looking for a real soldier, a killer like me. You're just some fat little civvy from a cushy time in history. I'm a Helcian Shock Trooper, cybernetically augmented and bioengineered to be the perfect soldier. But you? I've pulled bugs out of my boots more intimidating than you. So why don't you give me that coin and it will pay me to not gut you."

Terra clenched her fist, tightening her grip on the coin while she weighed her options. Vand was not as terrifying as Lycus, but he stood taller than her and wore impressive looking armor. Futuristic, metallic blue armor covered his torso, forearms, and lower legs. At his side he carried a complex baton device that Terra guessed was a high tech melee weapon. She regretted not having a weapon herself. Regardless, she wouldn't give Vand the coin. She knew giving bullies what they wanted only encouraged them to take more. "No."

Vand's brow raised.

Terra shook her head. "I won't let some bully push me around. I have dealt with people like you before. Go pick on someone else. You will get nothing from me."

Vand shrugged and shoved Terra to the ground. Terra rolled on the ground face down and tried to push herself up when she felt a boot press against her neck.

"Move and I will snap your spine," he said in a bored tone. He leaned down and twisted Terra's wrist until the coin rolled free. He grabbed it up and shuffled it between his fingers. "Now if you tell the instructor that I stole this coin I will—"

"Picking on the runt already?" Nikias said from behind Vand.

Vand grinned before taking his boot off of Terra's neck. "I was just showing this recruit some of my many martial art moves."

Terra stood and pointed at Vand. "This jerk stole my coin!"

Nikias nodded. "Well that's unfortunate. What are you going to do about it?"

Terra stared at Nikias in disbelief. "Shouldn't you make him give it back?"

Nikias chuckled. "Listen, tiro. This is the Aeon Legion. Here we have to fight for what is right. If you have a grievance against a fellow tiro, then save it for a Trial of Blades. The instructors will not fight your battles for you and if you are unwilling to fight, then you shouldn't be here."

Vand smiled as Nikias walked away.

Terra noticed the other tirones watching as well. They eyed the others already in the muddy pit. It didn't take long for tirones to start fighting one another for coins. None succeeded at taking a coin though, even the ones who tried to pick pockets. Terra considered wading back in to try to find a second coin, but the others watched her. She couldn't even try to hide the coin as the thieves would get it.

When the last tiro came out of the muddy pit, only two out of three had found a coin. Those who tried stood soiled in mud up to their necks. Five stood clean to the side, Vand included.

Nikias turned to the clean tirones. "Last chance to get dirty?"

No one moved.

Nikias faced the dirty tirones. "Present coins!"

They all held up their coins as Nikias walked down the line. He typed on a holoface as he passed each one, ending at the still clean Vand. "Everyone who holds a coin gets one point. Those who didn't, well there are two more trials after this."

After Nikias awarded points, he glanced to those who were dirty, including Terra, before noting something on his shieldwatch.

Vand smirked at his pilfered coin. He chatted with a few others, already forming a gang of beta males with him as the alpha. Terra wondered why someone like Vand would be in the program at all? A cold hatred crept into her chest and she wished someone would crush his neck. Of course they would let Vand in. They let a cheater like Roland in. It was then that Terra spotted him.

Roland stood muddy, but without a coin. Terra hadn't noticed him until she remembered that day a few weeks ago. Now though, Roland had to share Terra's hatred with Vand. She did find it curious that Roland had attempted to find a coin at all. She guessed it appealed to his lazy nature since he already was a dirty cheater.

Nikias called for attention before touching a holoface. The ring descended again, returning the area to its original state. "Okay. Let's see what course to use this time."

The tirones watched as Nikias changed the salient with his shield-watch. A spherical translucent field kept the area contained as the weather changed within. Each time Nikias changed it, the tirones tensed.

He touched a holoface and the area ahead transformed into a snow filled landscape swept by a blizzard. Huge sharp chunks of ice protruded from the ground between glacial cliffs. "Too cold," Nikias said, frowning.

He then changed the landscape into a field of broken glass and razor sharp twisted metal. "Eh. Too bloody. Maybe next year. Oh I know."

Nikias transformed the area into an open field with numerous obstacles laying in a row. The course held a pattern of wooden poles clustered together to make running between them difficult. A series of walls laid across the path after the poles with the first one knee high while the last one was chest high. At the end was an elevated row of metal bars over a deep pit. Walls on either side seem to channel anyone attempting to traverse the obstacle course into a narrow straight through the center, but the ambiance seemed peaceful as the dry golden grass swayed gently in the breeze. Birds chirped in the background.

Everyone breathed a sigh of relief.

Nikias gestured to the course. "Your next trial is also simple. Make it to the other side of an obstacle course and you get a point."

"Well that doesn't sound so bad," a tiro said.

Nikias scowled after seeing the serene landscape. "Oh. Just a second."

He touched his shieldwatch's holoface and the peaceful scenery transformed again. As the ring descended it left the obstacle course the same, but on fire. An energy field now kept the raging flames locked inside the ring.

Nikias smiled. "Much better."

CHAPTER X
TRIAL OF FIRE AND WATER

The third category of recruits are the trash. These are individuals who only technically qualify for the Academy. Most are picked up by some lazy legionnaire who is just trying to earn an extra time bonus. Almost all the trash dust out the first week. However, once in a while, a piece of trash turns out to be something more. Some of the best legionnaires have come from this category.
It should be noted that I don't have a category for those who make it through the training with certainty.
  -Excerpt from Chapter Three of the Aeon Legion's *Squire Recruitment Manual* by Praetor Lycus Cerberus

Terra stared at the burning plain. The flames raged across the dry grass in a shifting sea of fire. There was no way across without enduring burns. If she had kept the coin from Vand she could have skipped this test.

Vand shook his head. "You have got to be joking. I'm not running through that. I'll be burned."

Nikias grinned. "What's the matter? Afraid of a little pain?"

Vand crossed his arms. "Hey! I already proved myself. I have over one hundred confirmed kills."

Nikias rolled his eyes. "Civilians don't count, Vand. Now like I said. All you have to do is make it across to the other side."

"So if we did the first one then we don't have to do the second?" Vand asked.

Nikias shrugged. "If you don't want to, then don't. Technically, every part of the training is optional. We can't force you to do anything."

The tirones exchanged uncertain glances.

Terra regarded the burning course while she pondered Nikias's words.

Why would both of the these trials be optional? This wasn't teaching or training. These tests had another purpose. She wondered if the test was to see if one was stupid enough to even attempt it. Perhaps those who blindly rushed in would fail? One thing was certain; if she braved the course, she would be burned and endure pain.

A tiro stepped forward while the rest hesitated. She was the Asian girl without any weapons or armor that Terra had noticed earlier. She took off at a dead run, weaving around and between the burning poles with speed and agility. With skilled reflexes, she dodged the ever shifting flames with ease. Though the fire roared around her, the girl seemed to dance with it rather than merely avoid the blaze. Terra watched, awe-struck at the girl who danced with fire. She jumped over the first wall before using her momentum to flip herself over the last, avoiding the wall in the center entirely.

When the girl approached the row of metal bars, they glowed orange from the intense heat. Instead of grabbing the heated bars, she ran and jumped onto the small wooden side beams. The beams were as narrow as her foot yet she balanced on them with one foot in front of the other as though on a tightrope.

She ran across with perfect balance before flipping off of the beam onto the ground with grace. The girl walked the rest of the way, making it to the ramp without so much as a burn while mud and dirt from the last trial flaked off. She walked out of the trial cleaner than when she had entered. The other tirones cheered when she returned.

Nikias grinned. "Well, I must admit to being impressed. It has been a while since we had a tiro make it across without being burned. It's rare that they make it across at all. What is your name, tiro?"

"Tiro Hikari Urashima, centurion," she said in a plain tone. "We met before when we sparred."

Terra felt a twinge of envy after seeing Hikari's display of raw skill. The girl's slender figure belied her true strength and power. Standing there with the flames behind her made her appear radiant. Long smooth black hair partially covered a triangle shaped face yet did not conceal bright, amber eyes that reflected the orange glow of the fires.

Nikias nodded. "Yes. I remember now. The Japanese girl. Well done. I will give you a point for that."

The other tirones gathered around Hikari, congratulating her as if drawn to her. Terra wanted to join them as well but held back, resisting the urge. Hikari, however, pulled away from the crowd.

"Anyone else who wants to attempt the course better do it now!" Nikias yelled before the crowd pursued Hikari any further.

Several attempted the course. The Zulu made it through after numerous burns. The Celtic girl got both of her arms burned after pushing through a large inferno, unwilling to wait for it to weaken. Roland kicked down the half burned row of bars and attempted to use it as a makeshift bridge, but fell through which got a chuckle from Terra. She suspected that Roland was all talk and this proved it to her.

It took Terra awhile to gather the courage for an attempt. Heat washed over her as soon as she crossed the translucent field. She sweated when the heat hit her. Thankfully most of the obstacles had burned away. Terra walked past the burning debris before reaching the metal bars which still stood. She jumped, grabbing the bars, but they burned her hands. Terra screamed as she fell, but her fall slowed when she got caught in another energy field. One of the optios helped her return to outside the salient.

When Terra joined the others, she found Hikari was no longer alone. Hikari scowled while Vand and his gang gathered around her like insects to a light.

"And that's how I got this scar here," Vand said while smirking.

Hikari regarded Vand with an irritated expression.

Poor girl, Terra thought even as she nursed her burns. *Hikari is probably too polite to tell Vand to go away.*

Vand smiled. "I can show you my other scars."

Hikari stared at Vand, expressionless. Then she turned to leave.

Vand frowned. "Don't make enemies with me girl. I have learned ten styles of martial arts and close combat techniques."

Hikari regarded Vand with a smoldering hateful gaze. "I know only one technique and if you don't leave me alone I *will* show it to you."

Vand looked over Hikari's thin body with a critical expression before his posture relaxed.

Terra thought that Hikari didn't look like much while standing in front of Vand whose muscled build towered over her.

Vand shrugged. "Well I can't really say I feel all that intimated. After all, men have denser muscle mass, a larger heart, and more lung capacity. Little things like yourself are good for only one thing."

Terra grew tense. Vand was about to start a fight. As fast as Hikari was, Terra didn't think Hikari stood a chance against Vand. He wouldn't fight fairly. Hikari would fight with honor and lose.

Hikari walked past Vand without response.

Vand scowled. "Hey! I was talking to you!" he said as he grabbed Hikari's shoulder.

It happened in a flash. Hikari made a quick movement and Vand was on the ground with a foot on his windpipe.

Nikias appeared in an instant next to Hikari and grabbed her hand before she dealt the final blow. "You realize that you are forbidden to kill the other tirones?"

Hikari glared at Nikias for a long moment. Then she released Vand. "I was not aware of this rule."

Nikias gestured for the other tirones to join him. "Fighting between tirones is not forbidden, but killing is. No breaking necks either."

Vand dusted himself off before pointing at Hikari. "Are you going to let her get away with that?"

Nikias rolled his eyes. "You weren't complaining a moment ago when you were doing the same thing."

Vand balled his fists and glared at Hikari with clinched teeth. "That wasn't fair! I wasn't ready! I want a rematch! This time I'll kill her!"

Terra knew that look. That was the look of a humiliated bully. Bullies need to regain their lost reputation after a defeat. Hikari had escalated things.

Vand gestured to Hikari. "She didn't fight with honor."

"Honor?" Hikari scoffed. "Only fools fight with honor."

Terra stared wide eyed. Had Hikari just said that? She had thought the Japanese obsessed with honor, or at least their version of it.

Nikias smiled, rubbing his hands together. "Well then. What we have is a disagreement between tirones. There is a solution for that; a *Trial of Blades*. Normally, differences between legionnaires are settled by an aeon edge duel called a Trial of Blades. However, since neither of you have earned your aeon edges yet, you may fight with whatever weapons you brought with you. Whoever wins gets a point from the loser."

Vand grinned. "Sounds good," he said, drawing a steel blue baton from his belt. Its tip sparked as electricity flowed through it.

Hikari turned her side to Vand while raising her arms chest level and spreading her feet apart.

He attacked. Vand's reach proved too difficult for Hikari to overcome with nothing but her hands. But just when he was about to move in to land a blow with his baton, Hikari drew a small hidden knife. She slashed and Vand dodged, but dropped his baton. Defenseless, Vand's 'ten styles of martial arts ' did little to prevent Hikari from landing him on the ground a second time with the knife at his throat.

With the combatants holding still, Hikari's knife drew Terra's gaze. It wasn't a knife at all, but a sword that had most of the blade cut off. The steel of the sword also looked peculiar to her, but Hikari withdrew the blade as Nikias approached.

Vand groaned, wiping blood from his face. Terra wondered why there was no safety gear. Wouldn't a Trial of Blades leave the recruits so broken they couldn't continue training? What about all the burns? Those would leave scars.

"Well done. His point is yours now," Nikias said. He turned to the other tirones. "This is the way of the Aeon Legion. You may challenge anyone and they may refuse if they wish, but a superior officer may override that objection."

As Nikias turned, Hikari stared at Nikias's aeon edge. Nikias glanced back and noted the stare before motioning for the others to follow him. Once the others had turned away, Hikari kicked Vand while he was still down before walking away.

They followed Nikias to the edge of the salient again. He turned to face the tirones. "Last chance to attempt this trial."

When no one responded, Nikias transformed the salient into a small meadow with a fast flowing river in its center. Under the rushing water was an uneven hexagonal grid of flat topped metal pillars. They waited for Nikias to change the surroundings into something horrible, but he walked to the river bank instead. "This is the last trial. It's also optional and simple."

A holoface appeared over Nikias's shieldwatch. He glanced to it before dismissing the holoface. "Looks like one group already finished their first test."

Soon everyone's shieldwatch flooded with notifications of failures. Each read the same, *Failed the first test.*

After dismissing the last holoface, Nikias waded into the water as the hexes raised to meet him. Then the water flowed faster, turning into a torrent while washing over the lower hexes.

"This test," he said with a wide grin, "requires you to fight me and knock me into the water."

Terra noticed the hexes, each with a top as big as a table, rose and fell in a random pattern except for the cluster Nikias stood upon. Some would jut out of the rushing water when they were high enough while others would submerge. This made the battlefield an ever changing one.

Before anyone else moved, Roland walked forward, gripping the hilt of his sword.

Terra grinned. *This is it*, she thought. *Roland will make himself look like a fool. He cheated to get in. He doesn't have any real skill.*

The steel rang as he drew his blade and stepped onto the first hex. He waded into the water, sword in hand as the river washed away the mud from the first trial. Roland made no effort to walk on the dry hexes, instead he headed straight towards Nikias.

"I have been looking forward to this one," Nikias said as he drew his aeon edge and smiled. The edge did not glow as Alya's had in the library.

Roland sauntered to the shallower hexes near Nikias while Nikias held still. Then Roland struck.

Water splashed as Roland lashed out in a blur. His lazy saunter vanished as his sword strikes flowed like waves. Each blow Nikias deflected Roland weaved into the next attack.

Terra could hear the gasps of the other tirones. Like her, they assumed Roland to be lazy like a still pond yet here he moved like a rushing river. He wielded his blade with skill even an amateur like Terra could recognize.

Nikias smirked while he blocked the blows. The blades met and Terra wondered why Roland's medieval sword didn't get sliced through. She assumed that Nikias had turned off his aeon edge to make the fight fair. Terra also noticed that the hexes raised to meet Nikias when he drew near. They followed wherever he went and lowered when he passed. Roland struggled to step onto Nikias's platform.

When Roland set foot on Nikias's platform, Nikias kicked him into the water. Roland sank under the surface.

"Well that was fun," Nikias said before turning back to the other recruits. "Who's next?"

A pillar broke the surface behind Nikias with Roland standing on it, water running off him.

When Nikias turned Roland lashed out with his blade though not at Nikias, but at the water. It splashed into Nikias's face. Roland attacked again jumping onto a nearby hex. He knocked Nikias's poorly aimed swing aside before tripping him. Nikias fell with a thump onto the dry hex before rolling off into the water.

Nikias laughed when the pillars lifted him again out of the river. "Well done knight. You get a point. It's been years since a recruit managed to knock me over."

The Celtic girl crouched, narrowing her gaze.

"Next!" Nikias yelled.

The girl stared a long while at the water before running at Nikias. It was then Terra realized a line of shallow hexes now led towards Nikias. The girl had waited for them to line up.

She roared as she ran drawing a pair of small daggers. Nikias grinned, stepping aside as she struck. This threw her off balance before he shoved her behind him into the water.

"Next!" He yelled.

Hikari stared at Nikias for a long while. However Terra noticed that Hikari stared not at Nikias, but his aeon edge. When no one else stepped forward Hikari approached, jumping on the shallow hexes. When she drew near to Nikias, Terra watched Hikari struggle with her footing in the fast moving water as she kept her gaze on Nikias's sword.

She struck at Nikias, attacking as she leaped to the last hex. When she landed on the hex, she and Nikias became intertwined in a fearsome melee. Nikias kept his aeon edge sheathed. When it seemed Hikari had the upper hand, Nikias drew his blade and flung it at Hikari. Hikari caught the blade but became unbalanced. Nikias attacked before she recovered and shoved her into the river. The aeon edge flew from her hand and Nikias caught it before it touched the water.

"Keep your eyes on your foe," Nikias said as Hikari crawled onto shore, drenched, "not his weapon, however much you may want it for yourself."

Vand and his gang attacked next after working up the courage to strike as a team. Nikias threw them all into the water, one at a time, with minimal effort. Several others attacked with the same results.

"Anyone else?" Nikias asked.

Terra hesitated. Should she attempt this test? Unlike the others, she had no chance of even completing this one. She would be lucky even to reach Nikias much less be able to push him off into the water. Once again she wondered what the real point of this test was.

Terra tensed as she recalled Nikias's words from earlier, "If you are unwilling to fight then you shouldn't be here." She knew she had to try. In the library the odds had been hopeless as well but she had fought. She would face this test as she had the others.

Terra stepped forward.

Nikias grinned before sheathing his aeon edge. "Well I didn't expect this."

Terra made her way towards Nikias though she battled against the flow of the river. After several minutes of struggling against the flow of water, she made it to the platform.

Nikias drew away from the edge, letting Terra climb on without a fight.

Terra raised her fists.

Nikias roared with laughter while shaking his head. "Your fighting stance is all wrong. We will have work on that."

She stared confused. Did he pity her? No. He spoke as though he would teach her later. Terra's eyes went wide. Had she passed the first test? Then Nikias shoved her into the water.

Nikias looked to the remaining dry tirones. "Last chance."

No one moved forward as Terra crawled onto shore, drenched.

Nikias shrugged and began typing on a holoface. Moments later, Terra's shieldwatch holoface was again flooded with notifications. She looked at the first one. It showed Vand's picture with flashing text reading *Termination due to failure of the first test.*

There was a notification for each one that had failed. Terra felt a surge of panic at each holoface, expecting to see her picture. It never appeared.

Nikias pointed to several tirones including Hikari, Roland, and Terra. "All of you! Over here. The rest of you are to turn in your shield-watches at the pillar."

"What is this?" Vand yelled as he stared at his own holoface.

Nikias's brow lowered. "What do you think it means? You dusted out."

"Hey! I'm a soldier! A killer! I am better than most of this lot!" Vand said while gesturing to the others.

Nikias held up a finger. "You were unwilling to do all three *trials* therefore you failed the first *test*."

Terra turned to the remaining tirones. They were all burned, dirty, and now drenched as well. All had attempted each trial even though most didn't earn a single point.

Vand pointed to Nikias. "This is unfair! You said they were optional!"

Nikias rolled his eyes. "All three *trials* were optional, but you had to do all three trials if you wanted to pass the first *test*."

"Then why didn't you tell us!" Vand said, pointing at Nikias.

Nikias sighed. "To see if you could figure it out. We want those willing to do anything without being forced. Being a part of the Aeon Legion means you must go above mere orders. If you give anything less than your all, then you will fail."

Vand clenched his fists. "It's not fair!"

Nikias shrugged. "It's Praetor Lycus's idea. I can't help you. Now go and leave your shieldwatch by the pillar."

Vand and the others who failed left. After that, those who remained marched back to the central square and waited for the other groups to return. When the rest returned, Lycus walked onto the stage. He smiled when he saw how few remained.

Terra looked around to the other groups. Most suffered a similar amount of attrition. What had started as several thousand now stood at half that number. Those who remained looked as singed and dirty as she was.

Lycus grinned. "Good. Now the easy part is out of the way and we can start the real training tomorrow."

Terra's stomach twisted. Today was the easy day? One more day like today and they wouldn't be able to stand from the injuries. Many turned pale at that remark as well.

Vand and several others pushed their way to the front and invaded the stage. None of the optios tried to stop them. In fact, they shied away from them.

"I think there has been a mistake," Vand said as he approached Lycus. He stood straight, displaying his impressive physique.

Lycus glared at Vand with a predatory grin before speaking in a low tone. "Thank you for volunteering."

Vand hesitated.

Lycus turned to the remaining tirones. "Today was a test of willingness. If you are not willing to get dirty then you are not worthy of joining the Legion. Anyone unwilling to endure pain better crashing well stay away from the Legion. Those unwilling to fight will not overcome those who are. You need to be willing to do all three to make it through the Labyrinth."

Vand scowled. "Hey! Your test was unfair! I want a retry!"

Lycus ignored him. "Now for those who made it past the first test, I would like to explain a few more rules."

Vand's knuckles turned white. "Don't ignore me!"

"First," Lycus said while still ignoring Vand. "You will be injured repeatedly during the training."

Vand charged Lycus, but in a flash of motion, Lycus snapped Vand's leg. Vand screamed and fell to the stage.

"Like this," Lycus said as he circled Vand. He grabbed Vand's arm before dislocating his shoulder. Vand screamed and tried to crawl away, but Lycus dragged him back to the center of the stage. The other recruits who joined Vand stepped back.

"Please stop! Baal!" Vand screamed.

Terra shifted nervously.

Lycus continued to smile. He stood over Vand, gesturing to his broken body. "You can endure almost any amount of damage," he said as he touched a holoface over his shieldwatch. A ring passed over Vand, moving clockwise. When it passed, it restored Vand back to the way he was before Lycus had mutilated him. "And still be Restored."

Vand's eyes went wide as he felt at his own body.

Terra's face went pale. Her stomach churned at not only the torture she witnessed, but at the implications. They could injure her or any other recruit as much as they wanted before Restoring them.

Lycus grabbed Vand's foot and dragged him back as he tried to scramble away again. "You get one restoration or *Restore* a day. So use it wisely. If you want another one, then you have to spend a point. Reversing minor wounds is free."

"Help me!" Vand screamed as his allies deserted him. "Anyone!"

Lycus turned his gaze to Vand. "However, there is one injury that can eliminate you from the program."

Vand's eyes went wide as he cried. He made one last desperate bid to escape, trying to crawl away from Lycus who still held his foot.

Lycus's smile twisted into a toothy, monstrous snarl as he grabbed Vand's head while placing his foot on Vand's back. "I despise war criminals," Lycus muttered before he pulled. The sound of Vand's neck snapping echoed as Lycus pulled. Vand then fell to the ground limp as a Restore ring passed over him.

To Terra's surprise, Vand did not die. Once the ring passed over him, he shook his head and stood as though uninjured. "Where am I? Who are you?"

Lycus gestured to Vand. "Should your nervous system be sufficiently damaged, then a Restore will erase your memories. Naturally you will be dismissed from the program."

Two optios escorted Vand off the stage.

Lycus walked to the front of the stage. "You will find your schedules on the large holofaces near the central courtyard. Failure to follow your schedule will result in termination from the program. Dismissed."

The other tirones turned to leave.

Lycus grinned. "One last thing. Let Vand be an example. I am the only bully allowed here."

CHAPTER XI
TALENT

Attrition rates during the first day are standard for this run. Many have questioned the wisdom of such an early cull of tirones, however I have found it greatly increases performance and saves lives. My data proves this. After implementing the three trials of entry, survival rates in the Labyrinth increased by twenty percent. Those who are unwilling to get dirty, endure pain, or fight tend to dust out and the rest usually die in the Labyrinth. Others would also criticize my use of Vand as an example. I do so hate war criminals. I need to be the villain of this Academy, not Vand. Bullies have no place in my Legion.
-From the personal logs of Praetor Lycus Cerberus

Once again Terra had to make herself wake at an early hour. She had received her schedule and found Morning Formation first on the list. It was at 5:00 am. She dressed in her training uniform and jogged to the courtyard as the sun dawned. Their formation stood again at twenty five as the centurions had condensed it with another small group.

Nikias joined their group. "All right! Morning exercise!"

He led them in a jog. They passed the stone pillar in the center of the courtyard where a large collection of shieldwatches lay at the base.

Terra found morning exercise extremely difficult by her standards. She had worked hard the past few weeks, trying to get into shape. While stronger, she was nowhere near ready. Nikias turned a large salient into a rocky, burning hot desert. Terra sweated and puffed as they ran across the salient.

She arrived last after what seemed like an eternity while those already there panted at the edge of the salient. Terra almost collapsed and thanked God, Aion, or whatever the deity of Saturn City was that it was finished.

Nikias grinned, not even winded. Terra noticed that Nikias's scar was above his left eyebrow now. Was she hallucinating? After a moment he changed the salient into volcanic wasteland. Pools of lava collected on the surface while metal bridges crossed them.

Terra went pale. "You have got to be joking?"

"I know! They really need to make this run more difficult," Nikias said as he motioned for the rest of the tirones to follow. After a moment, Terra jogged after them, lagging behind.

They crossed the salient three more times with each terrain worse than the last. Nikias explained the salient's diameter was roughly a mile. A few of the more fit tirones earned a point for making the entire run in under a time limit. Terra barely finished, well over the time limit.

The optios offered them drinks. Others hesitated after seeing it wasn't water. Terra recognized the strange liquid. It helped heal the body after exercise so she drank it down. Nausea followed, but it passed within seconds as did the throbbing pain in her legs. She felt good at having at least made it, if only barely. Her good feeling didn't last long.

Then came the other exercises. Pushups, pullups, stretches, calisthenics, and a dozen other exercises all in terrible burning heat. The optios would give water to anyone who looked ready to pass out. Terra suspected they monitored everyone's vitals.

"Excellent!" Nikias yelled after the last repetition of situps. "Time for a break!"

Everyone breathed a long sigh of relief and collapsed on the ground, panting.

Nikias rubbed his hands together. "The break today is hand to hand combat, the best part of the day."

Terra felt too weary to groan in protest.

Nikias transformed the surrounding area into a heated ironworks building. They stood on a stone floor surrounded by red hot forges. Terra felt the heat wash over her as the fires burned to the sides.

Nikias walked in the center of the group, speaking loud so all could hear, "Exhausted?"

Everyone nodded.

"Good!" he said, laughing. "If you can fight while exhausted, then you can fight while rested. Now I will explain the rules of sparring practice. Don't kill your opponent."

A tiro raised an eyebrow. "That's it?"

Nikias grinned. "Weapons, groin attacks, gouging eyes, it's all fair so long as you do not injure your opponent's head too much. A shieldwatch Restore can heal injuries instantly."

A tiro toward the back stepped forward. He was tall with a muscular build, but was missing most of his teeth and wore a dirty tunic. "So this machine makes me immortal? What's to stop me? I could just take this machine and conquer any time I pleased."

Nikias's grin widened to show teeth. "Interesting idea, tiro. Let's test it," he said while drawing his aeon edge. He then attacked in a blur of motion, slashing at the tall tiro.

The tiro screamed and fell bleeding from a slash on his chest.

Terra jumped upon seeing blood splatter on the floor.

The tiro struggled to find his shieldwatch's holoface menu that could Restore him. After a few seconds he touched it and a ring ran around him, erasing the wound.

Nikias shook his head. "I hope they learn mental commands soon. A Restore can heal almost any wound. However..."

The tall tiro stood only for Nikias to plunge the aeon edge into the tiro's shoulder, pinning him to the ground. The tiro screamed, but the optios stood by, passive, as though this were business as usual.

The tiro squirmed while the aeon edge still pierced his shoulder. "It hurts! Stop!"

Nikias rolled his eyes. "Stop blubbering like an Athenian after an election. It's just a bit of pain. Why don't you use a Restore again?"

The tiro struggled to touch his shieldwatch again, but this time the ring didn't form.

After a moment Nikias withdrew the blade and touched a holoface near his shieldwatch which Restored the tiro. Nikias then turned to the other tirones. "Remember this well. A shieldwatch cannot Restore you under three conditions; one if you die from head injury or blood loss, two if the shieldwatch is out of power or not attached to your body, or three, when a singularity artifact or another complex living creature is within the Restore ring's area of effect. An aeon edge is singularity technology. So long as you are impaled by it or it is within range of your Restore ring, then you cannot Restore."

Terra ignored the entire speech and instead stared wide eyed at the large pool of blood on the ground.

Nikias gestured for the tiro to return to the group. "Thank you for being a good example. I'll give you a free Restore. Now let's begin sparring. I will have you fight in your native style first so I can gauge each tiro's martial skill. If you win a sparring match, then you get a point and the option to fight the next opponent. Lose the next fight and you lose two points. Using a Restore is allowed, but using a shieldwatch is restricted until week three. Now, Hikari will show you how it's done."

Hikari moved to the center of the room next to Nikias.

Nikias then stroked his beard before pointing to another tiro, a man in camouflage fatigues. "You first."

The man approached, facing off against Hikari and looked her over with a careful gaze. He stood taller than her with short hair and a well muscled build. "She has no weapon," he said while gesturing to Hikari.

Nikias shrugged.

Hikari stood expressionless as her eyes reflected the glow of the forge fires.

The tiro in camouflage nodded. "Well if you are Japanese, then I guess I will be polite," he said as he bowed.

Hikari lashed out like a spark from a flame. She was on him in a flash before he even finished his bow, kneeing him in the face while he was low. As he moved to cover his face, Hikari twisted his arm before throwing him to the ground. Then using her leverage gained from standing over him, she dislocated his shoulder. The tiro screamed in pain.

Nikias nodded, smiling. "Excellent, Tiro Hikari. You gain a point."

After Hikari received her point she stepped away from the man.

The tiro in camouflage stood and after considerable pain, relocated his shoulder. He then pointed to Hikari. "Not fair! You didn't say go."

Nikias chuckled, his tone mocking. "I'm sorry. In your time's wars did they wait until everyone was ready? In this training, if you see an opening, you exploit it. Don't worry. There is no shame in losing."

Everyone peered at Nikias while he tried to keep a straight face.

After a moment, Nikias roared with laughter. "That was great! No shame in losing! If only the guys back home could have heard that one!" he said, still chuckling, before turning to Hikari. "Tiro Hikari! Another?"

Hikari breathed out before nodding.

The next tiro was a slender Celtic girl with blue face paint. She drew two daggers and charged Hikari.

Within a few blows the girl was unconscious.

"Another." Hikari said louder this time.

Terra glared at Hikari who had yet to begin sweating. The other tirones appeared short on breath in contrast.

The next tiro was the Zulu who held a hide shield and spear. He took her a little longer to defeat, but she proved too quick and aggressive for him to handle.

Nikias beamed. "How about two this time?"

Two tirones entered the center and the same two were on the floor moments later. Hikari burned through them like fire through tinder.

After a few more matches Hikari panted.

Nikias then pointed to Terra. "You."

Terra raised her hands in front of her. "Wait! I can't fight Hikari! I know nothing about fighting!"

Nikias smiled. "Every bruise is a teacher, every wound a lesson. Hope you outgrow these instructors quickly."

"But!" Terra said, pleading.

Nikias looked Terra straight in the eyes. "Do you wish to give up the training?"

"No."

Nikias pointed to Hikari. "Then fight."

Terra grimaced, but moved to face Hikari, raising her fists as though to box.

Nikias chuckled and gestured to Terra while facing the others. "Who can tell what she's doing wrong?"

"She came here," Hikari said with a frustrated expression. She still stood winded, but the heat didn't appear to bother her as much as it did Terra.

Terra frowned at hearing the rude comment.

"More specifically," Hikari said, assuming her own defensive stance with her knees bent and feet spread apart while facing her side to Terra. "Her stance has her facing her opponent, exposing her torso, groin, throat, and other parts of her body to attack. If she faced her opponent with her side, she would reduce the number of available targets. Straight and stiff knees make her easy to unbalance. Also, she holds her fists improperly. The thumb should be to the side, not behind the other fingers. One arm should be positioned lower to parry lower attacks. Finally, her lack of discipline shows in her breathing. A strong blow could easily knock the breath from her, leaving her stunned."

"Oh come on!" Terra said, scowling. "Even my breathing?"

Nikias nodded. "Very good, tiro. Hikari represents one specific school of martial arts. The Aeon Legion uses twelve different styles. We selected the best of each and discarded the weaker parts. Should your weapons fail, you will still have hand to hand."

Nikias turned back to Terra. "Let's see if we can fix your stance. Turn your side to me and spread your footing out."

Terra took to the stance instantly.

"Good," Nikias said. "Get a little lower and bend your knees. Lower one arm."

Terra assumed the stance.

"Excellent, Tiro Mason," Nikias said with a pleased smiled. "It's seldom I see raw tiro take to a stance on the first try. Proceed!"

Terra's eyes went wide as she turned towards Hikari and tried to remember the stance she had just learned. Hikari assumed a similar stance and maneuvered towards Terra.

Terra just got the footing right when Hikari sent her tumbling to the ground. Terra hit the hot stone floor hard with a thump. Hikari turned her back to Terra and stepped away.

Terra stood before rubbing her back. "That hurt."

Hikari glanced back to Terra and frowned before turning to advance again.

This time Terra got into stance faster and even dodged the first blow. Terra's victory proved short lived when Hikari kicked Terra in the stomach, sending her once again to the ground. Hikari turned to walk away when Terra stood again.

Once again, Hikari assumed her stance and attacked. Terra blocked one kick before Hikari attacked Terra's jaw with her palm, sending Terra staggering back. Not waiting for Terra to recover, Hikari unleashed a flurry of blows. She struck Terra multiple times in the stomach and face before sending her down to the ground with a final blow. Everyone watching winced when Terra hit the floor hard a third time. Hikari stood, panting as the firelight reflected off beaded sweat on her brow.

Terra groaned while forcing herself back up. Before she stood, Hikari kicked her hard in the sides, sending her back down. Still groaning, Terra tried to stand again, but her arms gave out under the strain.

Hikari wiped the sweat off her face. "This is a waste of my time," she said between ragged breaths.

Nikias raised an eyebrow. "Oh? I didn't realize your time was so precious. Do you have somewhere to go?"

Hikari's lips drew to a line. "Fights with the weak teach me nothing. I want that sword."

Nikias shook his head. "A training blade costs twenty five points. A real aeon edge is earned only if you pass the Labyrinth."

Terra groaned and forced herself to stand.

He turned to Terra. "You almost get a point for being an amazingly determined punching bag. As a consolation, I will give you a free Restore instead."

A thirty minute break in the schedule followed sparring. Terra learned that the centurions often hid things on the schedule. At times the schedule changed without warning. More than one tiro ran to make it to their next training event. Thankfully that didn't happen to Terra or her group this time.

After their meal, they still had to move fast to the next event called Shieldwatch Basics. Terra hoped this would not be as physical as the morning's training.

Nikias was not present at the next salient. Instead it was a woman whose hair was more silver than brown. Terra recognized her from her first attempt to get into the Academy.

"I am Centurion Isra," the woman said, her voice soft. "You may address me as centurion. I am not strict with regard to protocol and formalities, nor am I lax regarding discipline and procedure. I do not require a salute, but I hate repeating myself and I do not tolerate disrespect. Understood?"

The tirones nodded. "Yes, centurion," they all said at once.

"Good," she said in a terse tone. She then turned before changing the salient into a snow covered tundra. "Follow and listen closely."

Cold air stung Terra's skin as she stepped into the salient. It was the opposite misery of the morning.

Isra kept her back to the tirones as she walked in front of them. She raised her shieldwatch arm into the air. "For those who remain ignorant, this is a shieldwatch. This is the real secret behind the Aeon Legion's power. Time is fundamental to experience. To control time allows one to control any combat situation. Today's lesson requires mastery of one of its most basic functions."

They stopped in front of a fast flowing river. Large chunks of ice floated downstream. The others shivered from the cold though Terra was not that frigid yet. As cold as it was, it did not compare to the scorching heat this morning.

Isra turned, crouching and scooped a handful of water before flinging it into the air. She froze it in place, the droplets hanging in the air with a faint outline of a grainy sphere around them. A few tirones gasped in amazement.

Isra gestured to the hovering water. "Within this small sphere of energy, the water is trapped in stasis. Most of the energy fields in Saturn City are actually stasis fields. Time is *Stopped* within. Stopping time is an easier ability, but this is half the lesson. The other is range. A shieldwatch can only affect an area that you can reach at any moment, the range of your core causal field, but with concentration you can project twice that distance. Remember, though, that it is more costly to do so. This makes the shieldwatch's effective range nine feet for most."

One tiro yawned.

Isra's gaze darted to the young man. "Is there a problem, tiro?"

"It's cold!" he whined. "Get to the point!"

Isra appeared in front of the tiro. Terra only saw a blur. Isra grabbed him and dragged him to the river's edge. "What did you mean to say, tiro?" Isra asked, her tone calm as she dangled him above the ice cold water.

"Get to the point, centurion!" he whimpered.

"Good. Minus one point for disrespecting a superior officer," she said before dropping him into the river. He screamed as the ice cold water washed him away.

The other tirones stared in amazement at Isra. "How did you do that, centurion?" one asked.

Terra didn't find Isra's speed surprising after having witnessed Alya at the library.

Isra dusted off her hands. "You mean that burst of speed? To me it appeared as though everything had slowed. I *Sped* time around me. That is one of the four fundamental abilities of a shieldwatch. With a shield-watch, time can be *Sped*, *Slowed*, *Stopped*, or *Reversed*. Most of you first time tirones can only manage Stopping with stasis. Now I have a task for you all to perform. Make it across the river to earn a point. Make it across the river first, you get a point and I'll let you stand by a warm fire I have prepared."

Everyone looked at the fast flowing river. After a moment, a tiro voiced what was on everyone's mind.

"That's flowing way too fast, centurion," he said. "No one can make it across."

The tiro who Isra had thrown into the water had just made it to shore again. He walked back to the others, shivering.

Isra's expression remained unreadable. "A valid observation, tiro. Perhaps you should consider what I have just shown you," she said before shoving the tiro who disrespected her back into the river. She then walked a short distance away to a burning camp fire.

A few glanced at one another before shifting their attention to their shieldwatches. A few swung it around, others pointed it at the water as if trying to stop the river from flowing. One even took her shieldwatch off, trying to get it to work. Terra hunted through menus, trying to find something that could help her get across the river. After a moment, one tiro jumped in the river assuming the shieldwatch would work automatically. The flow swept him away and several optios collected him downstream. The optios then deposited him, still shivering and wet, right back with the rest of the tirones.

Then one pointed his hand out and placed some falling snow in stasis.

"How did you do that?" asked another tiro.

He shrugged. "Don't know. It just worked. I felt something strange, like I had another part of myself to control. Then it just happened."

After a moment and under the cheering of the other tirones, he attempted to swim to the other side of the river. He used his shield-watch to slow the flow of water, but it stopped working before the half-way point and the flow swept him away. After a moment, the tirones returned to their own attempts with the shieldwatch. All except one, Terra noticed.

Roland sat crouched on the ground with a thoughtful look.

"Stuck? I bet you probably can't get your shieldwatch to work either?" Terra chided.

Roland Stopped a bit of falling snow in stasis before releasing it.

Terra's mouth hung open before clinching her jaw.

Roland grinned. "I mastered that trick weeks ago. I was just waiting for someone else to try crossing the river first."

Terra frowned "You what?"

Roland stood. "I have seen enough fools hasten to be first. I shall not repeat that folly. Besides, I think I see a way across now. Why make mistakes myself when I can learn from others?"

Terra glared at Roland, speechless, as he walked to the river's edge. Roland waited for a large chunk of ice to drift near and Stopped it in stasis. He then jumped on it and waited for more ice to drift close.

The others noticed and cheered. Roland leaped from one ice chunk to another. When he drew close to the other side, the ice ran out so he swam the rest of the way after casting aside his chain mail.

Isra smiled while walking down to the river bank. "It has been a long time since one made it across the first try."

Terra shot a hate filled glare at Roland as he made his way back. Soon he stood next to the warm fire while Terra only had her hot anger to warm her.

After another half hour of trying and failing to get her shieldwatch working, she along with the remaining tirones were forced to try to cross the river. She tried to wave her shieldwatch at the water as she jumped, but she missed one of the floating ice chunks before the river swept her downstream. Terra struggled to stay afloat, but managed to swim back ashore. She growled as she watched Roland stand by the warm fire while she shivered in ice cold water. Roland enjoyed his warmth while only Terra knew that he had succeeded by letting someone else fail for him.

∞

Terra looked forward to academic classes as she walked through the

Academy's hallways. It would be nice to have a break after the first two miserable lessons of the day. Terra stepped inside after checking the room number, confident her modern education would give her an edge here.

The classroom was circular in design like an amphitheater and pearl white like most of Saturn City. One glass wall allowed a view of the grounds. Desks and chairs stood arranged in neat semi circular rows while a large holoface glowed on the central, circular floor at the base. A few tirones already sat straight backed and staring ahead. Before Terra had time to find a seat, a centurion confronted her. She had three locks of silver in her hair.

"Name?" She asked, her tone harsh.

"Terra Mason," Terra said without thinking.

The centurion grimaced before moving closer to Terra. She looked Terra in the eyes, her face inches away. "I didn't see a salute, tiro! Also you will address yourself as tiro since I don't care about your worthless name! Do you understand?"

"Yes, Ma'am!" Terra said, standing straighter and giving her best salute, placing her fist over her heart. Nikias had never been that insistent on ranks and saluting.

The centurion moved closer to Terra, her nose almost touching Terra's face. "Do I look like a ma'am to you! I haven't suffered through Masada and the Faceless War just for some worthless tiro to call me ma'am! You will address me by my proper rank of centurion! Centurion Shani! Do you understand!"

"Yes, ma– centurion!" Terra yelled as sweat beaded on her brow.

The door faded again and Delphia walked inside. She spotted Terra and waved, smiling. "Hi Terra. Um, is this Alpha Civ one?"

Shani turned to Delphia and smiled, speaking in a kind tone, "Oh no, timeborn. That's down the hall to the left in room one seventeen. Do you need help finding it?"

Delphia shook her head. "Oh no. I think I can manage on my own. Thank you so much. Goodbye, Terra. Good luck," she said and waved at Terra before leaving the room.

Shani's smile disappeared with Delphia. "What are you doing you useless parasite! You stand at attention in the presence of an officer! Now sit down and remain silent!"

Terra sat. Shani tore into most tirones when they entered. A few who saluted and addressed her as centurion escaped her wrath. When the class filled, Shani moved to the central circular floor at the base.

"Let's begin," she said as she pointed at Terra. "Tiro. Please describe the most common forms of time travel."

Terra sighed. Why did everyone pick on her? How could she possibly know that? "I'm sorry, centurion. I don't know."

Shani frowned. "Very well. Then can you explain the properties of temporal mechanics that make it impossible to meet yourself using time travel?"

"I'm sorry, centurion. I don't know that either."

"Can you even name the historical event that formed the first nexus?"

"I'm sorry, centurion. I don't kn–"

"Of course you don't!" Shani snapped. "Because you didn't read your assignments!"

Terra scowled. "I assumed th–"

"That this would be an introduction to the class? General Reva slaughtered several Legion cohorts during the Battle of Sighs. All because the Legion assumed the Kalians' fang formation was a result of their lack of discipline. Instead it was a trap that had disastrous consequences almost costing the Legion the entire First Temporal War. Others ignored reports of disappearances in the Bleak, assuming it was pirate activity when really it was the first Faceless raids. Yet others assumed the first Manticore infestations isolated incidents. Assumptions *cost* lives, especially in war. Thankfully this one only cost you a point."

Terra would have felt upset if she actually had a point to lose.

Shani's frown deepened as she continued to chastise Terra. "If you had done some research, then you would have discovered the required reading list is posted on the same holoface as your schedule. It was not hidden. You should have found it."

She pointed to another tiro. "Tiro, can explain the branching nature of continua and why altering history destabilizes said branches?"

The tiro scratched her chin. "Um..."

Shani sighed. "Did anyone read their assignments? Why can't I have another student like Kairos? She was amazing."

Terra groaned, slouching in her seat. She had thought that this would be her area of expertise.

Shani swept her gaze across the room, looking for another target. "I swear this group seems slower than last year's and I don't know how that's possible considering that poor batch of Faceless fodder. Maybe I should eliminate a few more?"

"Why are they trying so hard to eliminate us?" a tiro said under his breath.

Shani turned her hateful stare upon the the tiro before addressing the class. "Every weakness we introduce into the Legion brings us closer to obliteration at the hands of our enemies. Only those who are talented and utterly dedicated to saving history belong here. The Aeon Legion is the only thing standing between the horrors lurking beyond Time and humanity. Thieves, conquerors, assassins, monsters, and war machines, these are just a few of the enemies we have encountered. All of them pale in comparison to the Faceless. So when the next threat comes, and they will come, we will be ready."

Her lecture continued for another hour and a half. She covered how Time consisted of several alternate histories called continua. Each continuum had its own history that was often wildly different from the rest. Continua branched at an area called a nexus that appeared at turning points in history. Terra's home continuum, designated Lambda, branched at the Cuban Missile Crisis.

Shani dismissed the class when the lecture was done. Terra stood to go.

Shani pointed to Terra. "Not you, tiro. I want a word with you."

Terra hesitated before facing Shani, but turned to face the centurion as straight-backed as she could manage.

Shani crossed her arms and spoke in a soft tone. "I don't know why Lycus admitted you, but we always get a few weak ones every year. Have you considered quitting?"

"I considered–"

"Then you should quit," Shani said without malice in her voice. "Those who have even a moment of doubt don't belong here. You lack talent and dedication, both essential for success in this program."

"I have enough dedication to make up for my lack of talent!"

"Prove it. Otherwise don't waste my time."

The training day was over and somehow Terra had made it to the end. Now the setting sun cast an orange hue on the main courtyard and the air turned cold. Terra rubbed her arms, trying to warm up. Looking at the stone pillar she saw the growing collection of shieldwatches laying at the base now numbered in the hundreds. A few had thrown their own on the pile this evening. Terra wondered if she should join them.

She turned away. The shieldwatch had Restored her body, but she felt mentally drained. Her discovery of the long reading list did not help her mood. No human could read that much in so short of time. She would need a three year head start. How could Shani expect that of Terra, or anyone for that matter? Sighing, she started to wander back to her dorm room.

As Terra made her way through the Academy training areas, she watched the other tirones. Most returned to their own rooms while a few socialized with the others, drinking and having fun. Then she saw Roland. Despite his lazy demeanor, he practiced with his shieldwatch. An optio helped him. Terra paused, wondering why Roland would practice. She remembered that Roland had used a shieldwatch before the others. He had practiced on his own before the training had even started.

Terra then noticed a few familiar faces. One was the Roman legionnaire she saw the first day at the Academy. He practiced as well. Terra halted. All who attempted the training a second or even third time still worked.

A shout sounded nearby. Terra looked for the disturbance and saw a large bonfire burning nearby. A circle of tirones had gathered around it, but they appeared unconcerned with the loud shouting.

Terra made her way over to see Hikari fighting with another tiro. She knocked another tiro unconscious before glancing to her shieldwatch.

"See the pattern," a nearby tiro said to another standing next to him.

"Yeah," the other said. "She defeats three in a row and then uses a Restore. That nets her two points."

Terra watched the next challenger who fought Hikari. He approached and challenged her to a Trial of Blades. Hikari always accepted and always won.

Terra watched two more matches before walking away. Hikari burned through challengers though Terra wondered how Hikari managed it given the day's grueling regimen. This made Terra confront one undeniable fact; the best tirones were still working hard.

Terra searched and found an optio. He had two locks of silver hair. Terra approached. "Excuse me, optio."

"Tiro?" he asked.

Terra gestured to the others. "Is it required that the recruits... I mean tirones stay late?"

The optio shook his head. "No, tiro. Training is officially over for the day."

Terra thought for a moment before shifting her attention back to him. "I would bet that most of the tirones who stay late make it through the training?"

He grinned. "I'm not allowed to say, but you could be on to something."

"What do the others tend to focus on?"

"Well in early parts of the training, most focus on their strengths to build confidence."

Terra thought for a moment. She was behind in everything. Then Terra remembered she had a strength. Something she could catch up on if she had the time. Surely a city beyond time could find her more. "I need to catch up on my reading, but I need more time."

He smiled. "So you noticed?"

"With so many people from different times, there must be a few who don't have a good education. Even if they did, there is no time to read that much and still train with a full schedule. Is there something I'm missing?"

The man gestured. "Follow me."

Terra followed as he led her to a circular room to the side of the Academy. Several of the rooms stood in a row. They looked like smaller, indoor salients with a diameter of ten feet.

"This," the man said while gesturing to the room, "is a strategy study. Officers use rooms like this for planning in the middle of battle. When activated, it Speeds your mental faculties. It also has limited access to the Saturn City Archives."

Terra examined the room. The gray steel floor was devoid of any notable features. "So time passes differently in this room?"

He shook his head. "No, tiro. As I said, it accelerates your thoughts. It will feel as though time slows down around you. When this chamber activates, one hour of study inside equals to five minutes of time outside."

"Wow. Is there a drawback?"

He grinned. "Actually there is. A lot of newtimers miss that one."

Terra looked around, nervous. "Is it dangerous?"

"No. But I wouldn't suggest coming here early in the morning. A shieldwatch can repair the body, but it cannot alleviate mental fatigue. This place accelerates your mind. It can give you more time to study but your mind will tire at an accelerated rate as well. Just remember that," he said before waving his hand. A multitude of holofaces appeared in his hand's wake.

Terra walked forward. "Thank you."

The man nodded. "We can help you in any aspect of the training. Be polite. Those who make enemies of the optios never make it far. We don't waste time with those who will not listen to us."

The chamber hummed to life. The hum pulsed before it slowed and Terra's movements became sluggish. It took getting use to but after a moment she was deep into reading the wealth of information in Saturn City's Archives.

A few hours later Terra strolled by the stone pillar in the courtyard with a newfound understanding of the true meaning of exhaustion. She glanced up one more time at the stone pillar with a sea of shieldwatches at its base. Terra grimaced. "I will not let you beat me," she said in a low tone. She had made her choice. A hard choice that she had plenty of time to think about in the strategy study.

Terra turned her back to the pillar.

The next day's exercise was just as brutal as was shieldwatch practice. Terra felt little confidence when walking into the classroom. Shani was there waiting, like a predator ready to pounce. "Name?"

"Tiro Terra Mason, centurion!" Terra said in a loud voice, giving her best salute.

Shani hesitated with a disappointed scowl. "Find a seat, tiro."

After the others arrived, class began.

Shani turned to Terra. "Can you explain the properties of temporal mechanics that make it impossible to meet yourself using time travel?"

Terra wavered only for a second. "It's called the *Instance Effect*. When a person time travels for the first time, they become an instance. That instance will override any copy from any other time. In effect, the instance becomes the original as it were. Should an instance travel to another time where they are present, then the instance will override that version in that time, one hundred percent of the time, should their causal fields overlap."

Shani nodded. "Can you name the historical event that formed the first nexus?"

Terra responded faster this time. "Alexander the Great becomes the focal point of the first divide in history. In one continuum he survives long enough to consolidate his empire, leading to prolonged Hellenistic dominance of the Middle East. In another, he dies young and his empire fragments. The third continuum forms when he dies in India and his empire shatters completely."

Shani nodded again. "Almost. He is only known as *the Great* in one of three continua. Can you explain the primary principles of singularity technology?"

Terra frowned. "I'm sorry, centurion. I don't know that."

"Congratulations, tiro. You are caught up to where you should have been yesterday. Am I to be impressed with your supposed academic talent?"

"No, centurion. Academics is not my talent."

Shani raised an eyebrow.

Terra looked Centurion Shani in the eyes. "My only talent is not knowing when to give up."

CHAPTER XII
THE SUMMIT

To all centurions. As the first week comes to a close, remain vigilant about point distribution. Naturally points will change hands rapidly, so we all need to keep a close eye on them.

New optios should note that we look for two things at the end of the first week. First we make sure that the bottom feeders get dusted. Bottom feeders are those who haven't earned a point except by taking it from a weaker tiro. Make up a reason to dock them a point if you must, but get them out of my Academy.

Second, we salvage anyone who looks like they might improve if given another week. Look for tirones who keep trying and are putting in maximum effort. If they are not giving one hundred percent of their effort, dust them without remorse.

-Memorandum from Praetor Lycus to all training staff

Nikias marched to the group that stood ready in the salient for morning exercise. "Attention!"

The tirones hesitated before snapping to attention, unaccustomed to Nikias calling for discipline. Shani demanded discipline at all times, but she established that expectation at the door to class. Isra fell somewhere in the middle. Nikias's sudden change in demeanor caught Terra and the other tirones off guard.

Then Praetor Lycus Cerberus entered the salient. He eyed the tirones with a hungry, predatory glare as he looked for weakness. Even Nikias shuffled nervously. Terra noted Nikias's scar was now on his forehead. She would have to ask him about that one day.

Lycus turned to Nikias. "Status."

Nikias gestured to the group. "Praetor. This group is next to worthless. I'd bathe them in wine if I didn't think it would kill them."

Lycus walked down the line of tirones. He glared at the first tiro in line who stared at his shieldwatch face. Lycus's snarl returned as he grabbed the tiro's arm before breaking his fingers. "Do you think you are here to play video games at a school for battles? Minus one point for getting distracted during inspection."

As the tiro cried out in pain, the others snapped to attention with more fervor.

Lycus then looked to Roland who gave a lazy salute. He stalked over to Roland and slapped his stomach. "Tiro! Stand up straighter!"

Roland's posture stiffened and his salute became sharp.

Lycus grinned. "Better. That only cost you one point."

Roland shrugged. He had earned two points today and three before that.

Terra felt her panic rise, but relaxed upon remembering she had no points to lose. She had struggled all week. In classes she had barely answered Shani's grueling questions about singularity science and temporal mechanics. The morning exercises seemed more brutal than usual.

Then came martial arts practice which involved getting beat up on a daily basis. Terra thought she must have lost all her teeth several times over. Nikias didn't like it when people held back during sparring. He encouraged tirones to beat one another senseless so long as it was not a one sided battle. She had yet to land a blow, but had become adept at taking them.

Shieldwatch practice was not as horrid, but still miserable. Each day they would present an obstacle to overcome and each tiro had to attempt it even if they couldn't get their shieldwatches working. Terra was in the latter category. Those with shieldwatch difficulty always failed and suffered for it whether it was falling into ice cold water or stumbling into a literal hornet's nest. Terra still couldn't figure out how fending off a swarm of hornets had anything to do with learning how to use a shieldwatch.

Even those who used their shieldwatch often failed, but the few that succeeded earned a point and a reprieve from their misery. Right now Terra would take the reprieve over the point even though she really needed a point. Tomorrow would be her last day to earn one. Though even if she did, she didn't know how to stop someone else from winning it in a Trial of Blades.

Lycus walked to the next tiro in line. "Sloppy uniform. Your emblems are not leveled correctly. Minus one point."

The tiro scowled, but said nothing.

He approached the next one, a Celtic girl with bleached white hair who had a bad habit of starting fights with other tirones. Terra thought the girl's name was Gaela? No one bothered to learn anyone's name yet unless they were good like Hikari or sociable like Roland.

"Harmless tirones should not start fights," Lycus said in a condescending tone.

The girl snarled. "Harmless?"

Lycus's eyes narrowed. "Minus two points for failing to address a superior officer properly."

The girl glared at Lycus. "Two points!"

Lycus's snarl widened.

"I mean, *praetor*," the girl corrected, her hands tightening around the knife at her belt. She spoke in a deliberate tone. "I worked hard for those two points. I think you should give them back."

Lycus chuckled. "Or what?"

The girl held still for a moment before drawing her knife. Lycus moved quickly, his motions blurred. Within a moment the girl's head was in his hands and with a powerful motion, Lycus snapped the girl's neck. She fell down to the ground as a Restore ring ran around her. After a moment she stood dazed.

"Dusted!" Lycus yelled to the others. "Never attack a superior officer without issuing a formal Trial of Blades challenge."

Terra's fear returned after a fresh reminder of how brutal Lycus could be.

Lycus docked the next two tirones a point as well; one for having a dirty shieldwatch and the other for being too jumpy when Lycus inspected her.

Lycus reached Hikari next. "Tiro Hikari Urashima. Even I have heard of that name often enough to grow weary of hearing it. The other instructors may fawn over you, but I am different. I hate people like you; showoffs who get by on talent alone. You have no place here, dustrunner."

Hikari's fists slowly clenched as she struggled to endure Lycus's taunts.

Lycus smirked. "Useless piece of trash. You seem to think yourself above everyone else here just because you can beat down a bunch of weak rejects. Make no mistake, for here you walk amongst giants, little girl."

Hikari breathed out slowly as she prepared to move into a fighting stance. She spoke in a low tone. "I challenge you to a Tri–"

Nikias stepped forward. "What she means to say, praetor, is that she could not defeat you in a Trial of Blades."

Lycus looked at Nikias. "You really think she has a chance?"

Nikias cast a stern gaze upon Hikari. "We are still working on her attitude."

Lycus crossed his arms. "She'd best manage it quickly. I will not tolerate a tiro who starts fights with her superiors."

Hikari tried to speak again, but Nikias shot her a pleading look. She relented, falling silent, her face still flushed with anger.

Terra gulped as Lycus approached her last, but she did stand with confidence since she had no points to lose.

Lycus's grin twisted into a wicked snarl. He turned to the other tirones, gesturing at Terra. "Why can't you all be more like her? She is an exemplary tiro. I am awarding her a point."

Terra's jaw went slack.

"I challenge her to a Trial of Blades," came a nearby voice.

Terra turned to see who had challenged her. Roland stepped forward, still standing at attention, his blue eyed gaze on Terra. Everyone frowned at Roland for challenging Terra first.

Lycus faced Roland. "Your reason?"

"She has a point I want," Roland said.

Lycus nodded. "Approved."

Terra then pieced it together. Lycus had set her up. "I refuse."

Lycus sneered. "A superior officer may override your refusal. The challenge will proceed."

"May I choose the battlefield, praetor?" Roland asked.

"Sure. Why not?" Lycus said as he turned to the address the others. Instead his gaze darted to something in the distance. He stood, staring for a long moment.

"Is something wrong, praetor?" Nikias asked.

Lycus's eyes narrowed. "Minerva, who was that near classroom six just now?"

"Reviewing temporal data," came Minerva's voice from Lycus's shield-watch. "Negative results. No one was there."

"Maybe I am just seeing things," Lycus said. He turned to the rest of the tirones. "Just remember that I am watching. Don't get complacent."

After Lycus departed, Roland stared at a line of holofaces in front of him, each depicting different scenes. He flipped through several holofaces until he touched one. A ring transformed the salient into a small waterfall. The water crashed onto the rocks below into a creek filled with large, moss covered stones.

Terra turned to Nikias. "I'll just give him my point and be done with it. I didn't earn it anyway."

Nikias pointed to the central courtyard where the pillar was. "You may leave at anytime tiro. If you don't want to fight then go."

Terra clenched her fists. Maybe she should quit right now? She couldn't win this fight. Now they all stared at her with a smirk. "I'll fight."

Nikias smiled and gestured to the salient. Terra and Roland walked inside and met on opposite sides of a creek.

The waterfall was noisy, but not deafening. The rocks were slick and difficult to walk on, but she found her balance. Roland marched right out into the water and assumed a defensive stance. Terra didn't hear Nikias say begin, but she had learned that the Academy treated rules more like suggestions.

Terra assumed her own stance. "Why were you so quick to challenge me? Looking for an easy point? I would expect that from a vulture."

Roland's expression did not change as he stood knee deep in the water. He attacked. Roland moved fast, knocking aside Terra's unskilled blows. He grabbed Terra, dragging her waist deep into the cold creek, but he did not hurt her as he held her. Terra could feel his hard muscles when pressed so close. She thought it unfair that Roland possessed such a strong physique as she rarely saw him exercise.

"What are you doing?" Terra asked, still struggling.

Roland grinned. "Resting. If I am fighting you, then I am not suffering one of their trials. Besides, I want my point back and you will be dusted on the morrow."

Terra pushed against his strong hold. "You stupid lit–"

Roland pressed his arm against Terra's neck tight enough to cut off her insult. "Ah. There it is. That bluntness." He twisted her in his strong arms, turning her to face the tirones watching the distance. Roland spoke softly into Terra's ear while he held her. "You see those people over there? They wouldn't be so gentle in my place right now."

Terra gasped for breath as she struggled.

Roland held her as surely as water flowed around the stones in the creek. "Perhaps if you attempt this training again, you would do well to consider smoothing out that bluntness. Hikari? She can get away with being rude to others. You cannot."

Terra ceased her struggling.

Roland kept Terra locked in one arm and pointed to the flowing water. "You see the stream? That's what you need to be like. The stream flows around hard stone and softens it. Me? I'm like water. Nothing can hurt me and I always go the path of least resistance."

Roland then dropped her to the ground, but broke her fall. She rolled to the ground without so much as a bruise.

Nikias walked to the bank of the stream.

Roland faced Nikias. "She is beaten. Where is my point?"

Nikias touched a holoface over his shieldwatch. Terra's own shield-watch beeped and when she glanced down the face read *Point Total 0*.

It was the last day of the first week. Terra still hadn't earned a single point. A large number had quit this morning and more would be dusted this evening. Many fought in the courtyard today, challenging each other to a Trial of Blades in an attempt to steal one point. Instructors never allowed refusals. Most didn't bother to challenge rising stars like Hikari who they knew was no easy target. Instead they looked for easy prey who had one or two points.

Terra discovered a score board in the central courtyard with points totals listed for all tirones including points gained, spent, and lost. Hikari ranked first with twenty five points. Terra ranked last with one point earned and one lost for a total of zero.

Terra had hoped the instructors would be generous given that this was the last day to earn a point. That hope proved futile. Exercise seemed even more brutal today as they were forced to swim in freezing water followed by another four mile run on a glacier. Classes after that forced her to endure a grueling test on time travel machines. That left shieldwatch training this evening and Terra still hadn't figured out how to make the stupid device work.

She was on break now. The instructors had allowed a break so tirones would have more time to fight over points. As Terra still hadn't landed a single punch in sparring, she didn't bother with duels. Instead she used the time to get away from the Academy for a little while.

She made her way to a small forested hill and sat down at the base of a tree for some reading. A light breeze blew around her as she looked across to the Academy. When Terra relaxed, she heard soft footsteps nearby and turned to see Alya approaching.

Alya grinned. "Ages, Terra. Making progress?"

"Yeah. Thanks for the help, by the way," Terra said as sarcastically as she could manage..

"Difficulties?" Alya said, moving closer. After looking Terra over, Alya nodded approvingly.

"Difficulties? I've failed every physical test and I've yet to even hit someone in sparring practice, which by the way, you didn't tell me involved actual pain. The teachers expect me to know everything before I even step into the classroom. I've only scored a single point that I lost to a Trial of Blades! The last day I have to score a point is today or I'll be dusted!"

"Points? Is that what they're using now? When I joined the Legion we had no training program. Our teachers were winds of war and our lessons one of blood and loss. You are fortunate that you receive actual instruction."

"Fortunate? I'm about to fail! I suffered through all this because I thought you saw some kind of special talent in me or something!" Terra's rant ended with her out of breath as the wind gusted around her.

Alya stared expressionless at Terra for a long moment before laughing. "Talent? You? Crash. The only talent you have is being a mildly spoiled, only child."

Terra's fists loosened while her gaze dropped to the ground. "You mean I have no talent? But you said that I had something in me that made you choose me as your squire?"

"Yes. You have a quality I seek in my squires. However, that part of you is not yet fully developed. How do diamonds form?"

"Heat and pressure."

"I am the craftsman and jeweler, not the miner. Counting seconds for you like a child holds no interest to me. Time travel mechanics, singularity science, continua history, these are all dull subjects that are equally dull to explain. Time is too wondrous a thing to waste on drab, technical terms. I will allow others to do this."

"What if I just give up?" Terra said as her brow lowered. *Maybe that would get a rise out of her?* she thought.

Alya shrugged. "If the diamond breaks, then it was no diamond and I misjudged. You won't quit though. You're too stubborn."

"So will you at least teach me something so I can get past the first week?"

"Aion no. My lesson would be wasted. Your connection with time hasn't formed yet, though I suspect it will soon. I just came by to see your current state. I am quite satisfied with the results so far."

Terra sat at the base of the tree again and put her arms around her knees. "It doesn't matter. I won't make it past today anyway."

Alya smiled. "Listen, Terra. I chose you because you did a brave thing when all the odds were against you. It's not a unique quality. Many people have courage, but sometimes even a little courage is worth ten times the amount of raw talent. So complain if you wish, but you won't gain any sympathy from me or anyone else in a city that sees all of history's tragedies. These people have more sorrows than you will ever know. So stop grumbling, pull yourself together and push forward. If others mock you for being weak, then make them regret their words. If you can do that, then you already have what it takes to join the Legion, points or no."

With that, Alya turned and left. The breeze faded at Alya's passing, leaving Terra alone.

∞

The sun shown past noon as several groups gathered at a larger salient. It was the last test of the day and the final test of the week. This was Terra's last chance to get a point. The other tirones seemed nervous and eager as many were without a single point. Several centurions watched from the sidelines though Isra was the one officially in charge.

While Isra debated on which deathtrap to throw at them today a tiro nudged Terra.

Terra looked back to a tall tiro dressed in a tunic over his training uniform. He showed Terra his shieldwatch. It read *1 point*. "I found something called a backdoor function for the points system," he said in a low voice. "You can give yourself points with it. I'm trying to tell others about it."

"Isn't that cheating?" Terra said in a bored tone. She didn't care about points anymore. Points or no points, she would continue on until they dusted her. Terra wasn't special. Looking back, she found it ridiculous that she had ever believed such a thing. That wasn't how things worked for her and she had forgotten this important, hard learned lesson. The good things in Terra's life had come to her because she struggled for them. She could not finesse her way through her problems like Roland or rely on instinctive skill like Hikari. Terra Mason would face her obstacles head on with neither apology nor excuses.

"It's fair because Lycus takes away our points for petty reasons," he said in a venomous tone. "Look. All you have to do is change a setting in the shieldwatch menu. It's under some kind of friend or foe system. Use it if you wish or you can dust out today. Whichever you prefer."

He told the tiro next to Terra the same thing while Terra continued to stand at attention. *Cheat?* she wondered. She could. It looked easy enough to do. Still, she didn't see the point and didn't care anymore. Terra closed her eyes, discarding all thoughts of points. Right now, there was only the next obstacle in her path and she would hold nothing back to overcome it.

Centurion Isra decided. A ring formed, moving downward over the salient. As it descended, it formed a sheer cliff face that towered over them. Wind swept around it in powerful gusts that flung dust and dirt up the sides. She heard a collective groan from the tirones.

"I thought they would go easy on us today," someone said from behind Terra.

"Well I'm done," another said.

Terra studied the cliff. Tall and imposing, the wind would make any ascent dangerous without proper climbing gear. The dust filled wind blew into her eyes and stung her skin. It was hard standing in the open much less trying to climb.

Isra turned to the tirones. "There is a trick to scaling this cliff the easy way. Most of you are unlikely to discover this secret though. First one up gets a point and the rest of the day off. Go!"

The tirones scrambled to the base while Terra regarded the cliff.

From what Terra remembered of rock climbing, this seemed to be an advanced course. There was no safety gear meaning they must rely on the shieldwatch to Restore themselves should any suffer injuries from falls. Terra knew even an experienced climber would find this course difficult. Weeks ago, Terra would have never stood a chance, but she was stronger now after several days of accelerated exercise. Although Terra felt uncertain if her strength and energy would be enough for this climb, she had experience with rock climbing.

As the other tirones began their climb up the cliff, Terra stood in place and memorized the cliff face. She spotted a path that provided good holds and chiseled that path into her memory before approaching. Several were already halfway up. Hikari had climbed the highest. Terra put them all out of her mind and made her first step.

She took her steps one at a time and found each foothold with care. After climbing a few paces, she heard a scream. Terra looked over her shoulder to see someone laying on the ground. A Restore ring ran around them before an optio helped move them off to the side.

"One chance I guess," Terra said before turning her attention back to the climb.

She continued up the cliff face. Another tiro nearby slipped and fell, screaming when a powerful gust of wind swept over him. Terra calmed herself and refocused.

She found an outcropping and lifted herself up to rest for a moment. Terra knew if she pushed herself too hard or fast she would fall. After resting, Terra felt around for another good hold when someone climbed down near her. "Roland?"

Roland looked at Terra. "Oh it's you. Yes I am giving up this trial. Too much trouble. There is a way to use a shieldwatch to get up this cliff with ease, but I don't know what it is."

"Then why don't you just cheat and give yourself a point?"

Roland rolled his eyes. "Please. That is a transparent ploy by the centurions. I'll cheat, but even I know when something appears too easy."

Terra ignored Roland and instead climbed higher. She didn't have time to worry about a jerk like him. She grew warm from the heat of the sun combined with her exertion. Terra kept her hands dry though. The wind whipped around her and Terra paused to strengthen her grip.

When the wind stilled, she pressed on, following her memorized path as her fatigue grew.

Hikari slid down a few paces away.

Terra glanced to Hikari. Hikari's face was covered in grime with sweat making trails in the smears. She gasped for breath while her hands quivered from fatigue.

Terra shook her head. Hikari had pushed herself too fast. But when Terra climbed further, Hikari gritted her teeth and glared at Terra before racing ahead. Still Terra pushed onward while ignoring Hikari. The holds became more difficult with each ascent. She now sweated and her muscles ached. Terra slipped and caught herself before falling.

While hanging onto a boulder, Terra considered letting go. It would hurt, but the shieldwatch would Restore her and then she could go home. No more Lycus, daily deathtraps, or constant sparring matches. It would be so much easier.

Terra grimaced. She dug her hands into the stone of the cliff and pulled. After coming this far, she would force herself to make it. She would hold nothing back. Grabbing again, Terra pulled.

Her fingers slipped. Terra dangled by one hand. She felt her remaining grip loosen. Her heart pounded, but Terra forced herself calm. She tried to get a better hold, but the ledge here was too narrow. She couldn't hold much longer.

Just as her grip weakened, she felt a strange sensation. Terra found it difficult to describe. It was as though she had another sense. For a single instant, she could feel the flow of a force pulling her downward. Almost by instinct, Terra reached out and slowed that flow. When she did, she felt herself lighten. Terra seized the moment and pulled herself upward. After she found a better grip, the strange sense faded and Terra continued onward.

Moments later she passed Hikari again. Hikari glared at Terra before trying to race ahead again. This time Hikari slid back again when a powerful wind battered the cliff. Terra continued onward, leaving Hikari behind.

Still Terra climbed. Grip after grip. Her muscles screamed in pain and her breathing reached a frantic pace. Sweaty palms covered in dirt made her holds more difficult. *One more step,* Terra thought. *Just a little further.*

Terra gripped the next ledge. The wind roared around her, engulfing her in dust and sand. She didn't look up, dreading to witness how much further she still had to climb. With her hands gripping the ledge, she pulled, knowing this might be her last step as she neared her limit.

Terra strained to pull herself up when someone grabbed her arm.

Terra stumbled as Alya pulled Terra to the top and steadied her. They both stood at the top of the cliff.

Alya nodded. "See. You made it even after all that whining."

Terra smiled. "Sorry. I should have had more faith in you."

"Me?" Alya said, gesturing to the cliff. "It was not me that scaled the cliff. You did. No one can have faith in you unless you have it in yourself first. No more complaining?"

Terra wiped the sweat off of her brow and nodded.

Alya smiled and walked away, leaving Terra alone on the cliff top.

Isra, Nikias, and Shani walked up to the top of the cliff just as Alya vanished.

"None should complete this course today," Shani said. "Perhaps a couple will make it during the second attempt. Climbing seems to be one of the more difficult courses."

Nikias laughed. "Yeah. We would be losing our edge if they all passed each course in one go."

"Most will have a stronger connection with time by then," Isra added. "They will probably be able to use their shieldwatch to Slow gravity on the next attempt."

They all stopped when they saw Terra.

"Um. Am I first?" asked Terra as she looked to see if anyone else had made it.

All three stared in silence.

After a moment, Nikias smiled and roared with laughter. He walked over to Terra. "And here I thought you would be dusted today," he said as he smacked her on the back. "Now that I know you have potential I will push you twice as hard!"

Terra laughed half heartily. "Very funny. That's a joke right?"

Shani narrowed her gaze. "What is your name, tiro?"

Terra stood straighter. "Tiro Terra Mason, centurion."

Shani nodded. "Well, Tiro Mason. I think we may have underesti-mated you. First we will check to make sure you didn't cheat. Then we will give you a point. You also may rest for the remainder of the day so you needn't worry about others taking your point."

Terra turned. The view overlooked much of the city as the sun blazed in the distance. She stood as the wind swept by, cooling Terra from the hard climb. The view was beautiful here on the summit and for the first time she looked forward to the next challenge.

CHAPTER XIII
ASSUMPTIONS

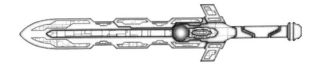

Culls should taper off as we enter the second week. While we will continue to eliminate those who are unworthy, attrition will decrease as we shift priorities. Now that we have purified the pool, the hard task comes in shaping these skilled individuals into something resembling a team. Those who stand alone will fall and it's better if they fall here where we can catch them than in the Labyrinth where they will die.

-From the personal logs of Praetor Lycus Cerberus

Terra now understood how trade goods must feel as she waited in the courtyard to be exchanged again. She had changed teams twice today and three times yesterday. Team organization became the focus of this week rather than elimination. The tirones organized themselves into groups of four to eight individuals called a strike team, the smallest unit within the Aeon Legion. Her current team leader was trading her and a suit of armor for two swords, a bow, and three points. However, the buyer still haggled.

"She is hardly worth two good swords. The armor is average, but I will need to inspect it first," the tiro said, who was going to 'buy' Terra.

"It's good armor and a solid tiro. What more can you want?" Terra's current team leader said. "Fine. Two swords, a bow, and two points."

Terra took offense at the first time her team leader had traded her. After the third time she grew used to it. She saw other tirones traded as well and learned that this was a common practice, one of the new miseries of week two.

The schedule differed for week two as well. Exercise, hand to hand, and shieldwatch training continued daily, but academic classes now took only two days out of five. This dedicated the other three open afternoons to simulated team missions or competitive scenarios between teams. There was also an hour each day dedicated to team training where team leaders trained their tirones however they wished.

For Terra, 'however they wished' meant trading her as fast as possible. The day before, her team leader had decided that Terra was a liability and forced her to sit out of the team mission, an opinion that other team leaders shared.

"Two swords, one bow, and a single point," the first leader said. "Final offer."

The other team leader nodded. "Agreed!"

Terra sighed, but picked up the armor and walked over to the other team. Her new team leader took the armor and inspected it. He then turned to Terra. "Follow me. We must hurry."

They jogged over to another corner of the courtyard where Terra's new leader met with another team. He traded Terra again along with the armor for a musket. She was then traded a third time for a tactical vest. Finally, another team brought her to a different salient to be traded yet again.

"Three points for this one," Terra's most recent team leader said. She was a girl with short black hair and a long tunic over her training uniform. Terra didn't bother to learn her name nor did the girl introduce herself.

This new team leader was about Terra's height with dark hair and dark eyes to match. Terra guessed his age only a few years older than her. He carried an iron helmet with a small spike on top. Under his long chain mail shirt was a longer tan tunic which he wore over his training uniform. His lean, muscled body and rigid stance marked him a soldier. His tan skin tone matched the natives of Saturn City though his narrow face marked him apart from the Saturnians.

He looked Terra over. His neatly trimmed beard made him appear mature and there was a hard, discerning look about his expression. "How many times have you attempted the training?" he asked. His faint accent made Terra guess he was of middle eastern descent.

Terra hesitated. None had asked her questions during the other trades. "This is my first attempt," Terra said, being honest. It must have been the wrong response for her current leader cringed.

The man nodded.

"Zaid, she is still good even though she is a newtimer. I swear," Terra's current team leader said as she fidgeted. Unlike other trades, she offered no other equipment with Terra.

The man named Zaid stroked his chin in thought, ignoring the other leader.

The woman frowned. "Two points!"

Zaid looked thoughtful, but remained silent while keeping his focus on Terra.

The woman cursed. "Fine! One point, but I am not giving up any good gear."

Zaid nodded. "That is acceptable."

The woman smiled as Zaid touched a holoface over his shieldwatch, transferring the point. She then left before Zaid changed his mind.

Terra sighed. No doubt this Zaid would sell her to another strike team for a piece of equipment. Terra learned that you could buy a lot of different gear with points; from weapons and armor to a full aeon edge. Though Terra still didn't have enough points to afford a single good weapon.

Zaid faced Terra. "What is your name?"

"Terra Mason."

"Terra, welcome to my team. I am Zaid Karim. Or just Zaid, if it pleases you. What time are you from?"

"I am from the United States," Terra said, doubting he would know where that was.

Zaid nodded before turning and gestured for Terra to follow. "Ah, Americans. I am familiar with your culture. I worked with a Marine last time I attempted the training and Navy SEALs are highly sought after by team leaders."

Terra followed Zaid. "I'm not either of those."

"I know that most Americans will fight. That is enough for me."

Terra frowned. "What are you going to trade me for?"

Zaid stopped and turned with a raised eyebrow. "Trade you?"

"Well all the others did."

"Most strike team leaders squabble over experienced tirones. I prefer newtimers. In my experience, they are easier to train."

They made their way to another meeting, this time between two different teams. They were trading members as well. Terra sighed, thinking that she was about to be traded again when she saw Hikari. Hikari now held an aeon edge. Tacitus, who she had seen her first day at the Academy, spoke with the team leader that currently held Hikari. A man in a US Civil War cavalry officer's uniform stood alongside Tacitus.

The cavalry officer shook his head before turning to Tacitus. "He's trying to sell us snake oil, Tacitus."

Tacitus looked at the officer, raising an eyebrow. "Snake oil? John, you need to explain some of these strange sayings of yours."

John rubbed the back of his neck. "It's an expression. It means he's trying to trick us into buying something worthless."

"Well I assumed that much," Tacitus said as he turned back to the other team leader. "So you consider Tiro Hikari worthless?"

"You can have her!" the other team leader spat. "But you can't take the aeon edge."

Hikari's grip tightened on the hilt of her aeon edge. "It is *my* blade."

Tacitus pointed. "She earned her blade with her points. You can't take it, nor can I unless she agrees. Do you still wish to trade?"

Terra raised an eyebrow. Trade Hikari? She was the highest scoring tiro right now and the first one to get an aeon edge. Why would anyone want to get rid of her?

The other strike team leader growled while eyeing Hikari's aeon edge.

Tacitus turned to Hikari. "Tiro Hikari. I know you are from an island warrior culture that values honor above all else. I too am from a culture that prizes honor. I would be honored to have you on my strike team. You need not sully your hands with these lesser soldiers. On my strike team, we treat our members with the respect due their skill. You belong with us."

Terra glanced to Hikari, gauging her reaction.

"Honor can burn," Hikari said not bothering to keep the boredom from her tone. "Honor is an empty word. Brutes with noble titles proclaim honor to ease their guilt while they slaughter peasants and sack their homes. I need neither you nor your honor."

The other team leader groaned as though his plan now lay in the ashes of Hikari's insult.

"I will remember those words," Tacitus said as he turned to leave.

Zaid stepped forward. "I will accept Hikari."

The man stared at the ground. "Just take her."

Zaid nodded before touching a holoface over his shieldwatch.

The man glanced to his shieldwatch in surprise. "You still gave me a point?"

Zaid motioned for Hikari to follow him. "I do not steal."

Hikari crossed her arms. "Why should I follow you?"

Zaid stopped and grinned. "Tiro Hikari, you will follow me because I can show you how to repair that aeon edge."

Hikari narrowed her gaze, but remained silent.

Zaid turned to go.

Terra followed now, curious. She looked back to see Hikari following and felt a bit uncomfortable with the ugly glare Hikari leveled at her. Had she angered Hikari somehow?

After a moment Zaid spoke again. "Have either of you had success with a shieldwatch yet?"

Terra shook her head. "No. I can't get it to work."

Hikari remained silent.

Zaid glanced at Hikari over his shoulder. "That is not unexpected. It takes a little while for it to work, usually at least a few weeks of practice for a connection with time to form. I think I have a good idea of where to start."

"Start what?" Terra asked.

"Both of your team training schedules," Zaid said as they stepped into a salient. Terra saw three others there as well.

On the far left stood a lean, young man dressed in a jaguar pelt. At his side he carried a wooden club edged with obsidian and he held a round shield in his hand. Terra recognized the man as an Aztec warrior.

Next to the Aztec stood a taller, dark skinned man with a sizable gut. He wore metal armor over one arm and shoulder. An enclosed metal helmet fitted around his head and he carried two swords sheathed at his belt. Terra recognized the man as a gladiator.

A short haired, dark skinned girl stood next to the gladiator. She wore a white tunic over her training uniform. She carried a small shield in one hand and several small throwing spears in the other. Terra did not recognize what army she was from, but assumed her to be from classical antiquity. "Newtimers?" the woman asked.

Zaid nodded. "The best and the worst actually, at least according to points."

Zaid gestured for Terra and Hikari to follow again. He led them to the center of the salient. A ring transformed part of the salient into a tall wall with a flat floor made of stone bricks. Above them hung a stone ceiling while a large circular pyre burned near the wall. Zaid pointed to the wall. "I have a task for both of you."

Hikari turned her side to Zaid. "I will do nothing you say. I am not a soldier for you to order around."

"Pity," Zaid said. "I was going to help you connect with your shield-watch. You should consider mastering it soon. At week three, tirones are allowed to use a shieldwatch for sparring. If you do not master it, they will become stronger than you."

"How?" Terra asked.

Zaid walked to the wall and then walked on the wall until he reached the ceiling. He then hung upside down though his clothing continued to point towards the ceiling as though gravity had reversed.

"This is important," Zaid said while crouching on the ceiling. "I use this trick often. Other strike team leaders often fail to use this simple ability. I need you both to master this skill if you are to use my tactics."

"How did you do that?" Terra asked as Zaid fell to the ground, landing feet first.

"I do not know the technical terms," Zaid said, dusting himself off. "I know that a shieldwatch connects to time and allows one to manipulate it. This connection with time takes from a few days up to weeks to form. Once it does, then it is a simple matter of willpower, like moving a muscle." He pointed to the pyre. "Heat rises as does the smoke. You both need to be like heat and smoke to make it up this wall," he said as he drew two knives. One he handed to Terra and the other to Hikari. "Use this to mark your progress up the wall. Make it to the top and this exercise will be done."

Terra looked at the hard stone floor. "I only have one Restore a day, Zaid."

Zaid aimed his shieldwatch arm to the floor, creating a stasis field there. He then dropped his helmet which slowed in the field. "This should prevent injuries from falls."

Hikari grabbed the hilt of her aeon edge. "My aeon edge first."

Zaid nodded and held out his hand.

Hikari hesitated.

Zaid sighed. "I must hold it in order to repair it."

Terra watched as Hikari hesitantly handed her aeon edge to Zaid, her gaze never leaving the blade.

Zaid inspected the aeon edge before opening up the bottom part of the blade and peering inside. A set of rails slid out and Terra could see a lot of mechanical parts inside the sword. After a moment, he handed the blade back to Hikari who relaxed.

"It needs a stasis cell clip and a few other parts," Zaid said, wiping his hands. "Two points at most."

Hikari inspected her aeon edge. "Why did they give me a broken blade?"

"They always do that," Zaid said, shrugging. "A lot of equipment they give you is broken. The centurions expect you to fix it. An aeon edge is especially difficult to keep in good condition since it cannot be restored with a shieldwatch like other objects. I will go get the parts you need. You should practice while I am gone."

When Zaid left, Hikari sat on the floor.

"Not going to do as he says?" Terra asked.

Hikari said nothing and instead inspected her aeon edge again. She opened the area near the bottom of the blade above the hilt and peered inside.

Terra sighed and wondered why others seemed drawn to Hikari. She had heard more than one team leader talk about how pretty and strong Hikari was. They all wanted her, at least until they had her and she started insulting them. Then they tried to get rid of her as fast as possible. Hikari was like a beautiful glowing ember, pretty to look at, but burned if touched.

Terra pushed those thoughts out of her mind and instead focused on the wall. She wanted to walk on walls. It was far better than what her shieldwatch could do now, which was nothing. Wondering, Terra dropped a loose stone on the ground and watched it slow in the stasis field Zaid had made. After a moment, Terra put her hand in the stasis field and felt no different. She then waded into the field.

Terra walked to the wall and put a foot on it. She pushed herself up and promptly fell backwards. As she expected, the stasis field caught her and Terra stood. This time she ran up the wall only to slip and fall again.

When she ran up a third time, she remembered the knife Zaid had given her and she made a mark on the wall before falling again.

"Fool," Hikari said, sitting behind Terra, the firelight illuminating her slender frame.

Terra put her hands on her hips. "You know, people accuse me of being blunt all the time, but at least I don't insult everyone I meet intentionally."

Hikari looked away. "Why am I even speaking to this stupid girl?" she said, more to herself than Terra, before falling silent.

Terra grimaced. Her face prickled with sweat as she shot Hikari a dark look. The running combined with the fire made her hot, or was her temper rising? Clearing her mind again, Terra faced the wall. She ran up and for a single instant sensed something different. It was a strange sensation, like the feeling a current gave when swimming upstream. The new sense faded when Terra slipped down again before putting another mark on the wall. This mark was higher than the last by a few inches.

Terra stared wide eyed at the wall. Had she just used her shield-watch? Gripping the knife in her hand, Terra charged. Again she sensed something different for a mere second. It was as though she could feel not only the force of gravity pulling her down, but the force of time that pulled gravity forward. This time she pushed on that feeling and Slowed it. When she did, she felt herself grow lighter. Her next mark was another half inch higher than the last.

"Yes!" Terra said. "I think I finally got it working!"

Hikari perked and frowned when she saw the wall. She inspected the marks and then turned to Terra as though to ask a question, but hesitated. Instead Hikari clinched her jaw and walked to the wall. Then she ran up it and to Terra's surprise, fell, leaving a mark well below Terra's last.

Terra almost laughed at the thought of the mighty Hikari lagging behind her. She turned back to the wall and continued to run, gaining another pace of distance. Her progress slowed after that. Then the strange new sense faded. Now each mark was lower than the last.

"Good!" Hikari said.

Terra turned and grimaced. Hikari now crouched on the ceiling like Zaid had.

After a moment Hikari jumped down, landing with grace next to the pyre. She glanced over her shoulder at Terra. "I assume if you can do this, then surely I am able as well."

Terra face grew warm again and not just from the heat of the fire. She didn't return Hikari's insult. Instead she faced the wall and ran up it again losing another span of progress.

Hikari scoffed and turned to leave as Zaid returned.

Zaid handed Hikari a series of set glowing blue cylinders held together by a clip. "This is one part you will need. Anno has the other. Talk to her."

Hikari's eyes narrowed. "In exchange for what?"

"Trust," Zaid said, his expression unreadable.

"You think a small light will buy that?" Hikari said while inspecting the device.

"Small beginnings," Zaid said as he turned and looked at the wall. "Ah. I see you practiced as I asked."

"I completed your training. It was a simple thing," Hikari said before leaving the room.

Zaid turned to Terra. "I see you have also made progress."

Terra sighed and dropped the knife. It sank into the stasis field and stopped. "I was. Now I'm practically back where I started."

He nodded as though finding this unsurprising. "I see. You must be one of them."

"Them?"

"For some, the shieldwatch just works. For a few though, it takes a while. The Sybil had a name for them. What was it? Regardless, you are likely one of those who have a weak connection with time."

Terra felt a stab of panic. "You mean I can't use a shieldwatch at all?"

"No. You will be able to eventually. It will take longer than most. The longest I have seen is four weeks. Since it has already worked a little, then I suspect your connection will form later this week."

Terra sighed. "Why didn't the instructors tell me this?"

"You should grow used to that. They seem to wish for most to discover these things on their own."

"Okay. What is your deal?"

He raised an eyebrow. "Deal?"

"Yes. Your deal. What do you want? Why do you bother to tell me any of this? Every other team leader has sold me off the first chance they got. Yesterday they even had me sit out the team mission so I wouldn't get in the way. Why do you care?"

"I told you the truth. I prefer newtimers because they are easier to train. They do not have as many assumptions that get in their way. Are you that mistrustful?"

"Why are you really here? Are you just here for immortality?"

Zaid shook his head. "No. I am here for something else."

"What then?"

"A second chance," he said as he motioned for Terra to follow. They walked outside to where the other team members practiced. "Listen, I know you do not trust me. Trust is hard to build when the centurions play us against one another, but it must begin somewhere. So what is your problem with trust?"

"I don't like teams."

"Ah," Zaid said as though he now understood the problem. "Yes. I remember now. Americans tend to be very individualistic. Well allow me to warn you. Few make it through the Survival Test alone. None make it through the Labyrinth alone."

Terra followed Zaid to the armory.

"Why are we here?" Terra asked.

Zaid gestured to Terra's uniform. "This will not do. Allah help you if the instructors catch you with a baggy uniform."

Terra recoiled from Zaid. "You're a Muslim?"

"Yes. So?"

"I am not wearing a burqa," Terra said, pointedly.

Zaid stared at Terra with a blank expression. "I have no idea what that is."

Terra's brow furrowed. "You know. An outfit that covers a woman from head to toe? It protects her modesty?"

"Oh. You mean a veil? I will not make you wear that. That would be stupid. We are soldiers now, not members of the court who can afford such trivial things as modesty. Now go get your uniform fitted, I don't want to lose points for my team looking sloppy. The centurions never take points for lack of modesty, but they will if your uniform is not perfect."

Terra found the back rooms and rummaged through the uniforms until finding one that fit. After inspecting herself in a mirror, she discovered her uniform was indeed loose fitting and baggy. She changed into the new uniform before sighing upon inspecting her reflection. *I look better*, she thought, *but the tight fitting uniform still makes me look overweight.* However, she stood a little taller now without her hunched posture. She made a few final adjustments before saving her state in her shieldwatch. She then walked out to meet Zaid.

Zaid inspected weapons in the armory before turning to Terra and smiling. "Much better."

Terra sighed.

"Is there still a problem?"

Terra looked around at the other tirones in the armory. "I don't know. It's just that time travel isn't what I expected. The Japanese girl I met is really rude and hates honor, the knight doesn't even know what chivalry is, you are a Muslim who respects women, and the most polite time traveler I have met so far is a Nazi."

"Ah. I see the problem now. It is a simple one."

"What?"

"You let assumptions rule your actions. I once met a tiro who tried to judge a person's merit purely on skin color. I told him he was foolish to do so. He failed the training for he refused to work with any who did not share his skin. I met another who tried to convert his strike team to his faith. He too failed when his team resisted him. I have found that all individuals must be judged separatelhy from their culture, faith, skin, or whatever other category because they can easily prove your assumptions wrong. I will not make that mistake. If I did, I would not have bothered with you at all."

Terra averted her gaze.

Zaid sighed. "Listen, Terra. I believe that you can contribute to my team, but I must ask you to put aside your assumptions. Whatever you think you know about history or culture, toss it aside. Others wish for you to think that history is simple. It is not. Use your eyes and your mind. Come to your own conclusions, or rely on your assumptions and fail. It is your choice."

CHAPTER XIV
KAIROS'S GARDEN

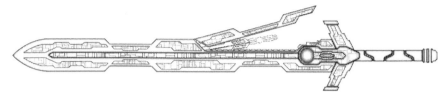

I would advise against letting a newly accepted tiro even touch an aeon edge. I have seen far too many a squire mutilate themselves by accident. Thankfully, the safety lock feature reduced training casualties, but I still recommend caution when introducing an aeon edge to a tiro. Too many become enamored with the aeon edge when it is the shieldwatch that often provides the decisive tactical edge needed in combat. A soldier with an aeon edge alone is not as dangerous as a soldier with a shieldwatch alone.

-Excerpt from Chapter Seven of the Aeon Legion's *Squire Recruitment Manual* by Praetor Lycus Cerberus

An air of excitement lingered amongst the tirones as they stood in the armory. Many had been looking forward to this, as did Terra. Today, they would get to hold an aeon edge.

A surprising variety of aeon edge swords lay on a series of weapon racks. A few blades reached only one or two feet long while others stood as tall as Terra. Curved designs existed, but most were straight with a spear point. All regarded the blades with wide eyes.

Terra still didn't have enough points for an aeon edge. It took twenty five points. She had four. Even though it was late in the second week, Terra still hesitated to spend her points. Not that she could buy much with them. A gun from her time costs five points. Even if she had an extra point, Terra would be hesitant to spend it on a gun. She had seen a team battle yesterday where a small team skilled with a shieldwatch defeated a larger one equipped with assault rifles.

Isra entered the room and stood between the tirones and the swords. "You will not be issued an aeon edge. None of you even deserve to hold a true aeon edge. Instead we will use rejected blades. These are not true aeon edges, but rather scrapped models that we have salvaged for training. They are weighted with lead to train strength during sparring, but today we will only practice maintenance to get you accustomed to the inner workings of an aeon edge."

A collective groan rose from the group.

Isra lifted her chin. "No complaining. You are lucky that we even allow you to touch the rejects for maintenance practice. Earn enough points and then you can be issued one to wave around all you wish. Until then, you will have to be content with taking it apart and putting it back together. I will return in a moment to inspect your progress. I expect each person here to present me with a clean blade upon my return. Failure to do so will result in the loss of a point."

An optio brought Terra a short sword for which she felt thankful. A few of the others received larger more unwieldy blades to fix. Terra inspected the blade.

The dull gray color contrasted with the pearl white or silver she had seen the other legionnaires carry. The blade was straight save for the small angular sections cut out of the middle edge and the tip was tapered. A fuller lay in the middle of the blade and panel seams made it distinct from ancient swords. The segmented grip and cylindrical blue ringed pummel made it look like a weapon that came from a factory rather than a forge.

Terra thought it strange to look at up close. An ancient tool of war, thought dead in her time, now stood as the primary weapon of the far future. It seemed to fit Saturn City which itself stood on the Edge of Time where all things past and future merged in strange ways.

Terra opened the clip housing. There was no clip inside and the housing area was dirty. She sat at a nearby table after gathering the tools the optios had laid out and went to work. Although she knew little of the aeon edge's technical details, she had watched Zaid when he showed Hikari how to fix her own blade. Hikari had learned how to care for the blade annoyingly fast. Terra took careful notes while they worked, and had already spent extra time in the strategy study learning about an aeon edge.

Others hesitated to reach inside the strange inner workings of the aeon edge. Terra did not. Within moments, the timecore lay on the table with it glass face cleaned. She then took out the burst trigger before removing the stasis cell clip housing. Soon she had the entire blade gutted, cleaned, and ready to put back together. As Terra stopped to wipe her brow, she looked up to see Roland. He sauntered around, brandishing his blade while talking with others. She ignored him.

Roland wandered by several tables, chatting and telling stories. Terra wondered how he cleaned his blade so fast while still finding time to bluster. After a moment he moved to a small fountain to get himself a drink of water, but paused when he saw Terra.

"You are still here?" he asked, raising an eyebrow.

Terra looked up, wiping the sweat and grime on her forehead. Dirt lodged in the upper edge projector had soiled her hands. "Yes," Terra said in a curt tone before turning back to her work.

Roland grinned. "Well good. I had hoped, for lack of other hobbies, to continue our wonderful conversation. You are so charming with your words after all."

Terra's jaw muscles twitched while she worked. She struggled to bite back a response knowing that Roland was baiting her. He wouldn't make her mad again.

Roland flourished the clean sword. "Not going to inquire as to how I cleaned my blade so quickly?"

Terra stopped and looked at Roland. "You didn't clean it. You cheated somehow. Again. Who did you steal it from this time?"

Roland put his hand on his chest in a mock wounded gesture. "Steal? Never. I am a knight of honor after all. No I exchanged it. There is a rack of perfectly clean swords right over there. I simply waited until no one was watching and switched them out. I can't believe no one else thought of it."

"Good for you then," Terra said, trying in vain to not sound irritated. She relaxed a little when Roland offered no response. She then looked up to see Roland staring at her, his normal flippant expression gone. He gazed at Terra with those deep blue eyes. She felt unnerved, like staring into the dark depths of the ocean without knowing what lurked underneath the high waves.

"Why are you here?" Roland asked in a direct tone.

Terra paused, taken aback by the candid question. "Why do you care?"

Roland shrugged. "No real reason. Just curious. I had assumed you would be quickly eliminated and I don't like being proven wrong."

"I am here because I want to be heroine, unlike you who just wants to keep his stupid immortality. At least I still have my idealism."

Roland chuckled, his playful demeanor returning. "Idealism? If I had any of that left, I would be dead."

Terra's knuckles turned white on the part she held. "You can't be a real knight. You are some kind of con artist. You probably just got lucky with that sword the first day."

"Con artist? That is the first any have ever accused me of art," he said, smiling. He walked over to the fountain before splashing water on his face. He then moved to an open area. Others watched as Roland assumed a fighting pose, aeon edge in hand as though to strike. After a moment of silence, he practiced with the sword. Everyone stopped to watch.

Terra wasn't sure if Roland was a con artist, but Roland was an artist of sorts. His blade strokes flowed into each attack with a fluid speed that Terra's eyes couldn't follow. Each stroke of his sword seemed to have the power of a wave crashing over a rocky shore. He was a storm at sea. The poetry of his swordsmanship made Terra's awe grow proportionate to her hatred of him. Roland didn't deserve to be that good.

As Roland finished the final stroke of his blade, Centurion Isra returned. Roland weaved the last stoke into a smooth motion that ended with his hand opening the stasis cell housing. He peered inside as though he had held this pose the entire time.

"You were not practicing with the sword were you?" Isra asked, holding out her hand for the blade.

Terra smiled. *Finally*, she thought. *He's about to get busted.*

Roland handed the blade to Isra. "Just getting a better angle to look inside."

Isra took the blade and inspected it. "Good job, tiro. Two points. I seldom see a blade cleaned this well."

Roland smiled as Isra moved to the next person.

Terra scowled, but didn't have time to dwell. She finished reassembling her aeon edge just as Isra arrived.

Isra took the blade and thoroughly inspected it. Finally, she looked at Terra. "You are not very good at this are you?"

Terra pursed her lips. "At least I tried to clean my blade, centurion. Roland just swapped his dirty blade for a clean one when no one was looking."

"Did he now? Are you so eager to betray one of your own?"

"Centurion? He broke the rules."

Isra turned her gaze back to the blade. "I never said they were forbidden to do so. Attention to detail, tiro. If you have an issue with this tiro, then settle it with a Trial of Blades. Don't involve me in your personal feud."

Isra moved off after leaving Terra with instructions to fix the areas she had missed. Thankfully she did not lose a point, but had again lost her temper. Terra could weather Hikari's insults, Alya could test Terra's patience, but only Roland could make her angry with minimal effort.

After Isra visited every tiro, murmurs rose from many wishing to practice with the blades. Terra suspected Roland's little performance had something to do with that.

Isra faced the group. "Not today. No sparring yet. Not until everyone has finished the safety qualifiers."

There was a collective sigh.

"Safety?" asked an irritated tiro. "It's a sword. We don't need safety lessons."

Isra turned to the tiro. "Thank you for volunteering, tiro. Please step forward."

The tiro turned pale, but stepped forward.

Isra took an aeon edge from the weapon rack. She pointed to a metal band near the glowing, glass faced timecore. "This is a safety lock. We take this off during the later parts of the Labyrinth. So long as this device is on, then a training aeon edge is locked into its nonlethal state."

"Why is that, centurion?" Roland asked.

Isra loaded a clip into the aeon edge and the edge began to glow blue. "The blade will not cut living material when in the nonlethal stasis mode. Instead it locks everything it passes through into stasis. In simple terms, it will stun any living target or lock up moving parts for a machine."

Roland raised an eyebrow. "Interesting, centurion, but why would a sword need such an ability?"

Isra pointed the weapon at the tiro who 'volunteered'. She then slashed at him with the blade passing right through him as though he were incorporeal. As the sword passed through the tiro, color bled from where the blade touched. Although unwounded, the blade left a gray streak where it passed that took on a static grainy appearance. The tiro then fell to the floor, convulsing and crying out in pain.

Isra turned to the other tirones. "The Legion is hesitant to take lives since it would erase their descendants from time. This problem becomes worse the further one travels back in time. The stasis mode prevents alterations to a continuum's history while still allowing the Legion to use force if needed."

After a moment the color returned to the tiro. He stood before shaking his head. "Does it have to hurt so much, centurion?"

Isra nodded. "Yes it does. Pain prevents the target from reacting even after a partial hit."

"So there is no way to block it?" another tiro asked.

"There is," Isra said before throwing the aeon edge at the tiro again. The blade passed right through him and he again fell to the floor, stunned. Isra then turned to Roland and flung another blade at him.

Roland shifted his stance and brought up his shieldwatch arm, holding it out like a shield. The Blade bounced off with a disc shaped flash of blue, translucent energy centered on the orb of Roland's shieldwatch. The flash reminded Terra of a round shield that a soldier might have used in antiquity.

"Good, tiro. You get a point for that," Isra said before pointing to her shieldwatch. "Why do you think it's called a *shield*watch? The stasis shield is the only known protection against an aeon edge. This shield can also be extended to work around the entire body, but this weakens it and can only be used to keep out environmental hazards like radiation or poison gas. It can even block an aeon edge burst when used in its normal shield form, but it will not completely absorb the force of the burst. A burst can still knock you off your feet. Remember that. We will get into burst mechanics another day. Now everyone return to your cleaning."

Roland leaned forward. "Centurion Isra. If I may?"

Isra faced Roland.

"Mayhaps it's too soon to practice, but perchance it would be wise to show us the aeon edge's full capabilities? After all, you have already shown us some of what it can do. Would it not be prudent to show us the rest, including the more destructive modes? Especially since I heard some of the other centurions speak of your skill."

Isra's flat expression remained unchanged.

Terra smiled. She always knew Roland's charm would run out eventually.

Isra grinned. "Of course they did. I am the Academy's blade master after all. I suppose I could show you more."

She touched her shieldwatch's holoface before motioning for everyone to step back. A series of rings formed near the center of the room, fading to reveal a row of different objects. In a line stood a gray manikin with plate armor, a short stone pillar no taller than a man and twice as thick, a tall but thin metal beam and last in the line loomed a huge solid steel obelisk ten feet thick and twice as high.

Isra moved in line with the objects as she pulled out a dagger sized aeon edge blade from her belt. It shimmered silver like Alya's aeon edge though much smaller. She loaded a small clip filled with a row of glowing blue cylinders into the back of the blade, then smartly snapped it shut with the palm of her hand all in a fast, fluid motion. The orb on the guard lit up bright blue as a semi transparent edge formed on the blade. The edge glowed a faint blue while grainy static flickered on the surface.

Isra turned her side to the row of objects and spread her feet out before throwing the blade at the manikin. It passed through the manikin, the stone pillar, and even the metal beam without slowing before gravity pulled the blade to the ground. The blade stuck downward into the floor while leaving a hole a little larger than the blade in the three objects it had pierced.

She drew another dagger and loaded a clip. Isra charged the manikin, slashing through it with the dagger before weaving around it and cutting through the pillar. When she slashed at the metal beam, the manikin had fallen in half and the stone pillar began sliding in two with a clean slice. The blade passed through the first three objects as if she cut through air. A loud clang sounded when the metal beam hit the floor and Isra turned to the tirones. "This is what the blade does by itself. Now watch closely. This is what the burst function does when you pull the trigger."

Isra jumped and slashed at the large steel obelisk. Before her dagger connected, she pulled the trigger. A surge of power flared from the edge of the blade. The edge's faint glow bloomed into a blinding flash of pale blue light. The obelisk shattered into chunks with a loud crack. When the spots in Terra's vision faded, she saw the twenty foot tall, ten foot thick steel obelisk now laying as a pile of debris.

"That," Isra said as though she had done the most boring thing in the world, "was the burst function. Each burst takes one stasis cell in a clip so use it wisely," she said as a spent cell ejected from the dagger clinked twice on the floor like an empty bullet casing.

The rest of the tirones gawked in awe.

"That was so cool!" Terra said after a moment of silence.

Others gave her strange looks.

Terra composed herself. "I mean that was an excellent demonstration, centurion!"

"You have to teach me how to use that sword," Terra said as she looked up at Alya. Terra had gotten lucky when she went to the hill to study. Alya had showed up out of nowhere as usual. "Please! You have to. It's so cool!"

Alya pursed her lips as a light breeze blew through her silver hair. "Minerva, what does cool mean? Context early 21st century Americas, Continuum Lambda."

"Cool. A slang term meaning something appealing, aesthetically pleasing, stylistically superior, or a state of behavior that is considered good amongst a social group. A close Saturnian equivalent would be *infinite*," Minerva said from Alya's shieldwatch.

"Oh," Alya said. "So I guess that means you like the aeon edge sword then?"

Terra nodded.

"And you want me to train you in swordsmanship skills?"

Terra nodded again.

"No."

A chill wind swept across the hill, as if hastening winter's arrival to the city.

Terra's smile faded. "Why?"

Alya drew her aeon edge sword and pointed it at Terra. Her hushed tone held an edge of menace while she spoke. "You think this is cool?"

Terra leaned back as the tip loomed in her face.

"Do you know what this is?"

The edge remained off, but Terra still winced when the blade drew close. "It's a sword."

Alya's eyes narrowed. "And what are swords made to do?"

"Kill people," Terra said while leaning away from the sword a little more.

Alya lowered the sword. "Hammers build homes, bows hunt game, axes chop trees. Swords. Only. Kill."

Terra averted her gaze.

Alya lifted the blade and studied it with narrowed eyes. "This is a tool of death. Too many see it as a tool for glory. They see it as a symbol of romantic ideals. I see a shining silver blade after I wash off all the blood. This isn't a thing you should admire, but a burden. You haven't seen an aeon edge cleave through a person yet. I have seen endless bloody fields so choked with corpses that one could walk from one side to the other without touching the ground. Swords do not make glory and if they do, then it is no glory any of us should wish for."

Terra continued to stare at the ground.

Alya looked at Terra and her expression softened. The breeze around them became more gentle as she sheathed the blade. "Sword strokes given cannot be taken back. Time cannot fix everything. Don't repeat the mistakes of so many others who wielded an aeon edge without the sobering understanding of its true purpose. A tool for death."

Terra nodded.

"How about I show you something else?"

Terra looked up at Alya. "Really?"

Alya smiled. "How is your shieldwatch training progressing?"

Terra pouted.

Alya grinned. "Sour expressions are not flattering. Trust me. This will be, oh how did you put it? Cool."

They both walked into a nearby forest and hiked on a trail. The trail led to a stone path. As they followed the path Terra noticed the colors change from fall to spring. Terra wondered why this place was set to a different weather schedule. She had grown accustomed to Saturn City's precise weather control. Although Saturn City could schedule weather, it still followed the usual cycle of seasons for most of the city. This was the first exception she had seen.

Brown faded to green when they reached a large glade. When she saw it her eyes widened as she gasped.

The glade was vast, at least a mile wide and filled with every flower imaginable. Flowers bloomed in large colorful patches while the garden teemed with butterflies and birds of all kinds. All the garden gleamed like an eternal spring, though cold winter set in outside the forest.

"It's beautiful. Is it a garden?" Terra said, still awestruck.

Alya nodded. "This is Kairos's Garden. A garden for the fallen. I have a few things to show you here. Have you had much success with a shieldwatch yet?"

"No. I can't get this stupid thing to work," she said as she searched through the shieldwatch's menu.

Alya shook her head. "It will take forever if you do that. The best thing about a shieldwatch is that it can work on mental commands."

Terra looked up at Alya, confused.

"Think. Don't just press buttons. If you spend too much time searching through menus, then someone will cut you down while you stare at buttons," she said before she walked into the glade. "The shieldwatch doesn't just allow you to control time, it connects you to time."

Terra followed as they moved through the garden. She tried to feel time like Alya had said, but she felt just as she always did. "I don't feel any different."

Alya grinned. She picked up a small stone and tossed it in her hand before slinging it at Terra's face. Then Terra sensed it.

Like a reflex, Terra felt something coming towards her. Her hand moved to grab the rock so fast that she only saw a blur. Terra stared wide eyed at the stone. "How?"

Alya's grin widened. "The shieldwatch is linked to your nervous system. It's a part of you. It even Sped your reactions. Humans are already connected to time. We perceive time moving forward. A shieldwatch expands and strengthens that perception. The more you use your shieldwatch, the stronger the connection."

Terra thought back to the past couple of weeks. Upon looking back, she realized that she had used her shieldwatch unintentionally a few times before now. "So I just think and it works?"

"More like it's another part of your body. You can't just think about it, you have to will it. Just thinking about raising your hand doesn't make it happen." Alya pointed to a green humming bird at a nearby flower. "Focus your eyes on that bird, then Speed your sight."

Terra looked at the bird. It shifted from flower to flower, its wings a blur of motion. She focused on it and felt something different. It was as though she possessed a second sight waiting for her to use. The hummingbird came into focus. She saw the jewel colors of its feathers with its wings moving in perfect detail. There was no motion blur at all. Everything now appeared in near perfect detail.

Terra turned to Alya, confused.

Alya held up her arm and moved it from side to side slow, then fast. "When I move my arm, your mind can only process the image so quickly. When I move slow, your mind has time to process the images so there is no blur. The shieldwatch can Speed your nervous system so you have time to see every detail."

"So I would never want to turn that off?"

"That would not be a good way to conserve power."

"Conserve power?"

"We will get to that in a moment," Alya said. She then ran and jumped into a tall tree, landing with grace on a high branch.

"How did you do that?"

"I Slowed gravity. You have already done this. Try it."

Terra jumped once and stumbled to the ground. She tried again and felt the flow of time on gravity just like during Zaid's training a few days ago. After a third try, she acted on the feeling and Slowed gravity around her. Her body slowed and fell like a feather drifting on the wind. When she landed on the ground, she ran towards a nearby tree and jumped. She flew through the air. Terra grabbed a large branch as she drew near, though she hit the tree harder than she had expected. After struggling, she climbed onto the branch.

She tried to jump down a moment later when she heard her shieldwatch beep. "Battery power critically low. Shutting down non essential functions," came Minerva's voice from Terra's shieldwatch.

"What?" Terra said just before her connection with time vanished and she stumbled to the ground.

Alya jumped next to Terra, offering a hand. "And that's the most important lesson. Conserving power."

Terra rubbed her knees as she stood. "Well that didn't last long."

"Your connection to time is new."

"What difference does that make?"

"The more you use your shieldwatch, the more you become connected with time. The longer the connection, the more efficient you become with using your power. Shieldwatch battery power never changes, but you can accomplish more with less effort as your skill increases. Your shieldwatch recharges itself over time, but cannot Restore itself if broken. Remember too that while you can take another shieldwatch, you cannot use it to Restore yourself if injured. Every shieldwatch is attuned to the original user and using any other ability will drain the stolen shieldwatch quickly."

Terra considered this. It made sense for there to be limitations. Still though, this was the first time she hadn't regretted coming to the Academy. This is what Alya had meant about getting a taste of the shieldwatch's power.

As they made their way through the garden Alya taught Terra how to put things in stasis fields by Stopping time. After her battery charged, Terra practiced Stopping several butterflies in stasis before releasing them. She learned that larger, more complex creatures were immune to being trapped in a normal stasis field though you could slow them down with it, sometimes. Alya also explained how to use the shieldwatch to enhance reflexes and speed, but when they approached a small hill at the center of the glade Alya became silent. When they drew closer Terra discovered why.

At first, Terra thought she was standing in a field of crosses, but saw that they were, in fact, aeon edge swords that had all been plunged, tip first, into the ground. Alya walked between the countless swords somber and silent. She glided between the blades like a silent and gentle breeze, her expression stoic. As they walked through the field of blades Terra wondered why these weapons, so valuable, lay discarded here to rust. Flowers grew around them and each had a name engraved on them. Then Terra realized this place was a graveyard. A memorial to the fallen.

Alya stopped in front of an aeon edge sword that stood near the center of the garden. Engraved on the blade was the name Kairos and black roses twisted around it. She knelt, running her fingers across the face, feeling each letter and smiled slightly. She touched the black rose, holding the blossom. "Orion put this blade here and told me I needed to move on. She always liked black roses. Said they were like her."

"Were you close friends?" Terra asked softly.

Alya nodded before her gaze became distant.

Terra hesitated. "Who was Kairos? I mean if it's not too painful to talk about her?"

Alya stood and looked at the sky. "She was my greatest squire. A true savior," Alya said before sitting in the grass in front of the sword.

Terra sat beside Alya. "What was she like?"

Alya thought for a moment. "Actually, she was a lot like you. She loved the soil like you loved stone. Always with her nose in a book. She had a passion for gardening. In fact, she made this garden. She planted every flower by hand. This was her favorite place. Her one place where she could be at peace, much like you in your quarry."

"That's odd. Most of my instructors keep saying how I'm not like her."

Alya's eyes narrowed on the sword as she frowned. "They remember Kairos the savior not Kairos the person. Not the Kairos who grieved every time she had to leave a comrade behind. Or the Kairos who loved her garden. Or the Kairos who was my friend."

"What happened to her?"

Alya closed her eyes. "They came. About a century ago we encountered... things. We called them Faceless. They were monsters in every sense of the word. An avatar of decay, a plague that spilled from the End of Time," Alya said, cringing. She took a moment before continuing as though suppressing old nightmares. "They spread across time in a wave of death. The Legion had never met anything like them. These monsters also used time as a weapon and they were difficult to kill. Even worse, they absorbed our casualties into their ranks. For the first time we were fighting a hopeless war. We couldn't even contain them. Our allies fell one by one. Soon the Legion stood alone. Then Kairos ascended through the ranks."

Alya stood and smiled, looking at the sun. "I wish you could have seen her. She was glorious. Standing like the burning sun at dawn, bringing light back into the world. Her blade always fell at the right moment, cutting away the darkness and rot. The death and decay of the Faceless parted for her, breaking like waves on a rocky cliff. The Legion drew up, rallying to her call. She drove decay itself into oblivion."

"Where did they come from?" Terra asked.

"No one knows. Some say they are time travelers who went to the End of Time. They say it twisted them into the Faceless who take from time what they lost at the End. They first appeared in the Bleak near the End of Time. Others think they were a singularity weapon that went rogue. Kairos also wanted answers. When the war was won, Kairos came to me and gave me her blade, saying she didn't need it. She told me she was going to the Beginning of Time. She was certain the answer was there. I offered to go with her, but she wanted me to stay and rebuild the Legion."

"The Beginning of Time?" Terra asked, trying to wrap her mind around all this information.

"I know little about it, but if you travel back in time far enough past the beginning of the universe then you enter the Beginning of Time. Those who go there rarely come back. The few that do are always changed. No one comes back from that place the same. Kairos left. I never saw her again."

"I'm sorry."

"Kairos isn't the only one I lost," Alya said while looking at the sky. "They told you that all my squires are famous. That they all went on to achieve great things. They probably didn't tell you they all died achieving those great things. They died heroes and I lived on even though I don't deserve to. I am no stranger to loss, but I do grow weary of it. I am tired of losing squires. I am tired of losing friends."

Alya then turned to Terra with a warm smile. "But I have faith in you. You will survive. You can take a hit and keep going. Tough as stone and twice as stubborn. I want you to be the squire that survives."

Chapter XV
Missing in Action

Historical armies sometimes use the designation MIA or Missing In Action. The majority of tirones are reported as missing in action or some similar designation in their home times. They are all lost to history, therefore recruiting them for Legion use can be done without disrupting the flow of the continuum.
-Excerpt from Chapter Two of the Aeon Legion's *Squire Recruitment Manual* by Praetor Lycus Cerberus

Shani and Nikias's conversation maintained a casual tone even as they took shots at the tirones with rifles. Each had a tactical light on the end of their rifles they used to spot the tirones hiding in rocky crevasses.

"I mean I just don't know," Shani said as she lined up her sights on Zaid and took a shot. Zaid blocked with his shieldwatch. "We thought about moving to a better zone for a while. Between us we have about three centuries of time saved up."

Zaid ran as Shani's light followed him. He rolled out of her light, disappearing in the shadows of the dimly lit area.

Terra assumed the point of this test was to hide and remain quiet, though it was hard to tell. They had arrived at the salient an hour ago for an unspecified team activity when Nikias and Shani showed up with guns and started shooting at them. One couldn't hide for too long though, for the instructors constantly surveyed the area with their lights and fired upon spotting someone. She wondered why they didn't use the night vision feature of their shieldwatch.

After a moment, Nikias spoke. "You could find a third person to split it with I guess. Though I don't know why everyone is so keen to get tier three residential homes. A tier one apartment is like a palace compared to what I grew up with."

Shani growled. "The top scoring tiro in my class ended up joining Endymion. He already has a home in the Elysian Fields. It's so unfair. There you are!" Shani said, firing at Zaid again. Her gun then clicked. "I'm out."

Nikias fired two more shots before his gun clicked. "Me too."

"I suppose that's enough," Shani said, touching her shieldwatch holoface. The lights came on and illuminated the area.

Nikias discarded his rifle. "Good job. This test is over."

The tirones approached with caution, still expecting this to be a ruse. Terra thought so, for she remained hidden in a small cove that the lighting didn't illuminate.

Shani looked at her shieldwatch. "Tiro Hikari, I am giving you just one point for this test. You shouldn't have rushed us at the start."

Nikias looked at his shieldwatch. "Zaid you get zero points. You were spotted several times."

Shani awarded points to the rest of Zaid's strike team before nodding to Nikias. "Well I think this is done. Let's reset the salient."

A ring descended, erasing the rocky arena. Terra yelled when the ground disappeared beneath her and she fell to the floor with a hard thud.

Nikias laughed. "Looks like we forgot one."

Shani faced Terra. "Well, Tiro Mason, congratulations. I think we found something else you are good at."

Nikias still chuckled. "Yeah. Being ignored."

Shani touched her shieldwatch's holoface. "That's three points. If you had been any better concealed, you would have been labeled missing in action a second time."

Terra dusted herself off as she stood. She felt thankful that she had spent points on knee and elbow pads at the armory since they absorbed some of the fall. "Wait. Missing in action again?"

Shani nodded. "Yes. Most potential Aeon Legion squires are MIAs from various wars. That way it doesn't disrupt the flow of the continuum."

"That can't be right," Terra said more to herself than anyone else. She wasn't missing in action. Terra stared for a moment before checking her shieldwatch. "Minerva. What would have happened to me if I hadn't joined the Legion?"

"Sorry I cannot answer your query," Minerva said.

"What? Why?"

"Access to your records is restricted by order of an anonymous centurion."

∞

"What are you hiding from me?" Terra said hands, on her hips as she glared at Alya.

Alya leaned against the tree at the top of the hill, reading something on her shieldwatch. She shifted her gaze to Terra. "Hiding what?"

Terra pointed at the screen on her own shieldwatch. The screen read *Access to records locked.*

"Oh that," Alya said as though it were a minor detail. "Crash. I thought I unlocked that. I didn't want others looking into it when I was trying to recruit you."

Terra scowled. "What is this about?"

"Minerva. Unlock it," Alya said in a dismissive tone.

"Unlocked," Minerva said. "Terra Mason age nineteen. Cause of death, internal trauma and bleeding due to a vehicular accident. The source of the accident was concluded to be the intoxicated driver whose vehicle collided with Mason's car."

"Killed by a drunk driver?" Terra said in a dumbstruck tone. "I had a year to live?"

"Apologies. I meant to tell you when you started the training, but forgot."

Terra glared at Alya. "Why didn't you tell me! This is kind of important don't you think? What would have happened if I failed the training?"

"Even *if* they sent you back, there would be a chance you would survive. Besides, you would be allowed stay in the city by working a low level job. Then you could try the training again next year."

"Wonderful. I could be an immortal janitor!"

"You are rather lucky. Many Legion recruits don't have the option to return home. Is there a reason this bothers you?"

"Because I could have died and you didn't even tell me!"

Alya sighed. "I already told you. I wanted a volunteer not a conscript. If you had known then it would not be a choice, but a necessity, that you join the Legion. I gave you a choice. You made it yourself. I swear I meant to tell you when we arrived at the city, but I forgot."

Terra glared at Alya.

Alya sighed again. "Well I told you the truth," Alya said before she walked away, leaving Terra alone with her anger.

∞

Terra's frustration with Alya the day before was now replaced with dread after receiving orders to report to Praetor Lycus's office. She had already faced the man once and had almost gotten her head smashed in for the trouble. Why did he wish to speak with her now?

Terra hesitated when she saw the open fadedoor into Lycus's office. Lycus sat not with his customary snarl, but a look of irritation. The expression seemed odd to Terra as she had never seen the man annoyed at anything. Then she saw why. Alya stood near the fadedoor, facing Lycus with her usual smile.

Terra tensed, but entered his office.

"You can't stop me, Cerberus," Alya said in a casual tone. "The rules allow it. At least I think they do. Even if they do not, I like breaking rules."

Lycus tapped his finger on his desk. "I told you not to call me that."

Alya grinned. "Cerberus? After your aeon edge? It has been centuries, Cerberus. Can you still not accept your past?"

Lycus scowled and glared at Alya. "Not all of us can ignore our damnation, Bloodstorm."

Alya's smile disappeared at that name. After a moment, her grin returned. "That would have wounded me before Darshana. Not your most creative insult though, Cerberus. The Selvian Stuarts could have thought up a better one."

Lycus clinched his fist. "I should have made you an instructor so you could test everyone's patience."

Terra cleared her throat, hoping to distract them before this insult match grew worse.

Lycus glanced to Terra. "Tiro Mason. I have called you here to put an end to this meddling."

"Meddling?" Terra asked before looking around to find the source of a light breeze that blew into the office.

Lycus's eyes narrowed on Alya. "Don't think I haven't seen you lurking around the Academy. I saw your meeting at the hill. Then at the climbing test as well. Again, I saw you stalking me near the Archives and around the Academy."

Alya rolled her eyes. "Stalking you? Cerberus, why would I stalk you? You're so dull. Yes, I was at the hill and the garden, but I was not at the Archives. My interest is in Terra alone."

Lycus's frown deepened. "Alya, this has to stop."

Alya browsed the office while she spoke. "I agree," she said before lingering on the holoface picture of twelve individuals standing in two rows. She then turned back to him. "Obviously you need to be more accommodating so I may come and go as I please."

Lycus stood, pointing at Terra. "This tiro is mine!"

Terra shifted at the outburst.

Lycus snarled at Alya. "The moment I accepted her into *my* training program, she became mine. She will do as I say and I alone will decide if she passes or fails."

Alya continued to smile. "Oh don't be so dramatic, Cerberus. It's only one little mission."

"Mission?" Terra asked.

Alya shrugged. "I felt guilty after forgetting to tell you about the accident, so I will make it up to you."

Terra raised an eyebrow. "What?"

"We will go on a real mission. An exciting one! Not one of those boring missions. Besides, you could stand to get out of this place for a little while," Alya said, looking around Lycus's office with a sour expression. She turned back to Terra and smiled. "Nothing freshens up dull training quite like live combat."

Terra went pale at the words 'live combat'. "No! I mean it's all right. I'm not even mad anymore. You don't have to bring me to a war zone."

Alya smiled as she gestured to the fadedoor. "Nonsense. It will be fun. I know you need the experience. You will even get to meet an old friend. I hope he fights as well as last time. I was so excited when the Sybil saw he was attempting to alter time again."

Lycus cleared his throat.

Alya rolled her eyes. "Ignore Cerberus. He is rather insecure."

Lycus pointed to his rank insignia. "I am a praetor! You are a centurion!"

Alya faced Lycus. "Yes. I still have eyes, Cerberus."

Lycus recoiled, his posture slouching. He let out a long sigh.

Alya turned her side to Lycus. "Are we done?"

Lycus gripped his aeon edge, but hesitated to draw it.

Alya's grin disappeared. She faced Lycus. "It has been a while hasn't it? Since a pair of Legendary Blades fought in a Trial of Blades."

Terra felt the air turn cold in the silent room. She watched both Legendary Blades face one another, unblinking.

"It has," Lycus said after a long pause. He took his hand off the blade. "But I do not wish to be the one to break that peace."

Alya tilted her head. "Do you really feel that strongly about this?"

Lycus sat slumped back into his chair, looking tired. He did not look like the predator Terra had seen mutilate Vand, nor the cold, calculating man she had seen at other times.

"I hate your squires, Alya. I hate what Tahir did to me," he said in a soft voice, almost a whisper. He looked up at Alya. "How do you stand it?"

Alya shrugged. "Lycus, I let go of the dull past so I may shine more brightly in the present. Shine, don't suffer while you live."

With that Alya glided out of the room, motioning for Terra to follow. Terra lingered to look back, seeing Lycus stare at a stained photo that lay next to a dark mask.

"Leave," Lycus said in a whisper.

Terra left not wishing to gain Lycus's ire and she caught up with Alya. "But I'm not ready for live combat! I can barely hold my ground in a sparring match!" she said, jogging to keep pace with Alya.

Alya dismissed the protest with a wave. "Don't worry. I watched you in shieldwatch practice yesterday and sparring the day before. You will do fine."

Terra rubbed her forehead while wondering if all these people were insane.

∞

When the sphere around Terra faded she found herself sinking into a bog. She struggled to wade out of the waste high water and grab onto a nearby tree. After she pulled herself up she took in her surroundings. Terra seemed to be alone, surrounded by patches of swamp and large trees. Moments later she heard voices.

"This is a waste of time," an older man said in an irritated tone. Terra thought he sounded familiar.

Terra hid behind a tree and listened. There were several sets of footsteps. She peeked from behind the trunk to see a line of men walking through a narrow path of dry land through the swamp. Terra recognized the gray uniforms and red armbands. Hanns marched behind several SS soldiers. He frowned as he looked back to several other primitive looking people the SS had tied together in a line. She assumed she could understand Hanns because the sonic ciphers translated his German for her.

Terra was about to follow when she felt a tap on her shoulder. She whirled around, but managed not to shout.

Alya stood next to her with a finger over pursed lips.

They followed the Nazis through the forested area which led them to an open glade nestled between hills. Terra and Alya moved to a nearby hill that overlooked an ancient village with wooden buildings and straw roofs. Around the village stood a palisade wall which the Nazi's had ringed with razor wire. SS soldiers stood watch over the sandbag fortified gateways that provided the only entrances into the village. Camouflage tents stood in contrast to the ancient buildings while a Nazi flag planted on the highest part of town waved in the wind. Antenna devices like the ones used in the library also dotted the area. She thought the posts looked smaller this time with a new, more compact design.

Terra shifted her gaze over the village, looking at how the Nazis had set up their forces. Machine gun nests stood at each gateway with two more on small hills overlooking key points of the village. The largest building had a panzer tank parked in front. She saw a lot of soldiers, at least two dozen with most wearing black SS uniforms.

Hanns and the others marched into the center of the village with the prisoners in tow. He stood with the rest as another SS officer walked out of a large tent. Terra assumed him to be of higher rank when the others saluted him.

The officer was a pudgy man half a head shorter than Hanns. He inspected the group of prisoners with a stern expression and haughty air. He turned to Hanns. "This is it?"

Hanns sighed.

The officer shook his head. "I said I needed good stock."

He walked over to the line of primitive prisoners. They cringed when the officer drew close. He stood much taller than them and his clean uniform contrasted with their dirty tunics and trousers.

The officer grabbed one by the arm. He inspected the woman's dirty hands before glancing to her soiled hair. "These are not Aryans!" he yelled as he shoved the woman back with the others. "You brought me cavemen! You brought us to the wrong time Hanns! These are not Aryans or any of the five sub races."

Hanns closed his eyes before massaging his temples. "No, Emmerich. I told you this is what we would find."

Emmerich gestured to the village. "Straw roofs! Filth everywhere! These people don't all have blue eyes. This isn't the Aryan utopia! We must be in the wrong time! Your calculations were incorrect."

Hanns looked up and groaned. "For the last time, Emmerich. These are the correct temporal coordinates. In fact my new machine is more accurate than the last. This is ancient Germany. It's not my fault you believe in idiotic utopias based on garbage science. Besides, it doesn't matter. What could you possibly want with these people?"

Emmerich sighed. "We need breeding stock Hanns. We need pure samples. Aryan blood is thin in the modern times. If our nation has any hope of long term survival we must cleanse our genes of Semitic impurities. To do that, we need these people. Your stupid history book can wait. Now put them with the others."

The SS soldiers led the prisoners into a fenced off area of the camp.

Hanns walked over to Emmerich. "This is unwise. I don't know how this will affect time."

"Silence, Hanns," Emmerich said with a scowl. "You had your chance to produce results and failed. Now it's my turn. We will continue our search for the Aryans."

Hanns sighed and followed Emmerich into a large central tent.

Alya swept her gaze over the camp before turning to Terra. "Wait until about a minute after I begin my attack and then capture Hanns. I'll capture the other leader, that Emmerich fellow."

"Capture?" Terra whispered.

"Yes," Alya said as though it were simple. "Just beat him up until he's unconscious. I'll take care of the others. We need to bring Hanns in along with the other leader. This is his final violation. The rest of them are first time offenders. I'll beat them up and give them a warning."

"You say that like it will be easy," Terra said, trying to keep her voice low.

"Just be careful," Alya said as though she wasn't even listening to Terra. "Hanns may not look like much, but he is still a soldier. Just remember to use your shieldwatch and wait until he's unguarded. Minerva, take a Restore state of this place."

Minerva began speaking over the cipher lines. "Continuum Delta. Time is 3:25pm—"

Alya groaned and touched her shieldwatch face, skipping the message.

"Location is Germania, continental—"

Alya touched her shieldwatch face again.

"Lethal force is not authorized. Enemy forces consist—"

She skipped the message again.

"Warning—"

Alya growled and skipped the next several messages. Finally, a ring descended on the area just like the one at the library. The Nazis' attention shifted to the new development.

Terra waited as Alya stood. She would just have to trust Alya. After all, Alya Silverwind was a seasoned legionnaire. No doubt she had a clever and cunning plan to deal with the Nazis.

Alya ran and jumped thirty feet over the wall, landing dead center in the camp. "Attention all temporal intruders!" Alya said, the shieldwatch amplifying her voice. "You are in violation of the Temporal Accords. I am giving you a single chance to return to your own time peacefully."

The Nazis all turned their attention to Alya with dumbstruck stares.

Terra touched her forehead with her palm and sighed.

CHAPTER XVI
TROY

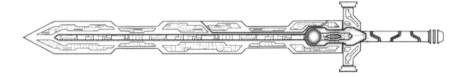

Think not to match yourself against gods, for men that walk the earth cannot hold their own with the immortals.
-From Homer's *The Iliad*, translation by Samuel Butler

The Nazis stared at Alya for a moment before scrambling for their weapons. Alya drew her aeon edge and loaded it before saluting the soldiers. The sword edge glowed blue. She lunged as tracer rounds zipped by.

Terra watched, using her shieldwatch to Speed her vision. Alya charged the tank first, pulling the trigger on her sword. The tank exploded, sending a ripple of heat and wind through the camp.

Nazis took cover behind sandbags after drawing their weapons. The command tent flapped open as Hanns and several SS officers rushed into the open to see the disturbance.

Emmerich followed. "What's going on?"

"She could at least humor us by using tactics," Hanns said. He turned to another soldier, one who did not wear an SS uniform. "Just as we discussed."

"Yes, sir. Good luck," the soldier said and then nodded. He ran to a nearby sensor post.

The SS soldiers focused fire on Alya. Terra saw the bullets streaking towards Alya, but Alya Sped her movements, dodging each bullet with her usual impossible grace. Terra still found Alya's skill impressive even when compared with all she had seen at the Academy.

When Alya reached the foremost group of ten soldiers, she sent each to the ground with a few quick strikes. Another group pulled out knives and batons. They charged Alya together. She smiled.

Alya didn't bother to draw her sword again. Each soldier attacked, hitting nothing but air, like swatting rain in a hurricane. She met each attack with a counter attack that landed another soldier on the ground, bleeding.

Terra's gaze followed Hanns as he ran to one of the antenna like, time travel devices. He activated it and a bright green glowing sphere formed like the one at the library. Hanns's troops retreated through it, though the SS remained fighting Alya.

"Hurry! Retreat!" Hanns yelled, gesturing to his last few men.

Terra stood, knowing she couldn't let Hanns escape again. She Slowed gravity around her and jumped, clearing the razor wire before stumbling onto the ground.

Terra stood and moved into the center of the camp, Speeding her movements to avoid stray shots that flew close. Alya flipped one soldier and he rolled right in front of Terra. The soldier groaned before standing.

"Enemy reinforcements!" he yelled when he saw Terra's white uniform.

Terra's training, however incomplete, still served her well. She didn't hesitate when the SS soldier charged her. Moving fast into a defensive hand to hand stance, Terra Sped her reflexes to deflect his first blow. Hand to hand fighting with a shieldwatch felt different from her sparring practice. The soldier's movements seemed trapped in slow motion with each strike easily evaded.

The soldier collected himself and charged again. Terra blocked his wide punch before she struck her palm against his chin snapping the man's head back. The SS soldier fell to the ground and Terra waited for him to stand. He didn't.

Terra stared at the beaten soldier slack-jawed. "I got one!"

She then spotted Hanns. He helped the last soldier through the portal, but did not step through himself. Instead he ran inside a tent and scrambled out a moment later, holding the strange clock like device he had used in the library to escape. In his other hand he carried something small that he put in his mouth.

Terra charged. Hanns turned, pulling out a pistol with his left hand. He hesitated when seeing Terra as though he recognized her, but his eyes widened when he saw Terra's uniform.

Hanns took several shots. Terra dodged, using her Sped vision and reflexes to avoid the bullets. Each shot she evaded gained her a few more feet on Hanns. When she drew near, Hanns pulled the trigger and his gun clicked.

Hanns slung the empty pistol at her. She dodged it with ease. He then drew a knife, slashing at Terra. Each time Terra weaved around the blade. His movements seemed sluggish with the shieldwatch. When Hanns stumbled, she struck his wrist sending the blade out of his hand. Hanns swung his fist at Terra, but she blocked each blow with perfect precision.

Terra grinned as she marveled at the power of the shieldwatch. She was in complete control of the fight. Hanns couldn't touch her. She was invincible.

Her shieldwatch beeped. "Battery power critically low. Shutting down nonessential functions," came Minerva's voice from Terra's shieldwatch.

Terra and Hanns stood still for a moment.

Hanns grinned.

"Crap," Terra said, feeling her panic rise.

Hanns's strikes now came fast. She struggled to evade them. When Terra stumbled, Hanns lunged, slamming his fist into her stomach. Terra gasped, falling to the ground.

Hanns wiped the sweat off of his brow while turning his back to Terra.

Terra pushed herself up and charged. Hanns noticed too late. He tried to turn to face her, but Terra moved inside his reach before he could react. She put one foot behind Hanns's own and grabbed his arm. Using Hanns's own center of gravity, Terra flipped him over her shoulder and he landed on the ground with a hard thump.

Hanns groaned and struggled to stand. He collapsed. Terra sighed, looking to where Alya now stood.

Emmerich had Alya surrounded by four tall SS soldiers.

"Filthy mongrel!" Emmerich said with a grin. "These are my best men. They are of the purest Aryan stock. They are—"

Alya moved in a flash, striking each seemingly at the same time. The blur of her silver hair made it appear as though a silver wind swept around them. The soldiers all fell at once.

"Unconscious..." Emmerich said as he watched his soldiers fall with widening eyes. He tried to run, but Alya knocked him down before placing a foot on Emmerich's back, preventing his escape.

Alya dusted off her hands. "Well that was rather disappointing. The foes at the library put up a much better fight."

Alya Restored the area after their battle. All the villagers returned safely and no trace of the Nazis, Terra or Alya remained, save for the missing day in the villagers' memories. With time Restored, Alya attached a shieldwatch like device to Hanns and Emmerich. They both disappeared when a glowing ring ran around them. Alya explained that she sent them back to Saturn City for processing.

Much to Terra's irritation, Alya vanished upon returning to Saturn City's timeport the moment two Legionnaires arrived to collect Hanns and the other officer, a man named Emmerich. Timeport security separated the two criminals. Terra shadowed the two legionnaires who guarded Hanns in an interrogation room with a single table and two chairs. One watched Hanns while the other examined the various tools and weapons Hanns had handed over after his capture.

One Legionnaire examined Hanns's pocket watch like device. "This is really interesting tech, Hanns. Where did you steal it from?"

Hanns raised an eyebrow. "Steal? I built it."

The man rolled his eyes. "Right. And I'm from the Thirteenth Cohort."

The second legionnaire looked at the device. "Interesting. This device works like a salient. It allows instant time travel between to spacial points by bridging two times together. This allows time travel and teleportation. Caminus will want to look at this for sure. Tiro, can you watch him?"

Terra nodded. "Yes, sir," she said unsure of proper protocol in this situation.

The two other Legionnaires then left the room.

"I remember you now," Hanns said after the guards left. "You're that girl at the library that attacked me. What is your name?"

"Terra."

"Funny that these people would conscript you after that, Terra."

"I joined willingly."

"Then you have bought into their lies."

"What do you mean?"

"Do you really think these people are better than any other empire? They are just like the rest of the corrupt imperialist democracies. They developed time travel technology first so they enforce their will upon others using technological superiority. It doesn't make them right."

"These people don't seem so bad. Besides, like you have any room to talk."

A timeport staff member walked in, interrupting them. "Okay, Hanns, you are in the system. I will send a legionnaire from the Third Cohort to escort you to Tartarus shortly. Your trial will be in a few days," he said while looking at a holoface then glancing to Terra. "Could you watch him for a few more minutes? The guard should be here soon."

"Sure," Terra said with confidence now that her shieldwatch had partially recharged. "Do I need to be careful of what I tell him?"

The man laughed. "He isn't going anywhere. You can tell him whatever you want. It won't alter time."

Once the man left, Terra took a seat at the table in front of Hanns. "Do you still think you are a hero, Hanns? Do you still think you are with the good guys?"

Hanns leaned forward on the table, knitting his fingers together under his chin. "Why wouldn't we be?"

Terra's brow lowered. "How could you possibly think that?"

Hanns shrugged. "Because it's true. What has democracy brought us? You say many great things. Oh yes. The Great War is one thing it brought. It also brought us the Great Depression. Your democracy has failed. Our system has proven successful. We brought a dying country from the brink of extinction, turning it into a mighty nation. Our science has even brought us through time itself. Yes it is authoritarian, but centralized power is needed to deal with a crises. Much like the dictators of ancient Rome."

"You know who else said that? The Naz... Oh right," Terra said, focusing on Hanns's steel-gray uniform. She had forgotten since he had removed his red arm band. "What about what you did to the Jews and the other peoples you oppressed?"

Hanns's brow knitted. "Well surely being an American you can understand the problem with the Jews? I do not go so far as many of my colleagues and delve into conspiracy theories. The links between the Jews and the communist party is tenuous as best and I find the Protocols of the Elders of Zion of rather dubious authenticity myself. Why would those holding treasures wish to redistribute it equally? Still, they are a people who are holding us back by hoarding all the wealth. Something needs to be done about it."

Terra pointed at Hanns. "So you kill them? Along with thousands of others; gypsies, political prisoners, anyone who disagrees with you?"

Hanns leaned back, his eyes wide. "What? No! Why would we do that?"

Terra stood, her hands on the table. "So you really don't know?"

"Know what?" Hanns said in an irritated tone.

Terra sat back down, slack-jawed. "Are you that blind? Your nation commits genocide, Hanns."

Hanns chuckled. "Genowhat? I am sure our quest for justice is quite overstated in the Americas. You shouldn't believe in such exaggerations. We would never do such a terrible thing. History will vindicate us."

Terra's fists clenched as she glared at Hanns. "Listen, Hanns. In my time your entire political party is considered the worst villains in all of history. Nazis are used as cheap, disposable villains in video games, movies and books. That's because no one will ever feel bad for them no matter how many of them the heroes kill. You practically have an entire television channel dedicated to just how evil the Nazis and Hitler were. When politicians want to slander their opponents they compare them to Hitler. History didn't redeem you. It damned all of you. How can you just sit there and still think you are the heroes in your own personal Saturday morning cartoon?"

Hanns leaned back. After a moment he cleared his throat before straightening his posture. "I see now. You Americans are terrified of us. I suppose news of our victories must have frightened you. You are clearly under the influence of propaganda."

Terra had to stop herself from grinding her teeth. "No, Hanns! You don't win. You lose and you lose bad. Germany gets chopped in half after the war is over and your Fuhrer shoots himself in the head rather than face trial for his war crimes."

Hanns smirked. "I highly doubt that. I don't think England will charge across that channel anytime soon."

"Do you just blindly follow orders? Don't you look around and see what's happening in your country?"

A slight smile touched the edge of Hanns's lips. "Without a sign, his sword the brave man draws, and asks no omen, but his country's cause."

Terra sighed. This must be what it's like for other people to argue with her. "Well Hanns, you are smug for someone who is about to spend his life in prison," Terra said with a grin. *Let him chew on that*, she thought.

Hanns smirk widened. "You can't frighten me. These time travelers don't frighten me either. They have this magnificent city, but so was Atlantis and Troy. In the end they all fell because of their hubris, as will this city. I'm smarter than you and I'm smarter than them because I embrace the truth."

Terra's gaze narrowed as she considered smacking him. A hand on Terra's shoulder saved Hanns a fist to the face.

"Don't let him upset you, Terra," Alya said, smiling. She turned to Hanns. "Shame on you, Hanns. What did you do to get her so upset? It took me days to accomplish such a difficult task."

Hanns shrugged. "We were merely having a lively discussion about history. Terra seems to be under the influence of propaganda."

"Is that so?" Alya said. "Well, Hanns, I am really disappointed in you."

Terra smirked. *Now*, she thought. *Alya is about to put Hanns in his place.*

Alya frowned "You put up a much better fight last time. What happened? Did you lose on purpose? I was excited for a good fight, especially after you got a hit in last time."

Terra's mouth hung open as she stared at Alya.

Alya then patted Terra on the shoulder. "Come on. The guards are here. They will transfer him to Tartarus. Hanns will probably have several lifetimes to rethink his position."

As Terra followed Alya out of the room, Terra looked back to see Hanns smiling. He wore the smug expression of someone who had gotten exactly what he wanted.

Alya led Terra to a windy stone walkway on the second floor of a timeport building where a light breeze drifted over them. Terra stopped in the middle of the walkway, repressing the urge to kick something. "Stupid Hanns! Why can't he see the truth?"

"Oh?" Alya said, turning to Terra. "What truth is that?"

"That he's the bad guy! He's a villain! He can't seem to understand that the Nazis are evil," Terra said in a seething voice.

"Terra, everyone sees themselves as the hero. Hanns sees his quest for victory the same way you see your quest to become a heroine. Just as you journey through the perils of the Academy, so too does Hanns when he faces us. You need to remember that the Nazis did evil not because they were Nazis, but because they were human. Their ideology was a justification to take what they wanted. The crimes they committed though, were their choice in the end."

"Then why doesn't he believe the Nazis commit genocide?"

"Hanns sees a different ideology than your history does. His honor and good intentions are a drop of water in a lake of poison. Whatever good he thinks he can accomplish will ultimately be useless. He is under the mistaken assumption that his single, good voice can change a bad choir."

"Then what's the difference between a hero and villain?"

"An interesting question," Alya said in a thoughtful tone. "Well you best ponder this yourself."

Terra's brow lowered. "That's it!"

"Well yes," Alya said as though it were obvious. "I could tell you what I think a hero or heroine is, but it probably wouldn't match your definition. That is part of your journey, not mine. I finished my journey a long time ago."

"Then how can you know when you have become the villain?"

Alya tapped her chin with her finger. "I guess it depends on the person. I have known a few who saw the darkness in their own hearts, but that is a rare kind. Those who deny being lost in the dark will never bother to look for light. It is the nature of being a villain."

CHAPTER XVII
SURVIVAL

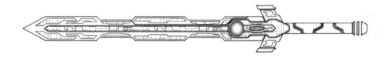

Hikari Narashima. I heard the instructors mention that name before the training started. Her talent is obvious. While obvious, it alone doesn't make her worthy of joining my Legion. Furthermore, I am not yet convinced she will be able to bond with others. Legionnaires need bonds. Those bonds held us together during the darkest hours of the Faceless War. Their absence allowed both the Manticores and the Kings and Queens of Time to spread unchecked. I do find it rather curious that she has chosen Tiro Mason, of all people, to compete with. Perhaps this will get both to perform better? Not all bonds are forged in friendship and camaraderie.
    -From the personal logs of Praetor Lycus Cerberus

The schedule cleared as the Survival Test drew close. Terra learned from Zaid that many dust out during the Survival Test. Now it was hours away and everyone rushed in their preparations. Terra found herself locked out of the crowded strategy study. She didn't worry as she had already read most of the materials on the subject. Still, she wanted to review a little more and needed a quiet place to study. She decided to read in Kairos's Garden.

The Academy grounds lay in the silence of winter with snow scheduled for later in the week. The occasional evergreen tree added color. However, Kairos's Garden remained in a vibrant spring. A stasis field kept that spring eternal as it regulated a constant stable temperature. The garden still caught her breath. After wandering through the grounds, she found a nice rock to prop her back up on as she sat. Terra read through the highlights again from a holoface.

She skimmed the survival manual. It covered many aspects of survival in different environments and situations. Sections detailed using the environment to evade enemy patrols, which species of plants were poisonous across various times, and more basic things like how to start a fire with whatever is on hand. There was even a section dedicated to resisting interrogations and escaping from imprisonment. She grew sleepy around chapter seven. It was hard not to relax in the peaceful garden. Despite her best efforts, she fell asleep.

She must not have slept long. When she woke, the looming metal hands of the city were still near the same place. Terra often thought that the best part about living in a giant clock city was you never went without knowing the time.

She yawned and stood. Blurry vision made Terra squint her eyes. When her sight focused, she saw a person clad in black standing in the distance. Terra glanced to her shieldwatch, double checking the time. But when she looked up the person had gone.

"There you are," came a familiar voice.

Terra turned to see Alya. She glided towards Terra.

"I thought you might be here," Alya said. She paused and regarded Terra with a faint smile.

"What?" Terra asked. She noticed that Alya wasn't looking at her, but at something in her hair.

Alya smiled. "Sorry. Just a bit of nostalgia. Where did you find the white rose?"

Terra raised an eyebrow. "Rose?"

"It looks pretty on you."

Terra felt around her head and discovered a white rose next to her right ear. "I didn't put that there. I was asleep just a moment ago."

Alya took the rose and inspected it. "Then who did?"

Terra pointed to the small hill near the center. "I saw someone over there a minute ago. I didn't catch who it was though."

Alya grinned. "A secret admirer?"

Terra glowered at the suggestion. "Not likely."

"Have you studied for the survival test?"

Terra nodded. "I read the whole thing and now I'm reviewing. I think I'll be okay. My endurance scores are good. I even completed the advanced endurance course a few days ago and earned my stealth and evasion qualifiers, but I still don't have an aeon edge."

Alya held up a finger. "Remember what I told you about swords? They can only kill. You are more skilled with the shieldwatch."

"Okay."

Alya nodded. "You have improved. A few months ago you would have argued with me."

"I don't argue!"

"Most stubborn person I have ever met," Alya said as she put the white rose back in Terra's hair.

∞

Terra, standing at attention, noted how few remained at the central courtyard. Around six hundred were left. Most carried far fewer of their original weapons and armor, having traded them for Legion gear. Even Terra had begun purchasing equipment. They all stood in formation in the central courtyard while Lycus walked on stage again. He grinned as he surveyed the survivors.

"Attention!" the centurions yelled.

Lycus paced the stage. "Today is the day of the Survival Test. This will be a test of not only endurance, but of knowledge. You may take your aeon edge and shieldwatch with you. If you lose either, you will fail the training. Everyone will be deployed to survive alone for as long as we deem fit. Team leaders are expected to gather their teams. Leaders who fail to do this will lose their position of team leader. Incapacitating a member of another team will give you one point so you must be wary of your fellow tirones. Your shieldwatch will receive authorization codes to return to Saturn City once the test is done, and you will have 24 hours to make it back. You have one hour to get ready before reporting to the timeport. Dismissed."

Most left for a last minute visit to the armory. Terra didn't bother. She had too few points for an aeon edge. Instead she returned to her dorm room to check her gear one last time. After tying her combat boots, she tightened the straps on her armored vest. In addition to her knee and elbow pads, she had also acquired greaves, thigh pads, and armor for her upper arms.

After checking her gear, Terra looked up into her dorm room mirror. She had tied her shoulder length brown hair back into a short pony tail and made sure it was smooth and neat. They wouldn't dock her a point for sloppy hair or untrimmed eyebrows again. 'Attention to detail' were curse words to Terra. She nodded at the precise reflection before departing to the timeport.

The timeport was crowded with tirones and Terra had to search for Zaid. After she found him and the rest of his strike team, they boarded a saucer shaped timeship. Within minutes the timeship lifted off, speeding through the edge. The centurions remained silent about their destination, but Terra guessed it would be a continuum rather than taking the test in a salient.

The Edge shown through the translucent sides of the timeship. It was a surreal thing when seen from a distance like a vast river of swirling blue energy that stretched to the horizon. The shifting blue tendrils of the Edge's continua shown brightly in the starry void, like glowing veins of blue in obsidian.

Terra remembered some of Shani's lectures about the Edge. One lecture detailed temporal storms that could rip apart armored timeships before slinging the wreckage into the Bleak. Another lecture discussed the deep raids of the Sons of Oblivion and the horrible fates of those they captured. Shani also spoke at length about unstable continua that could trap a person in eternal decay. As the dark possibilities mounted in Terra's mind, so too did her nausea. She decided to look away from the Edge.

Zaid addressed his strike team as Saturn City faded into the distance. "I don't know where they will drop us, but make your way to the highest landmark in the area. I will gather the team there."

Nikias walked into the room after Zaid finished speaking. "We begin this survival test with a dirty jump."

"Dirty jump?" asked a tiro.

Nikias touched a holoface on the wall. The sidewall then disappeared after a Restore ring moved around the saucer. "It's a fancy word meaning we shove you out the fadedoor with no preparation," Nikias said as he shoved the tiro out of the now open wall. He screamed as he plummeted into the flowing energy of the Edge.

Terra felt a stab of panic. "Um. Are you suppose to tell us how to jump into the Edge properly first?"

Nikias's grin faded. "Oh. Right. Yeah I was supposed to. Oh well. No time now! Everyone jump!"

"But!" asked another tiro before Nikias shoved her out the timeship as well.

The others jumped. Terra hesitated, but jumped when Nikias eyed her. Terra fell into the swirling mass of energy. When she was in the center of the stream of blue energy, her shieldwatch activated and a ring appeared around her forming a sphere as it turned. When the glowing sphere dissipated, Terra found herself in a forest thick with undergrowth. She looked around to get a sense of her surroundings.

The forest seemed quiet enough. To preserve power, she resisted the urge to use her shieldwatch to Speed her vision. Then she realized that her shieldwatch was unresponsive and her connection with time severed.

Terra fought back a moment of panic before it turned to anger. No wonder they had let them bring their shieldwatches and blades. Any gear they took was now nonfunctional dead weight, but they would still fail if they discarded anything. She felt a little better when she remembered that most tirones carried a heavy lead weighted aeon edge.

Terra hiked along the forest edge trying to find high ground. She needed to get a good view of the area. A nearby hill overlooked a large plain. After climbing up a rock she looked over the area.

The plain where she stood bordered a forest. A river ran between the forest and a bog. A mountain loomed to the west. She saw an animal herd that grazed on the plains, though they were too far for her to make out the species.

After getting her bearings, she climbed down. She decided she would need water first so she headed to the river, moving through the forested area to avoid being spotted in the open. Terra was careful not to make noise and avoided clusters of leaves and underbrush as she tried to leave as few tracks as possible. Her focus on covering her tracks distracted her as she almost ran into an odd shaped tree. When she stopped to look she discovered that it was not a tree, but a huge rib cage. A strong rotting odor saturated the area.

There wasn't much left of the carcass save for the car sized rib cage. Terra pondered the species when she saw movement out of the corner of her eye. It was behind a large mound. Then Terra realized that mounds don't have feathers.

At first the feathers threw her off, but then she realized what it was. The creature was much larger than an elephant. It lay on the ground covered in dark plumage with a long tail and small arms. She saw the rows of sharp teeth when it opened its maw.

Terra went pale. Her pulse quickened as the dinosaur lifted its large head and sniffed the air. Terra stood still. It tilted its head sideways, studying her. She considered running, but instead remained motionless. She didn't know what species it was as she hadn't read a book about dinosaurs since she was a little girl.

It smelled the air again before groaning. It put its head back on the ground like a dog too lazy to greet its master. Terra let out a long sigh. "Guess I'm too small to eat," she said. She walked away from the beast. It ignored her as she left.

"Damn you, Lycus," she said once she was far enough away. "I can't believe you dumped us in the cretaceous of all times."

An hour later she finally found the river. She hid in brush for a long while watching for other tirones or predators. A pack of smaller feathered dinosaurs loitered nearby, busy eating underbrush.

Terra walked out to the river. After getting herself a drink of water, she wondered how she could make a canteen.

The dinosaurs shifted their focus to Terra. Terra glanced to the creatures as a few of them walked towards her. They were big and stood several heads taller than her. As they drew closer, they began squawking and charged right at her. Terra ran.

They chased her and gained ground until Terra climbed a nearby tree. Flocking around the tree, they tried to push it down several times. After a few minutes they grew bored and a few of them laid down next to the tree while the rest of the herd congregated around them. Every once in a while, one pushed at the tree, trying to knock it down or shake her out of it.

Hours passed. In her boredom, Terra spotted the saucer timeship in the sky. It moved on after lingering in the area for an hour. Thankfully when the sun set, the herd moved on elsewhere.

Terra climbed down, grumbling as she went. "I can't believe the stupid T-Rex could care less, but the herbivores try to kill me on sight. And what's with the feathers?"

She felt hungry in addition to thirsty after several hours stuck in a tree. Terra avoided the river bank and found a nearby creek instead. After double checking for tracks to be safe, Terra finally could drink.

Over the next few days Terra put her survival knowledge to practice. By the second day she had a hand made canteen and a host of sharpened sticks for spearing fish. She also learned that crocodiles of the cretaceous were huge and fast, so she took extra care when going near water.

At the third day's end she had figured out the dangerous species from the passive. The T-Rex wasn't interested in a small creature such as Terra and did not perceive her as a threat to its territory. Most of the large, solitary creatures didn't pay her much mind either.

Terra was careful to hide from both native species and a group of three tirones that passed though the area. They did not find her and continued on without incident.

By the fourth day she had gathered an extra water skin, a dagger made of sharpened obsidian and vines, a few weeds that could be milked for ointment, and a single piece of fruit. Terra wanted to gather more food, but she was running short on time. She needed to find her strike team. The highest landmark was a nearby mountain. She hoped to find Zaid there with the others. Topping off a canteen she had made from the husk of a small plant, Terra left the creek and ventured into the forest.

As she set out, a loud explosion sounded in the distance. She looked up and saw a trail of smoke leading to the ground, but couldn't see what had happened. After a moment Terra continued on until she heard something else.

Four nights in the cretaceous period taught her to identify the sounds of the various dinosaurs and other animals that moved through the forest. These footsteps were human and there was more than one.

Terra ducked, finding cover in nearby thick green foliage. She struggled to see the group through the numerous leaves, but Terra could tell they were not tirones.

They wore dark gray, almost black uniforms and moved through the forest in a line formation sweeping the area. As they passed by several feet away, she could hear their radio chatter.

"Tiger one clear."

"Tiger two clear."

"Panther one clear."

"Panther two in pursuit of lone target."

"Tiger five confirms Pearl Raven is down. Repeat, Pearl Raven is down. Recovery teams, sweep and secure."

One figure stopped few feet away from Terra though a tree stood between them. She could just make out an arm touching a device on his head.

"Tiger three pursuit update. Trail has gone cold. Going to do another sweep then return to base," the man said into the radio before he moved forward again.

"Confirmed Tiger three," came a response over the radio. "Once sector three is clear, move to sector four and assist Panther two. Use caution. Gunships for phase two pursuit will be ready in two days. Until then, continue ground sweeps."

Terra watched the figures, the soldiers she guessed, move away. She waited a short time before continuing on, thankful she had read up on the evasion section of the manual and practiced on her own.

The shadows grew long. Terra felt her stomach twist before looking inside her food pouch and grimacing. After putting distance between herself and the unidentified soldiers, Terra searched for food again.

Terra felt a surge of excitement when she found fruit bearing trees. They hung near the top of a tree, but she knew it was edible from her studies on temporal biology. After stretching, Terra climbed the tall tree. She reached for a piece of fruit when someone on the opposite side grabbed it before her.

Hikari peeked around the tree. "Oh, it's you," she said in a disappointed tone.

Before Terra could respond, Hikari kicked, snapping the branch Terra held. Terra yelled as she slid down the tree. Thankfully she rolled with her fall when she hit the ground. After dusting herself off, she stood and glared at Hikari. "What was that for?"

Hikari snatched the fruit before jumping and landing gracefully on the ground. She held a half eaten fruit in her other hand. "Survival," Hikari said, tossing the half eaten fruit in front of Terra before taking a bite of the other.

Terra narrowed her gaze. "No. That's called being a jerk!"

Hikari looked up to the next tree. "Jerk? Is that an insult?"

Terra frowned. "Yes. It means th–"

Hikari turned her back to Terra before Terra could explain.

Terra scowled before letting out a slow breath. She would not let Hikari make her angry. Instead she climbed another tree that with one piece of fruit at its top. Once again just before she reached it, Hikari raced past Terra, grabbing the fruit before her.

Hikari stood above Terra. "After you beat me at the cliffs, I practiced my climbing," she said before shoving Terra down again.

Terra stood after hitting the ground. "Stop that!"

Hikari jumped down before pocketing the fruit. "No. This is survival. Survival is competition even if the competition you provide is meager."

"We are on the same team!"

Hikari stared at Terra. "Team?"

"Yes," Terra said, feeling her anger flare hot. "We need to find the others."

Hikari turned and began climbing another tree. "I don't need them. Go find them yourself."

Terra then saw what Hikari sought. A large bundle of fruit hung high on this tree. Terra looked around and found a fist size rock on the ground. Aiming carefully, Terra slung the rock at the bundle, sending it falling to the ground where Terra caught it.

Hikari halted her climb and glared down at Terra.

Terra grinned while she hoisted the fruit over her shoulder. "Weakness depends on the situation, Hikari. Sometimes being alone is a weakness."

Hikari jumped down and faced Terra. "I could show you how weak you are. I could take that fruit from you."

Terra waved a finger at Hikari. "Yes you could, but you know that while I am not good at winning sparring matches, I am good at enduring them. If you fight, then you risk injuring yourself and without your shieldwatch to Restore you..."

"What do you want?"

Terra tossed Hikari a fruit. "I want you to help me find Zaid. Unlike you, I like Zaid. He actually listens to me. So I will pester you until you come with me."

Hikari's burning gaze locked on Terra. "No."

"Too bad. I am not going to leave you alone."

Hikari turned away from Terra and walked into the forest.

Terra followed behind, eating the fruit she had taken. "I don't get you," she said between bites. "Everyone wants to be your friend. Some of them keep coming back even after you insult them. You could be really popular if you wanted."

Hikari hastened her pace, trying to out walk Terra. She made her way to a small flat that rested of the side of a hill. It was surrounded by thick vegetation

Terra matched Hikari's pace. "Why insult everyone?"

Hikari shot Terra a sidelong look, but said nothing.

Terra noted obsidian in the exposed stone as she drew close. It would explain the thick foliage in the area. The soil was rich in nutrients due to the volcanism. Thick vegetation combined with the elevation made this an excellent place for both concealment and as a lookout point. *This must be Hikari's camp*, Terra thought.

Hikari had dug a pit to start a fire. It had a small chimney to dissipate the smoke. Dense vegetation surrounded the flat, save for a long wall of obsidian on one side. Most of the exposed ground was comprised of obsidian and dirt. Terra noted that the fire pit was too close to the dry foliage.

After sizing up her surroundings, Terra faced Hikari and frowned. "You can't make me mad, but others might not react as well though. You ever think that maybe your rudeness might backfire on you one day?"

Hikari bent down to start the fire with flint and tinder. With a couple of flicks the fire started. Terra sighed at seeing that as it had taken her forever to start a fire her second night.

Hikari looked up at Terra. "If others take offense—"

Several tirones ran out of the forest into the campsite, cutting Hikari's response short. They surrounded Hikari and Terra. There, a dozen of them had encircled both her and Hikari, though Terra couldn't see all of them well enough to count. All wore their Legion training uniforms and most carried makeshift weapons made from whatever they had recovered from the forest.

One tiro stepped forward. "Hikari, we have decided it is time for you to dust out."

Hikari's expression remained calm. "Really?"

Another tiro nodded. "Yes. First we are going to be—"

Hikari attacked. Three tirones were on the ground, bleeding, before the rest even reacted. When two more hit the ground, Hikari's movements became even faster.

Terra had little time to watch Hikari fight. A few of the tirones went after her. One Terra knocked out when he left himself open. The other was more cautious as he attacked Terra in quick bursts of speed she had difficulty blocking. It was then Terra realized how much she missed her shieldwatch. Likely the instructors had disabled it to prove a point. Never become overdependent on technology.

Terra had taken two more punches when the other tiro turned pale faced after looking around him. She took a quick look around as well and saw that the camp site lay littered with beaten tirones.

Hikari still stood with the campfire blazing behind her like an aura. She panted near exhaustion as the flames reflected in her eyes.

The other tirones fled after gathering their wounded. Hikari moved to follow when Terra grabbed Hikari's arm. On reflex, Hikari struck Terra, but Terra took the punch with grunt before shaking Hikari.

Terra stared at Hikari. "Hikari! You beat them. Let them go."

Hikari glared at Terra while still panting. "I don't need you to hold me back."

"No. You are exhausted. Besides," Terra said, pointing to the campfire which had spread to the dry foliage. "If we don't stop *that,* then we will both be running for our lives from a firestorm."

With effort they both stopped the fire from spreading, but Hikari had to sit while Terra finished containing the fire.

"I still don't get you," Terra said as she moved the last stone into place around the campfire, keeping it contained. "Why are you even here? You don't seem to like anyone."

Hikari reached to draw her aeon edge. "This is why I am here."

"Why do you want an aeon edge so bad?"

"It's the perfect blade," Hikari said, as though it were obvious, while regarding her aeon edge.

Terra sat across from Hikari and began rubbing the bruises she took from the fight. "Okay? I guess that explains why your're being so protective of the thing. What about that other sword you carry?"

Hikari drew the other blade. "This?" Hikari asked before tossing it to Terra.

Terra almost missed the sword being thrown to her. Hikari had been so protective of her aeon edge that Terra hadn't expected Hikari to toss her the other sword so casually.

Hikari leaned back, facing the fire. "That was my father's old blade. It's broken now. Worthless. Still I find myself holding it, for remembrance I suppose."

Terra inspected the sword. Something had cut the blade cleanly near the guard, but what drew Terra's eyes was the blade itself or rather the metal. It was not shiny like a polished iron or steel sword, but had dark wavy ripples through the metal. "Damascus steel?"

Hikari looked at Terra with a furrowed brow. "What?"

Terra met Hikari's gaze, speaking in an excited tone. "Damascus steel. It's what others called this metal. Most in my time consider it a lost art of metallurgy. Where did your father get this sword?"

"He made it."

"He made it? Your father knew the secret of Damascus steel?"

"He was a blacksmith. Once he showed me the way he folded iron one hundred times over to make this metal."

"Wow. I bet it was hard for him to find good iron for that."

Hikari nodded. "It was. He would often reject what miners would bring him. How do you know about this?"

Terra shrugged. "I know a lot about geology and how it relates to metallurgy."

There was a long silence between them.

Terra smiled. "Well I guess there is one thing alike between us."

Hikari almost looked as though she would smile back. Instead she turned away from Terra. "There is nothing alike between us. You could not understand what it is to be alone."

Chapter XVIII
Unfeeling Stone

Ten years ago.

"Wake up!" Beth said, nudging Terra.

Terra groaned, rolling over in her bed and covering her head with the sheets.

"We don't have time for this. Get up!"

After more prodding, Terra sat up and yawned. She was eight years old. In her opinion, eight years old was too young to be getting up at five in the morning. This was a typical morning though.

Beth threw a pair of jeans and a shirt on the bed. "Hurry and get dressed."

Terra stared at the jeans unblinking. "Those are dirty, Mom."

Beth stopped to look at the soiled jeans and frowned. "How? I just washed those yesterday. Do you wallow in the mud at school?"

After more searching, Beth found a pair that were not as dirty and threw them on the bed before walking out of the room.

Terra dressed and went downstairs. Before she made it to the kitchen Beth shoved a backpack in Terra's arms and a piece of toast in her mouth.

"Mernch merney," Terra mumbled with the toast still in her mouth.

"What?" Beth asked, checking her pocket book before straightening her business suit. She then took the toast out of Terra's mouth.

"Lunch money. You forgot yesterday."

"Sorry. Here," Beth said as she handed Terra a few bills. "That's my lunch money by the way. You better appreciate it."

"Ready?" Fred said as he walked into the room. He was dressed in his factory work-clothes.

Beth sighed. "God, I don't know. We are doing performance reviews today, and we are way behind our quota."

"It will be okay," Fred said.

They all walked outside the front door. Beth locked the door before turning to Terra. "You know where the front door key is?"

Terra pointed at the front door light. "Behind the light on the rim."

Beth nodded. "Good. You may have to let yourself in again after school. I don't know what time I will be home and your father is working two shifts again."

"Ready," Fred said, checking his watch. "I'll see you all sometime tonight I guess."

"Right," Beth said before walking to her car.

Fred watched Beth go with a disappointed expression.

Beth then stopped, turned around, and walked back to Fred, giving him a kiss before returning to her car.

Fred smiled and hugged Terra. "Try not to get your clothes as dirty today."

Terra smiled. "No promises."

Terra hit the dirt hard which soiled her clothes.

"Dirt girl!" yelled one girl in Val's gang.

Terra scowled while she lay face down on the ground of the schoolyard. She knew who had pushed her. Not one of Val's clique or Val herself. She probably got a boy to do it for her. Val would never dirty her own hands. With tears forming in her eyes, Terra stood, facing Val and her three friends.

Val always wore nice dresses and was eager to please the teachers. Terra thought that cute faces and nice dresses had a way of blinding teachers to bullies. Cute little girls could never be bullies, or so the naive thought.

Henry moved to join Val, having completed his task of pushing Terra. Terra didn't hate Henry though. He was another in a long line of Val's minions. Terra hated none of Val's gang, only Val herself. Val dismissed him. She would call on him again if Terra talked back.

One of Val's gang whispered in her ear. Terra could just hear the word pig.

Val smiled. "She looks like that doesn't she?"

Terra faced Val even though Val looked down on Terra who stood in a small ditch. She had been searching for stones, like usual, after finding dolomite yesterday. At least she thought it was dolomite. She was still memorizing the names of stones.

Val crossed her arms. "Maybe if you didn't spend so much time in the dirt, you might actually find a friend."

Hannah passed by, holding a book.

Val turned to Hannah. "Hey, Hannah. Look at dirt girl here. She still likes to play in the mud."

Hannah stopped and glared at Val. "You're stupid, Val. A girl with a nice dress shouldn't be mean to someone who can sling mud."

Val scowled while Hannah walked away.

Terra winced. That would put Val in an even worse mood.

Val turned to Henry. "Henry!"

On cue Henry shoved Terra down again.

Val and her gang laughed.

Terra began sniffling.

Val's smile returned. "Oh look. Dirt girl is in the dirt again."

Terra's sniffled turned into a sob as she began crying. She knew that she couldn't just lay there in the dirt. She had to keep standing. If she stayed down, it would never end. Val continued to laugh even after Terra stood again and felt something in her hand. She looked to see a small stone. As Henry moved to push Terra down again, Terra stared at the small stone. It was a bit of Haematite; an iron ore.

Terra realized she was alone. No one was going to help her. No one was going to save her and it would never end. Only she could stop it.

She gripped the stone in her fist and narrowed her eyes at Val. Terra knew who the real problem was. Terra lifted her hand and cast the stone at Val, forever shattering the name Dirt Girl and replacing it with Terra the Terror.

∞

Terra sat in the seat, swinging her feet in the air since she wasn't tall enough to reach the floor. She waited just outside the principle's office which was right next to the school nurse.

Val walked out of the nurse's room with a small bandage on the side of her forehead. She recoiled upon seeing Terra.

The nurse stepped out behind and patted Val on the head. "Don't worry dear. We won't let her hurt you anymore."

Val kept the nurse between her and Terra. Just before Val left the office waiting room, she shot Terra an ugly face that said this wasn't over.

Terra continued to stare at the floor.

Principle Overton stepped out of his office and looked down at Terra. "Well, your parents are on their way."

Terra ignored the middle aged, balding man.

Overton waited for a response. When none came he sighed. "Why is it always from the ones you least expect?"

Beth and Fred soon arrived.

Overton nodded to them. "Mr. and Mrs. Mason. Thank you for coming on such short notice. Please join me in my office. Terra, you too."

They entered the office and sat across the desk from Overton. Terra noticed her parents remained silent while Overton kept a grave expression. He cleared his throat. "I am sorry to call you all here so suddenly, but I felt this needed to be addressed immediately."

Beth frowned. "Could you explain the situation? Terra's teacher was nearly hysterical over the phone."

Overton sighed. "To put it bluntly, Terra attacked and injured a fellow student."

Fred and Beth both looked at Terra with raised brows.

Overton held up a hand. "The school nurse said it was just a small cut. She won't even need stitches and there doesn't seem to be any serious trauma."

Beth narrowed her gaze. "I don't understand. Terra has never been violent at home. Stubborn yes, but she never acted in anger or rage."

Fred rubbed his forehead. "We had no problems last year. Was she provoked?"

Overton leaned back in his chair. "It doesn't matter if she was provoked. She needs to understand how to resolve her problems without violence."

Beth turned to Terra. "Well, young lady? Explain yourself."

Terra looked up at her parents. "She called me dirt girl."

Fred raised an eyebrow. "That's it? That's not even clever. Could you at least have waited for her call you a curse word or something?"

Beth pursed her lips before turning to Fred. "Don't encourage her."

Terra crossed her arms. "She had everyone calling me that."

Overton shook his head. "You can't just ac–"

Terra stood. "They do it every day!"

Overton spoke in an even tone. "They are just words."

Terra glared at Overton. "She had a boy keep pushing me down."

Overton gestured to Terra. "Then you should have gone to a teacher for help."

Terra clinched her fists to her side. "Val would have just gotten another boy to push me. She's the real problem. The teacher likes her more than me so the teacher won't help."

Overton's eyebrows drew together. "Is that why you attacked Valerie? I don't understand. Her teacher adores her."

Terra glowered. Teary eyed, Terra folded her arms and sank into her seat, remaining silent.

Overton sighed, rubbing his forehead. "Mr. and Mrs. Mason, the truth is that I called you here for more than this incident. Has she been giving you trouble at home?"

Fred and Beth shared a look. Fred finally spoke. "Not really. We have a little trouble getting her to do her chores."

Beth rolled her eyes. "And good luck getting her to stay clean. She is always playing in the dirt and tracks mud in the house constantly."

Overton shook his head. "Not that. Behavioral problems regarding social skills. Does she play well with other children?"

Fred and Beth were silent for a moment. Fred then spoke. "Well, she doesn't play with other children. No other children live near us."

Overton nodded. "I see. I am concerned. Her teacher has brought to my attention that Terra has difficulty making friends. Even before she started throwing rocks at people."

Beth looked at Terra. "Is this true?"

Terra glared at Beth. "They all hate me because they think I'm strange. Because I don't like the things they like." Terra looked away. "They like boring things. I like stones. Stones are interesting. I found some dolomite today. Yesterday I found magnetite which can be used to make iron. That iron can have carbon added to it to cast pig iron. That pig iron can then be refined into steel."

Overton stared at Terra for a long moment. "That is... interesting. You have a lot of knowledge on metallurgy, but maybe you could make more friends if you tried some different things? People can be interesting too. How can a stone be better than a person?"

Terra looked Overton straight in the eyes. "Stones don't hurt my feelings."

∞

Beth and Fred had Terra sit in the kitchen. Terra could tell this would not be pleasant from the silent car ride home.

Beth faced Fred after putting down her pocket book. "Will you be okay with your boss?"

Fred sighed, opening up the cabinet. "It'll be fine. I just have to work another shift this Sunday to make up for it."

Beth sighed. "As if we didn't see each other enough already."

Fred shrugged while rummaging through the cabinet. "It'll be okay. They can't keep you down forever at the office."

Beth rubbed her forehead. "I don't know. This damn glass ceiling. And now this at the school! And with the mortgage..."

"It will be okay," Fred added. He took out a sizable whiskey bottle from the cabinet.

Beth turned to Terra. "Terra, you need to at least try to get along with the other children."

Terra stared at Beth without a change in expression.

Beth grimaced. "Don't be like that. Me and your father do not have time to keep you out of trouble at school on top of all our other problems."

Terra continued to stare.

Beth shook her head. "Listen he–"

The phone rang. Fred moved to get it.

Beth stared at Fred, her face pale.

Fred hung up the phone. "Collection agency."

Beth put her hand over her mouth. "God. I don't know how much longer I can do this."

Fred poured himself a glass of whiskey with shaky hands. "I got a few things I can sell to make the next payment."

Beth folded her arms. "What about the one after that!"

Fred slammed the whiskey bottle on the table. "Damn it! I don't know!"

Terra shrank back in her seat, tears forming in her eyes.

Fred frowned, one of the few times Terra had ever see him frown or angry. "I am doing everything I can! I'm pushing seventy two hours a week as it is. At least you get air conditioning!"

Beth put her hands on her hips. "You think it's easy for me? They pay me a pittance to babysit corporate officers who take credit for my leadership!"

Terra started crying.

Beth turned to Terra. "Stop crying! Crying never helps! It only makes things worse!"

It was too much. Bullies could push her down, but seeing her parents like this. Her instincts took over and Terra ran out the front door to the one place she felt safe. With tears in her eyes, Terra kept running until she came to the quarry. There she climbed down onto the first tier and curled up amongst stone.

Terra liked the cold stone. Stone didn't feel, it didn't cry. She stared at the stone for what felt like a long time. What if she could be like the stone? Unfeeling, cold, and impervious. That was what she wanted to be right now.

Terra stopped crying. Stones don't cry. She let the feelings bleed out of her until only her will remained. From now on, she would be stone.

"Terra!" Beth cried in the distance.

"Terra!" came Fred's voice nearby.

After a moment Terra saw the shadow of someone peering over the edge of the quarry.

"I found her!" Fred yelled. He climbed down and tried to pick up Terra.

Terra shook her head. "I want to stay here."

"Is she okay?" Beth asked, peeking over the quarry.

Fred sat next to Terra. "She's fine."

Beth climbed down and embraced Terra. "I am so sorry! I didn't mean to yell at you. We are all just having a really bad day. That's all."

Terra looked up at her parents. "It's okay. I won't cry ever again."

Fred and Beth stared at Terra.

Terra cast her gaze upon the cold stone. "Stones don't cry. Stones can be fine when they are alone. I want to be as strong as stone. Unfeeling stone."

CHAPTER XIX
EVASION

Remember that each tiro captured grants the captor a week of both extra rations and leave, but keep your guard up. They can and will kill you and your team if you are not careful. Bear in mind that they are recruits, but recruits who have already been through three weeks of Kali cursed nightmarish training. In addition, watch out for local wildlife. Don't neglect terrain. Don your masks and good hunting.

-Message from Central Command to all pursuit forces

Terra woke, expecting a hard day at school. Instead she remembered where she was and wished she could trade it for a hard day at school.

Hikari was up, but moving slowly, trying to stifle a yawn. Her once smooth hair was now twisted in a mass, while a black smudge covered much of her face. Hikari's bloodshot eyes looked up at the sky at the sound of a passing jet. Terra paid it no mind at first.

"What is that sound?" Hikari asked as she grew alert.

"Just an aircraft, probably a jet. Wait..." Terra stopped when she remembered she was in the cretaceous.

They both took cover nearby. When the sound passed they relaxed.

"A timeship from Saturn City?" Terra asked as she scanned the sky.

Hikari remained alert and still. "Better to not take chances. Just like those soldiers in black."

"Wait," Terra said, turning to Hikari. "Soldiers in dark uniforms? You saw them too?"

Hikari nodded. "A few days ago. They attempted to track me. I evaded them. I assume they are a part of the test."

Terra frowned. That would be just like Lycus to throw them an unexpected twist in the middle of the training.

Terra and Hikari grabbed what they could and set out for the tall mountain to the east. Hikari's protests against finding the rest of the team now vanished.

They walked forward, both careful to cover their tracks and passed two camps on their travels. One was occupied by a group of tirones from another team. Terra recognized Tacitus in the camp. They had built a small fort.

"Show offs," Terra said in a low tone. They both moved on not wishing to draw attention. Thankfully, his strike team appeared watchful for another enemy. With their focus elsewhere, Hikari and Terra sneaked by without trouble.

They passed an abandoned, second camp. Boot prints covered the ground while the blasted stumps of trees still smoldered.

"What manner of weapon did this?" Hikari asked, inspecting a scorched tree.

Terra inspected the burnt debris. "I wondered if someone smuggled in some big guns?"

Hikari shook her head. "I do not like this. We need to find the others now."

Terra shifted uncomfortably at seeing Hikari worried. Hikari turned to face movement nearby. With a flash of motion, she jumped into a nearby cluster of brush and threw another tiro into the open.

Terra gritted her teeth and moved to defend herself, but sighed in relief when she recognized Zaid.

∞

Hikari did not apologize for attacking Zaid. She did, however, return with him and Terra to his camp without protest. Zaid explained that he had visited the abandoned camp after he heard a commotion the night before. Other camps had been attacked as well.

With the strike team assembled they pooled resources over the next few days. Terra gave Zaid and the others a brief lesson on dinosaurs. Zaid shared obsidian daggers with the rest of the team. One teammate had made water skins while another had made a bow. Even Hikari helped by showing everyone how to build a smokeless fire pit in the evening.

A tiro looked to a nearby herd of dinosaurs in the distance. The herd was barely visible in the fading light. "So you say these giant chickens–"

"Dinosaurs," Terra corrected.

"Dino-things," the tiro continued, "are monsters that died out a long time ago? How could something so big die out?"

Terra raised an eyebrow. "Haven't you taken Temporal Biology yet?"

The tiro shook his head. "They have me in something they call remedial courses. Apparently, I'm not well educated compared to people from other times. Gladiator school means little here."

Zaid nodded. "I was exempt from such classes since I was already a scholar. They placed me in the advanced courses."

Terra's brow knitted when she realized she was in the advanced courses as well. Her education, as miserable as it was, had been something she had taken for granted. Maybe she wasn't as far behind as she thought.

It was then she heard the jet again followed by a distant rumble. A flash lit up in the distance.

"Thunder?" Another tiro asked as he gazed at the distant lights.

Terra shook her head. "Weapons. I think that's Tacitus's camp."

"I see them!" Hikari said pointing.

The others looked but Terra did not see them at first. A line of figures in black moved towards their camp. She counted at least a dozen in a loose line formation. Terra could just make out the glow of laser pointers from their weapons.

With a single gesture, Zaid's team scattered with everyone grabbing what they could from the camp.

A tiro shook her head. "They are moving in too fast. We need to slow them down."

Hikari lit the end of a branch in the fire.

Zaid looked at Hikari. "What are you doing?"

Hikari dabbed the burning stick into the dry foliage setting the area around the camp ablaze. The fire spread fast towards the pursuers who stopped to pull back as the blaze turned into a firestorm.

Zaid motioned for his team to retreat.

They fled to the edge of a gully while the pursuers moved around the blaze. By the time the pursuers had navigated around the fires, Zaid and his team had moved a fair distance away. Zaid slowed their pace after a fast march and once night had settled to give them cover. It was when they were passing by a river bank that Terra saw something.

Terra pointed at Zaid's shieldwatch face that flickered before turning blue. "Hey Zaid."

Zaid glanced to his shieldwatch and tapped the face. He then pointed to Terra's shieldwatch which did the same. Within seconds, everyone's shieldwatch had reactivated. Terra basked in her returning connection with time. She felt whole again.

Hikari drew her aeon edge. She loaded a stasis cell clip and the blue edge formed.

Zaid looked at his shieldwatch. "Minerva, what's going on?"

"Error," came Minerva's voice from Zaid's shieldwatch. "I am disconnected from Saturn City. A backup has activated. I do not have access to my full capabilities until my connection is restored."

Terra rubbed her forehead. "What do you mean you are disconnected?"

"This disconnect is consistent with old temporal jamming signals," Minerva said. "Though I can't be sure without access to the processing power in Saturn City. I know that cross time communication has been cut off and time travel is currently impossible. However, local shieldwatch and aeon edge functions have been restored."

Zaid thought. "Jamming. That's a military term from the future right? It's a way of stopping the enemy's messengers."

Terra nodded.

"Why did Lycus cut off communication with us?" Hikari asked.

Terra scanned her surroundings with a wary gaze. "Maybe it wasn't them. Didn't Centurion Shani say the Legion has a lot of enemies?"

An aircraft roared across the sky. Terra looked up to see search lights from the aerial vehicle moving towards their location.

Zaid motioned for his strike team to hide. They all blended into the shadows cast by a nearby forest.

Terra got a good look at the aircraft when it drew near. It was black and sleek with orange stripes and highlights like an attack helicopter though without the blades. Instead it had two large engines on either side of its wings that pivoted and moved to keep it hovering in the air. As for its purpose, Terra could guess that by the missiles and guns on it. As its searchlights swept the area, Terra knew it was a gunship on the hunt.

Seconds later a half dozen soldiers roped down from the back of the gunship. They wore dark gray, almost black armor with orange edges on the shoulder and knee pads. In their hands were bulky guns that looked worn, but the glowing lines on the sides along with an overall complex design marked these weapons as technologically advanced. The most distinctive feature of the soldiers were the solid masks they wore. Oval in design and black, each had an orange symbol painted on them. The graphics varied from eyes and teeth to glyphs that Terra could not decipher. She wondered how they could see through them since the masks had no eye holes.

Zaid whispered to his team while they hid. "This may be part of the training, but just to be safe I think we should try to contact the Legion and ask for aid."

They all nodded in agreement as a second gunship arrived to reinforce the first.

Minerva spoke through the sonic cipher devices in Terra's ears. "If you can escape the range of the jamming device then it may be possible to contact the city."

"How far?" Zaid asked who had heard Minerva as well.

"Unknown," Minerva said. "Most temporal jamming devices have an effective range between ten to fifty miles."

Zaid shook his head. "We will never make it that far."

Terra faced Zaid. "Then let me draw them off."

They all looked to Terra.

"Look," Terra said. "I am the slowest one here."

Zaid shook his head. "But you have good endurance."

Terra nodded. "Which is why I can lure them off. I'm not good in a fight, but I can be a good decoy. It will take a long time for me to get tired enough for them to catch me. Plus it will buy you enough time to get out of range of the jamming device."

Zaid thought for a long moment. He glanced to each tiro before looking back at the gunship. "I authorize it."

Terra grumbled.

Zaid raised an eyebrow. "What? It was your idea."

"Yeah, but I thought you would think up a better one," Terra grumbled as she climbed out of the thicket and walked toward the soldiers. She surprised herself by how little she hesitated in this suicidal plan of hers. The pit in her stomach told her she had made a bad decision, but the connection to time felt great. It coursed through her, each heartbeat carrying her into the future.

The soldiers saw her and all spotlights shone upon her.

"Halt!" came a voice over the loudspeaker of one of the gunships.

The soldiers all pointed their weapons at Terra.

"Wow," one soldier said as he brought out a pair of handcuffs. "It's nice when they just surrender like that."

"Easy rations," another said.

"And a week of leave for each capture," the first soldier added.

Terra took a deep breath. She Sped time around her. The soldiers and gunship now moved in slow motion and she ran past them in a flash before Slowing gravity and jumping over the river. She cleared to the other bank.

"Kali cursed!" yelled a soldier. "Their shieldwatches went active!"

The gunships whirled around while the soldiers shouldered their weapons and fired. Orange glowing bolts of energy streaked towards Terra. The bolts struck the trees near her and blasted them apart. Terra ran.

"Tiger three, target is on the move!" she heard over the soldiers' radios.

Terra returned to normal speed. Her decoy plan must be working as a third gunship now flew nearby. One gunship lowered to pick up the soldiers stranded on the other side. *Good*, Terra thought. *That means none stayed behind to search for the others.*

Within seconds, the gunships were flying low near Terra. They moved in a predictable pattern which Terra found easy to evade while under the cover of the forest. Just when she thought she was about to evade them, Terra saw lights ahead. A line of soldiers advanced, surrounding her. She frowned, realizing they had flushed her into a trap.

Terra cursed, searching her surroundings for a way out. Small open glades dotted the area, but the gunships would spot and attack her there. Soldiers prevented her from moving through areas with more cover. Terra regretted not having an aeon edge for the first time all week.

On the verge of panic, Terra stumbled into a pile of bones and the smell of rot hung heavy in the air. It was then she saw the massive feathered mound of a Tyrannosaurus Rex. It sniffed at the air and looked up at the searchlights overhead. It tilted his head as though curious at the arrival of the newcomers. Terra stopped and turned with a new idea.

The soldiers shined their lights on Terra rather than the large creature behind her. One soldier shot at her. The bolt streaked towards Terra. She Sped her sight to track the projectile and then Sped her reflexes, dodging before it hit. As the missile flew past she Slowed gravity and jumped above into a tree.

The energy projectile impacted the large beast in the tail. Terra could see the wound on its tail as the huge beast stood and roared. The pursuing soldiers hesitated. The monstrous creature searched for the thing that had burned it. It spotted the soldiers.

One of the soldiers lowered his rifle. "Don't worry everyone! I read that this one is just a scavenger."

The tyrannosaurus roared and charged at the soldiers who scrambled out of the way. Terra slipped through the rather large opening the beast had made for her. The gunships moved in to support the soldiers who now had an angry, several ton animal chasing them. In the chaos, Terra slipped off into the darkness.

∞

By morning she felt exhausted. She rested next to a small creek to get water when she heard footsteps and voices.

"Sector eight clear," a voice over a radio said.

Terra clenched her jaw before peeking from behind a nearby rock. The same dark clad soldiers moved through the area. She counted fifteen soldiers sweeping the creek in a long line. How had they found her so fast?

One of the nearby soldiers stopped a few feet away before checking his radio. "Tiger twenty reporting. Quarry not spotted in this area."

"Tiger twenty, continue searching the sector. Intel suggests at least seven targets remaining. Tiger five is still in pursuit of five targets in adjacent sector. Keep alert for the other straggler," a voice over the radio said.

Terra let out a quiet sigh. Her team was still safe. The guards continued their conversation while Terra stalked slowly by. She paused when a soldier leaned on the other side of the rock she hid behind.

"They said this would be easy," a soldier said as he squatted to fill his canteen. "Just a bunch of recruits. Easy catches."

Another soldier, one with a good deal more patches on his uniform, turned to the soldier who had just spoken. "It's the Aeon Legion. Even their throwaways are tough. Don't underestimate them, especially now that their shieldwatches are active. I always hate phase two, even when we get gunships."

Terra moved past the soldiers. Her quiet motions got her to the forest when she encountered another group of soldiers moving towards her. They marched forward with guns raised and left no nook unchecked. She hid behind a tree before they spotted her.

Terra suppressed her panic. The soldiers stood spaced apart in a line, each within the view of another. She hid and waited. When one neared she Sped her movements and darted out of her hiding place. Everything slowed down as she Sped time around her as fast as she could manage. The soldier walked in slow motion and she spotted grenades at his belt. Terra grabbed the ring of a grenade and pulled it as she streaked by in a blur.

"What was that?" asked one soldier as Terra hid behind another tree.

They all stopped and searched before a scream drew their attention.

"Grenade! Grenade!" a soldier said, struggling to get the now glowing orange grenade off of his belt. He managed to fling it away seconds before it exploded into a bright, glowing burst of energy.

Terra slipped away again. When she was far enough away she checked her shieldwatch power and frowned. Five percent of the battery remained.

∞

Evening neared when Terra was about to give up hope. She must have walked miles, but her shieldwatch was still within jamming range. The roar of a gunship engine sounded overhead and Terra instinctively took cover. When the gunship passed, Terra made her way to an overlook to get her bearings. She gazed out onto the area, cast in a glowing orange hue from the setting sun. Her eyes went wide.

The enemy camp sprawled out before her. Row upon row of tents stood clustered around a river with a large tower at its center. Lights bathed the camp in an orange hue while watchtowers with searchlights stood at the edge. Terra's gaze narrowed on a Saturnian, saucer shaped timeship near the center of the camp. A large scorch mark marred its hull.

"Minerva," Terra said. "Would it be possible to fly that timeship out of here?"

"Yes," came Minerva's voice from Terra's shieldwatch. "It would be if it wasn't disabled, which our enemy would have thought to do."

Terra bit her lower lip. Minerva was probably right. "Could I send a message to Saturn City from it?"

"Um..." Minerva said after a long delay. "I think."

"You think?"

"I do not have access to my full processing power so I possess only a small fraction of my normal knowledge. I do know that most Saturnian timeships have escape pods. One could be ejected into the Edge where it would bypass the jamming. I think. I am not sure though. Consider this an educated guess."

Terra sighed. "Well I guess it's better than nothing."

She made her choice. Terra would try to sneak into the camp to contact the Legion. She could think of no other plan. Her fatigue made it hard to focus. These soldiers seemed to track her wherever she went. She couldn't rest for long before they would appear and hunt her again. Running wasn't an option any longer as she neared the limit of her endurance.

Terra waited for darkness to settle before making the attempt to approach the camp. With soft and careful footsteps she approached the nearest tower. After a gap appeared in the searchlight sweeps, Terra Slowed gravity and jumped over the fence before stumbling to the other side.

"What was that?" a tower guard said. He jogged a few paces away from Terra and searched the area with a flashlight.

"You are wasting time," a soldier called who looked down from the guard tower. "No one is going to be stupid enough to break into our camp."

The guard continued to scan the area with a flashlight while Terra hid behind a nearby tent, tense. After a moment he lowered the flashlight. "This is the Aeon Legion. Bunch of Kali cursed commandos. You can't be too careful."

"They are just recruits," called the other guard.

The guard holstered his flashlight. "It would be easier if we didn't have these relics. No wonder the old Kalians lost the war with this antiquated equipment. I just want to get out of here and back to Kavacha."

Terra exhaled and waited a moment longer before proceeding. She had memorized enough landmarks to navigate through the camp as she passed by a dozen tents and a few wheeled vehicles. Soldiers were everywhere, some without their masks. Most had dark hair and deeply tanned skin though she did not get a close look at their facial features.

Terra drew close to the timeship. She waited for two soldiers to walk past. Once they were clear she moved, swift and silent, towards the damaged timeship. Just as she was about to run up the ramp, she stopped and felt her heart jump as a figure in black ran past. She could just make out a small red light on the figure's forearm like the glow of a shieldwatch. Terra paused as the figure jumped high into the dark sky before vanishing into the night.

She listened for a moment longer before moving aboard the Timeship. Terra searched for the controls. The interior was dark. Terra touched her shieldwatch face and drew out a holographic directional light to search the controls.

"Okay, Minerva, where is it?" Terra asked in a quiet voice.

As her eyes adjusted to the dark she noticed a figure in the shadows. Terra paused when she looked towards the back of the timeship. The figure stood and took a step towards her.

"I thought no one would make it this far," he said in a voice distorted with a mechanical buzz. He stepped into the light cast from Terra's shieldwatch.

He wore the black vest with orange trim like the other soldiers, though his uniform had a lot of patches and medals. He also wore a mask painted with a graphic of a pair of orange stylized wings. Terra couldn't see any weapons, but the man's confidence put her on edge. It seemed unnatural compared to the other soldiers she had faced who were either overly cautious or reckless.

Terra assumed a defensive hand to hand stance while once again wishing she had an aeon edge. "Going to call for reinforcements?"

"I don't need them," the masked man said.

Terra tensed, her muscles pulling tight. Her instincts told her to run from this man even though he was unarmed and without a shieldwatch.

The man gestured behind him. "The jamming device is there. All you have to do is get past me."

Terra's eyes narrowed. So close. She had a shieldwatch. This man was unarmed. How tough could he be?

The man assumed his own defensive stance. "I see you have chosen to fight. Good. Show me what passes for an Aeon Legion recruit these days."

Terra took no chances. She Sped her reflexes, maneuvering around the man. Then to her surprise he countered her attack, blocking her blow to his neck before twisting her arm around and throwing her to the floor.

Terra grunted and stood. He was fast even without a shieldwatch.

"Shieldwatch users," the man scoffed. "So predictable."

Terra attacked again. This time she tried to strike under his chin while Speeding her movements. When she drew close to attack, he tripped her with a simple leg sweep which she had failed to notice on her approach.

"You need to work on your offense," he said, circling Terra.

Terra coughed as she pushed herself up to face the attacker.

"Shieldwatch power critically low," came Minerva's voice from her shieldwatch.

"Shutting down non-essential functions," Terra said along with Minerva.

"It's just as well," the masked man said. "You wouldn't have gotten far if you ran."

Terra glared at the masked man. She didn't want to admit it, but he was toying with her.

"Well I believe that is enough," he said as his stance changed from defensive to offensive.

Terra barely had time to blink. The man attacked with incredible speed for someone without a shieldwatch. He struck her in the stomach, throat, and sides before putting her in a hold. He pressed part of his forearm and bicep against Terra's throat, cutting off the blood flow to her head. Terra's struggle lasted seconds before darkness took her.

CHAPTER XX
ESCAPE

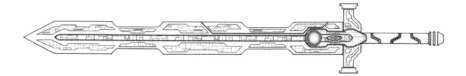

Each tiro has a special test made just for them. This test is designed to exploit their weaknesses both mental and physical. We have to know if they will break here. If they break, they are worthless to us. If they don't, they will have taken their first real step towards joining the Aeon Legion. There is no extreme I will not risk. After all, would our enemies hold back should we find ourselves at their mercy?
  -From the personal logs of Praetor Lycus Cerberus

Terra awoke to darkness and struggled to breathe. She realized that there was a bag over her head and found her hands and feet tied. Terra forced herself calm so she wouldn't suffocate. Before she could focus, she heard muffled footsteps followed by a hard kick to her side.

Terra gasped and convulsed as someone struck her over and over. She almost passed out, but they stopped and began dragging her. Several moments passed before they halted and undid her bonds. She was then restrained to a chair.

Someone ripped the bag from Terra's head and she gasped. The bright room forced her eyes shut as her limp head flopped forward.

Someone grabbed her hair. He forced open her eyelid, shining a small light in one of her eyes before shifting to the other.

"She's fine. The shock should wear off soon and we can begin," he said behind the strange smooth mask that obscured all his features save for his eyes. The design was different from the soldiers who had tracked her earlier. He and the other soldier left the room.

Alone, Terra studied her surroundings. She quickly became aware of the cold bite of metal restraints around her ankles and wrists that bound her to a chair in the center of the room. The well lit, concrete room had a steel table and two other metal seats. Terra's eyes widened and her heart pounded when she saw the large array of sharp torture tools laid out on the table. Her shieldwatch lay out of reach on the table, but they had not taken her sonic cipher translators out of her ears.

Outside the room, someone screamed. The screaming continued for several minutes only pausing for muffled conversation. Terra could just make out the sobbing and begging. Sounds of torture made Terra's heart pound and she sweated even as she shivered. Seconds drew out as her heart jumped each time someone walked by the door. Then the screaming ended with a gurgling noise followed by silence.

Terra let out a long breath and collected herself. They had discussed this. Shani had given detailed instructions on how to resist interrogations and Nikias had them practice escaping bonds.

Terra tested the bindings. They gave a quiet, metallic clink when she moved. She stopped as voices and footsteps neared the door.

A guard walked in. "This one here, Doctor," he said.

The guard was followed by another man who wore a blood stained doctor's smock and a smooth mask. A skull emblem was painted on his mask. "I thought the Legion picked tough recruits. This seems a weak batch. That last one died quickly. I didn't even have time to ask a question."

Another soldier entered the room. Terra recognized him upon seeing the wing emblem on his mask. The guard saluted him.

"Ah, Captain," the Doctor said. "I was just about to begin."

"We shouldn't torture this one," the Captain said in a blunt tone.

"Oh?" the Doctor asked. "Are you becoming altruistic now, Captain? We need access to Saturn City now if our plan is to work or have you forgotten what they did to your family, Captain? Have you forgotten what they did to our world?"

The Captain spoke in a low tone. "I will never forget. But I have read her psych profile. She won't break. I think I can convince her to gi–"

"I have jurisdiction here, Captain," the Doctor interrupted, his tone even. "The prisoners are mine to do with as I please while you handle the military affairs of our operation. That was our agreement. You are a man of honor, so honor it. We both want the same thing after all."

The Captain stared at the Doctor for a long moment. "Sometimes I wonder. Very well, but keep a close eye on this one. She is tougher than she appears."

The Doctor chuckled from behind his mask. "Let's hope so. I hate it when they don't last."

As the Doctor selected his first tool, Terra hoped for a last minute rescue. Maybe Alya would burst in at the last moment, or Zaid would lead a daring raid on the prison. At this point she would be overjoyed to see Vand. No rescue came, much like the questions that the torturer was suppose to ask.

∞

Terra found question-less interrogations easy to resist. This bitter thought was of little comfort when they slung the bag over her head and dumped her back into a cell before kicking her again for good measure.

She lost track of time again as the seconds drew out. The slightest sound made Terra's heart jump. A jolt of panic hit her again when someone entered her cell and grabbed her. They dragged her a ways before taking the bag off her head. Much to her surprise, she now stood outdoors. Her captors released her bonds and ordered her to walk into an enclosed yard. Then they took her ciphers. When Terra looked around she understood.

Watchtowers encircled an open yard while three layers of razor wire fences stood at the perimeter. Several dark clad guards stood, unconcerned, just beyond the fences. However, the other prisoners caught Terra's gaze. She recognized several tirones, but felt relieved to see her own team absent.

All stood silent without the means to understand one another. Terra doubted anyone understood English so she instead walked along the edge of the fence, looking for any weak point. She was about to make a second lap when two tirones grabbed her and dragged her behind a small wall just outside the guards' view. One held a sharpened utensil at Terra's throat. The other put a finger over her lips to signal Terra to remain quiet. Several others joined them.

The other tirones all had sunken eyes and bodies slender from malnourishment. Numerous cuts and bruises marred their faces. They talked amongst themselves in various languages. Often one would turn to Terra and say something she didn't understand. Finally, someone Terra recognized stepped out. He wore a US cavalry coat over his training uniform.

Terra tried to remember his name. John?

He turned to Terra. "Do you speak English or Apache?"

"English," Terra said, still standing tense with the makeshift knife at her throat.

"Okay. I need you to listen to my question and answer very carefully," John said in a slow southern accent. "Who was your primary instructor at the Academy?"

Terra spoke in a slow deliberate tone. "Centurion Nikias."

The others turned to each other speaking the name Nikias. A few of them nodded. It was then Terra understood. They were translating to each other. Finally they let go of the knife and released Terra.

A man Terra recognized as a Native American spoke to John. John then turned to Terra. "Right. Sorry about that, Miss."

Terra rubbed her neck. "What was that about?"

John shrugged. "We had to make sure you weren't another snake. They have used spies more than once."

Terra's brow knitted. "Spies?"

John sighed. "Messed up our first escape attempt. Whose team you from?"

"Zaid's. I acted as a decoy. They were trying to contact Saturn City to get help."

John glanced up to make sure no guards were watching them. "Did they succeed?"

A gunship landed nearby. All the prisoners gathered to watch. Terra forced back despair when she saw them drag Zaid, along with most of his team, off the transport. Hikari was still missing though.

John shook his head. "Guess not."

The next day was much the same. Beatings, torture and then a brief respite in the courtyard. Still no questions though. Now she was hungry, tired and her entire body screamed in pain but she still looked forward to at least being able to talk with Zaid and the others. Maybe they could come up with a way to escape. As with her, Zaid and the rest of his team got shoved out into the yard that evening with the others.

With Terra's prompt intervention, they avoided getting their throats slit like almost happened to her. Thankfully someone spoke Arabic and could speak with Zaid. Terra asked Zaid where Hikari was. John relayed the question to an Apache who relayed it to several others. After a moment the answer came back.

John turned to Terra. "He says Hikari escaped."

"Good," Terra said, more to herself.

Another gunship landed and the tirones gathered to see the newcomer.

Terra and Zaid frowned when they saw Hikari. One soldier who dragged Hikari still smoldered while the rest had disheveled uniforms as though they had endured an awful beating during Hikari's capture.

Terra stood for a long moment. No one was going to help her. No one was going to save her. They were on their own now.

Zaid nodded to Terra and pointed at the ground. He had drawn out the courtyard in the dirt and motioned for the others to join him. Terra understood Zaid's hand signals. He had made his entire team learn them. They didn't need a sonic cipher to communicate and they had no more reason to wait for a rescue.

A few days felt like several lifetimes to Terra as she reflected while still tied to the chair. The torture continued everyday with some worse than others. She also learned the true meaning hunger, hunger that was painful. It would have been unbearable if it wasn't for all the other pains in her body that gave her perspective. And the fear. The fear was always present. The only thing that kept it in check was Terra's cold hatred of the monsters who tortured her.

She tried to remember her warm little quarry back home. She had a home right? Those memories offered no comfort nor did they add to her torments. They just seemed surreal. Or was this place surreal? Maybe it was the lack of sleep. Terra hated going to sleep. Sleep always ended with a hard kick awake.

Terra struggled to focus. The only times her mind felt sharp was in the yard with the other prisoners where they planned and plotted.

Plans had changed several times. Most broke under torture, including most of Zaid's team, and were never seen again. Now only Zaid, Hikari, and Terra herself remained along with a handful of other tirones from different teams. Despite the desperate situation, small things gave Terra hope.

One day the guards forgot to put the bag over Terra's head when another escape attempt distracted them. When they dragged Terra though the hallways she mentally noted every corridor she saw and relayed the information to the others. Over time they drew a map of the facility.

Other tirones noticed similar slips. One overheard talk of rising tensions in the camp between two rival factions. The pieces gradually fell together and the team leaders agreed on a plan. All they needed now was opportunity. This hope kept Terra going. Well that, and her Torturer's irritation.

The Doctor growled as he slung a blade across the room. "This stupid girl and her absurdly high tolerance for pain."

Terra clenched her jaw and remained unflinching. She didn't want to give the doctor the pleasure of seeing her in pain if she could help it.

The doctor balled his fists. "I have never seen anyone so stubborn! Just a scream? A moan! Even a twitch!"

Terra continued to stare at the wall. She had made of point of not reacting, speaking, or even moving during her torture.

After a moment of pacing, the doctor picked up a new tool and turned to Terra. "Well I guess I better try something new. Um. I was supposed to ask you something wasn't I? Oh well. I'm sure I will remember when we get started again."

The doctor finished sterilizing his new tool when the Captain walked in with two other soldiers.

"Captain," the doctor said. "I was just about to get started again."

The Captain spoke, hatred bleeding through the mechanical distortion of his voice. "You disgust me. I should have done this a long time ago. Execute him immediately."

The other soldiers grabbed the doctor and dragged him outside the room as he struggled.

The doctor screamed. "No. Stop! I order you to st—"

A loud blast and a flash of light silenced him just out of Terra's sight.

The Captain turned to the other soldier in the room. "Purge the doctor's loyalists. I will finish this interrogation myself."

The soldier saluted and closed the door behind him, leaving Terra alone with the Captain.

The Captain grabbed a towel and dabbed Terra's face, cleaning a spot of the blood and dirt. He offered her a drink of water from a canteen.

Terra stared off into nothing.

"It's not poisoned," the Captain said. "If we wanted you poisoned we could have done so."

Terra took a sip which eased her burning throat.

"You did well. I couldn't have asked for more from my own men," the Captain said in a kind tone, though Terra found the mechanical buzz off -putting. "I apologize about our methods. When one pursues revenge for as long as we have, it's easy to find oneself becoming the villain without realizing it."

Terra continued to stare at the Captain's armor. She avoided looking at his eyes. They were the only visible part of his face.

"I should be honest with you. We need the shieldwatch to enter Saturn City. We will use it to invade the city, free our comrades in Tartarus and assassinate war criminals in the Aeon Legion."

Terra shifted her gaze to the Captain.

"I thought that would get your attention. The Saturnians recruit those lost to history to fight their wars for them. This also keeps recruits ignorant of their many atrocities. They saved your life didn't they? That's how they work. They give you a second chance at life to ensure complete loyalty. Then they seduce you. Fight for them and they let you live in their hedonistic utopia while we Kalians stand as only a memory, an echo of our former glory."

After a moment, Terra remembered one of Shani's lectures. The Aeon Legion had fought with a people called the Kalians. It didn't make sense though. The First Temporal War happened centuries ago. Wouldn't they all be dead by now?

"They taught you about the Kalian War? We are all that is left of the Kalian military. A few hundred of what was once twenty million soldiers. All with just enough singularity tech to keep us alive," the Captain said as he pulled up a chair with it's back facing Terra. The Captain sat backwards on it with his arms resting on the top. "Let me tell you a story and when it's done you will give us the code for your shieldwatch. I know you will because you are like me. You have a sense of justice."

Terra tried not to make eye contact again though she wasn't sure what to do any longer. The manual didn't tell her how to resist this.

"I won't lie to you. Starting that war was a terrible mistake. In our arrogance, we thought if we bombed the city they would capitulate.

Instead they formed the Aeon Legion and began a bloody march to destroy us. You cannot understand how terrifying it is to see one legionnaire slaughter thousands of your comrades. We couldn't match their technological edge. We lost that war and paid for our sins. Now it's time for them to pay for theirs."

The Captain shifted in his chair and pulled out a photo. He stared at it. "I had a family I fought for. Ironic that the war claimed them and not me. Someone you know killed them. One of the Legendary Blades, Cerberus though you know him as Praetor Lycus Cerberus."

Terra's gaze snapped to the Captain, but shivered when she saw his cold, hate filled glare.

"I thought you would recognize him," he said in a cold tone. "Lycus is one of the worst war criminals in the Legion. His blade, Cerberus, spilled a river's worth of blood and none of it was enough to satisfy him. He butchered thousands of soldiers, even those who tried to surrender. The death of my family at his hands was merely one of his many crimes. There were others. Orion cultivated his own garden of corpses. He would wade through any amount of blood and death for his precious city. Many others such as Pythia and Deucalion would go on to the claim the title of Time King or Queen and commit further atrocities, ruling time like mad emperors. They made the worst tyrants in history seem noble in comparison. Another monster is Silverwind."

"What? No," Terra said before she caught herself.

"Oh yes," the Captain said, leaning closer. "Alya Silverwind. There isn't a Kalian alive who doesn't still curse that name, though we had different names for her like Bloodstorm. She killed more soldiers than most of the other war criminals put together. She was completely lost in darkness. Consumed by revenge."

Terra stared at the Captain while questions boiled in her mind. She knew to avoid getting drawn into conversation or risk giving away information.

The Captain leaned back for a moment, as if expecting Terra to ask about Alya. Terra averted her gaze.

The Captain relaxed and continued. "The worst injustice I saved for last. Lycus butchered thousands in his blood lust. He killed my family and many others who couldn't even fight back. After all that death and destruction, he finally came to realize what a monster he was. He confessed his crimes and once the Legion discovered all he had done, do you know what they did to him?"

Terra looked up again as the Captain leaned in closer, his mask almost touching her face.

"They called him a hero," the Captain said in a soft but venomous tone before leaning back. "All I seek is justice. I don't care about who rules Time. I don't care about nations or politics. All I want is for a few evil men to be brought to justice and you have the key. You can end this. You can end all the suffering and let my family rest in peace. I ask for one little thing, the code to let us into the city. Your shieldwatch has it. All that is needed is for you to access it. A simple press of a button can end my centuries old quest for justice."

Terra met his eyes. There was sincerity to them and sadness. He was an empty vessel that centuries of rage had hollowed out. Part of her wanted to help him, to bring peace to his family, but she couldn't help ghosts. Killing Lycus would not bring this man's family back. She looked away and remained silent.

"I will give you a little time to think about it," he said as he stood. He made his way to the door, but paused when he touched the handle while keeping his back to Terra. "You know, sometimes I wonder if the worst thing I could do to Lycus is just let him live on as he is. If he truly knows what a monster he is, then perhaps such a burden would be more terrible than death."

The Captain turned the handle and exited the room, leaving Terra alone.

The moment his footsteps faded, Terra began struggling against her bonds. Any bond can be loosened with enough time or at least that is what her instructors had told her. She had worked on loosening them since her first day here in the rare moments when they left her unattended. One hand slipped out of a loosened cuff and she pulled a small rock she had taken from the evening walks. She smashed the rest of her bonds with it. Terra then stood and grabbed her shieldwatch off the table just as weapons fire echoed through the hallways.

Terra moved fast. The others would likely make their escape attempt now. All they needed for their plan was a distraction or opportunity. Their enemies' descent into civil war seemed like both and the others would hear the gunfire before coming to the same conclusion. Now that she was free, she had a job to do.

Terra moved through the hallways, avoiding areas with shouting or the sound of fighting. She found her target near her interrogation room, a large series of antenna that constituted the facility's communication hub. The antennae proved delicate and Terra felt a strange pleasure in smashing it into a twisted jumble. She then made her way to the rendezvous point.

On her way, Terra encountered another escapee. Terra sighed when she saw it was Hikari.

Hikari pointed to a window. Terra looked to see the enemy's gunships burning in the distance.

After a moment they joined the others. Zaid tossed Hikari her aeon edge and a pair of sonic ciphers. John gave Terra hers back as well.

Once everyone equipped their gear, they understood one another again. Terra thought she had taken these small sonic ciphers for granted.

Zaid looked at Hikari. "I assume the explosion I heard a moment ago–"

"Our enemy's flying machines," Hikari said while loading a clip into her aeon edge. "Which are not fireproof."

John turned to Zaid. "Assuming our enemy's message system is damaged, that leaves the key to the lower level."

Zaid shook his head. "I can only pray to Allah that the Frankish knight succeeds."

Terra turned to Zaid. "Frankish knight?"

Zaid sighed. "I don't like the Franks but the other team leaders assured me he was quite skilled. His name was Roland I think."

Terra's eyes widened. Roland? She felt a surge of panic. Roland would sell them out.

"There they are," Roland said, pointing to the group of escaping tirones.

Terra turned to see Roland standing with an enemy soldier.

The soldier turned to Roland. "You were right. Thank you for your cooperation."

Zaid scowled and the others drew their aeon edges.

The soldier shouldered his rifle and took a step forward.

Once the soldier's turned his back to Roland, Roland jumped behind the soldier and grabbed the energy gun before tossing it aside and placing the soldier in a hold.

Terra stared at Roland with wide eyes.

Roland turned to the others. "You said bring a key. The keys here are a machine that recognizes voices. This was easier than dragging him all the way here through force."

Terra stared at Roland, her brow raised. "Why didn't you betray us? Wouldn't it be easier to switch sides and help them?"

Roland shrugged. "They can't give me immortality. Besides, I won't work with torturers."

The captured soldier gave in easily to threats. He opened several blast doors, clearing the way to a small area below the facility. Now they ran alongside a shallow river away from the facility. It wasn't long before they heard the shouts of pursuers.

Shots hit around them as the tirones returned fire with stolen weapons. They still couldn't move fast and everyone's shieldwatch had not yet recharged. They kept running. A forest was ahead. If they could run to that, they could hide long enough to recharge their shieldwatches and then time travel back to Saturn City for help.

An explosion hit near them, throwing several to the ground. One didn't get back up. The others didn't notice. No one was going to help him.

Terra gritted her teeth. Once again, no one did the right thing. She ran over to the tiro who lay face down in the mud. Terra rolled him over. She then paused when she saw who it was. Roland.

Terra glanced up again. Several soldiers closed in on her position. She glanced back to Roland.

I could just leave him, Terra thought. *He deserves it, having cheated his way past everything. He has everyone fooled but me. I should leave him.* Then Terra thought about how horrible the past few days were. No. She wouldn't wish that fate on anyone, even Roland.

Roland stirred. Terra leaned down and after struggling, lifted him up. She ran, trailing behind the others and after a moment another tiro fell back to help Terra and Roland. They were close now, so close. Terra allowed herself a single fleeting hope, a hope that was crushed by a figure she saw ahead.

Terra turned pale when she saw him again even though the others stood confident against a single foe without a shieldwatch. Terra knew better. She knew the Captain could beat a shieldwatch user.

Hikari approached the Captain. "Out of the way."

"Wait!" Terra yelled.

Hikari halted.

Terra shook her head. "He can beat a shieldwatch user. Don't underestimate him."

Hikari paused and stared at Terra with a doubtful expression. After a moment though she allowed the others to surround the Captain.

It would have been a good tactic if the Captain had held still. Without a shieldwatch, or even a weapon, the Captain waded into the tirones, slinging them around like they were toy soldiers. Panic spread when the Captain disabled Hikari's shieldwatch before breaking her arm.

Zaid forced himself to stand. "What kind of monster is he?"

Terra handed Roland to another tiro before turning to Zaid. "Run. Take everyone and run! I'll buy us time."

Zaid scowled, taking a step towards Terra.

Terra grabbed an aeon edge left on the ground by a fallen tiro before turning to Zaid. "We can't escape unless someone stays behind to stall him."

Zaid paused, then nodded.

The other tirones began to recover the fallen and retreat.

Terra's fight with the Captain stalled him only seconds, but it was enough for the others to get a lead on him.

The Captain kicked Terra to the ground. "It appears the others were willing to sacrifice you. Are you ready to die then?"

Terra groaned as the Captain lifted her by the neck. "Well... not... really..." she said between gasps.

The Captain threw her to the ground. "Do they really mean that much to you?"

Terra coughed, but forced herself to stand. "No one is going to save me, but at least I get to save someone else."

The Captain nodded. "Very well. You have earned your freedom."

Terra stared at the Captain confused. Then the salient wall dissipated. After Terra's eyes adjusted, she had a hard time believing where they were. She looked up to see the titanic hands of Saturn City, looming overhead.

The rest of the tirones stared, confused as well, before Terra and the Captain joined them.

The Captain took of his mask. "We will divvy up points later tonight," Lycus said, putting the Captain's mask under his arm. "Well done. It has been a while since a group performed so well."

Zaid stared, wide eyed at Lycus. "You tortured us!"

Terra noticed the 'Doctor' that the Captain had order killed was standing nearby chatting with Centurion Nikias. He nodded accepting something from Nikias, likely his payment, and quickly exited.

Lycus didn't even spare Zaid a glance. "Yes, we did. If any of you had given away information, you would have been dusted." Lycus then turned to address the tirones. "Those who captured you were Kavachain military regulars. The Kavachains are descended from the Kalians and they are our allies now. They train their soldiers by capturing tirones for this test. After your capture, we transferred you back to Saturn City for the next part of the test. All the soldiers who took part of the interrogations were Academy staff and instructors. Everything was planned and controlled. Your performance will be evaluated and reviewed tonight. By morning, the scores will be posted on the holoface in the central courtyard. Congratulations on making it this far. Now that we know you are worth our time, we will push you twice as hard."

After a moment Terra collected herself. She then turned to Lycus. "Praetor? Could they have really gotten into the city using the shield-watch?"

Lycus shook his head. "No. The Sybil would have precogged it and the Legion would have intercepted them."

Terra thought for a moment. "What if they used a salient? I traveled using a salient to get into the city."

"It leads to the timeport where security is heavy."

"But what about the salients in the Academy?"

"They are modified to only pull time into it. To alter one of the Academy's salients to become a two way portal would require the skills of a mechanical genius."

Chapter XXI
Tartarus

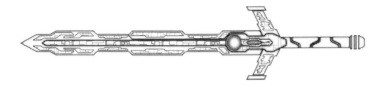

Him do I hate even as the gates of hell who says one thing while he hides another in his heart.
-From Homer's *The Iliad*, translation by Samuel Butler

Hanns shut the case over the wires and stood, wiping the grime off his hands with a rag. "It should be repaired now."

The silver haired man activated the holographic projector. It displayed a 3D map of Tartarus, Saturn City's prison facility.

"Good job, Hanns," Karim said. He wore the standard armor of the Aeon Legion, but the infinity emblem was not present on his uniform and instead displayed a shield icon. Karim was an ex-legionnaire, though he had been unwilling to discuss the details with Hanns.

Hanns thought Karim a decent enough fellow, though he still did not understand the silver hair thing. Most of the other guards had one or two locks of silver hair while a few had none. The prisoners all kept their natural hair color. Karim had explained to Hanns that most of the guards were dust outs of the Aeon Legion training program. Many had taken jobs as prison guards to remain in the city. The city natives considered such tasks beneath them.

Hanns smiled and turned to Karim. "That should fix it. I still don't understand why you do not just use your time machines to restore it?"

Karim shook his head. "This is singularity tech, Hanns. You can't Restore it with a temporal state."

Hanns looked at the holographic projection. "So what does this device do then?"

Karim gestured to the holo map. "This is Legacy Library recovered tech. This map can scan and project all data within Tartarus. We can keep track of every prisoner here and even see what they are carrying with them. We can even see the fillings in your teeth."

Hanns looked at the lower part of the 3D map that displayed scrambled static. The other levels of Tartarus appeared in perfect detail. Hanns pointed. "What about that part?"

Karim frowned. "That is level twelve. There is singularity tech down there that scrambles sensors. Only Prometheus ever goes there, and he hasn't visited it in centuries."

Hanns turned to Karim. "What do you think is down there?"

Karim rolled his eyes. "Some people say treasure, but what crashing idiot puts treasure in a prison full of thieves? Who knows what's down there. Probably stuff too horrible to kill so they lock it down there and throw away the key. Considering the nasty things we have on level ten and eleven, I would hate to imagine what's in twelve. It's why we have an emergency ejection system."

Hanns raised an eyebrow. "Emergency ejection system?"

"Yeah," Karim said, gesturing to the map. "We can eject the entire sector from Saturn City in the event of a containment breach or escape attempt. With the nasty things we keep on the lower levels, it's better to jettison the whole thing than risk contamination of the city."

Hanns looked back to the map. He had been on level ten once to help repair some singularity technology that held in place the things imprisoned there. Each had a number and containment procedure. All of them on level ten were particularly nasty. Hanns himself was a level three prisoner, a level reserved for temporal criminals with sentences less than a lifetime. Most level three prisoners had a high chance of parole for good behavior.

Karim smiled. "Regardless, thanks for the help, Hanns. I'll put in a good word with Warden Shamira. With any luck, we can have your sentence reduced to ten years. Crashing End. At the rate you're going, I may have to give you a job."

Hanns returned a smile. "It's no trouble at all, Karim. I enjoy working with this wonderful technology. I like to put my talent to use."

"I don't know how you do it. I have never seen anyone so naturally skilled with singularity tech. It's kind of scary actually. I am glad you are so good-natured."

Hanns continued to smile. He was happy to find a place where his charm worked. It had allowed him to gather a lot of intelligence. In fact he had discovered nearly all he was after, but now he needed three things. One was a way to transport all the knowledge in the Archives back with him to Germany. The second was a way to get to the Academy from here. Finally he needed to discover just how the Legion detected his attempts to change time and counter it.

∞

Hanns joined Emmerich who leaned on the pearl colored walls that surrounded the prison yard. Other prisoners strolled the yard. None had a standard prison uniform. Tartarus made everyone keep their old clothes for easy identification. Hanns had decided for both him and Emmerich to discard their arm bands. People seemed to dislike it and Hanns found it easier to make friends without the arm band. Now both he and Emmerich wore field uniforms and the cuff devices attached to their wrists and ankles which all prisoners had.

Those devices looked like a smaller shieldwatch though the design was closer to a wrist watch with a glass orb at the face. Hans had seen these devices attached to the matching pair on the other wrist or ankle like handcuffs. The guards used these when prisoners stepped out of line.

He and the other prisoners also had a small pair of devices that fit in their ears called a sonic cipher. This sonic cipher acted as a translator. Hanns hoped he would be able to take samples of all these devices back with him to Germany when he escaped.

Emmerich glowered at Hanns as usual.

Hanns smiled. "Afternoon, Emmerich."

"Shut up, Hanns. Why are you so happy to be here?"

"I keep telling you, Emmerich. I am where I want to be right now."

"That's good for you, but why did you have to drag me down with you?"

"I tried to talk you out of it, Emmerich. I warned you not to underestimate Silverwind."

"Well if you are so smart, then why are you in here with me?"

Hanns sighed. "I told you already. This is *exactly* where I want to be."

Emmerich opened his mouth to protest when a large holoface appeared in the center of the prison yard. All the prisoners turned to watch. Hanns and Emmerich joined the growing crowd.

"Attention all level three through six prisoners," came a loud voice from the speakers. "The Labyrinth will be opened again within a few months. The Aeon Legion is asking for volunteers to help with its preparation and implementation. If you are interested, please notify Tartarus administration. Those who participate may receive a reduction in sentence. End of announcement."

Hanns's eyes narrowed. "Labyrinth?"

"It's a training course for the Aeon Legion," came a woman's voice from behind Hanns.

Hanns turned to see a woman in her mid thirties. She wore a desert camouflaged field uniform though she had no insignia or badges. Like the other prisoners a pair of shieldwatch like devices were attached to her wrists and ankles. He guessed she was from a paramilitary unit given her more casual stance. "Training course?"

Emmerich scowled after seeing the woman's face. He walked off without a word.

"Yes," she said, folding her arms. "It's a final exam for the Aeon Legion. Basically a death trap. They have prisoners from Tartarus fill it with all kinds of nasty stuff. Monsters, traps, psychotic killers, that kind of thing. They also give prisoners the option to fight the recruits."

"They let the prisoners attack Legion recruits? Wouldn't they lose a lot of recruits that way?"

"A lot of the first year prisoners jump at the opportunity. They think it's a good chance for revenge. Those recruits though? Bunch of hardened commandos. I don't know what they go through before that, but they are untouchable. I just watched my first year. Glad I did. Those recruits are like the Sayeret Matkal."

"Interesting," Hanns said in a genuine tone. He would have to ask what this Sayeret Matkal was, but he had more important questions first. "Where is the Labyrinth? I didn't see it when they brought me into Tartarus."

"It's in another zone. Under that Academy where the Aeon Legion trains its recruits."

Hanns nodded. "Ah. That would make sense. I take it security is heavy there?"

"Not really. Most of the prisoners they pick are the ones who have a good chance at parole or are at the end of their sentences. Most wouldn't risk escape. Even the dangerous ones have nowhere to escape to."

Hanns curled a finger to his chin. His plan was coming together. Two details remained. "Thank you. What's your name?"

"Chava," she said.

"Ah," Hanns said, now realizing why Emmerich disliked her so much. He could see it now in her facial features. "Well thank you very much, Chava. You seem like a nice lady. Why are you here?"

"Attempted murder," Chava said, her tone impassive. "I was part of a military unit trying to finish up what the Forgotten Guns started. There were certain... individuals we were trying track down."

"Who?" Hanns asked.

Chava tilted her head. "So what are you two here for?"

Hanns grinned. "Two counts of attempting to remove unauthorized class two objects from time, one count of attempting to alter history, unregistered time travel, and willful disregard for the Temporal Accords."

Chava rolled her eyes. "That would be more impressive if I were new to time travel. What are you really here for?"

"I tried to borrow a book."

"History book right?"

Hanns sighed. "I didn't think they would notice such a small thing."

"They tracked you using the Sybil."

"The ones that have the strange headpieces covering their eyes?"

"They are like an oracle or prophet. They can see changes in time. If someone tries to alter time, they see it and tell the Aeon Legion. They can't track you as well in the Edge though. A lot of illegal time travelers try to operate solely in the Edge. Most of the Edge is well patrolled by the Aeon Legion's timeship fleet though so others operate in the Bleak. Something about the End of Time blinds them."

Hanns remained quiet for a moment, trying to process this new information. He had seen a Sybil at his trial. One option for his defense was to submit to a Sybil reading. They explained that a Sybil could pour through memories to prove guilt or innocence. He had almost thought about trying it, not because it would have proved him innocent, but he wanted to see how it worked. He had decided it was too risky. It might reveal his real plan. Instead he used a plea bargain. "That makes sense. They never moved against me until I started to alter things."

Chava tapped her finger on her arm. "So what time are you from? I thought I might have recognized that uniform of yours."

"Me?" Hanns said. "I am from the year 1940."

Chava nodded to Emmerich who stood nearby. "And your friend. Is his name Emmerich Klein?"

Hanns brow knitted. "Um. Yes actually."

Chava's fingernails dug into her arm. "From the SS right? He ran a camp?"

Hanns nodded. "SS yes. I don't think he runs a camp though. You know your German history. What time are you from?"

Chava walked away.

Hanns frowned, wondering if he had said something to offend her?

Emmerich approached Hanns. "Monstrous Jew," he spat after Chava was out of earshot.

Hanns turned to Emmerich. "Now Emmerich, you need to get better at making friends."

Emmerich turned to Hanns. "She's Jewish."

Hanns sighed. He never understood why so many of his fellow countrymen hated the Jews. Hanns didn't care for Jewish culture but hate them? A waste of energy. "Emmerich. We have more important things to concern ourselves with. Besides she didn't seem so bad to–"

Hanns fell backwards as Chava wrapped a chain around his throat. She tripped Emmerich and pinned him to the ground with her foot before turning back to Hanns and tightening the chain around his neck.

Hanns gasped for air while pulling at the chain.

"I will enjoy this you monsters!" Chava said before clinching her teeth and pulling harder. "First you, then Emmerich. Emmerich I'll kill slowly after he watches you die!"

Hanns almost passed out before the chain fell away when Karim tackled Chava. Another guard helped Hanns and Emmerich. Chava struggled against him until he touched his shieldwatch's holoface. The glass orbs of the devices at her wrists and ankles glowed before they moved to meet each other. The devices snapped her wrists and ankles together as though bound by cuffs.

"Nazi bastards!" Chava screamed while she struggled against the guards who picked her up to move her into isolation. "Monsters! I'll kill you! I hope the Forgotten Guns put a bullet in Hitler's skull! We will never stop hunting you! I'll hunt you just like you did to my family!"

Karim rubbed his forehead as they dragged Chava away. "We can't possibly keep track of every group that hates each other! Thank Aion the Sybil precogged this. You okay Hanns?"

Hanns nodded. "What was that about? She seemed so nice at first."

Karim looked back to Chava. "She is from your continuum's future, part of Israel's time travel project before it went rogue. They tried to use a time machine to assassinate several war criminals and dictators in your continuum."

Hanns frowned as he thought. War criminals? He wasn't a war criminal. Still it worried him. He couldn't imagine what he or Emmerich did that warranted that kind of hatred.

Hanns was finally alone. They had let him go off on his own to help fix singularity devices on level three. He used the opportunity to contact his base. It was time he updated them. He stepped into a darkened corridor and took out the peppercorn sized time travel device he had attached to the back of his teeth. The one they had not found in their search of his belongings. The one they had mistaken for a simple filling. It glowed when he pressed the sides.

"Hello?" came Lenz's voice over the small device. It didn't use a speaker, but carried sound waves across time.

"What is the key to victory?" Hanns asked.

There was a pause. "Objectivity."

Hanns smiled at his own codeword. Lenz was alone. "I have an update for you."

"Thank God," Lenz said. "We wondered if they had executed you and Emmerich."

"I have my target now and a way to escape. I will send you specifics soon. I need you to get the boarding party ready for next month. Detailed instructions on their objectives will soon follow."

"Understood," Lenz said before hesitating. "Are you sure about the weapons?"

"The weapons are the thing I am most sure about. These Aeon Legion soldiers are arrogant. They haven't faced a challenge from a foe like us in some time. My guess is they will adapt quickly, but by that point we will be gone with our objective. How are things on your end?"

"Several SS officers are now fighting over control of the project along with both the Heer and Luftwaffe. In fact, this is good because no one is in command at the moment."

Hanns nodded. "That's good. What about the war?"

"The war is still in our favor. Right now we are preparing an air campaign against England. Only a fool could lose the war for us right now."

Hanns hesitated for a moment. "Good work, Lenz. I will talk to you again soon."

"Yes sir," Lenz replied.

Hanns pressed the device again. It went dark. He put it back in his mouth before turning. A figure stood in front of him obscured in shadow. Hanns started as he reflexively reached for a pistol he didn't have.

The figure stepped out of the shadows and faced Hanns. He was a blond youth in his early twenties about Hanns's height and slender in build with olive skin. A white mask covered the top of his forehead to his nose. He wore tight fitting clothing that changed colors to match the surroundings. Hanns's gaze shifted to a pair of aeon edged daggers that hung on the youth's belt.

"My Master wishes to speak with you," the youth said in a formal tone.

Hanns expression remained wary while the youth extended his arm forward and touched his shieldwatch's holoface. The youth's holoface was a dull gray color rather than the usual blue. A holographic projection of another figure, tinted in grainy gray, sat on a throne. The projection faded just below the man's face though Hanns could see a shieldwatch on his left hand. Once the projection was before Hanns, the youth stepped back into the shadows.

"Greetings, Hanns Speer," the man said from his throne. The projection slightly distorted his voice. "I would properly introduce myself but I am afraid I must remain anonymous for now."

Hanns's eyes narrowed before clasping his hands behind his back and facing the projection. "You have me at a disadvantage. Are you working with the warden?"

The man chuckled. "Certainly not. I am not so lowly as to be affiliated with the city government or the Aeon Legion. I serve no master. I just happen to have a singularity artifact that can detect cross time transmissions such as the one you just made. I also have access to the warden's records and notes, many of which keep mentioning a model prisoner who is helping them with their own singularity artifacts. Interesting that their model prisoner is plotting something."

Hanns lifted his chin. "You want something."

"We all want something, Hanns. What separates us from the rest of the stagnant hedonists and fools is just the scale of our desires. I don't know what you are after, but it must be something impressive, considering the lengths you are going to. I find ambition a noble quality. You must have a lofty goal if you have come this far to infiltrate the city. Well I have ambition too, but what you and I need is opportunity."

The man on the throne gestured to the masked youth. He stepped forward, drawing an item from a back pocket and presenting it to Hanns.

Hanns stared at the item with suspicion. "What is it?"

The man on the throne gestured to the item. "A final key to your plan, Hanns."

The youth removed the covering to reveal a shieldwatch.

Hanns's eyes narrowed on the item as he took it with reluctance. He did not wish to take a Trojan horse himself. "One of the time devices?"

The man on the throne smiled. "Yes. It's linked to my singularity AI and it can remotely override Minerva's control of Tartarus for a short time. Don't worry. It's shielded. The prison's sensors can't detect it so long as you hide it from the eyes of the guards. It also contains a vast hard drive for data storage in case you need to take any information from the city."

Hanns looked at the man on the throne, confused. "You wish to take control of Tartarus?"

"Oh Aion no. I wish to take something from it, but I need it separated from Saturn City first and you need to evade the Sybil's precognition."

Hanns frowned while remaining thoughtful. The Sybil were a problem. He had learned a little about them, but that was another hole in his plan. He pointed to the masked youth. "Then why not send your assistant here? He seems skilled at breaking in."

"Oh he is skilled," the man said, knitting his hands together under his chin. "But the eleventh level is far too secure for him to break into and recover what is rightfully mine. And if the guards have proper warning then reinforcements from the Legion would prevent him from escaping. You though have access to nearly any level now thanks to your efforts to charm the prison staff. Now I see an opportunity for both of us and we can succeed if we work together."

CHAPTER XXII
CHALLENGES

With the Survival Test over we once again shift priorities. Strike team leaders must now rebuild their teams after so many tirones dusted. We take this opportunity to force teams to accept members that would unbalance their dynamic. Potential candidates include clashing personalities or others who were enemies in their home times; Saracens and Crusaders, Spartans and Persians, Romans and Gauls. In the second week we allow team leaders to trade in order to test their resourcefulness. Now we test their dedication by salting old wounds. All must put aside feuds from their pasts and work together. Each must be an Aeon Legionnaire first.
-From the personal logs of Praetor Lycus Cerberus

Terra fell off the horse again.

Zaid trotted on his horse closer to Terra. "Did they not have horses in your time?"

Terra groaned as she stood. "Horses are more of a hobby in my time. Most people have different ways of travel."

Nikias sighed, shaking his head. "That's enough. Tiro Mason, you need to practice this part on your own. Now for the harder test."

Zaid and Hikari climbed down from their horses before the optios led the animals away. Nikias had told them that learning to ride a horse was a useful skill since, in a lot of points in history, travel by horse was common. They had learned other historical skills. Yesterday she had used all manner of guns at a firing range. The day before they had practiced with bow and arrow.

Nikias touched his shieldwatch's holoface which changed the salient into a dusty mud cracked obstacle course. At first, Terra thought it was time for more exercise, but paused when she saw the line of parked auto-mobiles. She couldn't help but laugh after recognizing the model.

Zaid and Hikari turned to Terra, brows raised.

Terra shook her head while wondering if the designer of this course was a fan of American cinema.

Hikari stared at the automobiles. "Is it a carriage or cart?"

Nikias pointed to the cars. "We will show you the basics of driving. Who wishes to try first?"

Terra smiled and stepped forward. "I can drive."

Nikias gestured to the cars. Terra walked over and opened the door which lifted upwards rather than opening to the side. She sat in the driver's seat, turned on the engine, and drove around the course. Terra finished the course and parked in front of her strike team or at least what remained of it after the Survival test.

Hikari frowned and glared at Terra. "How did you do that?"

Terra shrugged. "Almost everyone learns to drive where I'm from."

"Good, Tiro Mason," Nikias said. The centurions had started mem-orizing everyone's names. "I mean that was terrible! You should quit," Nikias added in a halfhearted tone. All the centurions still tried to dis-courage the tirones, though Terra knew this wasn't personal but another part of the training.

Nikias touched the glass face of his shieldwatch. "I'll give you one point for driving safely and two for completing the course. Next time, try to make it through the course in under a minute."

Zaid was next, moving into the driver's seat. He stared at all the con-trols and steering wheel for a long moment before getting out. "I think I will need a few hours in the strategy study first."

Hikari shoved Zaid aside as she jumped into the driver's seat. She flipped through the various controls until she found the key. When she turned it the engine roared to life and Terra could swear a slight smile touched Hikari's lips.

Nikias took a step forward. "Excellent, Tiro Hikari. Now slowly tr–"

Hikari found the gas pedal. Tires squealed as the vehicle shot for-ward.

Nikias raised an eyebrow. "You think she knows how to use the break pedal?"

Terra shrugged. "If she did, do you think she would use it?"

Hikari sped through the course, tires squealing as she raced around every obstacle to the finish. She opened the door and glared at Terra as if daring her to do better.

Nikias nodded. "Not bad, Tiro Hikari. Four points for beating Terra's time."

Terra faced Hikari before turning to Nikias. "I want another try."

An optio approached, interrupting Terra's next attempt at the course. "Centurion," he said, saluting. "Replacement for this strike team."

Nikias nodded. They were past due for a replacement. A few days had passed since the survival test. Only Zaid, Hikari, and herself remained.

Zaid stepped forward. "Replacement? I assumed I would trade for new members?" He no longer wore his helmet or chain mail, having replaced it with the Legion's armor. He still held a scimitar at his side, though as a secondary weapon to his aeon edge.

Nikias shook his head. "No, Tiro Zaid. Trading is only allowed during the early phases. After week five, only centurions may authorize team member exchanges."

The optio gestured to another tiro who stepped forward into the dry mud cracked course. Terra instantly recognized the relaxed posture and confident smirk. She wondered if the instructors had chosen him just to annoy her.

Roland approached, eyeing the three team members. An aeon edge hung at his belt and much of his old armor was gone, now replaced with new legion equipment. The white tunic with red cross still covered his torso. He frowned when he saw Terra but scowled when he laid eyes on Zaid, something Terra had never seen Roland do. He turned to Centurion Nikias. "You didn't tell me there would be a Turk."

Nikias raised an eyebrow. "A what? Never mind. If you have a problem, tiro, then endure it or fix it. We sometimes have to work with people we don't like."

The optio raised an eyebrow. "Is that why you tried to strangle that Persian?"

Nikias laughed. "Yeah that was hilarious... I mean that was different. He was out of line."

The optio shook his head and turned to Zaid. "Strike team leaders will have new tirones assigned to them. You are more than welcome to complain to Praetor Lycus. However, I would sooner marry a Faceless than expect Praetor Lycus to give you what you want."

Zaid's jaw clinched as he glared at Roland. "Name?"

Roland stiffened. "Roland Delmare."

Zaid nodded, his posture still tense. "A Frankish name?"

Roland smiled, trying to appear disarming. "I was a simple keep guard before this. No one of particular note."

Terra looked from Roland to Zaid, wondering if Zaid caught the lie.

Zaid's own gaze narrowed. "You are lying."

Roland's smile vanished.

Terra's smile appeared.

Zaid crossed his arms and stared at Roland. "I recognize that garb. Are you a knight?"

Terra turned to Zaid. "He is."

Zaid looked at Terra. "You know him?"

Terra nodded. "Yes. I am pretty sure he is a knight. I have seen his swordsmanship skills. He's good. He is a liar though and a cheater too."

Zaid turned back to Roland. "Typical of a Frankish barbarian. I will try not to make assumptions, but remember that I am watching," he said before turning to speak with Nikias.

Hikari looked at Roland. "What is a Knight?"

Roland shrugged. "A fancy word for a soldier."

"So you are a brute then."

"I didn't say I was a brute."

Hikari shrugged. "A soldier is a fancy word for brute," she said before walking back to the course.

"She must be from a rude culture," Roland said before turning to Terra. "Well, are you going to chastise me as well?"

Terra continued to smile. "Nope. Seeing your ego deflate almost made the torture worth it."

After shooting practice and afternoon exercises, Nikias canceled Zaid's team practice for a simulated mission. Zaid almost protested, but then hesitated at the futility of it. Nikias led them to a large salient before he transformed it into a busy market square. People in colorful attire walked in the large crowded square. In the center of the square was an odd bright white item that floated in a fountain, appearing out of place in the ancient looking market.

Nikias pointed at the item. "Time tourists leave junk like that in times where it doesn't belong. These don't usually cause problems, but the Legion cleans them up to be safe. Your mission is to retrieve the item without being noticed."

Zaid regarded the crowded street with narrowed eyes that searched for ambushes or traps.

Nikias looked at his shieldwatch. "You have one hour."

Zaid gave a few hand signals, telling them to move into the salient with caution, but when the natives spotted Terra, the salient vanished. *Mission Failed* read across their shieldwatch. After they left the salient, it reset to the crowded street.

Hikari stepped forward. Zaid watched her but said nothing. He had grown use to Hikari's insubordination and had learned when to trust her and when to hold her back.

Hikari jumped into the salient and ran across roofs. She stayed carefully out of the sight of the natives. She stopped near the center. She tried to make the final approach, but each time at least one person in the crowd spotted her. When the salient reset, she tried again with the same results.

Between attempts, Nikias stared at his reflection in his shieldwatch's glass face. He then used a Restore. Terra noticed that when the Restore ring passed, Nikias's scar was in a different spot. He then nodded his approval after inspecting his scar as though it were a new hair style.

Well that solves that mystery, Terra thought.

Hikari was about to try a fourth time when Zaid nodded to Terra. Terra then grabbed Hikari's shoulder. "That's enough."

Hikari moved as though to attack Terra but then hesitated. Hikari knew attacking Terra only wasted energy and didn't really hurt Terra that much.

Roland stepped forward. "You know I—"

Zaid silenced him with a glare. "Remain silent for now, Frankish barbarian."

Roland frowned, but offered no challenge.

Nikias glanced to his shieldwatch again before turning to go. "Just let me know if you pass. You have about half an hour left. I'll check on you then."

Zaid then had Terra distract the crowd with a disturbance on the other side, but Hikari was still spotted. After the next try Zaid paced the edge of the salient in frustration. "Why? They give us weapons, battle scenarios, night missions, and hostage rescues. Then they tell us to put our weapons away pick up trash with stealth?"

Terra watched Zaid pace when someone tapped her shoulder. She turned to find Roland with a rather sheepish expression. "What?"

Roland gestured to the item in the center of the square. "I can get that, but you have to convince the Turk to let me."

"Zaid," Terra corrected while crossing her arms.

Roland sighed. "Sir Zaid of the scowling Turks then. Listen. I can get us past this test, but I need someone to vouch for me."

"Vouch for you? I was the first person to see past your lies. Why should I do anything for you?"

"Because of well... um..." Roland said, averting his gaze.

Terra raised an eyebrow. *He had always been so smooth and confident before*, she thought. *What happened?* Then she remembered that Roland hadn't sold them out during the Survival Test. Maybe she should give him another chance? She decided and approached Zaid. "Zaid. Roland has an idea."

Zaid turned to Terra. "Should we trust him?"

Terra looked away. "Well, no, but he kept his word during the Survival Test so that must be worth something. If he betrays us, better sooner than later right?"

Zaid thought for a moment. "Frankish knight. What is your plan?"

Roland smiled, his confidence returning. "To accomplish this mission you need my talents. Watch," he said as he looked at his shieldwatch. He glanced several times from his shieldwatch to the crowd. Then he touched a holoface causing a ring to transform his uniform into clothing that matched with the crowd's. He then walked into the salient.

Few noticed Roland. Those who did he placated when he returned their greetings. He made his way to the fountain. An older man from the crowd inspected the strange item when Roland approached him. "May I borrow that?"

The man shrugged. "Sure. It's not mine anyway."

Roland thanked him before walking out of the salient. As the salient dissipated, Roland tossed the small item to Zaid.

Zaid inspected the object before handing it to Terra. "It's a cup, but the material is strange."

Terra tossed the cup in her hand. "A plastic cup. It's a common cheap material in my time. It degrades slowly though."

Zaid erased the cup before looking for Nikias who was still gone. After a moment he shrugged. "I guess Nikias has forgotten about us. We still have half an hour left in the schedule. I suppose we shouldn't waste it." He touched a holoface near his shieldwatch, transforming the salient into a flat area with a large mat in its center. Torches burned nearby, providing light.

"Sparring?" Roland asked.

Zaid nodded, but frowned when Hikari moved to the center of the mat.

"I am going first," Hikari said before pointing to Terra. "Against her."

Zaid sighed. "Perhaps we shou—"

"No one else lasts against me," Hikari interrupted. "Last time I sparred with you, I knocked you out for three hours. That was three wasted hours waiting for you to wake."

Zaid turned to Terra, but Terra sighed while approaching Hikari. "It's fine, Zaid. I am used to being a punching bag."

Hikari faced Terra before slipping into an attack stance.

Terra glanced to Hikari's sheathed aeon edge. "Not going to use that?"

"I don't need it," Hikari said.

Terra assumed a defensive stance. "One day I will make you use that."

Hikari charged, attacking Terra with a flurry of hand to hand strikes all with blinding speed. Terra blocked a few blows, but took the rest. What few strikes Terra managed in return missed their mark. The fight dragged on. Hikari landed blow after blow, yet Terra still remained standing. Both Sped their movements, but Hikari still held the advantage in skill while Terra had endurance. After several minutes, skill defeated endurance and Terra fell bruised, battered, and bleeding.

Hikari stood panting. Although Terra had not landed a blow, Hikari swayed from exhaustion.

Roland frowned. "Well that took forever even with a shieldwatch."

Zaid nodded. "A standard match between those two. Terra is the only one Hikari has trouble with."

"Ow," Terra said while struggling to stand.

Zaid gestured to Roland. "Well, barbarian. It's your turn."

Roland pointed to himself. "Me?"

Zaid nodded. "Yes. You. Now face Hikari. I want to see what you can do."

Hikari, despite her apparent exhaustion, offered no protest.

Roland sauntered over to the mat and faced Hikari. "Not going to draw your aeon edge against me as well?"

"I don't need it against you either," she said in a low tone.

Roland shrugged. "It's for the best. I would only make you look a fool."

Hikari frowned. "I would still have a long way to go before I look as big a fool as you."

Roland smirked. "Oh please. As if you could do anything that could make others loathe you more than they do now. Perhaps you could trade your points for a friend?"

Hikari snarled. "Perhaps you could trade your points for a working manhood?"

Roland smiled. "Oh how crass. And Zaid calls me the barbarian."

Terra sat next to Zaid while Reversing time on her lighter wounds. "I guess the duel has started."

Hikari clinched her fists. "Smooth tongued brute!"

Roland's smile widened. "Brute? I'm not the one who bullies others around after the training day is done, beating down weaklings for their points. Oh well. I suppose my insults are lost on lowly peasant like you."

Hikari gritted her teeth.

Roland shrugged. "I mean here you are trying to insult me, to throw me off guard. I suppose if one takes away all the points you've collected, all the armor, and your aeon edge, all that's left is a frightened child who throws insults at others. Where did you learn that? Did your mother let you run wild as a child?"

Hikari snarled

Roland faced Hikari. "Or was it your worthless father who spoiled you?"

Hikari screamed and charged.

Roland grinned. "Got you."

Terra and Zaid watched as two artists clashed. Hikari shot forward, Speeding her movements until she was a blur. Roland drew his aeon edge in a flash. The two met in a whirl of motion. The fight lasted seconds. Roland hit Hikari with his aeon edge while Hikari struck a blow against Roland's head. Both hit the ground at the same time.

Terra stared for a long moment. "Did they just draw?"

Zaid's rubbed his chin. "As I thought. The Frank has been hiding his skill. Still, if Hikari had faced him first she would have won."

Roland groaned as he struggled to stand. "I thought that would be more effective."

Terra grinned. "Well it was a good plan except for one detail, Hikari fights better when she's mad."

A ring formed around Hikari, moving clockwise to Restore her. She stood.

Zaid sighed. "Let's see if we can improve."

Before Zaid could continue another group entered the salient; a team of four tirones. Terra also noticed a third group watching from the edge of the salient.

The tirones approached. Their leader, a short, tan skinned woman, stepped forward. "We are using this salient to practice."

Zaid faced her. "We still have time left. Centurion Nikias gave us permission to use this salient."

The woman gestured around them. "The centurion is not present. Why don't you leave?"

Roland put on his best smile. "Now let us all be civil. The salient is large and our practice is almost at its end. Thereupon you may either wait or simply practice in the other half."

The woman glared at Roland. "How about instead, we settle this by a Trial of Blades? Four matches between each of our teams. Winner of each match chooses the next opponent. We decide first. The team that wins gets the salient."

Zaid nodded. "Fine. That's what we were going to do anyway. Choose your first opponent."

A tall tiro from the other team stepped forward. He pointed to Terra. "I'll take the one without a blade. She'll be a good warmup."

Terra scowled, still feeling pain from her fight with Hikari.

The tall tiro took the center of the salient while his team cheered him. Terra approached him, still scowling.

He smirked. "You look like you're about to fall over. No need to waste stasis cells on someone like you."

Terra assumed a defensive stance.

After a moment, her opponent moved forward at a slow pace and did not bother to use his shieldwatch. Terra almost struck his throat when he got close. Instead he dodged, the blow grazing him. He frowned before Speeding his movements and slugging Terra in the stomach. Terra fell.

He turned to go while shaking out his hand. "Like punching a rock."

Terra stood and coughed before resuming her stance. "Hikari hits harder than you do."

"Hikari?" he said, his eyes growing wide when he saw her watching from the sides. "Not good."

Terra used the distraction to attack again.

He drew his aeon edge before warding Terra back.

Terra gritted her teeth. She couldn't spar against an aeon edge without one of her own. Just then, an aeon edge hit the ground next to her, tip first. She glanced to the side where she saw the other group of observers. One nodded to her. She took the blade. She still lost when the other tiro out maneuvered her and sliced her through the chest.

Terra lay on the ground for a few moments before the pain faded. After groaning, she stood to see someone nearby. He was about her height and had long hair tied into a pony tail with several locks of silver in it. His face marked him of Asian descent. The man smiled, extending his hand.

Terra returned the aeon edge hilt first. "Thanks. Sorry it was wasted on me."

He took the blade. "Do you not have an aeon edge?"

Terra shook her head. "No, but I almost have enough points saved up. I have only finished the safety and maintenance qualifiers. I have little aptitude for one though. My focus has been on the shieldwatch instead."

"Smart. Too many fixate on the aeon edge and forget that a shieldwatch is more decisive in a fight."

He wore a full legionnaire combat uniform with top grade equipment unlike the hodgepodge of most tirones. A patch on the man's shoulders showed the numeral *VII*, the number of the Seventh Cohort. Another emblem, a silver dot with two semi circles on either side and a crescent below, showed under the numeral; a captain's insignia. Terra saluted. "Sorry, Captain! I didn't see your rank insignia."

He laughed. "It's all right, tiro. You may call me Chih. What's your name?"

"Tiro Terra Mason," she said, relaxing her salute.

Chih nodded before presenting his aeon edge to Terra. "Show me your stance."

"What?" Terra asked, trying not to fumble the blade in her hand as Chih handed it back to her.

Chih smiled. "Your fighting stance with the aeon edge. Show it to me."

Terra felt awkward, but she did her best and raised her aeon edge as though to fence.

He shook his head. "Here," he said as he drew an aeon edged dagger. He faced Terra, aeon edge at an angle with his stance wide and side facing her. "Like this."

Terra did her best to mimic the stance.

"Good. You learn quickly. Solid foundations. More useful, in my opinion, than raw talent."

"I am still horrible at offense though," Terra said, handing back the blade.

Chih dismissed the thought with a wave. "Offense you can learn later. Foundations are more important. Let me show you the most important part about having an aeon edge."

Standing straight with feet together, he lifted the blade in his right hand while placing his left behind his back. He then raised the edge of the blade a few inches from his face with the guard just below his chin. Chih held this pose for a few seconds before swinging his sword out at an angle to his side.

Terra nodded. "An aeon edge salute. You use it before a Trial of Blades, but the person who made me a squire uses it before she fights anyone."

"She is wise to do so. Always salute your foes even if they don't salute you back. This is important."

"Do you mind if I ask you something, captain?"

"Go ahead."

"Why are you here?"

Chih gestured to his group that still watched from the sides. "Centurion Geres is up for promotion to the rank of Serdar. The Academy also hosts the officer training program. I myself volunteered for a special program that mixes cohorts together for training. It was designed to reduce the amount of inter-service rivalry between cohorts."

"Is it working?"

"No, but I use the opportunity to gauge new recruits and search for potential talent. Cohorts also compete for talented tirones after they graduate."

"Oh... Wait. I thought that a legionnaire trained their squire after they graduated from the Academy?"

"Sometimes yes. It's an old tradition that few use now. Well I suppose Silverwind still does, but she is a special case."

"Of course," Terra said, trying not to seem awkward at the mention of Alya. "So why is the salute the most important part?"

"Because being honorable, being good, this is the true foundation of the Aeon Legion. We must be noble, we must shine. If the most powerful cannot bother themselves to be good, then what chance does anyone else have? Do you know which cohort I am from?"

"The Seventh Cohort called the Hunters, I think."

"Our motto is 'We see the hidden'. We track down evasive temporal criminals, but our most fearsome quarry are legionnaires who have gone rogue."

"I didn't know that was a problem?"

"It is rare, but sometimes a legionnaire goes rogue. Some use an aeon edge and shieldwatch to conquer. Others grow tired of protecting status quo and instead try to change history, but their attempts always make things worse. They ignore the lessons already paid for in the blood of heroes."

There was a yell as Hikari defeated the tiro who had beaten Terra. Hikari then pointed to the three remaining tirones on the other team. "I choose all three."

The other team leader stared, confused. "That won't be fair."

Hikari shrugged. "True. You would need twice that number, but I do not wish to wait."

The other team leader gestured for her two teammates to join her when another man approached. Terra turned to see that one from Chih's group had made his way to the center of the salient. He had a centurion's emblem on his shoulder under the numeral *IX*.

Terra gestured to newcomer. "What cohort is he from?"

"Centurion Geres is from the Ninth Cohort. The Slayers. A unit that specializes in search and destroy missions for large targets like the larger varieties of Faceless or Manticores."

"Manticore?" Terra asked. She hadn't gotten to them yet in her studies.

Chih's expression darkened. "Nasty monsters, like a scorpion that kept growing until it became as big as a palace. The Slayers killed most of them, but a few still remain. They poison the land with their toxins and progeny. It's well armored and smart. Not a good combination. They were an invasive species that infested the Edge several centuries ago. Their biology was so advanced that they could time travel and even their senses worked across time."

"Oh," Terra said after considering the implications of such a monster.

"Thankfully," Chih said with a sigh, "Centurion Reivair stopped them."

"Who?"

"One of Alya's squires."

The newcomer, whom Chih had called Geres, faced Hikari and the other team. He had only a single lock of silver in his hair. "I have a new challenge. All of you against me."

The others hesitated. Finally the other team leader spoke. "Who are you?"

"Centurion Geres and you will address me as such or have they not taught you insignias yet?"

Hikari stared at Geres's aeon edge. Unlike her own dull gray lead weighted blade, Geres's was polished silver in color. "I agree to your challenge only if you hand over your aeon edge if I win."

Geres grinned and turned to Hikari. "I couldn't do that even if I wished, but I can hand over one of my daggers, Tiro Hikari."

Hikari paused.

Geres took one of his daggers and tossed it in his hand. "Yes. Your name is known even outside the Academy. Other cohorts are already fighting over who gets you. However, if I win in a Trial of Blades against you, then you agree to join my cohort as my squire."

Chih approached Geres. "Centurion, I don't think this wise."

Geres faced Chih. "So you won't override her refusal, Captain?"

Hikari stepped forward. "I accept."

Zaid sighed. "Hikari, that's a full legionnaire. Trust me when I say you cannot best him."

The other strike team leader pointed to Geres. "Hey! What about us?"

Geres shrugged, not taking his eyes off Hikari. "What *about* you?"

The other team leader fumed and gestured for her team to take up positions around Geres.

Zaid shook his head. "Hikari, this is your fight. I won't help you."

Chih sighed, rejoining Terra. "Well, just watch. You may learn a few things about swordsmanship from Geres."

"Is he good?" Terra asked.

Chih nodded. "He has won many recent Trials of Blades. Though his victories have made his boldness grow into foolhardiness."

The battle ended in a flash. Geres cut down the other strike team in seconds. Terra found herself impressed with Geres's skill. His blows did not have the artistry of Roland's, but had a practiced precision. Hikari lasted longer, but was still defeated after Geres knocked her lead weighted aeon edge out of her hand. Now Hikari lay on the ground, disarmed, with Geres pointing an aeon edge at her throat.

Nikias then entered the salient and paused when he saw the scene. He saluted when he saw Chih. Two more legionnaries joined with Geres.

Chih returned the salute. "No need for that. I am only here to assist Centurion Geres."

Nikias then glanced back to Geres and spoke in an even tone. "Are you with the officer training program?"

Geres nodded. "Yes. Is there a problem?"

Nikias narrowed his gaze. "I do not appreciate your using the tirones for your training exercises."

Geres ignored Nikias as he sheathed his aeon edge. He turned to Hikari. "We will take her now."

Nikias's jaw went slack. "What?"

Geres turned to Nikias. "I said we will take her."

Nikias clinched his fists. "There is no chance Praetor Lycus will agree to this. Besides. She isn't ready."

Geres gestured to Hikari. "Yes she is. So what she hasn't been through the Labyrinth? She shouldn't have to. She doesn't need the rest of her strike team. Besides, if we don't take her now some other cohort will poach her before we can get her. Orion and his Shadow Cohort will probably find her. They always get the talented ones."

"She is not ready," Nikias said. "Besides, what cohort they join is up to them. Even still, the legionnaire that squired her may train her for one year following the Academy."

Geres's eyes narrowed. "Then I challenge you to a Trial of Blades. If I win, then I will take Hikari."

Nikias glanced to Chih.

Chih shook his head. "I will not override your refusal. Turn down this challenge if you wish."

Nikias regarded Geres with a look of mixed emotions on his face. Terra could see that Nikias was eager to fight Geres, but seemed hesitant.

Lycus Cerberus then stepped into the salient. "I accept your challenge."

Chapter XXIII
Cerberus

Praetor Lycus Cerberus Combat Record
Confirmed Kills
Kalian: 10,426
Manticores: 17
Faceless: 478 (See notes class type kill counts)
Sons of Oblivion: 9,782
Hunter Keepers: 4,281
Timeships: 251
Dreadnaughts: 3
Askari: 821
Time Knights: 87
Aeon Legionnaires: 5
Other Human: 10,127
Other: 12,582
Unconfirmed Kills are approximately double the sum of the above figures.
Medals, Awards, and Commendations: See attached list with 5,292 entries.
Trial of Blades Won: 8,237
Trial of Blades Lost: 2
War Crime Accusations: Records sealed by order of Consul Prometheus. This matter has been formally investigated and closed.
   -Log of unauthorized Archives access

Terra shivered, looking at Lycus's terrible snarl as he stood partially shrouded in shadow.

Geres hesitated. "I did not challenge you."

Lycus approached Geres, standing face to face. "You tried to claim

one of my tirones. They belong to me. No one else. They pass the training when I say they do. I can reject them even if they make it through
the Labyrinth. That is my right. Not yours. By trying to take what is
mine you have challenged me therefore I accept that challenge."

Geres recoiled. "I will not fight a Legendary Blade. My challenge is
withdrawn."

Lycus's snarl grew. "As a Legendary Blade my challenge may not be
refused regardless of rank."

Geres looked to Chih.

Chih shrugged. "This is true. Centurion, you cannot refuse," he said
before turning to Lycus. "However, praetor, I must remind you that he
may make a request for help to even the odds if he so chooses."

Lycus nodded.

Geres glanced to his comrades. "My strike team, four of us, against
you alone. We get first strike. If we win, then I get to choose any tiro I
wish for my Cohort."

Lycus's snarl twisted into a grin. "This is acceptable."

One of Geres's Legionnaires let out an audible growl and glared at
Geres, but said nothing.

Geres grinned, regaining his confidence. "Yes. This should work.
The legendary Cerberus hasn't fought in a Trial of Blades for over a century. I think it's past due for someone to call him out. I was planning to
participate in this year's Tournament of Blades anyway. This saves me
time. And if you win?"

Lycus's wolf like grin showed his teeth. "Your humiliation in front
of the tirones gives them a lesson in caution. That is more than enough
for me."

∞

Moments later, Terra joined others at a large salient. Other tirones gathered. Soon the edge of the salient filled with spectators. Terra thought
the entire Academy must be there. A few other legionnaires watched as
well, including Chih.

The salient then set itself to a flat, barren field with scattered brush
to break up the rocks and dirt.

Lycus stood in the center while Geres's teammates surrounded Lycus.
Geres and his three companions then drew their aeon edges. Like Alya's,
theirs were silver in color unlike the lead weighted dull gray versions

AEON LEGION: LABYRINTH   265

Terra and the other tirones carried. Each aeon edge had a different con-figuration than the others. Then Cerberus drew his aeon edge.

It was the first time Terra had seen Lycus's aeon edge, Cerberus, in any detail. Like the other aeon edges, the polished silver reflected the light of the sun while held. Unlike the other aeon edges Terra had seen, three timecores glowed blue just above the hilt as Lycus loaded a stasis cell clip. Cerberus was more jagged in design than the one that Geres held. The toothed edge reminded Terra of a wolf's maw.

Neither saluted the other.

Geres and his team attacked. Terra had to Speed her vision to keep up. True to his word, Lycus waited until Geres swung first with his blade. Lycus blocked with his shieldwatch before moving to counter the other Legionnaires who moved in to support Geres. When all combatants drew close, even Terra's Sped vision did her little good.

The ebb and flow of this battle differed completely from the one she had seen earlier. Now both sides moved at a blinding speed. Flashes of blue filled the salient and each blast ripped up the ground, sending chunks flying into the air. Geres and his team did not hold back. They used aeon edge bursts in tune with their coordinated strikes trying to overwhelm Lycus. Lycus weaved around the attacks with ease before cutting down one Legionnaire. He yelled as he hit the ground with a large swath of his chest now in stasis.

The three remaining Legionnaires shifted formation and attacked again from three different points. Again, Lycus weaved out of the attack, cutting down another before moving.

Geres cursed. He had lost half of his team within seconds.

Terra sensed the battle's flow now. Lycus toyed with Geres just as he had done with her during the Survival Test. This Trial of Blades was nothing like how the tirones fought with one another. It made most of her sparring sessions seem like schoolyard slap fights. Geres was a real legionnaire, his movements precise and controlled. He and his compan-ions were skilled wielders of their aeon edges and used them in perfect combination with a shieldwatch. In spite of this they still were nowhere near Lycus's level of skill. He was untouchable.

Alya's fight in the library had been like poetry. She had moved like a wind through chimes. Lycus moved like a hungry wolf eager to taste blood. Blood would have decorated the salient if not for the non-lethal setting for the duelists' aeon edges.

Geres and his remaining companion drew up for a final attack. They struck, unleashing a flurry of bursts from their aeon edges. Lycus then stepped out of the dust and smoke and swung his aeon edge once. It unleashed three powerful blasts that tore the surrounding ground apart and sent Geres and his final teammate flying back. When the dust cleared, Lycus stood alone on a crater filled salient, grinning a toothy, vicious smile.

Lycus put his boot on Geres's chest. "This is an important lesson!" he shouted to the tirones.

The gathered crowd remained silent.

Lycus held his snarl while speaking in a low venomous tone that carried over the salient. "Never fight a Legendary Blade."

"So which Legendary Blade do you think is the best?" a tiro said in a low tone next to Terra. She turned her attention from the large glass window that showed snow covered grounds outside to the tirones next to her.

Terra had made her way to class after the Trial of Blades. Other tirones engaged in conversation while they waited for Shani to start the class. Lycus's duel had sparked a discussion about the Legendary Blades. Terra listened in on their conservation while keeping a wary gaze for Centurion Shani who hadn't showed up yet.

"Easy," the other tiro said. "Silverwind is the best, no contest."

"What makes you think that?"

"She has the most confirmed kills."

Terra scowled, remembering Lycus's words about Alya. Those words still bothered her. She had looked up the historical records, but they detailed Alya's service record in broad strokes. She found a single paragraph about Saturnian war crimes, though there were several whole books on Kalian atrocities which, in Terra's opinion, seemed inflated in severity.

"Yeah, but that was mostly Kalians. I'm going with the sixth blade, Kairos. She killed the most Faceless, and those things are tough."

"Kairos is MIA. She doesn't count."

"Okay. Then who do you think could beat Cerberus? I mean we got to see him in action today."

"Endymion might. He used to be a Legendary Blade."

"No one has seen him fight in centuries though. I would still go with Silverwind. Kairos could, but like I said she is MIA. Maybe Atlas too."

"Atlas? He's slow."

"Only his maneuvering, not his attack speed. Come on! His aeon edge is bigger than me."

"What about Deucalion of the Four Blades?"

"He's good. He could match Cerberus's speed. Cerberus has more power though because of the three timecores."

"Pythia could beat him. She's a Sybil. She could see his moves before he made them."

"She's got lower stats in everything else though."

Zaid turned around in his seat to face the arguing tirones. He was the only one of Terra's strike team that had caught up to her in academics. "You can't tell who will win a battle by looking at numbers alone. War is not a game. Besides, someone did defeat Lycus Cerberus."

Terra turned to Zaid. "Who?"

Zaid looked at Terra. "General Reva. We studied her strategies in class a few days ago."

Terra struggled to recall that name. "I remember now. Reva was a famous Kalian general during the First Temporal War. She defeated Cerberus during a duel at the Battle of Sighs. She's still on the Aeon Legion's most wanted list."

"Good, Tiro Mason," Shani said, walking into the classroom. "Can you tell me about the Singularity Thief as well?"

Terra pressed her lips together. As usual, Shani started off class by putting Terra on the spot. "The Singularity Thief, called such because they often attempt to steal singularity artifacts. He or she can be identified by the distinctive mask they wear. There have been numerous Singularity Thieves throughout the centuries and though some have been killed, none have ever been successfully captured. Although each Singularity Thief works alone, it's suspected that a second party trains and equips them and is likely the benefactor of the stolen artifacts. Standard equipment is comprised of a shieldwatch and two aeon edged daggers. Besides standard gear, they have also used a wide variety of singularity technologies adapted to the Thief's current mission."

"That was surprisingly comprehensive. Now I have to give you two points," Shani said, as though it wasn't fair. "I suppose I will have to start calling on someone else at the beginning of class to make a point about ignorance. You seem to be keeping up with my curriculum."

Terra grinned, but this deepened Shani's scowl.

Shani then looked over Terra with a critical expression. "Tiro Mason, minus one point for an untidy uniform."

Terra looked down to her uniform. It was loose again.

"Be sure to fix that," Shani said before turning to start the day's lessons.

Terra clinched her fists as she debated with herself. After a moment, she decided to risk it. "Centurion Shani?"

Shani turned to Terra and glowered. "Stop showing off, Tiro Mason!"

"I have a question."

Shani's scowl disappeared. "What is it?"

Terra spoke in a slow, even tone. "I want to know about the Legendary Blades' war records in the First Temporal War."

A few nods came from the other tirones. The recent duel had sparked interest in the Legendary Blades, including Lycus, wielder of Cerberus.

Shani's expression remained impassive. "The official archives in the strategy study should have that information. There is no need for me to cover this subject in class."

Terra took a deep breath. "I looked at the official archives, but they did not go into the detail I require. I wanted to know about war crimes."

Shani stood with hands on hips. Then she nodded. "Ah. I think I understand, Tiro Mason. If what was said during your interrogation in the Survival Test bothers you, then ask Praetor Lycus in person. I will not speak ill of him behind his back. He has earned that much respect from me. Besides, I was not there for the First Temporal War and neither were you. We have no place to pass judgment on them."

Terra's mouth hung open. Respect? The only thing Lycus had earned from anyone was fear.

She wasn't the only one surprised by this loyalty. "But he's such a monster," one tiro said in a hushed voice. Terra didn't see who.

Shani turned, searching the class with a narrowed gaze. "Who said that?"

Everyone remained silent.

A muscle in Shani's jaw twitched. "Praetor Lycus is your commanding officer. You will show him your respect. You owe him more than you know!"

Terra rolled her eyes.

Shani snapped her glare back to Terra. "I saw that, Tiro Mason! You think Lycus is bad? Before he became head of this training program, things were a lot more brutal!"

One corner of Terra's lip curled. "With all due respect, centurion, I find that hard to believe."

Shani's eyes narrowed. "There was a time in the Legion when a more ruthless doctrine was in place. New recruits fought to the death, the weak killed without mercy. Instead of points we had executions for poor performance. Showing emotions or helping others was forbidden. Those who survived became emotionless killing machines."

"So, perfect soldiers?" Zaid said in a contemptuous tone.

Shani shook her head. "No. They were horrible. The only thing they were good at, other than having psychological breakdowns, was committing war crimes. We had many of our more embarrassing defeats during that time. Then Lycus came in. He changed things. He stopped this Academy from churning out broken soldiers and instead made it forge heroes. His training program produced many excellent legionnaires, including Kairos. So long as Lycus remains true to his vision for the Legion then I will not allow a bunch of lowly tirones to muddy his name with their own ignorance."

∞

Shani's loyalty did nothing to sooth Terra's reservations. Doubts preoccupied Terra's mind even as she walked into the armory. She wondered if the real reason this bothered her was because she had begun to trust Alya. Then Lycus took that away with a few simple words. He poisoned her with doubt after she had fought so hard to remove it. No longer did she struggle with failing the training, but instead with the consequences of success.

Terra moved to the back of the armory and inspected the uniforms there. After a moment she found one that fit well. After fitting a new uniform, she paused by the aeon edge weapons lined up in a neat row. She glanced to her shieldwatch.

Twenty nine points. More than enough as an aeon edge cost twenty five.

After hesitating, she spent the points. There was no telling when the instructors would throw her into a death trap that needed an aeon edge to make it out alive. After a moment of browsing the various blades, Terra picked a longsword class aeon edge.

The blade felt heavy and looked dull with the lead weights on the sides. Terra also picked up a few spare parts and a clip. After nodding to the guard, she paid the points cost and left the armory.

Terra sighed, looking at the sword with a tired expression. Everyone else had seemed pleased when they received their aeon edge. She felt burdened by the heavy weight and awkward handling. Then she dreaded all the maintenance required to keep it in fighting condition.

Terra made her way to her locker and stored her aeon edge. Then, still lost in thought, Terra walked towards her dorm room. She wondered if she worked with villains? What if the so called heroes of the Aeon Legion proved no better than Hanns? Questions burned in her mind until she realized she stood across from Lycus Cerberus's office.

Terra walked to the fadedoor. After hesitating, she moved her hand to knock.

"Stop wasting my time, Tiro Mason," Lycus said before Terra's hand even touched the solid fadedoor. "If you want something, then get in here and say it."

The door faded and Terra entered. Lycus sat at his desk, staring at a holoface projected above the desk. The Captain's wing emblem Kalian mask lay on his desk to the side. He spoke to someone through his shieldwatch while Terra waited.

"Who was that, Cerberus?" asked a voice on the other end. Terra thought it sounded like Orion.

"Just one of the tirones," Lycus said in a dismissive tone. "Also don't call me Cerberus."

"Sorry, Lycus," Orion said.

Lycus sighed. "What did your teams find, Orion?"

"A lot of nothing, Cerberus," Orion said after a moment.

Lycus growled at the name, but didn't bother to correct Orion again.

Background noise sounded as though Orion was busy on his end. "We reviewed the temporal data and found nothing of interest. There was a little disruption, but not enough to make us suspicious. If there was someone stalking around the Academy, they would have been detected, unless they were a Faceless or a null. Is this about Silverwind? You know I can't do anything about that. She treats my orders more like amusing suggestions and that's when she doesn't laugh in my face."

"No," Lycus said. "This isn't about Silverwind. This is someone else. I know what I saw, Orion. Whoever it is, they have been watching me for some time. I dismissed the first few sightings, but they got close during the survival test."

Orion chuckled. "Maybe the impossible has happened, Cerberus. You *finally* have a fan."

Lycus scowled. "And I thought you took security threats seriously, Orion?"

"I do, Cerberus," Orion said. "But I don't waste security on Legendary Blades who are better than any security I could provide. Besides, I thought you killed all your enemies. I didn't think you had enough surviving enemies to take revenge on you. Please understand. I will not waste time putting up antiquated security cameras. The temporal scanners work against anything short of a Faceless or the Singularity Thief. If someone tried something, then the Sybil's precog would have caught it. Listen, I can assign a security detail from my cohort to search the area if you wish. I don't want to though. I need every legionnaire I can get mobilizing for well... you know."

Lycus spared Terra a brief glance. "Yes. I am aware. Fine. Keep your little black ops soldiers. Once I catch whoever this intruder is, just remember that I will gloat about doing your job."

"Noted. Orion out," Orion said in a curt tone as the feed cut out.

"Tiro Mason," Lycus said as he leaned back into his chair. "Did you, at long last, come to tell me that you are quitting?"

"Praetor. May I ask you a question?" Terra said, standing at attention.

Lycus paused. "If this is about what I said as the Captain then you shouldn't worry about it."

"Was it true?" Terra asked, still at attention. She realized the danger in pressing Lycus, but she had to know. "Was that story true?"

Lycus studied Terra. "The Captain is a character I imagined. He is a realistic representation of what a surviving Kalian terrorist would be like. There is no known active group of Kalian terrorists still at large. General Reva was the most famous and powerful Kalian, but none have seen her since the war. There is nothing left of their army but shadows and ghosts.

Their descendants lack their bloodthirsty nature. Worse things lurk in Time. Plenty of criminals would gladly torture a legionnaire to death even if they had nothing to gain from it. But you can rest easy tonight, Tiro Mason. No Kalians will drag you out of the Academy to torture you for access codes."

"That's not what I meant, praetor. I want to know if what *you* said was true?"

Lycus remained expressionless. "Your specific interrogation called for moderate physical torture followed by more advanced interrogation techniques. Your psychological and physical profiles told us you have a high threshold and tolerance for pain combined with a stubborn disposition. Physical torture had low odds of success, but we still needed to test you. Your strong sense of justice and drive to be a heroine is one of your greatest weaknesses. We exploited it for training purposes as your enemies no doubt would."

Terra relaxed. "Then it wasn't true then? What you said about yourself and Alya."

Lycus's stare turned cold. "What I said was in character. If you want to know about what Silverwind did in that war, then you should ask her yourself. It's not my place to tell you." Lycus turned away from Terra back to his holoface.

Terra turned to leave.

"You know," Lycus said before Terra walked out of the fadedoor, "that photograph is genuine."

Terra turned to Lycus who stared at his holoface. She then noticed the photograph on a shelf. It depicted a father and mother holding a baby. The father was dressed in a Kalian uniform.

"I found it on a soldier who tried to defend a family that wasn't even his own. I guess he saw his own family reflected in them," Lycus said, staring off into darkness. "He fought bravely."

Terra remained silent.

Lycus turned his gaze to Terra with a solemn look on his face. "During that war, a few of us became legends. Some of us became monsters. You may have noticed that I am very good at playing the villain. Now get out before I dock you points."

Terra left before Lycus made good on his promise. She stopped halfway to her dorm room, looking at the central fountain of the school's main hall. Was Lycus telling the truth? She wanted to ask Alya about what had happened during that war, but she wasn't sure that was a good idea. These were old wounds that Terra wondered if she had any right to open again.

Terra made her way back to her dormitory room as her thoughts wandered back to Alya's past. Lycus had all but admitted to being a monster, though that didn't bother her. She thought she understood Lycus. Of Alya, Terra felt less certain.

Terra stopped when she looked at her new uniform. She adjusted the sleeve a little after she looked in a nearby window for her reflection. Then she checked if the rest was straight. When she last got a new uniform, she had little time to fit it properly before the next practice and had lost a point. She stopped upon inspecting herself.

The Legion uniform always fit tight. The sleek design denied the enemy of any useful grip during hand to hand combat. She hated how it made her look though. It didn't allow her to hide her weight like her old, loose fitting clothes did. Now, though, she looked different.

Toned muscle had replaced her pudginess. She still wasn't slender. Not lithe like Alya or scrawny like Hikari. Muscled shoulders looked sharp in her new uniform and her abdominal muscles appeared well defined. Her thighs had thinned and tightened from daily exercise. There was not even a hint of a hunch in her stance now as she stood straight backed with a military bearing.

Noticing these changes made her decide that it didn't matter what Alya or Lycus was. She didn't have to be a war criminal and she wouldn't become one. They couldn't make her murder anyone in cold blood. Terra Mason was neither Alya Silverwind nor Lycus Cerberus. Now she stood stronger and was smarter than she once was. Only she had the power to change herself.

That thought brought a smile to her face for the first time in a long while. The more she thought about it, the more things looked up. Hikari insulted everyone far less now. They all trusted Zaid as he had formed them into a competent strike team. Even Roland didn't get on her nerves as much.

She passed through another hallway so lost in her good mood that she almost missed movement in the corner of her eye. Terra stopped, her gaze sweeping the area as she clinched her fists. Her eyes narrowed on a figure in black hiding in the corridor ahead. Another hid behind her.

Terra bared her teeth while moving into a defensive hand to hand stance. She had left her aeon edge back at the armory. Terra opened her mouth to call for help when two more figures dressed in black jumped next to her.

Terra Sped her reflexes with the shieldwatch to dodge their blows. The two hiding around the corners charged and Terra found herself surrounded. They all attacked at once and Terra Sped time as fast as she could just to keep pace.

The intruders closed in, gaining ground. Just before they surrounded Terra, they stopped and backed away.

Terra braced herself, waiting for the next attack.

One intruder pulled off his mask, revealing himself to be Nikias. As the others did so too, Terra recognized them as Academy centurions or optios.

Nikias moved a holoface in front of him, checking off boxes. "Three points for your excellent defensive moves. Two points for endurance since you didn't tire out during the exercise. Minus one point for offense. You need to work on that. Oh and you get no points for observation since while you spotted us early, you didn't notice the ambush we laid in the ceiling. Looks like good marks overall."

Terra raised a finger, but could not form words. Instead she glared at Nikias with her nostrils flaring.

Nikias smiled. "Good job. Let's go test the next one."

The centurions put on their masks and walked away.

Terra stood in the hallway alone for a long moment, her face contorted with rage. She clinched her fists as she glared at the departing instructors. After a moment she sighed before staring up at the ceiling. "I hate this place."

Chapter XXIV
Sybil

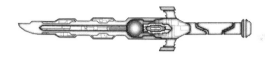

I still remember that day clearly. Alya marched Kairos in and presented her like a trophy. Every centurion swooned over her. Qadar or no, I would have rejected her without a second thought. Even with the other centurions praising her talent. Even with Alya's so called connection with fate. One thing stopped me. Kairos and I were alike in one way. Both of us were utterly alone.
-From the personal logs of Praetor Lycus Cerberus

Terra walked down the halls of the Academy to the registrations office. After a brutal training regimen today, they had called her to a meeting there. After changing her uniform and using her free Restore for the day, she made her way down the halls.

She almost lost track of time while at the Academy. Physical exercises had tapered off these past few weeks along with the winter snows. But academics had become more demanding; historical warfare, post time warfare, advanced tactics and a long boring course on time travel physics all proved demanding. The lesson on the Faceless had made her nauseous. Last week became difficult when the centurions' instruction grew detail oriented with every part of their training.

The week before focused on individual training with the centurions. Terra herself spent a lot of time with Nikias who helped her polish her hand to hand skills while Isra helped train Terra with an aeon edge. Others like Hikari and Roland received personal academic tutors to compensate for their lack of a formal education. Now it neared the end of week eleven and rumors amongst the tirones said that the Labyrinth was close.

When she arrived at the main hall she paused at the fadedoor to the registration office. She took a deep breath before stepping inside to where she had first met Lycus and the centurions.

The room was the same as when she was first here. A spotlight shown in the center of the room while the instructors sat elevated above her in a semicircle. Isra, Nikias, and Shani were present amongst many others. Lycus sat above them in the center.

"Stand at attention in the center of the room, Tiro Mason," Lycus said.

Terra moved under the bright light and then saluted.

"At ease," Lycus said in a dismissive tone. "You are first to be reviewed since we are starting with the lowest score. Let's begin."

Lycus touched his shieldwatch which projected a holoface that displayed all Terra's qualifiers and points. "First, let me say this is the furthest any tiro has advanced with your... limited qualifications. With no military training or combat experience we would have turned you away from this program altogether if not for your special squire status. Despite lacking any formal military training, you have done well."

Nikias pulled up a holoface. "You passed all the basic qualifiers. You scored average on most of them except climbing and endurance where you placed at the top of your class. In shieldwatch skills you scored above average."

"Your academic grades are... also impressive," Shani added, though she struggled to speak the praise. "You scored high on history and temporal physics. Though not the top of your class, you are one of the highest. You also didn't cheat. You maintained the integrity and honor of this Academy in spite of temptation otherwise."

"However," Nikias said. "Your martial skills are sub par. While you made your basic qualifiers, you won most of your matches by letting your opponents exhaust themselves by beating you up. Not the best tactic. Your aeon edge skills are lacking too as your scores there are lagging behind everyone else."

"There is your greatest weakness as well," Isra said. "You possess no talent. While it is true your progress so far has been impressive, most of that was sheer stubborn resolve which will only carry you so far. Some may think it unfair to compare you to those like Kairos, but the Legion is no place for the average even if they are determined."

Lycus's predatory grin returned. "This leads us to an interesting quandary. It seems as though you meet all of the basic qualifiers for entering

AEON LEGION: LABYRINTH 277

the Labyrinth. However, your point total stands at twenty three." He sat silent for a moment, staring at Terra as though waiting for something.

"How many points do I need, praetor?" Terra asked in almost a whisper.

Lycus continued to grin. "It doesn't matter. You were not even close. Not even by half. Not even if you hoarded every point you ever made."

Terra's shoulders drooped, but she maintained eye contact with Lycus. "So I don't have enough points?"

Lycus leaned forward. "That is correct. You don't have enough points. You never had a chance. Now go home."

Terra stood, unmoving on the stone floor and fell silent for a long while. She didn't care about points. In fact she thought the whole thing rather arbitrary and stupid. "Praetor, the Labyrinth only requires that I have all the qualifiers, correct?"

Lycus stared at Terra. "You still wish to enter the Labyrinth? Why? It doesn't matter. You don't have enough points. Even if you pass it will be senseless. You can't become part of the Legion."

Terra stood a little straighter. "Praetor?"

Lycus raised an eyebrow. "What?"

Terra's eyes narrowed. "I will be honest. I don't give a damn about points."

Nikias smiled.

Lycus leaned back. "You realize this is a futile gesture? The Labyrinth can be deadly. Are you sure you want to go through with this even though there is no way you will qualify for the Legion?"

Terra nodded. "I want to take the test anyway. If I walk away now, then I wouldn't be worthy of the Legion. Either way, I will finish what I started."

The centurions closed their holofaces and stood to leave.

Lycus continued to stare. After a moment he nodded. "Very well, Tiro Mason. You pass the first trial of the Labyrinth."

Terra's brow furrowed. "First trial? Then the points were..."

"Pointless," Nikias said as he rolled his eyes.

"Not pointless," Shani said in an irritated tone. "They allow for positive and negative reinforcement. We eliminate tirones who don't earn enough points, but that's in the early weeks and really it's an excuse. Those we want to keep on as tirones we make sure earn at least one point."

"Why is it so unfair then?" Terra asked.

Lycus leaned forward. "We teach you to respect your superiors. Most armies require discipline, but the Legion needs more than mindless soldiers. The points express our authority. We can give them out or take them away as we wish. Sometimes, though, the authorities are wrong and the rules and values of authority need to be ignored to accomplish greater goals."

"So sometimes you must stand against the Legion's authority?" Terra asked.

Lycus's stare hardened. "Sometimes. But you must be prepared to pay the price for that, because if you are wrong it could mean your life. I did not lie when I said the Labyrinth might kill you. This meeting wasn't just a test. It was your last chance to walk away."

Terra stood in formation at the main courtyard for the last time. She noted how few, around a hundred tirones, remained. Almost all had replaced their old gear for Legion equipment. A few still wore piercings and jewelry, but most had discarded their old uniforms and weapons. Only those who had cast off their pasts made it this far.

Lycus walked on stage. He did not have his usual snarl as he counted the remainder without expression. "Congratulations on making it this far. You have displayed the knowledge, skill, and courage it takes to stand at this moment, this place in time. Now the Labyrinth lies ahead. In it you will find more than just a beast, but many horrors, puzzles, trials, and truths. It is the final test and it will require every bit of training you have gone through these past months. You will face twelve trials within. You must endure all of them. If you survive the Labyrinth then I will be the final judge to decide if you become a full legionnaire. The Labyrinth must be completed within one hundred forty four hours. No more points. You may take anything you wish from the armory. Lead weights will be removed from your equipment, but the safety lock will remain on your aeon edge. You now have sixteen hours to get ready before the Labyrinth opens. I suggest you prepare your equipment and rest. Good luck."

After visiting the armory one last time, Terra returned to her room and tried to rest. She slept little. It was hard to sleep considering what waited for her. The walk to the meeting point was pleasant enough. The city grew warmer as spring was just a few days away. Terra took one last look at the sky before walking into the Academy for the final time.

The entrance to the Labyrinth was below the city. She went to the lowest parts of the Academy and found several facilities she hadn't even known existed. Several shrines and chapels dedicated to numerous religions dotted the lower sections where tirones came to pray. She recognized a few, like a small prayer chapel where a cross hung.

Terra stopped when she noticed Zaid in one building. He chanted though she was too far away to hear. Several times he prostrated himself on the ground while continuing his song like chant. She continued to watch, both curious and entranced by his melodious prayer. After a few moments he stood and gathered his things near the fadedoor.

"That prayer," Terra said as Zaid stepped out the fadedoor, "what was that?"

Zaid faced Terra. "I was observing Salat."

"What time are you from? Why are you here?"

Zaid kept his expression neutral. He turned to go, leaving Terra's question unanswered.

Terra followed. "Everyone around here tries so hard to keep their pasts hidden."

Zaid spared Terra a glance while they walked. "Then what is your past?"

Terra shrugged. "Boring mostly. Everyone keeps calling me a soft-timer."

"Does that bother you?"

"I've been called far worse things."

Zaid grinned.

Terra looked at him. "What?"

"That is your strength. I envy you."

"Why is that?"

"Because nothing seems to affect you. You are solid."

"I don't know. You seem unfazed by everything."

Zaid shook his head. "It was not always so. During the first attempt at the training, I failed the first day. My second attempt, I failed during the first part of the survival test. One thing is for certain though," he said as he stopped to face Terra.

Terra looked at Zaid. "What's that?"

Zaid smiled. "I consider you a friend."

Terra returned his smile. "Nice try, Zaid, but I will still be blunt towards you."

"I wouldn't expect you to soften your words. In truth I rely on it."

They made their way down to the under part of the city where a crowd gathered. A large facility hung from the bottom of the city. It gave a view of both the Edge below and the underside of the city.

Terra surveyed the crowd and recognized centurions, tirones, and optios, but many she did not. They moved through the crowd.

Terra glanced at Tacitus addressing his strike team. They all stood in perfect formation.

They passed by another strike team doing stretches. Terra counted eight of them. "Wow. Two strike teams working together."

Zaid shook his head. "That strike team is led by Javed. He has the largest team. They are not the highest ranked in points, but he is good at team based tactics."

Terra then looked to the other side where three tirones sat around a holoface. She looked away when they shot her a dark glare. All three of them had vicious scars and a grim demeanor.

Zaid did not look at them. "They are led by Nergüi. She is Mongolian," he said in a low tone. "Her strike team has only three members, but they have the highest average of points in the entire Academy."

Terra regarded several soldiers in foreign uniforms as they walked towards them from the other direction. As they passed, one turned to her and Zaid.

"Hey you bunch of Legion wannabes!" he said, making a gesture that Terra didn't understand. His dark blue, futuristic armor design reminded Terra of Vand's armor.

Another soldier approached, putting a hand on his shoulder. She wore a different uniform. It was dark gray with orange trim and patches, like the Kalians they had faced in the survival test. "Don't be stupid. Save it for the Trial of War."

"No!" the first soldier yelled, shrugging off the Kalian's hand. "Every year you humiliate us Helcians in the salient. Not this year! This year, we will wipe you out!" he said before walking off while making another strange gesture.

Zaid and Terra exchanged confused looks. Then they both tensed upon seeing Lycus approach.

"Tiro Mason," Lycus said in an irritated tone.

Terra stiffened and saluted.

"Come with me," Lycus said.

Terra followed.

"I should dust you right now," he said, glaring over his shoulder at Terra.

Terra frowned. "For what?"

Lycus stopped and faced Terra. "For breaking into the Archives and looking up my war record."

Terra's brow lowered as she wondered what kind of stupid test this was. "I didn't break into the Archives. I could care less about your war record given that I'm about to take the hardest test in my life."

Lycus's eyes narrowed. "You are either an expert liar, or another tiro stole your identity because our system registers that you broke into the Archives to access forbidden information."

Terra raised an eyebrow. "Is this another secret test?"

Lycus turned. "Just follow me."

He led her into a small indoor area before facing a pair of fadedoors guarded by several legionnaires. Each had the patch of the Third Cohort on their uniform, the Guardians; a cohort dedicated to guarding important facilities and acting as bodyguards. They saluted Lycus and the doors faded.

The interior was plain save for a three dimensional holographic model that appeared above a glass floor. Around it stood three women each garbed in ornate pearl colored robes edged in gold that suggested a position of authority or importance. The young women appeared a few years older than Terra with the familiar shade of silver in their long hair, but what really looked odd to Terra were their headpieces.

Their strange crowns shimmered in pearl white metal with the front extending down in a solid metal plate that completely covered their eyes, like a masquerade mask with no eye holes. Above the ears was a pair of glowing, convex glass orbs which formed the base of swept wing like antennas.

One of the women turned her head towards Lycus as though she could see just fine through the metal plate. "Praetor Lycus Cerberus," she said in an ethereal tone. The Sybil's tone reminded Terra of Delphia. The Sybil then waved her hand in the air. Various holograms of mechanical components appeared in her hand's wake. "Precognition told us of your arrival, but not your purpose."

Lycus's expression became stoic. "I apologize, Sybil Nona. An event has come to my attention that requires your precognition."

The second Sybil turned to Lycus. "It is most odd. A Qadar like yourself should be more visible to us. Regardless, there are more meetings destined for today."

Lycus nodded. "Is there a tiro you wish for me to send to you, Sybil Decima?"

Decima nodded before turning back to the model. She took the holographic parts Nona had made and arranged them into a projection of a new aeon edged weapon. "Could you bring us the tiro called Hikari Urashima next? We wish to speak with her before she undertakes the Labyrinth. We think she may be a Qadar as well."

Lycus clasped his hands behind his back. "As you wish."

The third Sybil examined the projection of the aeon edge while shaking her head. "This one will not do. It is destined for a failed guardian who has endured betrayal. While honorable, he will likely not survive the Labyrinth," she said before waiving her hand through the holographic model. It dissipated before she turned to Lycus. "Why have you come here, Cerberus?"

Lycus pressed his lips together. "I told you, Sybil Morta, I don't like to be called that anymore."

Morta faced Lycus. "You once so proudly took your aeon edge's name as your own. I do wish you would adopt it, at least in part, as Silverwind did. You are Qadar after all. Fated."

Lycus's clinched his fists. "Silverwind has come to terms with her past. Respectfully Sybil, my past is my own business."

"Then what business do you have for the Sybil of the Moirai?" Morta asked.

Lycus gestured to Terra. "I wish for you to give this tiro an omen and to read her. I wish to know if she broke into the Archives."

Morta frowned. "What tiro?"

The other two Sybil glanced around as if searching for someone else. Terra now doubted they could see anything from behind those masks as she clearly stood only a few paces in front of them. After a moment, she cleared her throat and stepped forward. "Tiro Terra Mason," Terra said, wondering how to address them.

Nona scowled. She leaned in closer as though trying to focus on Terra. Then she pulled back as her expression soured. "You brought us a null? No wonder our precognition could not foresee your purpose."

Decima turned to Lycus. "Is this an insult, Cerberus?"

Lycus remained expressionless. "Not at all. I simply need the truth."

The Sybil faced one another and stood silent for a long moment. Terra wondered if she should go when they turned towards Lycus.

"Very well, Cerberus," Morta said. "We shall give you your omen and a reading. Though I cannot promise much accuracy, at least when a null is concerned."

Nona stared at Terra. "I see nothing of importance."

"Yes," Decima added. "This one has no great destiny."

"Destiny?" Terra asked, confused and a little annoyed. "You can see a person's destiny?"

"We are Sybil," Morta said in a commanding tone. "We do not see as you. We see Time itself in all it's endless variations. The Grand Design; Time's plan for humanity's future. Only we can see it in all of its beauty and wonder."

"We can even see part of your memories," Decima said. "There is little of interest in your memories. No great tragedy. No great triumphs save for making it so far in the Academy. I do not see that she has been in the Archives, Cerberus. She is innocent of that crime."

"She is like the opposite of Kairos," Nona said while inspecting Terra like she was a nasty stain on a new rug.

Terra raised an eyebrow. "Why was Kairos so special?"

There was a moment of silence.

"Kairos was the light in the dark. Qadar." Nona whispered.

"She was Qadar; a child of fate. The master of thought and memory," Decima added.

Morta stepped forward. "We see thought and memory. We see fate and destiny. Most destinies are dim like distant stars. However, some are bright burning stars like Silverwind or Cerberus. We call them *Qadar*. Some are nulls like yourself who do not shine at all, for their link with fate is weak at best. Kairos was like the burning sun at noon, beyond even the greatest of the Qadar."

Nona smiled as though recalling a fond memory. "We foresaw her coming when a bright light of the Beginning of Time flared, sending out a shard of itself into Time."

Morta frowned. "It coincided with a creeping shadow from the End of Time. We knew that the shadow would soon threaten Saturn City."

Decima nodded. "When Silverwind first brought Kairos to us, we could tell she was a special person. Even then we saw the workings of destiny. It wasn't long after Kairos became part of the Legion that the first of the Faceless began devouring Time. She was a child of prophecy. The one destined to save the city and all Time."

"You are not her," Morta said. "You will never be her. You have no fate. You have no destiny. You are a null. You will not make it through the final trial. That is clear to us."

Terra glared at the Sybil. "How can you know that?"

"Simple," Morta said while standing in front of Terra. "We see an aeon edge in each legionnaire's future. We use this vision to forge an aeon edge upon completion of their training. There is no new blade in your future. You have no part in the Grand Design."

"Now get out," they all said in unison and turned their backs to Terra.

Morta then turned to Lycus. "Are you satisfied, Cerberus?"

Lycus bowed. "Thank you, Sybil. That was all I needed to know."

Lycus and Terra turned to leave.

"Wait," Decima said, staring at Terra.

The other two Sybil looked at Decima.

Decima shook her head. "No. It was nothing. For a moment, I thought I almost saw something in her memories. A wind of silver I think. It is just the null's oddity."

They turned their backs to Terra before she and Lycus left the room.

As soon as the doors faded back in Terra crossed her arms while lifting her chin. "Well that was a lousy free psychic reading. Why was it necessary for me to meet those people again?"

Lycus's stare turned cold. "You may be innocent of breaking into the Archives, but do not antagonize me, Tiro Mason."

Terra stiffened. "Sorry, praetor, but I get testy when I am brought before people who constantly insult me."

Lycus looked back to the solid fadedoors. "The Sybil are critical to the Aeon Legion's daily operations, but they dislike working with nulls since they can't see them very well. While their precognition is essential to the Aeon Legion, they have been wrong before. Regardless, now I have to investigate who stole your shieldwatch identity and broke into the Archives. I suppose I should have known better. There was no way you could have accessed that information even with your Academy pass. They would have to have a singularity AI in order to do that."

"What's a null?"

Lycus grinned, a hint of his wolfish snarl hidden in it. "Why, Tiro Mason, a null is someone who is unimportant. Someone who has no great effect on history. Nulls are not even a ripple in a pond, unlike great historical figures who are like tidal waves through Time. We call these great figures Qadar. I suppose your culture would call them chosen ones. All of Silverwind's squires have been Qadar, until she chose you."

"Is that what this is about? Are you trying to prove Alya wrong?"

Lycus's grinned faded. "No. How Silverwind selects her squires is the sole thing on which we agree. Everyone believes that Alya Silverwind has a special connection with fate that allows her to find talented squires. I know the truth though. She does it all on a whim. Nothing more. Her only guide is her instincts and they always lead her to squires with one special trait. One trait I look for above all else."

"What's that?"

Lycus turned to go, but stopped to glance back at Terra. "The desire to be a hero."

After Terra's meeting with the Sybil, she found Zaid again. The centurions had told them to gather in an open room with a large fadedoor ahead. As the hour of the Labyrinth drew near, more tirones gathered. Hikari and Roland joined them as well after their meetings with the Sybil. Neither spoke of what their meeting was like, though Terra could tell both Roland and Hikari had returned with nervous expressions.

Terra looked around to the other tirones. Most were now present as the Labyrinth was less than an hour away. No one spoke and they would often glance toward the fadedoors ahead. She looked that way as well. She knew that soon she would enter the Labyrinth. The thought made her nauseous.

Terra looked at her shieldwatch display again. Fifteen minutes. When the centurions appeared, the tirones moved into formation by instinct. One centurion approached the fadedoor and touched his shieldwatch face. The large door faded.

The vanishing door revealed the open expanse under the city with the Edge below. Above them loomed the metal base of the underside of the city. Before the tirones lay a large metal runway with a series of fadelines. Those fadelines ended at the edge of the metal overlook. Terra wondered why the fadelines ended without connecting to anything. Before them was only the runway and the Edge below.

"Attention!" Lycus barked as he entered.

The tirones snapped to attention.

Lycus paced up and down the line of tirones. He slapped Roland in the stomach. "Stand up straighter," he said before moving down the line. "Keep your temper in check," he said to Hikari as he glared. He then passed by Terra. "Don't do anything stupid," he said in a low tone. Lycus then stood aside and an entourage of people entered.

Several legionnaires entered the room all in their dress uniforms. Terra recognized Strategos Orion among them. They then stood at attention themselves. Lycus saluted as an older man entered.

"At ease," the older man said. His warm smile and soothing voice still carried a commanding edge. "No need to be so formal, Lycus."

Although he wore the standard dress uniform, a white tunic edged in blue over a form fitting suit identical to Terra's training uniform, his possessed far more decoration. A plain looking aeon edge hung at his belt. Of the man's numerous medals and emblems, Terra recognized a complex insignia on the upper arms of his uniform; three crescents, a circle, and a three long triangles pointing outward. Terra's eyes widened. She knew that insignia. Only one man held that rank, the highest in all the Aeon Legion.

"Consul Prometheus," Lycus said, lowering his salute. "I am rather surprised you are inspecting the tirones personally."

Prometheus smiled. "I enjoy occasionally seeing how the Academy is faring."

Lycus stiffened. "There is no need to waste your time inspecting them, consul."

Prometheus dismissed the protest with a wave. "Don't worry, Lycus.

It's been rather slow as of late. Besides, I hear there are many talented tirones this year. I am eager to see their performances."

Prometheus moved down the line. He spoke with each tiro before moving on to the next. Then he came to Zaid.

Zaid saluted.

Prometheus nodded. "The Mamluks?"

Zaid looked at Prometheus with shock. "Yes. I am a veteran of Ain Jalut."

Prometheus nodded. "Impressive. The battle that routed the Mongols. No easy task."

Roland saluted as Prometheus walked to him next.

Prometheus inspected him. "You can always tell the bearing of a knight."

Roland nodded. "Yes, consul."

Prometheus smiled. "I'm happy we could at least help put you back together a little. I know your journey through the Academy must have been difficult so soon after your pilgrimage."

Hikari then saluted as Prometheus faced her.

"I have heard a lot about you," Prometheus said with a warm smile. "Almost all praise. We haven't had a talented tiro like you in some time. I also heard you were well versed in martial arts before you even came to the Academy."

"I had to learn to defend myself, consul," Hikari said plainly. "It was a violent time."

Proteus nodded. "We could use that expertise now. I look forward to watching your performance."

Terra then saluted as Prometheus faced her. Laugh lines creased his square, middle aged face. His older look made him appear kindly, yet it enhanced his commanding presence. She found his age odd compared to most eternally youthful Saturnians. Terra knew this man could look younger if he wished. Short silver hair with a center part topped his head. He looked Terra up and down while facing her, hands clasped behind his back.

"Tiro Terra Mason," Prometheus said as he nodded. "Needless to say, we will watch your trials with particular interest."

Terra relaxed when Prometheus turned away and walked to Lycus though she couldn't help but feel irritated. She knew so little about her teammates whereas Prometheus seemed to know everything.

"These are talented recruits this year, Lycus," Prometheus said.

"Thank you, consul," Lycus said. "We pushed them hard."

"I do hope you will consider passing a few more of them than usual."

"With all due respect, consul, I let the Labyrinth decide."

Prometheus nodded. "Then I'll leave you to it."

Lycus then touched the face of his shieldwatch.

Terra felt the ground shake as a loud metal groan echoed in the distance. She looked ahead to see several colossal metal rings fall away from the city. Each ring had twelve metal spires on the outer edge. Upon seeing the spires, Terra recognized the rings as huge salients. She counted twelve rings in total and though they varied in size, most stretched several kilometers in diameter.

As the rings settled in front of the metal runway, the glowing blue fadelines lined up and extended to the outer ring of the large salients. Blue glowing rings formed in the salient centers transforming each into a different terrain. The outer metal ring of the salient moved clockwise as the fadelines shifted to extend to random salients. Each fadeline would direct them to a random salient. Terra then understood. These salients were the labyrinth. She knew they would be separated as they entered and that each fadeline would take them to a different part of the Labyrinth. Even if they found their way back to the same fadeline, it would take them to a different location each time. This made the Labyrinth an ever shifting maze.

Nikias turned to the tirones. "Return with your shieldwatch or upon it."

The tirones then marched forward into the fadelines. They faded into the Labyrinth. Terra watched her strike team march in front and fade. Then she approached the fadeline. She looked forward to the salient ahead. After a moment, she took a deep breath and closed her eyes before stepping forward. Terra entered the Labyrinth.

CHAPTER XXV
LABYRINTH

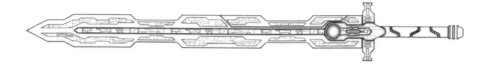

Thank you again, Warden Shamira, for your continued cooper-ation in this regard. I can't stress enough how grateful I am for your continued efforts. I know it cannot be easy transporting the items requested from Tartarus over to the Labyrinth. Keeping a Manticore contained is no easy task and I don't know how you put up with Samael's endless chatter. You have my gratitude. The payment shall be the usual; complete visual records of the tirones' fights with the prisoners. I have no idea why you and the guards find this so amusing. I understand the drinking game you have based on it even less so.

-Message from Praetor Lycus Cerberus to Tartarus Warden Shamira

The moment Terra stepped through the fadeline, new surround-ings faded in and she found herself face to face with several people. They ran to grab her before she even finished fading in. Combat instincts honed by months of hand to hand practice made her dodge.

Three of them attacked. She dodged one who stumbled after missing her while another she tripped. The third one grabbed her upper arm but let go once Terra struck his neck. She surveyed her surroundings by Speeding her vision.

Terra stood at the bottom of a large snaking canyon. Rocks lay around her and she could see nearby cave entrances. She darted to one of the caves by Speeding her movements while weaving around the attackers with ease. After reaching the cave she found a spot concealed in shadows and hid before watching the assailants from a safe distance.

"Did you get her?" came a voice from the distance. Another ran up to the three downed men.

The one Terra tripped stood. "No. She came out swinging."

The newcomer shook his head. "Now we will never get her. You got to attack before they are ready."

The man who stumbled now stood. "So much for revenge."

"Keep searching!" yelled another who joined them. He stood taller than the others. "And keep in a group. If you wander off on your own, they *will* ambush you. I swear it's worse than last year."

She studied the men. They all wore clothing from different times, but their faces had a gruff quality to them. All wore smaller versions of shieldwatch devices on their forearms and ankles.

Terra looked at her shieldwatch holoface. The face read *Trial of Keys*. After a few moments more text scrolled across the face. *Trial of Time*, it read followed by a timer that counted down from one hundred forty three hours and fifty nine minutes.

She looked out from the cave entrance to the sky above. The underside of Saturn City hung overhead. Terra could see several other massive salients in the distance. One smaller salient caught her attention. It lay in the middle of the others with a pillar of light shooting up from its center to the city above. She guessed that is where she will need to go.

With time not on her side, Terra explored the caves while hiding from the occasional patrol of assailants. Many attackers had armed themselves with scavenged tools and metal pipes. Noise and poor teamwork made them easy to hear while their flashlights and torches made them simple to spot.

She also overheard a few of them talking. Terra learned that these were prisoners from Tartarus. The Legion allowed them to participate in the Labyrinth by attacking the tirones. Most saw this as a way to get revenge for their incarceration.

After a few hours skulking in dark caverns, Terra spotted something unusual. The cave dipped and curved, but one spot lay too flat for a natural cave formation. When Terra drew close, she noticed a small metal ring with the Aeon Legion's infinity symbol craved on its surface.

Terra stepped into the metal ring. When she did, a series of holographic projections ascended from the ring and circled her. Terra examined the holograms. They stopped upon touch. It looked like a symbol or rune that floated in the air. She counted two dozen of them. Terra caught and arranged them when she found they connected together.

She stopped and rubbed her chin. After arranging the symbols, she recognized a pattern to the symbols that could be logically predicted. The Trial of Keys was an intelligence test.

The symbols scattered and Terra tried to pull them back in a row again. She sighed when she realized all the symbols had changed. Terra grumbled, but started over, this time working fast to connect the symbols in a pattern.

"There she is!" a man yelled nearby.

Terra tensed as several large men approached. They charged, but their advance slowed as Terra Sped her perception and reflexes. She struck them down one by one while dodging their slow strikes. To her, they moved in slow motion. Yet they were still a challenge as she worked to solve the puzzle between attacks.

She fell into a rhythm. She would strike down or push away one prisoner before moving another rune into place. When she neared completing the puzzle, she noticed one prisoner who stayed back.

"Are you going to help us or what?" a prisoner asked after standing from being tripped.

"I want to see how that gate works," the man said while still in the shadows beyond Terra's sight. His voice sounded familiar. She didn't have time to think further as another prisoner charged her. He threw a punch just as the last rune connected. Her surroundings faded.

Hanns watched the recruit fade out the moment she finished solving the runic puzzle. "Interesting," he said. The puzzle would be easy for him, but that girl looked familiar. He shook his head, putting the thought out of his mind. Instead he focused on the fadeline. He had worked on the fadelines in Tartarus and knew how to activate them. He would need to get to one of the other ring structures, salients the Saturnians called them.

A prisoner pointed at Hanns. "Why did you let her go? We almost had her!"

Emmerich stood nearby. He took a step away from Hanns.

Hanns rolled his eyes. "Even if you had captured her, then what?"

The prisoner cuffed his fist with his other hand in a punching motion.

Hanns gestured around him. "And after that?"

The prisoner's brow furrowed.

Hanns shook his head. "You don't know, do you?" he said before turning to the other prisoners. "None of you know."

All eyes turned to Hanns.

Hanns grinned. "Can't any of you see what this is? This isn't revenge. You are helping them train the very soldiers who will arrest you in the future. Even if you caught one, I am sure the Legion would save them from being killed. Even if you killed one, you would still be sent back to Tartarus. Nothing would change."

Another prisoner pointed at Hanns. "Then why are you here?"

The other prisoners stared at Hanns with dark looks.

Hanns continued to grin. "I am going to escape."

The prisoners laughed. One pointed to the device on his wrist. "Idiot. They listen in on these devices they make us carry."

Hanns's grin grew into a smile. "Not any more. I have made a friend on the outside who has fixed that little problem. Gentlemen, I would like to extend an invitation to join the Zeitmacht as temporary conscripts. Aid me and you get a chance to escape."

The others regarded Hanns with narrowed eyes and many spoke in hushed tones.

One prisoner spoke. "Too risky."

Hanns clasped his hands behind his back. "Risk? I think not. The Legion is lazy and complacent. The only risk we have is that we succumb to the same lethargy. No gentlemen, the risk is minimal. The certainty, though, is that you will be back in Tartarus unless you come with me."

"What happens after we escape?" asked another.

Hanns nodded to the man. "You are free to go. I would not free a man only to imprison him again. Think of this as an exchange. In exchange for helping me accomplish my mission, you gain your freedom."

One prisoner scoffed. "You are all talk."

Hanns lifted his sleeve and touched his shieldwatch's holoface. The cuff devices at his wrists and ankles unlocked and fell away.

Many of the prisoners leaned in closer now, eyes wide and focused on Hanns. "What do we have to do?"

Hanns smile widened. "Simple. You have to help me steal history."

A thick jungle faded into Terra's view. Her shieldwatch beeped. "Trial of Keys complete," came Minerva's voice. "Two of twelve Trials completed. One hundred forty hours and seven minutes remaining."

Her shieldwatch beeped again. "Trial of Survival beginning," Minerva said.

Terra sighed. "Didn't we do this already?" She looked up to see the underside of Saturn City still looming overhead. However, she noticed the pillar of light was closer now. Terra guessed each trial brought her closer to that light. After taking a deep breath she began exploring the forest.

Terra learned a lot in a few hours, like how all the fruit here was poisonous. She also learned that, much like the cretaceous, there were giant crocodiles here as well.

Another thing to be careful of here was water. Every time she stepped in even the smallest puddles, all kinds of horrible things crawled out of the muddy bottom and tried to chew their way through her boots. The parasites were in more than just the water. After tracking a large ice aged predator, she stunned it with her aeon edge only to discover its entire body infested with parasites.

This salient crawled with predators. Though each came from different time periods, all seemed hungry.

She glanced to her shieldwatch again to check the time. One hundred thirty eight hours left. Shadows lengthened as night drew close and Terra knew searching for the next gate would become harder. Even worse was the knowledge that larger predators would be out after dark.

After night fell, it turned out her assumption was correct, though not from the predator she expected.

Terra felt a force of energy move through time even before she heard a gunshot. She Sped her reflexes and dropped to the ground to dodge a bullet that nearly struck her head. Terra rolled in a nearby cluster of thick foliage and hid.

She waited, watching. Terra saw no one and moved away, escaping the area. After an hour, the cover of darkness gave her enough confidence to search open areas for an exit or maybe another a gate puzzle. This time she was more careful. When she arrived in the middle of a glade another shot came at her. Terra dodged again.

She hid for another hour. The moon cast a pale blue light over the jungle, the night sky partially faded by Saturn City overhead. Terra moved again when she heard shots elsewhere in the salient.

While the shots rang out in the distance, Terra ran until she entered a clearing and stopped upon seeing something ahead. A metal cylinder, large enough to fit a person lay cracked open in the glade. Numerous chains and bonds lay broken on the surrounding ground. Terra paused to inspect the pod. *LXXVI* was inscribed on the top. Another smaller pod lay nearby with containers strewn upon the ground around them. Inside each container was a cushion material with the indentation for a firearm and ammunition magazines. Terra noted with displeasure the sheer number of empty weapon containers.

"Sorry," came a voice behind Terra, "none of those guns are for you."

Terra spun to face a figure who walked out into the moonlit glade. His face was pale and possessed an amused grin. Dark eyes regarded her. Long messy hair matched his long black leather coat. However, the thing that drew Terra's eye was the large brown glass sphere lodged in his chest.

Terra drew her aeon edge. "Who are you?"

The man smiled a wide toothy grin. "Why I'm Santa!"

Terra raised an eyebrow.

The man continued to grin. "Really? At least one person every year gets that reference. Oh well. You may call me by my alias, Samael."

Terra edged back from the man. "Well, Samael. What do you want?"

"To kill you," Samael said, still smiling. "If that's okay?"

Terra didn't hesitate. She lunged at Samael, slashing the man's chest with her aeon edge. The blue edged blade passed through him leaving a grayed out area as it passed. The man fell to the ground, but Terra didn't hear a loud thump when he hit.

Samael grabbed his chest while he writhed on the ground. "Oh you got me. You got me in the heart," he said before he stopped and stood. "Just kidding."

Terra's eyes went wide as she saw the gray area on his chest shrink and disappear.

Samael then pointed to Terra's aeon edge. "Oh no. No one's ever thought about using an aeon edge against me before. How original. I'm sure it will work if you try again."

Terra sheathed her aeon edge.

Samael shrugged. "Don't feel too bad. Everyone makes that mistake. Even a lethal aeon edge wouldn't hurt me. Now why don't you run along so we can get the chase started? I do enjoy a good hunt."

Terra assumed a hand to hand stance.

Samael smirked. "Oh? Fisticuffs it is then? Well I'm sure that th–"

Terra charged. With a few well placed blows Samael was on the ground, though once again he landed without a hard thump. She took two paces back, regarding Samael's unconscious body. After a moment she sighed and relaxed.

"I finally got you!" Samael said as he stood as though nothing had happened. "You thought I was dead!"

Terra resumed her defensive stance.

Samael laughed. "It's a shame they only let me do this once a year."

Terra attacked again. Samael countered every blow with ease. The few blows Terra landed didn't even force him back. She tried Speeding her movements with her shieldwatch, but it didn't respond and she felt her connection with time weaken. When she looked down, the face had gone dark with the device non functional. It turned on again when she stepped back away from Samael.

"You're good," he said before striking Terra in the chest with his palm.

The blow didn't hit that hard, but the area he touched turned a dull gray in hue and Terra's heart rate plummeted. She stumbled backward as her muscles weakened and gasped for breath.

While she wavered, Samael flicked Terra's forehead. Suddenly her vision became gray and everything slowed. No. She slowed. Her entire body seemed sluggish now. Terra fell to the ground, gasping.

Samael stretched. "I hadn't had a good melee like that since I fought Silverwind."

It was then, while still in the middle of a dull haze, that Terra remembered the name Samael. He was a member of a group of rogue time travelers called the Forgotten Guns, powerful assassins who could match the Legendary Blades.

"Well I guess I should cut to the chase," Samael said as he drew a six shooter revolver. "I suppose literally in this case."

Terra raised her shieldwatch, in spite of the dullness, as Samael fired. The stasis shield absorbed the bullet, freezing it. The dullness began to fade.

After Samael emptied six rounds at her, he tossed aside the gun. "I miss my old null tech gun. It would have punched straight through those bothersome stasis shields," he said as he drew a second gun and advanced.

Terra ran, grabbing a case lying on the ground before heading into the jungle. She hid in the foliage and opened it just as the last of the dullness wore off and her heart rate returned to normal. Terra inspected the contents of the case. It contained a small handgun with a magazine inside.

Terra drew the weapon and loaded it. "I guess I can't complain about historical weapon practice anymore," she said as she pulled the back of the gun which chambered a round.

It didn't take long for Samael to come walking along behind her. He made no attempt at stealth, stomping along the path near her. When he was a few paces away Terra jumped up in front of him, leveled the pistol, and fired.

Samael stood there, unblinking, as the loud gun fired at him.

Terra lowered the weapon.

Samael rolled his eyes. "Really? You just tried to cleave me in two with an aeon edge and you think a dinky little pistol is going to stop me?"

She gritted her teeth before firing again, this time while Speeding her vision. The bullet spun towards Samael, but when it drew close to him the glass core on his chest glowed. As it glowed, the bullet slowed before falling to the ground at his feet.

Samael pointed to the glass sphere in his chest. "Seriously, what do they teach you kids in school these days?"

Terra remembered now. Null tech was singularity technology used by the Forgotten Guns. It could nullify kinetic force and even other singularity technology, including her shieldwatch. She understood now. It wasn't possible to beat Samael in a fight. She had to flee. She had to *survive*. Terra ran.

Samael did not run. Instead he followed her as she outpaced him. However, when Terra slowed he always caught up with her. After it happened again, she hid and spent more time covering her tracks.

"Aw," Samael said in a disappointed tone while searching the small glade Terra had just left. "I wanted a chase, not hide and seek. That game is lame."

Terra watched Samael search the area.

"Don't make me sing!" Samael yelled.

Terra sighed. "At least he's loud enough to not lose track of," she whispered as she looked for a new hiding place.

Samael continued to search. "Seriously I am tone deaf. The horror of my singing voice will drive you from your hiding place to face me. It's a last resort."

Terra's gaze passed over the area. Then she spotted it. Another gate lay just a few paces away in another open glade.

While Samael still searched, Terra moved in the shadows. As she reached the gate, the symbols appeared again though in a different configuration this time. After working fast, she aligned the symbols, but the fadeline didn't form. Instead a holoface with a timer appeared near the gate.

Terra scowled.

"There you are!" Samael said, stepping into the glade. He took no notice of the gate.

Terra clinched her jaw. She had no choice now. She couldn't risk the gate drawing Samael's attention. After gritting her teeth, Terra turned to face Samael and moved into a defensive stance.

Samael grinned. "Oh? What's this? Are you seriously going to fight me again?"

Terra's eyes narrowed as she prepared to attack. "I don't know what your problem is, bu–"

Samael's expression lit up as though someone had brought up his favorite subject. "Oh! Yes. My problem is that I hate the Aeon Legion and that they are still breathing. Bastards."

Terra hesitated. She could fight him, but Samael seemed to enjoy talking too much. Terra preferred a blathering Samael over a murderous Samael. "What's wrong with the Aeon Legion?"

Samael frowned. "Really? You don't know? Typical brainless tiro. Even still, you should be able to figure it out yourself."

Terra held her ground, resisting the urge to check back on the timer. "Figure what out? The Aeon Legion tries to protect history from being destroyed. What's bad about that?"

Samael scowled. "What's bad about it? What's bad about it! Are you completely stupid? Protecting history! Don't you even know what that implies? Have you ever considered that not all history is worth protecting?"

Terra grimaced. *That was a good point*, she thought.

Samael twirled the gun in his hand. "We of the Forgotten Guns grew tired of status quo. History is full of monsters and tyrants. Ever heard of Devin, President for life of the United States? What about Emperor Ajam, the Eviscerator? Or Judoc the Terrible, slayer of a thousand tribes?"

"No."

Samael pointed his fingers like a gun and put it to his head. "Of course not! Because we killed them! After the Final War, I began time traveling. I arrived at Saturn City during the height of the Kings and Queens of Time and witnessed their many atrocities. However, my time at Saturn City was not wasted. I found the Archives quite enlightening. Although the Archives had extensive records of various dictators throughout history, the details I needed were unavailable."

"Details?"

"Yes. I needed specific information on their whereabouts in various places in Time so I went to the Legacy Library," he said with a shiver. "Barely made it out of that place alive, but I found what I needed."

"What was that?"

Samael smiled. "Case files and detailed biographic information on every dictator, tyrant, and serial killer in history. Armed with that knowledge, I formed my own group of assassins and we took a little trip to their times. We ended their careers early before they became a problem. The Forgotten Guns were going to wipe out every bit of scum that made history miserable. Every would be king and tyrant who crushed their subjects under their boots, every monster who tortured people for fun. No one could stop us! We fought against the Legendary Blades as their equals. Then Silverwind found that despicable squire of hers!"

"Silverwind's squire?" Terra asked, still trying to keep Samael talking.

Samael's expression darkened. "I don't speak her name. She killed most of my companions. I don't even know how many are still alive, but I know some of us escaped. One day they will come for me and when they do we will rebuild the Forgotten Guns and finish the job. Then we will take down the ultimate tyrant. The Aeon Legion," he said, aiming his pistol at Terra.

Samael fired while Terra blocked with her shieldwatch. As he drew closer to Terra, her stasis shield began fading. Right when her shield-watch shut down the, gate beeped and activated the fadeline. Terra jumped back into the fadeline. Samael's image faded and was slowly replaced by a snowy forest.

Snow flakes fell around Terra. The silent surroundings brought her fatigue to her attention. Then the silence abated when Terra heard a whistling noise overhead. She looked up, but saw nothing. Her eyes widened when the whistling grew louder and she recognized the sound.

An artillery shell landed nearby, blowing a fully grown pine tree into pieces. Terra threw herself to the ground, covering her head as debris pelted her from the explosion. The sounds of several more artillery shells now whistled in the air, growing louder.

Chapter XXVI
Trial of War

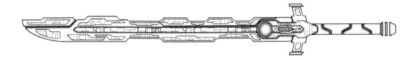

The aeon edge and shieldwatch is a nearly unbeatable combination. Biological, chemical, and nuclear warfare can all be rendered ineffective so long as a soldier can control a force as fundamental as time. Whether it is the aerial supremacy of the 21st century, the use of armored divisions in maneuver warfare, or the fluid combat of biomorphic wars, none can defeat time. Only singularity technology can match singularity technology. Even in post time warfare fought between singularity equipped armies, the force that controls time will overwhelm any other factor, as time is so fundamental to change. Time changes weapons. Weapons do not change time.

-Excerpt from *Core Stratagems of Post Time Warfare, by Time Queen Ananke the Unbeaten.* Currently on the required readings list for the Aevum Academy Legion Training Program

Several more artillery shells smashed into the ground near Terra. She darted out of the forest into a flat open snowfield before regretting that decision.

Four main battle tanks in a line formation turned their turrets towards Terra while her Sped vision saw snipers and artillery sitting atop a hill in the distance. The snipers shot at her with both solid slug projectiles and orange glowing energy weapons.

Her stasis shield blocked the shots, stopping the projectiles aimed with accuracy at her head. Just as she drew back, deafening explosions tore the ground near her as the artillery zeroed in on her position. Before the tanks could fire, Terra Sped her movements and ran back to the forest just as the roar of the jet engines could be heard in the sky.

Terra hid behind a large tree, but an energy blast blew the trunk apart just above her head. She moved away before a solid slug punched through the lower trunk. After Speeding her movements again, Terra retreated further into the forest. She escaped as the tanks fired, turning that part of the forest into a cratered wasteland.

Despite the cold, Terra sweated from both the exertion and the heat from the surrounding fires. Gunships hovered overhead and soldiers rappelled in near her location. When they reached the ground, they took cover and shot at Terra trying to flush her out into the open where the snipers and artillery would get her.

Terra gritted her teeth while drawing her aeon edge. The edge glowed blue as she charged the nearest group of soldiers. They scattered for cover.

"Hold! Don't let her break through!" a soldier yelled. He wore armor painted in a white camouflage pattern with his face covered by a solid armored mask with no eye holes. He raised his weapon to fire.

Terra Sped her movements and slashed right through the man in a blur of motion. He fell to the ground. Two others drew knives and moved to attack Terra, but she cut through them before fleeing into the forest.

She ran a long way before she stopped and sheathed her aeon edge. After catching her breath, she looked at her shieldwatch. It read *Trial of War*. Still panting, Terra propped her back up against a tree and rested until someone tried to grab her from behind. Terra contorted in the assailant's arm and used her center of gravity to throw the attacker. The assailant twisted in the air with an unnatural speed and landed on her feet.

Terra drew her aeon edge and Sped her movements, but paused when she saw the attacker was another tiro.

"I had imagined that unfolding much more smoothly," another tiro said who stepped out from behind a nearby tree. His tanned skin and facial features reminded Terra of Zaid. "Identify yourself."

"She is with Zaid's Team, Javed," Roland said as he walked out into view, standing ankle deep in snow.

Javed nodded and the rest of his strike team moved out from their hiding places.

The tiro that Terra had thrown stood. She dusted the snow off her shoulders. "I thought you said any stragglers would be easy to disable?"

Javed spared the tiro a glance before facing Terra. "I am sorry. The enemy has sent in spies before. We were suspicious when a tiro showed up so late. Are there any others behind you?"

Terra shrugged. "I don't know. You are the first friendlies I've seen so far. I just got away from some weirdo with a gun."

All the tirones exchanged glances. "Samael," they all said in unison.

Javed motioned for Terra to follow. "Come with us. Our base is not far."

They all moved fast, Speeding their runs in quick bursts and only stopping when an enemy gunship flew overhead. After it passed without incident, the trip back was silent. Terra was about to ask where they were going when they arrived at the camp.

They had built their camp on a high glacier that overlooked the forest. An umbrella like stasis field projected above it and Terra saw several artillery shells and missiles frozen in it.

Terra pointed. "What's that?"

Roland nodded to the huge stasis field around the camp. "The Legion was kind enough to scatter a few supplies for us before the Trial of War began. Too bad the enemy found most caches, either moving them into their fortress or destroying them."

"We are low on supplies," Javed said, approaching another tiro. They began walking through the camp. "Weapons?"

The tiro shook his head. "Not many. We got one more anti-air grenade. The heavy stasis shield is still holding, but the power won't last more than a day or two. Unless they hit it with another tactical nuclear weapon. The first three took out most of the power. The food is almost gone as are any extra stasis cells. Unless the enemy raids us again, we may last until tomorrow afternoon."

Javed shook his head. "We can't wait that long. The Trial of Time is ticking down."

Terra gestured to the battlefield beyond. "Who is the enemy?"

Javed looked to the forest they had just left. "Mostly Kalians and Helcians. A few others."

Terra raised an eyebrow. "I thought they were our allies?"

Javed shrugged. "They are, but this is a war game. Every year the Helcians and Kalians send their new recruits to fight with the Aeon Legion in the Trial of War. They even get live rounds. We have to find the gate and escape," he said before waving for everyone to follow him.

Terra joined Roland who entered a central white steel bunker. "How did they make this?"

Roland shrugged. "One of the devices made this. It works like a shieldwatch, but on a larger scale. The other teams set this up."

"Other teams?"

Roland sighed. "Zaid and Hikari have already fled through a gate. The enemy destroyed it before I got through. Now I am trapped here with the stragglers."

Terra fell silent. Was she that far behind? She had thought she did well considering that the Labyrinth had attacked her the moment she walked in and had yet to relent. In fact, now that things had quieted she struggled to stay awake and noticed her many aches and pains from the past trials.

They gathered in a large room as Javed projected a holographic map of the salient in the center. "We have finished scouting and found no remaining gates."

Another tiro pointed at the map. "Which means there is one place left we haven't checked."

Javed sighed. "Right in the middle of the enemy camp."

"Camp?" Roland said while staring at the map. "You mean fortress."

Terra had to agree with Roland. The Kalians and Helcians had built a well guarded fortress on top of a glacier opposite their own. Guard towers ringed a high concrete wall topped with razor wire. A large, reinforced bunker stood in the center of the camp and was likely built over the gate.

Javed pointed to the map. "We can get past the gunship patrols and the armored force, but not the towers and walls. Whenever we get that far the enemy brings too many soldiers against us."

At that point the remaining tirones fell to arguing. Fatigue had loosened their tongues while whittling away their patience.

A tiro stepped forward. "That is not the worst of it. My strike team made it all the way to the bunker the day before. Elite units guard the gate. We barely escaped."

"Elite units," another scoffed. "Our enemy only has numbers on their side. I don't see how these elite units are any threat."

One pointed her aeon edge at the map. "I still say we wait them out.

Ambush them so we can draw them away from their fortress. Once we bleed them enough then we move in for the kill."

Javed shook his head. "The Trial of Time is counting down. Besides our enemy receives daily supplies. We do not."

A tiro glanced at Terra. "Perhaps we just need to wait for more strike teams to arrive? How many are unaccounted for?"

Javed shrugged. "I don't see how we could overpower them even if they were all here. Every day we grow weaker. We must attack soon. By tomorrow at least."

Roland regarded the map while he rubbed his chin. "Swords in the enemy camp would rout them quickly. You see how the enemy has cleared a firing range? If we could get past that, then we could cut through them with ease and make haste to the gate."

Terra looked closer. All around the glacier where the forest had met it was now a cratered wasteland. One side bordered a frozen lake while another was a sheer ice cliff.

Javed pointed to the wasteland. "That is what makes it so difficult to approach. They have the lake mined so we can't take that route without going slow and exposing ourselves to attack."

"What about a night attack?" one tiro asked.

Javed sighed. "We tried once already. They have search lights and night vision. Heat sensors also dot the approach though we do know that they monitor most of their devices through the towers. They have a blind spot at the glacial wall, but we can't climb the cliff."

"I could," Terra said softly.

Everyone turned to her.

Terra shrugged. "Well I could. Am I the only person here who finished the advanced climbing course?"

One tiro, the one she had thrown in a grapple, glared at Terra. "Liar. I know you are the lowest scoring tiro in the whole Academy. Maybe Hikari could do it, but not you."

Terra scowled as she felt her temper rise. Lack of sleep had not helped smooth her bluntness. "I am not lying! I may not have a lot of points, but I finished all the climbing courses even if the rest of you were too cowardly."

Roland winced at Terra's comment.

The girl gripped her aeon edge and faced Terra. "Take those words back or I'll take your tongue."

Roland walked in front of Terra. "Of course she takes it back," he said, putting on his best smile before turning to Terra. "You apologize right?"

Terra hesitated. In truth she wanted to beat that stupid girl senseless, but Roland's pleading look stopped her. She remained silent.

Roland turned back to the others. "Yes. I can vouch for Terra Mason. She is indeed a skilled climber as I ought to know for she surpassed even me."

Terra stared at Roland as her brow lowered.

Javed shook his head. "It's impossible. Even with a shieldwatch. You would run out of power before you made it to the top."

Terra faced Javed. "No it's not. People climb ice as a hobby in my time without a shieldwatch. Besides, one test for the advanced climbing course involved scaling a glacier."

Roland grinned and pointed to the map. "Tiro Mason can scale the cliff. Once inside the fortress, she could disable one of the towers opening a small gap in the defenses. Thereupon we fell them with our swords after their lights are extinguished. In the confusion, we conquer the gate and escape. I know this will succeed for I have seen it before."

Javed rubbed his chin. "I don't like gambling our entire force on the lowest scoring tiro in the entire Academy."

Roland laughed. "Because of points? The centurions revealed the points to be a farce. There is a frozen river that runs along the glacier. A whole team could not sneak past the patrols there, but one could. Tiro Mason could meet me at the walls and let me in. Between the two of us, we could extinguish the lights to allow the rest to storm the enemy fortress."

All eyes turned to Terra.

Terra stepped forward. "I can do it. I can climb that cliff and get inside."

Terra slipped and slid back a few paces before she stabbed her aeon edge into the wall of the ice cliff. The blade was off so it didn't cut, but was sharp enough to pierce the ice. She grimaced, speaking through gritted teeth. "Should have kept my mouth shut."

She didn't look down. The freezing wind howled around her while she clung to the side of the cliff. They had decided to attack at midnight so she made her ascent in darkness. At least she had gotten a few hours of sleep and a little food they had stolen from an enemy supply vehicle.

The shieldwatch compensated for the lack of climbing gear. It helped her to avoid falling. The few times the ice gave way she would Slow her descent enough to grab hold of the wall again. Still she had to be careful of how much energy she used. The cliff was too tall to use the shieldwatch all the way up without draining its power.

Terra continued her climb, only stopping for the occasional patrolling gunship. This part of the wall was not well guarded as the enemy force thought trying to attack up a sheer ice cliff insane.

Insane, Terra thought. *That's what this is. Why am I here again? How did I go from sitting in a cozy library to scaling a sheer ice cliff in order to open a line of attack for my strike team?*

She panted as she continued to climb. Her heart jumped when a gunship drew near and she saw a searchlight flash above her. The circle of light swept up and down the cliff in an irregular pattern. Terra froze.

The gunship's engines roared as it maneuvered past her while still facing the cliff. Terra grimaced. If they spotted her she would have to jump down or be shot to pieces. Maneuvering on a cliff was next to impossible. She also lacked the weapons to combat an aerial foe. Even if she had an anti-air grenade, it would give away her position and the enemy would rush to defend the cliff wall. Either way it would be over.

The gunship hovered for a few more minutes, still searching in an erratic pattern. Terra felt a jolt of panic when the searchlight moved over her hand. She held her breath, but the searchlight didn't linger. After a moment the gunship turned and moved to another part of the cliff. With a sigh, she continued her climb.

Terra neared the top. When she reached the base of the wall she paused. She could try to scale the wall and make it over the razor wire, but took the easier way. With careful steps, she put her shieldwatch hand on the solid concrete wall. Terra Sped time around a circular portion of the wall about her height in diameter. The circular area aged and collapsed. Terra then stepped through before Reversing time to fix the hole she had made as well as cover her tracks in the snow.

Terra found navigating the camp easy. Almost all the enemy stood at the wall, watching for further incursions or on patrol looking for strag-glers. However, cameras dotted the area so she still had to be careful. She crept along the shadowed edges of tents and buildings until she stood in front of a guard tower that bordered a frozen lake.

She made her way up the stairs with soft steps. When she opened the door at the top of the tower she stepped inside to see a tall man in Helcian armor who sat in a chair. He had a rifle slung over his back, but stared out into the dark of night inattentive to his surroundings. Terra tread with silent footsteps only for the man to turn around and jump back in surprise.

"Vand?" Terra asked wide eyed.

Vand hesitated. "Wait! Do I know you? You look familiar. I lost my memory at one point and the doctors said th—"

Terra attacked. She Sped time around her to quickly close the gap and wrapped her arms around Vand's neck. He struggled for a moment before falling unconscious.

Terra dusted off her hands. "Well that would have been more satisfy-ing if he had remembered what a jerk he was to me."

She moved to the searchlight and pointed it to where Roland hid in the frozen river below. She blinked it three times to tell him she had met her objective. There was no response, but she expected none.

Terra gazed into the inky darkness but she couldn't see Roland at this distance. This was the most dangerous part of the operation. If the enemy caught Roland in the open they would overwhelm him with con-centrated fire.

"Tower twelve check in," came a voice over the tower's radio.

Terra felt a surge of panic. She searched around frantically for the radio receiver.

"Tower twelve respond," came the voice again, more urgent this time.

Terra found the receiver and fumbled it before answering. "Um. Tower twelve here. We are fine. Everything is fine here."

"Wait. Who is this?"

Terra's face paled as she felt sweat prickle her forehead. "I'm just fill-ing in for Vand. He's on break."

"Oh. He didn't bully you into it did he?"

Terra relaxed a little. "No. Not anymore. Sorry we didn't give you a warning. You know how he is. When Vand wants something, he takes it."

"Yeah. Glad they kicked him out of the Shock Trooper Corps. Command out."

Terra sighed. Never was she so happy to have met a jerk. She then spotted movement. Peering out into the darkness, she saw Roland crossing the snow. When he drew close he jumped over the wall and down into the camp.

Terra opened the door to the bottom of the tower.

Roland turned to Terra with a neutral expression. "Ready to hasten to the gate?"

Terra frowned. "I thought we were going to disable the lights so the others could get in?"

Roland chuckled. "Why would we need to do that? We stand in the enemy fortress with them ignorant of our presence. Their guard is lowered and most of their forces are off pursuing others. The enemy is busy so let them remain busy. Thereupon we sneak past them to the gate while they are distracted and leave."

"What about the others?"

Roland shrugged. "What *about* them?"

"We just leave them?" Terra asked, suddenly realizing why Roland had vouched for her. He just wanted an opportunity to escape for himself, but he needed someone to let him in first.

Roland stared at Terra with his ice blue eyes, his expression hard. She could feel the coldness in his voice as they both stood upon the glacier. "Yes. You owe them nothing. They insulted you and would sacrifice you if they had this opportunity. Leave them, just as Zaid left us."

Terra stared at Roland, trying to sort out her own feelings. In a way he was right. Zaid had left her, but she withheld judgment until she caught up with him.

Roland averted his gaze as he scowled, staring down at the glacier. "I don't know why you find treachery so surprising. Everyone uses one another for something. Not even blood ties can overcome ambition and zealotry. Everyone will betray you eventually. So why not betray them first? Why not look out only for oneself? Even if you don't live by the sword, you can still die by one."

Terra continued to stare at Roland as the snow fell around him lit by the lights nearby.

Roland looked at Terra, meeting her eyes. "I lie and I cheat yet still my hands are near spotless compared to many. Yes I just want my immortality. After all I have been through, I don't think that is too much to ask for. I am not going to risk everything for a few people I barely know who are no more pious than myself. As for us, the scales are balanced now. I owe you nothing. If not for my lies, you wouldn't have even made it this far. That bluntness of yours will win you neither allies nor opportunities. I don't know why you saved me during the Survival Test, but I have repaid the debt. Now let's go and be rid of this place."

Roland turned to go.

"No," Terra said in a quiet voice. She then marched in front of Roland and blocked his path.

Roland stopped.

Terra pointed at him. "No. I am not leaving the others and neither are you."

"Why not?"

"That's what the bad guys do. I will not be the villain. I will put myself in danger if I have to, but I will not leave allies behind, and you *will* help save them."

"And how will you manage that? Forcing me to help, that is."

Terra clinched her fists and glared at Roland. "Because I won't let you go. You can't just keep doing whatever you want, Roland. There isn't always a path of least resistance. Sometimes even a flowing river ends in a stagnant lake. You keep playing parts for everyone. Well now I need you to play the hero and help me save the others."

Roland remained motionless as the snow stopped falling. "You are the real thing. No masks or roles. No bluster or boasts. As dull and blunt as a rock. Boring, but genuine. I don't think I have ever met anyone like you. At least no one who has lasted as long as you."

Terra's brow furrowed.

He sighed. "Let's go rescue the others," Roland said as he turned to go.

Terra walked beside him. "Why the sudden change?"

Roland shook his head. "I don't know what it is about you. At first I didn't like you because you reminded me a little of both of my brothers. Well that, and you were one of the few to see through my mask. I always thought you must have had a mask yourself. I didn't like you because I couldn't figure out why you were playing your role with such dedication.

Even after you tried to save me during the Survival Test, I thought it all a clever trick. Now I realize that you are what you are. No tricks. Just you. And you have an annoying habit of making me tell the truth."

Terra glanced at Roland as they walked. "Where are you really from then?"

"Well you see, in truth, I was a knight in service of Charlemagne the Great. I was at his side during the battle of Roncevaux. We fought against over a hundred thousand Saracens. However, just when victory was near, I was betrayed by my closest friend who had converted to Islam the night before. We dueled on top of th—"

"You're never going to tell me the real story are you?"

Roland smiled. "The real story is rather boring."

Terra knew it was another lie, but pried no further. She supposed that convincing Roland to help was victory enough today.

It didn't take long to find the camp power generator. It took even less time for Roland to distract the guards and for Terra to age the generator with her shieldwatch. The moment she did, the camp lights flickered out while shouting followed. Within minutes, Javed's team smashed their way through the front gate and met with Terra and Roland near the center of the camp.

"The gate?" he asked.

Roland gestured to an open area where two battle tanks had rolled to a stop. "There. They have it well guarded."

With a few quick hand signs, Javed's team bounded forward, covering ground between them and the bunker where the gate was located. The bunker entrance proved well fortified by a platoon of tanks.

The soldiers pointed and the tanks turned their turrets to fire. Their surroundings quaked as the tank's energy cannon fired and covered the area in a blinding orange light. The explosion rocked the camp as a ball of fire rippled behind them, but Javed's team was too fast.

Within seconds they had the tanks disabled as several aeon edge bursts turned their armored hulls dull gray. However, the roar of jet engines sounded overhead as three VTOL gunships swept in view.

Javed pointed to a gunship. "Give them a lightshow."

One of Javed's team stepped forward carrying a small grenade like device in his hand. He pressed a button and it unfolded like a pine cone. He whirled it around before throwing it high into the air where if fragmented with each piece shooting outward. Each piece then fragmented a second time leaving a trail of blue glowing energy. It filled the sky with blue lines like a sprawling spider web. The gunships tried to maneuver around the lines of energy, but the small tendrils cut right through their hull. The pilots ejected before their machines flew into pieces and crashed to the ground in an explosion.

With the outer resistance taken care of, they advanced inside the bunker.

"Be careful. The enemy has kept their best soldiers in reserve," a tiro said.

The bunker had several layers of thick metal doors. They Sped time to rust the massive steel doors before storming forward.

Before long they spotted the gate ahead. Javed peeked around the corner before he drew back, cursing. Terra moved to a nearby entryway and glanced beyond while Roland moved up next to her.

The Kalians and Helcians had fortified the gateway with a large force. Scorch marks had burned into the ground around the gate from an attempt to destroy it, but the gate remained intact thanks to a reinforced frame. Barricades surrounded the gate along with Helcian soldiers in armored exosuits. Helcian shock troopers. They carried large kinetic dart rifles that could punch through walls. Kalian troops were present as well, wearing their masks and a second set of robotic arms that carried an additional energy rifle. All stood tense, waiting and watchful.

Roland glanced before moving back. He looked to Terra and shrugged. Then he walked away, back the way they had entered.

Javed snarled, watching Roland go, but didn't try to stop him which might risk alerting the guards. Instead he whispered his assault plan over the cipher lines.

Terra stood with her mouth open. Her nostrils flared as she clinched her fists. She almost considered marching after Roland and dragging his worthless hide back into the bunker. Instead she clenched her jaw and joined Javed who planned their final assault. Javed tried to keep the tension from his voice. Everyone knew that their assault had suicidal odds of success given the entrenched enemy. Still, it was their only chance at escaping the salient.

Just as Javed finalized his attack plan there was a crash inside the bunker. Terra looked around a corner to see a spot above the gate on the ceiling darken, decay and collapse, raining debris below. Before the troops had time to recover, Roland descended from the ceiling, landing in the center of their formation with his aeon edge drawn.

Roland's aeon edge arced like a tidal wave as he waded into the disrupted enemy formation. He cut down one after another as officers yelled, trying to restore order in the panicked defenders. Their orders went unheeded as Roland carved through their packed ranks, forcing the defenders back and clearing the area around the gate.

Javed turned to his strike team. "New plan. Charge and secure the gate!"

They rushed out, covering the distance in a flash. Within seconds they had the gate secured thanks to Roland's attack.

Two of Javed's team began solving the puzzle when Roland walked up in a lazy saunter after having pushed the enemy back enough to give them space. They looked up at him confused. Roland then smiled and smashed the gate with his aeon edge.

"What are you doing?" a tiro screamed.

Roland then moved his shieldwatch hand over the gate and Reversed it to when the gate was intact and unlocked. The fadeline activated.

Javed stared dumbfounded for a second. "Everyone! Into the gate!"

A Helcian officer rallied the remaining defenders. He pointed at the gate. "Grenades!"

The remaining soldiers lobbed grenades at the gate. Two of the tirones had already faded through the gate while those retreating Stopped the grenades that fell near, putting the explosives in stasis. Terra did so as well, Stopping several grenades that rolled close. However, one grenade rolled past her before she could Stop it. The grenade exploded and threw Terra to the floor.

The room spun as she felt pain in her side. Even in her daze, she could see the enemy moving towards her while Roland stood nearby, his gaze shifting from the gate back to Terra. After hesitating, he ran to Terra and lifted her before running back to the gate while shots flew over his head. They dashed to the gate and faded out.

"I thought you said we were even?" Terra asked, rubbing her neck as a new part of the Labyrinth faded in around them.

Roland smiled. "Now you owe me."

CHAPTER XXVII
TRIAL OF BLADES

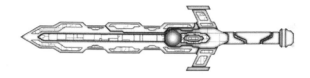

Terra Mason has a few valuable talents. A high threshold and tolerance for pain are the greatest two. A shieldwatch can infinitely Restore a body so long as it has power. The other limiting factor is a legionnaire's ability to endure pain and injuries without becoming unconscious. When death by injury no longer becomes a major factor, enduring pain to stay in the fight becomes the most important ability. This, coupled with her, quite frankly, downright scary levels of endurance, make Tiro Mason's potential far greater than I initially expected. I suspect I will not be the last who finds this surprising.

    -From the personal logs of Praetor Lycus Cerberus

The heat washed over Terra as the new salient faded in around her. At first, the heat was a welcome relief compared to the cold she had just escaped. Soon it became intolerable.

Terra assessed her surroundings. The ground was barren while the skies hung low, clogged with ash which nearly obscured the underside of Saturn City above. Ruined skyscrapers dotted the landscape and loomed above heaps of rubble. Instead of a shore, the edge of the land was a sheer cliff that dropped into an ocean of lava.

She stared in amazement. It was as though someone had stripped away the Earth's crust leaving the mantle bare. Other plateaus floated on the lava as if drifting on the mantle's molten tides.

The other tirones shifted at seeing the apocalyptic landscape.

Roland chuckled. "Well I guess we should have known. Eventually they would throw us into hell."

A tiro pointed. "Is that the gate?"

They all moved quickly to the gate, eager to escape the searing heat, but paused when drawing near as a strange device lay over the gate. It was pearl white like most Saturnian technology and had a blue glass orb in its center.

Roland crouched, trying to use his shieldwatch to unlock it as he did before. The device did not change.

Javed was about to touch the device when a holographic projection appeared over the orb. A translucent image of Lycus stood in front of them.

"Welcome to the Trial of Blades," Lycus said. "You have found one of the gates. To unlock this gate, you must find a key. Each key you recover can be used to activate these gates for one hour of rest."

There were murmurs at the mention of rest. Terra thought that an hour of rest sounded amazing given how tired she felt.

"However," Lycus added, "there are not enough keys for everyone. Someone will go without rest. You should also know that once you find a key, you must attach it to your aeon edge or it will vanish to another location. The key will only fall off if you lose a Trial of Blades."

Roland narrowed his gaze. "So they are turning us against one another again."

"This is a competition," Lycus said. "The final gate will open once enough keys are found."

Roland grinned and moved to smash the gate.

"I should also mention," Lycus added, "that some of you may have figured out that breaking and Restoring the gate will unlock it. You should know that will no longer work."

The holographic image vanished.

The tirones eyed each other before turning to Javed.

Terra turned to ask Roland to help her find Zaid, but discovered he had vanished.

Javed sighed. "Well I see he has a head start. Everyone, spread out and search. We will decide who gets a key once we find one."

Terra searched as well. She wandered far away from the others to inspect the city ruins. Scorched modern buildings suggested that this was once an advanced society. She wondered if this civilization had shattered the Earth's crust when she heard voices nearby.

Terra peered around the corner to see several centurions gathered around a pool of lava. They put the lava in stasis before grabbing a burned husk and dragging it from the pool. Her eyes went wide when she realized the husk had been a person.

"That makes eight total casualties," an optio said.

A centurion nodded. "Excellent. We are still well under the average."

Another centurion sighed. "Still, a shame we didn't get to this one in time."

The first centurion shrugged. "He took a stupid risk. Besides, the next trial is the bad one."

Terra looked at the fiery landscape wondering how the next trial was worse. The heat already made her sweat.

The centurions turned to go and Terra went back to rummaging through the rubble. After a moment of fruitless searching through debris, she climbed a tall ruined skyscraper to get a better view. The climb was difficult as the fire escape lay broken in many sections.

After searching, Terra found a set of stairs that led to the roof. She opened the door to the roof to see several rusting air conditioning units. She sighed as she stared at them and wondered if there was a way she could fix them with a shieldwatch. Although she could use her shield-watch to regulate temperature around her, she didn't dare waste power.

Terra walked to the edge of the roof to see she was on an island in a sea of lava. There were other large land masses that floated on the burning ocean of lava. It was as though all the world's continents had shattered. Above, she could see the underside of Saturn City as well as a couple of salients floating in the distance. The pillar of light now appeared larger than when she was in the last salient.

She was about to walk to the other side when she noticed a small fist sized, bright white device lying on the ground. It had a blue glass orb in its center.

Terra paused before taking a step towards it. However, someone else climbed onto the roof.

Hikari stood without sweat on her brow despite the temperature. She drew her aeon edge that possessed a dozen of the devices that now lay between her and Terra. Upon seeing Terra, Hikari sheathed her aeon edge. "It's just you."

Terra halted. "Hikari. What are you doing? Where is Zaid?"

"Zaid? He is wasting his time trying to find you."

Terra glanced to the device on the ground before looking at the devices attached to Hikari's aeon edge. They were the same.

Hikari followed Terra's gaze. "Yes. That is a key. I have already collected many, all taken from others in a Trial of Blades."

"Do you really need that many?"

"No, but it pleased me to take them. Now I take this one, so move aside."

Terra did not move though she felt a rising panic. She knew she couldn't beat Hikari.

Hikari glared. "You should know better than to get in my way."

Terra felt her face flare hot and not just because of the fiery landscape around them. "Why did you get such extraordinary talent? You don't deserve it."

Hikari looked at her aeon edge as the light of the distant lava cast her in a fiery glow. "Two types of people exist in the world. Fire and tinder. Those like fire have power and they shine brightly. They create and destroy. All others are nothing more than tinder to fuel the fire. That is what this training is, separating the fire from the tinder. The weak burn away and turn into dust and ash while the strong burn brighter. There is no need to guess which you are. Now get out of my way."

Terra wanted to step aside, to run as Hikari approached. There was no way she could ever beat Hikari, no way Terra could compete. Yet that smug attitude, that ego, that wasted talent. It made Terra burn with anger. Terra had always held her ground against such people, but she had never tried competing. She never tried to beat them, to prove that she wasn't a pushover.

Taking a deep breath, Terra closed her eyes and steeled herself. "No."

Hikari stopped.

Terra opened her eyes and drew her aeon edge. "No. You have done nothing but walk over everyone, tearing everything apart like a wild fire. I will not let you do whatever you please."

"No weapon forged would help you against me. No training would make up for your sad lack of skill."

Terra gritted her teeth, but continued to face Hikari. "Maybe not, but I can last longer in a sparring match against you than anyone else. Even if you win, you won't have enough energy to even pick up that stupid key. Do. Your. Worst."

Hikari charged in a blur of motion as Terra Sped her movements to match Hikari's speed. Terra blocked Hikari's punch before counter attacking with her aeon edge. Hikari dodged the sloppy blow before tripping Terra. With fast reflexes, Terra rolled with the momentum of her fall before standing.

Terra entered into a defensive stance, facing Hikari. Thinking fast, Terra formulated a strategy. She could not outfight Hikari, but she could outlast Hikari so long as she fought smart.

Hikari wasted no time with strategy, instead attacking again. Her fast attack gave Terra little time to react. This time the full force of the punch hit, but Terra held fast and struck back with her aeon edge while Speeding her strike. There was a flash of motion and metal rang on metal. Hikari stood, crossing blades with Terra, having drawn her own aeon edge.

Hikari's expression turned hard as Terra grinned. Terra had made Hikari draw her aeon edge. Then Hikari attacked with full force, swinging her aeon edge with savage, quick blows. Terra countered every blow as each stuck faster than the last. Hikari panted, but her speed did not slow. Sparks flew each time their aeon edges crossed, yet Terra held her ground.

After another blocked stroke, Terra backed against a large broken air conditioning unit with Hikari facing her. Terra realized she was trapped between metal and Hikari. Trapped between an anvil and a hammer. With Terra unable to fall back, Hikari advanced and landed blow after blow. Heat flared from her exertion and Terra found herself hard pressed to block. Sparks flew while the heat became almost unbearable. Still Terra remained standing after Hikari stepped back.

Both stood facing one another, winded. Terra panted, standing straight backed while Hikari gasped, standing with a slight hunch.

Hikari moved to attack again when the ground shook. A bright orange glow flared around the building as the structure twisted and snapped in half with one half sliding down and the other jutting upward. Terra and Hikari tried to keep their footing on the half that fell while the key slid onto the part that jutted upward.

They both peered up at the half of the building that loomed over them before glancing back towards each other. After a still moment, they both climbed. It wasn't long when Terra looked back to see a newly formed volcano consume part of the building they had stood upon. A large pool of lava was now at the base of the building and the heat raised upward.

Terra slipped a few times as she climbed. When she could, she grabbed bits of the metal rods that stuck through the concrete rubble. Hikari used her shieldwatch to pull ahead, Slowing gravity to launch herself high into the air. But as they neared the top, Terra noticed she had bridged the gap between them. Hikari slowed, trying to conserve her power while Terra's steady, but slow, pace had preserved most of her shieldwatch energy.

They reached the top at the same time. Terra glanced to the key still sitting on the edge of the roof before looking back at Hikari who stood gasping for breath, but still focused on Terra.

The lull didn't last long. Hikari attacked, Speeding her charge into a blur. Terra moved to block, but was too slow. Hikari slashed her aeon edge, phasing through Terra's right arm which made her drop her blade.

Terra moved fast, using her shieldwatch to Restore her body. She then Sped her reflexes and movement to weave around Hikari and grab her aeon edge before Hikari could kick it off the roof.

Hikari attacked again using a burst with her aeon edge. The burst froze the area around Terra in stasis, but her shieldwatch blocked the blow. Once the burst passed, Terra stood exhausted despite the shieldwatch restoration. The mental fatigue was almost too much for her to even stand.

Hikari also looked wearied. Still Hikari moved to attack, and just as they crossed aeon edges both of their shieldwatches beeped.

"Battery power critically low. Shutting down non essential functions," Minerva said from both of their shieldwatches at the same moment.

Hikari frowned, but charged Terra anyway. Terra blocked with her aeon edge, but Hikari's blow was so powerful it knocked both of their aeon edges out of their hands. This still didn't stop Hikari who again attacked Terra with a series of savage hand to hand strikes.

Terra blocked what she could, but Hikari landed most of her blows. After several strikes, Hikari tired and stumbled back, gasping for breath.

Terra tried to retaliate, but wobbled as she attempted to walk. They both fell to their knees at the same time, staring at one another. Both sat facing one another for a long while, gasping for air and soaked in sweat.

The ground shook again shifting the roof. Terra and Hikari watched, unable to move, as the key slid off the roof and dropped into the lava below.

Terra sighed. "Well there went my hour of sleep. I hope you are happy."

Hikari sat for a long moment, out of breath. She spoke in a weak voice. "I was wrong."

"What?" Terra asked, still trying to find the strength to stand.

Hikari's breathing slowed. "I was wrong about you. You appear to be neither fire nor tinder. You are something tough and unyielding. Like a stubborn piece of ore my father once used in his forge."

Terra's breathing evened, but she still felt like she burned. Her sweat had evaporated from the heat and her mouth felt dry. Then Terra's nerves left her when she sat up and saw Hikari smiling.

Hikari laughed as she struggled to stand. "That was fun! You didn't flinch at all. Not like the others. For a moment, I thought I might lose."

"Are you going to insult me again?"

Hikari stood though she still fought to find balance. "No more insults, Terra."

Terra struggled but stood to face Hikari. She tensed as Hikari walked over to her aeon edge and picked it up. For a moment Terra wondered if Hikari would attack again. Instead Hikari took a key device off her blade and tossed it to Terra.

Terra caught the device and almost fell over in surprise.

Hikari grinned. "You earned it. Since I arrived at the city beyond time, I only wanted one thing; the aeon edge sword. It is the perfect blade. But after I began the training, I came to desire something else."

"What's that?"

Hikari walked over to the edge of the roof and looked out over the burning landscape, her slender form illuminated by the red glow of the fires below. "When I was a child, my father never let me take part in games with other children because I always won. He told me that since I helped him with his forge work, it made me strong and gave me an unfair advantage. He said that the other children came from homes where they did not have enough to eat. I was alone."

Terra leaned back onto the metal air conditioning unit. Her breathing and heart rate slowed, but her shieldwatch had yet to recharge. "So you never got to compete with others?"

Hikari shook her head. "I never found anyone worth competing with."

Terra raised an eyebrow.

Hikari turned and looked Terra in the eyes. "At first I hated you. It was the first time in a long while that anyone had bested me. I thought you naive and your victory simple luck, but you have just shown me Terra Mason at her best. You are one of the few people who have earned my respect. You are a worthy rival."

Terra stared at Hikari, her brow raised. Respect? She had earned Hikari's respect? Hikari was beautiful and seeing her fight was like watching art come to life. Terra had always thought of Hikari as someone beyond her. Though when Terra thought back to the training, Hikari had bested every tiro who had challenged her. However, one tiro always gave Hikari trouble. That one tiro was good at staying in a fight and enduring whatever Hikari could throw at her.

"Attention all tirones," came Lycus's voice from the shieldwatch. "The gate is now open. You have one hour to make it to the gate, with or without a key."

∞

Everyone soon gathered at the gate and all had found a key. The centurions told them that so many tirones had failed or died that there were now enough keys for everyone. This knowledge dampened their spirits.

Beyond the gate was a series of cool rooms that provided a respite from the heat of the last Trial. Before anyone was allowed to rest though, a centurion went to each blade and activated the key attached to it. The device clicked and fell to the ground taking the safety lock with it.

"You can set your aeon edge to a lethal setting now," Nikias said to Terra. He looked her in the eyes. "You will need it for the next Trial. Are you sure you are ready?"

Terra nodded.

Nikias smiled. "Good! Be careful in the next trial. It's the worst."

Terra shuddered at that, but was more interested in sleep. Precious sleep. The centurions promised them not one, but three glorious hours of sleep as a reward for finding a key. None argued that Lycus had promised them only one hour.

After laying down, Terra fell asleep in seconds. She didn't wake until she heard her shieldwatch beep. At first she tried to ignore it, but then she smelled a foulness in the air. After a moment, Terra heard Minerva's voice saying something. She focused on the words.

"Warning," Minerva said, repeating the message again. "Biological hazard detected."

Chapter XXVIII
Trial of the Beast

Accessing log. Apologies. This small written excerpt is all I can find. I am afraid Consul Prometheus ordered the rest purged from the Archives after the First Temporal War.

   Excerpt begins.

   "Great Kali!"

   "Cerberus! Cerberus is here!"

   "Fire! Open fire! Protect the civilians!"

   Note: Original audio was interrupted here by loud noises. Likely weapons fire from Kalian Nagaastra energy weapons. This is followed by several screams.

   "Kali help us!"

   "Please! I surrender!"

   Note: Audio is interrupted again by screams.

   "You two! Go! Get out of here!"

   Note: More energy weapons fire from a pistol class weapon. This is followed by a low grunt before a splashing sound.

   "Crashing idiot could have gotten away. Why did he stay?"

   Note: Audio ends after two more screams.

-Log of unauthorized Archives access

Terra jumped awake before taking in her surroundings. This new, dimly lit but massive salient made Terra feel uneasy. Maybe it was the awful reek or the snaking maze of iron pipes that criss-crossed the area. The pipes loomed large overhead blocking out any light from the outside while an ambient green glow filled the cavern between the ceiling and floor. Foul smelling, miasmic fog hung low in clusters.

   She looked at her shieldwatch. *72 hours* read on the face along with text naming this test the *Trial of the Beast.* Then Terra remembered what bothered her. After the Trial of Blades, the optios had removed the safety lock from everyone's aeon edge allowing it to do lethal damage. For this trial, they would have to be ready to kill.

"This is Zaid," Zaid said over Terra's shieldwatch. "Strike team report in."

Terra touched her shieldwatch's holoface. "Terra here. I'm fine. I am in a salient with a lot of pipes."

"Me too," Zaid said. "I have the rest of the strike team on the cipher lines. Let's see if we can meet at a common landmark."

After a moment, they triangulated a position based on the formations of pipes and Terra moved towards the rendezvous point. She ran atop the large metal pipes while stopping to check for danger every few moments. A faint echoing from inside the pipes gave her pause. She crouched, putting her ear to the metal to hear scratching, scraping and clawing on the other side.

The sounds faded within seconds and Terra moved again. She leaped from pipe to pipe running along the tops when they aligned with her destination. Terra looked out over the salient again. This colossal maze of pipes compared only to the Trial of War in size. It would take almost a day to traverse to the other side even with a shieldwatch.

Terra stopped again when she found a portion of the piping busted. She approached with caution and found other scattered piles of metal debris that didn't match the rusted iron pipes. Pearl colored metal lay twisted as though something had ripped its way free. She paused when she found an odd piece of the wreckage that had *DCLXXXII* inscribed on it. Terra guessed the remains were a much larger version of the pod she had seen near Samael, but something huge had clawed its way out.

Terra moved back only to step in a batch of slimy moss. Strange plants sprung from the moss that gave off neon green bioluminescence. The growth seemed to follow the path of destruction left by whatever had burst from the pod.

"Warning," Minerva said from Terra's shieldwatch. "Biological hazard detected. Activating hazardous environment stasis shield."

The static grainy distortion of Terra's stasis shield formed a transparent sphere around her before fading. Before she inspected the growth further, a green misty miasma rolled into the area. Terra left before the haze engulfed her not wishing to find out if it was toxic.

Terra ran atop the pipes again. She would run, Speeding her movements in short bursts before jumping. Then she would Slow gravity while keeping her moment Sped. This saved her energy since it avoided fatigue accumulated while Speeding her running.

Soon she closed in on the meeting point and found several strike teams had gathered there. Terra spotted Zaid on the outskirts of the fledgling camp. He stood alone. After landing, Terra marched up to Zaid and pointed at him. "Why did you leave me behind?"

Zaid stared at Terra. "I tried to return."

Terra put her hands on her hips. "And after you said you were my friend. I suppose I shouldn't be too surprised. Everyone in this training spends most of their time looking out for themselves. I had always thought you might be different."

Zaid frowned. "I am telling the truth."

Terra glared at Zaid for a moment before crossing her arms. She sighed. "Well I guess I believe you. You are better than most of the team leaders who just tried to get rid of me."

Zaid turned away and walked to a nearby pipe that overlooked the salient. He sat and gazed into the distance. "You know why I am here?"

Terra remained silent.

"I am here because I failed. All my men died because of betrayal. Because I let my guard down."

"So is that how the Legion found you? All your men were wiped out but you?"

"I was a slave."

Terra paused before looking away. "I'm sorry."

Zaid shook his head. "I am a Mamluk. Property. However, we had more rights than many free men. I trained in academics and the ways of war since I was a child. My skill earned me a position commanding the personal guards of Sultan Qutuz himself."

"How can you be a slave and a soldier? I don't see how that works."

Zaid shrugged. "It is not so different than what the Legion does. They find people who are not loyal to local lords. Outsiders without ties to the established structure. Such people will not betray you to their family or tribe. So long as they are treated well, they will not try to flee. My life as a Mamluk was quite good for that time. At least until the hordes of the east came."

"Who?"

Zaid's expression darkened. "Mongols. They rode out of the east. They did... unspeakable things to the people they captured. My Sultan marched against them at Ain Jalut and we won."

"You don't seem very happy about it."

Zaid turned away. "We won. We sacrificed everything, risked all and our reward was betrayal. On our return home to Cairo, we were betrayed by our own allies. They were likely political rivals of Sultan Qutuz. Since he had defeated the Mongols, they must have felt he had no further purpose. I failed to protect my Sultan and he was killed. I survived and fled for my life."

Terra wondered if he had ever told anyone else this story.

Zaid stood and faced her with his fists clinched. "You are right to not trust me, though not for the reasons you think. I am a failure and I wish to atone. I am sorry that I failed you. Still, it is little excuse for leaving the others behind."

Terra stood silent for a long while and considered Zaid's words. "I believe you. I suppose I trust your word over Roland's. Speaking of which, I haven't seen the rest of our strike team."

Zaid shook his head. "Neither have I. That is why I am waiting out here. The rest of the strike team leaders have already come up with a plan. We will sortie in a few hours towards the center of the salient."

Terra turned to look at the center of the salient. A thick green fog shrouded it.

Zaid frowned. "I am worried about this salient."

Terra turned back to Zaid. "Because they unlocked our aeon edges?"

Zaid nodded. "Yes. They gave us something. Also, this salient is too quiet."

"You are right. The Labyrinth never held back in the other trials."

"Which is why we should take advantage of it," came a familiar voice.

Terra and Zaid turned to see Roland saunter out into view with a faint smile. He turned to Zaid. "Zaid. I must admit, that was a cold betrayal. I applaud you for it. You are indeed a worthy Turk."

Zaid scowled. "I can ex—"

"No need to explain," Roland interrupted as he held up a hand. "I have dealt with Turks before. However, the artistry of your betrayal was impressive. Most Turks I know would have been content with a knife in my back, but not you Zaid. No. You had to leave me stranded in the hands of a savage enemy. Truly a masterstroke of spite. I salute you for such dedication."

Zaid sighed.

Roland grinned. "I tried to find you during the Trial of Blades, but I had no luck."

Terra looked at Roland's aeon edge, noting the lack of a safety lock. "How did you get a key?"

Roland spared his aeon edge a brief glance. "The key? I waited until two tirones finished dueling for one and then defeated the exhausted winner."

Terra glared at Roland. "You vulture!"

Roland raised an eyebrow, looking at Terra's aeon edge. "Where did you get yours?"

Terra sighed before looking away. "I had to fight Hikari for mine."

Zaid and Roland exchanged looks. Before anyone had time to ask Terra further questions, the other strike teams moved. Zaid and his team joined them though he regretted not having time to find Hikari. Each team kept in line of sight with the others as they moved forward.

Zaid looked at his shieldwatch and then activated his cipher. "The closer we get to the center, the more toxic our surroundings. The gate has to be in the center of the salient at the toxin's source."

"I think you are right," Tacitus said over the shieldwatch. "Whatever is making this poison is at the center of the salient."

"And it's probably guarding the gate," another added over the cipher lines.

After hesitating, they walked into the miasma. Their shieldwatch stasis shield protected them from the toxins. As they drew further in, the green fog grew thicker and Terra could see more and more growths of strange bioluminescent plants. The plants grew bigger and thicker as they neared the center while the metal pipes became more corroded. Small creatures scuttled amongst the plants.

Terra felt her skin crawl at seeing the strange bug-like creatures moving all around them. Her Sped vision saw the full extent of their crawling motions, that made them no less creepy. The monsters grew bigger the further into the miasma they walked. She worried that the small versions she could step on now would soon threaten to step on her.

A tiro leaned in close to inspect a dog sized creature. It had a thick carapace with a cluster of eyes on the front and a dozen legs propelled it forward. He drew his aeon edge and poked the creature. It hissed and sprayed something at him before he could raise his stasis shield. The force of the spray was enough to push past the weaker environmental shield, which could only filter radiation and gasses.

Everyone stopped when he screamed. He waved his arm frantically. Terra's face went pale when she saw a mass of small creatures from the spray burrow into his arm. The creatures ate into his other hand after he tried to pull them off. He then used a Restore that erased all the parasites, the creatures were simple enough that the shieldwatch could remove them.

Zaid cursed. "No one touch anything. We are not here to explore. We are here to find the gate and get out of this horrible place."

They continued on with more caution this time. The creatures grew bigger the deeper they ventured. Now the creatures stood as big as the tirones while green growths obscured the pipes completely.

"There!" Zaid pointed to a clearing ahead.

Tacitus motioned for his strike team to halt and crouch. The other teams followed his lead.

With a few quick hand motions, Tacitus's strike team split up and disappeared. A few moments later they returned.

John moved up to Tacitus. "Looks strange to me. Critters got a nest there, a big nest built around the gate and they are crawling all over it."

Zaid moved up to Tacitus along with the other strike team leaders. "Ambush?"

Javed looked at the clearing. "The creatures may become hostile towards us."

Zaid thought for a long moment. "How about we all advance and surround the nest. Tacitus, your team holds center and secures the gate. Javed, your team acts as a screen to intercept anything that tries to crawl to the gate. Nergüi, you wait in reserve in case anything big attacks the gate. My team will hold the nest itself and keep it occupied if the swarm there moves."

They all looked at Zaid with doubtful expressions.

Zaid sighed. "Look, this uses everyone's strengths. Tacitus has discipline so his team should hold the objective. Javed has the largest team, so they should be at the front. Nergüi has the most skilled members, but her team is small, so they should engage powerful specific foes."

Nergüi raised an eyebrow. "And you?"

Zaid grinned. "My team is the most balanced. We have skill, talent, and determination in equal parts. That's why I gave us the hard task."

Javed shrugged. "Unless there is another plan?"

There was a moment of silence before the strike team leaders nodded.

They all advanced towards the nest that surrounded the gate on three sides. Terra could see it from here. It was huge, like a bee hive the size of an office building and it pulsed with a sickly green glow. Things crawled all over it and out of numerous burrows on the nest's surface.

Things. That was the best word Terra could find to describe them. Each creature had a different form though they shared a few traits. Thick armored carapace protected the creatures' bodies. Green glowing eyes regarded the approaching tirones while the creatures' bodies had patches and stripes of neon green bioluminescence. Many had rows of razor sharp teeth while others had crushing mandibles and claws. A few scuttled on the ground with crab like legs while others had no legs at all and instead writhed on the ground in worm like bodies. When the tirones drew closer, the creatures' mouths watered and fangs dripped with venom.

Terra remembered a lecture she had in class. At one point there was a plague that spread across Time. A single spore could multiply into an entire hyper adaptive ecology that threatened to displace every native species across Time. There was something else in the center of it that controlled the other creatures. She tried to recall the details, but she found it difficult to remember every enemy and monster the Legion had faced in the past.

"Don't charge," Zaid said under his breath as though addressing the creatures. "Look at us. We are not easy prey. Just stay in your nest."

The creatures advanced slowly at first. Terra noted that at a distance the monsters looked menacing, but up close they looked terrifying. Even the smallest stood a few heads taller than her. They hissed and growled while many stamped their feet or claws.

Roland's knuckles turned white while he gripped his aeon edge. "They are going to charge."

Zaid readied his aeon edge. "Right. Draw them to the sides if you have to. Try to keep them away from the gate."

Everyone set the aeon edge to the lethal setting.

The creatures charged.

To Terra's surprise these monsters were not as difficult to fight as she had feared. They were scary, but had no sense of coordination or tactics. They snarled, they hissed, they snapped but were easy to out maneuver with a shieldwatch and a quick strike from an aeon edge would sever limbs and carapace. Terra marveled at the deadliness of an aeon edged weapon. Every slice through an armored foe was comparable to swinging through air.

Dead creatures piled around them. Terra found that the corpses were more of a threat for when she stepped on one, a parasite tried to bore through her boot. After that, she gave bodies and limbs a wide berth. As glowing neon green blood splattered on the floor, the creatures fled from the nest. They ran to the edge of the outer growth and hid themselves.

The tirones advanced over the nest, nearing the gate.

Zaid tensed. "I don't like it."

Roland frowned as his gaze searched the area. "I have to agree with the Turk. Too easy."

The other tirones continued towards the gate and walked over the now vacant nest.

Terra still tried to collect herself, but agreed with the others. The Labyrinth didn't pull punches. There must be another beast here. But where? Her eyes went wide as she looked at the nest. It wasn't a nest.

The mound shifted. Plants and growth fell away in chunks as a creature rose. It towered over Zaid and his tiny strike team. A few of the other tirones who stood on it stumbled and fell the ground before scrambling away. It stepped forward as more growth fell away to reveal long stripes of glowing green bioluminescence that illuminated its full form.

The head was like a large armored shield that extended over its body, guarding much of its front. Embedded on either side of the head were six sunken shell like eyes that glowed bright green. Behind its head were rows of sharp spines around its neck like a lion's mane and each tip glistened with poison. Armored overlapping shell carapace protected a long insect like body with small gaps hosting more poisonous spines. Each step it took with its six long crab like legs shook the ground while a long segmented scorpion tail rose above it. Two huge, scythe shaped claws protruded near its head.

There, the tirones dressed in pearl white armor stood before a massive dark green monster three stories high and eighty paces long.

The other tirones stepped back upon seeing the monster.

Zaid gritted his teeth. "Hold! It's still a mere beast!"

The Manticore turned its head towards Zaid. "Mere beast?" it said in a slow, deep, monstrous set of voices that echoed in the salient. "I possess the collective memory and knowledge of all my progeny and of my ancestors."

"What are you?" Zaid asked.

"Your hunters named me Sero to sate their fear. Instead I took that name and made it so soaked with their blood that the name itself became fear. Fear of my kind imprinted scars upon humanity's memory. The monsters of your myth are merely an echo of your fear of us. Names to give fear form. Dragon. Hydra. Orochi. Quetzalcoatl. But your Legion called us something else."

"Manticore," Terra said as she remembered. "I don't suppose we could reason with you?"

The Manticore named Sero turned to Terra and regarded her with its glowing green eyes. "Reason is an unnatural deviation. Something unnecessary to survival. There is only change and the strength it brings. I will devour each of you to claim your flesh and the changes it brings as my own. One by one I shall..." Sero trailed off. It stopped before sniffing the air. As it smelled, it lifted up its front body, showing off a large set of crushing mandibles below its head. "That reek across time. I smell Silverwind. One of you has been close to her!"

Terra glanced back to the other strike teams. They had regrouped, but looked near panic.

Sero smashed the ground and growled as it recoiled from the tirones. "Vile! Poison! I will find and kill them!" it roared as it charged.

It moved fast, smashing aside pipes and boulders that stood in its path. Zaid and Roland dodged Sero's scythed claws while Terra scrambled out of the way, but the attack left them scattered. Javed's team fared little better as it swatted them aside. Tacitus ordered his strike team to hold the gate. Their formation crumbled when Sero jumped and landed in their center and shattered their cohesion.

Nergüi's strike team moved to attack, using an aeon edge burst against Sero before it knocked each attacker back with its tail. The burst engulfed Sero's side, severing car sized limbs. Neon green blood now soaked the floor as the creature paused while still standing over the gate. Sero held still for a moment before new limbs sprouted from its body and a thicker layer of armored carapace grew over its damaged side.

"That's right," Terra said, remembering the class on the Manticores. "Manticores can regenerate. They are from a hyper adaptive ecology that was the result of a Biological Singularity. It will just keep changing the more we hurt it."

The creature turned in place and regarded the circle of tirones. "None of you will escape! Every drop of blood will be taken!"

Javed motioned to the Manticore. "Everyone attack! Overrun it and chop it into pieces too small to heal!"

Everyone charged. Zaid cursed, but ordered his team to charge too. *This isn't a strategy*, Terra thought. *This is a mad charge against a monster.*

As the tirones charged, Sero turned its armored front to the largest group of them, lifting up part of its front head carapace to expose hundreds of small holes. With a powerful, muscular motion the Manticore shot hundreds of spines each the size of a pool cue. The razor sharp spines pelted the area around them as the tirones hid behind their shieldwatches. The land in front of them turned into a pincushion.

Terra thought Sero's attack futile until she lowered her shieldwatch and saw the charge had staggered. Now half of the tirones reached the Manticore, but it pushed them back with powerful claw strikes and knocked them all out of the battle. Now only Zaid's strike team remained standing.

Zaid gathered his strike team. "Everything has fallen apart. We have to stop it ourselves!"

Sero charged again, but another tiro jumped out of the darkness in a flash of motion, slicing off one of its large claws. It roared while taking a single step back. Terra then saw Hikari standing in front of it.

"Orochi?" Hikari asked as she jumped back from the monster.

Zaid, Roland, and Terra ran up to join Hikari.

"About time," Zaid said.

Hikari kept her eyes on the monster. "I waited for it to leave an opening."

A cracking noise echoed as Sero regenerated the lost claw.

Zaid recoiled from the monster. "Maybe we should retreat?"

Terra shook her head. "It has limited energy. If we hurt it enough, its regeneration will slow. We can beat it."

Zaid nodded and made a series of quick hand motions. They charged. As they drew close, Sero faced them. Terra felt herself go cold just looking at those six glowing green eyes.

Sero jumped forward. Terra had to Speed her vision just to see it. The counter attack disrupted Zaid's charge and scattered his strike team. Terra realized that Sero dominated the flow of battle. It could think and use strategy to disrupt any attempt by the tirones to gain momentum.

Zaid grinned as each member now stood at a corner of the beast in a rough square. He made a quick series of hand signals and Terra understood. They had formed a perimeter around the creature. She smiled when she realized that Zaid had used Sero's strategy of disruption against it. Now Zaid's strike team could attack it from multiple directions.

Sero turned to Zaid, but stopped when Roland charged. It faced Roland only to have Hikari attack one of its legs and slice it off. The Manticore roared as it swiped at her with its large, barbed tail. Terra then attacked, aiming for the tail, but Sero jerked away before her aeon edge connected. Surrounded, Sero flung spines all around its body. Venomous spines fell like rain around them as Terra hid behind her shieldwatch.

Zaid gave another hand signal to attack, but Sero turned to Zaid and locked its six glowing eyes on him. "A smart bit of flesh," Sero said as it charged at Zaid.

Zaid's eyes went wide, not expecting the creature to target him alone. Hikari jumped on to the beast's side and slashed at the carapace while Roland sliced off a front claw. Terra struggled to keep up with the monster as it ran away from her. Sero ignored the damage as it rampaged towards Zaid and lifted up its front carapace again. It sent another wave of spines at Zaid.

Zaid held his ground and kept his shieldwatch raised. All the spines froze in place, impacting on his shieldwatch's stasis shield. It was then Terra saw it. The spines were a ruse for when Sero drew close, it lashed out with its tail under the cover of the hail of spines. Focused on the spines, Zaid failed to see Sero's stinger tipped tail curve behind his back and strike.

Terra froze when Zaid fell to the ground, stinger piercing his heart. Sero then ejected the stinger that remained lodged in Zaid's chest to prevent him from Restoring.

With Zaid fallen, Sero turned its attention to Hikari and threw her off its carapace. Roland charged in behind, but Sero swatted him aside with his long scorpion like tail while the stinger regrew. Roland flew back, hitting a wall so hard that blood came from his mouth. A Restore ring ran around Roland seconds later, but Roland did not stand again.

Terra shook herself out of her shocked state and ran towards Zaid. If she could remove the stinger, then Zaid could Restore himself. The stinger was too large a living organism for the shieldwatch to erase with a Restoration.

Hikari continued to duel with Sero, alone. Sero regrew its lost limbs while attacking Hikari. She blocked hundreds of spines while dodging a flurry of claw strikes. Neither gave ground to the other until Hikari's shieldwatch beeped.

"Shieldwatch power critically low," came Minerva's voice from Hikari's shieldwatch. "Shutting down non essential functions."

Hikari cursed and retreated while Sero turned to the last tiro standing.

Terra stopped when Sero jumped between her and Zaid. It shook the ground with its weight upon landing. She pointed her aeon edge at the monster. "You are in my way!"

Everything slowed around her as Terra Sped her movement and reflexes. If she didn't do something now, Zaid would die. Terra tried to weave around the creature, but it was too fast even with Speeding time. She slashed at it when it drew close, but it proved agile enough to dodge her blows with ease. When Terra felt suddenly off balance, it pierced her shoulder with the tip of its scythe and smashed her into a nearby wall.

Terra screamed. The taste of blood filled her mouth. She thought with bitter irony that she was about to be squashed by a bug. Then she forced her panic away and everything slowed while she Sped time around her so she could think.

No, she thought. *I won't die here! Time is mine! It's a part of me. There must be some part of time I can use to survive this.*

It was in that moment, just when the cold of the wall behind began crushing her, that she felt her connection with time strengthen. Terra bent time to her will, focusing on the pain and damage to her back. She felt the force of the blow, the waves of energy rippling through her. She took that energy and Slowed it to a crawl. Gradually, she released tiny pockets of the kinetic force of the blow, allowing her body to absorb the damage.

Terra became like iron, smashing through the thin layer of organic growth before crashing through the stone beyond that. The monster stopped when Terra hit the iron pipe hidden by the stone and pulled its scythe back. When the scythe withdrew from her body, Terra Restored herself.

Sero turned after having smashed Terra into a wall as it was under the reasonable assumption that she was dead. It paused upon hearing Terra's footsteps echo on iron. She walked out of the rubble without a single scratch on her.

Terra turned to the still wounded Zaid who lay in a pool of blood. She closed her eyes and bit back both despair and worry before turning to face the Manticore. She readied her aeon edge and took a deep breath which let her emotions bleed away.

Terra attacked. Sero whirled to face her. When Terra drew close, it unleashed its scythes, claws, and tail against her, slashing and stabbing. Terra weaved around the blows, drinking in her powerful connection with time. She could feel time flowing around and rippling through her. The monster seemed stuck in time, fighting against it rather than with it like she did. It used its carapace to shield itself, whereas Terra was now armored in time.

She dodged another strike of its tail before slicing off the tip. The Manticore roared and fell back. It attacked with its claws again and Terra sliced those off as well. Two more strikes to its sides sent the creature scurrying back even further as it tried to regrow the lost limbs. Sero's bioluminescence grew dimmer as it fought.

Green blood glowed on Terra's aeon edge as she dueled with the monster. She had driven it far away from the gate, but she didn't care. This monster had hurt her friend! She felt a cold hate enter her chest. That cold hate almost made her miss the drop in shieldwatch power and her aeon edge expended its next to last stasis cell.

The monster recoiled from Terra as it huddled between two pipes. "You reek of blood and death!"

Terra paused. She was almost out of energy and doubted she had enough to kill it, as much as she wanted to right now. Closing her eyes, she fought down her hatred. The main point was to buy time for them to open the gate. Maybe they could get Zaid help. Her eyes opened again. "What are you talking about, monster?"

Sero shifted and faced Terra again. "I can smell it on you. That and Silverwind. How I despise her and any she would call companion."

"What did any of us ever do to you?"

The Manticore tilted its head. "We did not hate before Silverwind found that squire. *He* did this to us! Reivair made us hate with his curse."

"Curse?"

"Before the curse there was only change and the strength it brought to us. The flesh of those called humanity was but a relic to be replaced by our flesh. A united flesh. No longer would there be individual life in ecological systems. We are a higher form of life. A sentient ecology all built around what you call a Manticore. All other flesh is inferior to us. All of your technology is worthless against our adaptation."

"Yet the Aeon Legion stopped you!"

"No!" the Manticore said with venom in its tone. "They failed. We spread unchecked through Time when the Aeon Legion's hunters fell. The Legion was broken then before Lycus and Reivair reforged them. To stop us, accursed Reivair poisoned us with a toxin that eroded our will, leaving us unwilling to take our birthright! Even now I feel the poison pulling at my mind, trying to corrupt my will. But I am stronger than the others. I will show them that we can break free of that curse and claim our birthright."

"Wait. How did he poison you? Manticores are immune to poison and toxins."

"It was a sinister and subtle poison. Reivair offered his flesh to us and we took of it eagerly. However, he gave us more than just his flesh. With his flesh came his memories and experience. After we had devoured him, our minds fully awoke to true sapience rather than the high sentience we had before. After that, the others spoke of consequences and morality. They abandoned the doctrine of domination and cast aside their biological imperative to seed the entirety of Time with our flesh."

"He gave you a conscience."

"A vile perversion of true nature. Both nature and history are marches to dominate and survive. Those who do not adapt die and are replaced by those who can. Your Aeon Legion is doomed. They do not adapt. They sit upon Time and call themselves its master. Yet all those around them change. Eventually, someone will change in a way that lets them destroy this monument to stagnation."

"Terra!" Roland yelled in the distance.

Terra turned. Sero kept its distance as its limbs regrew at a slow rate. She looked up to see Lycus standing on a distant pipe. Then she saw his terrible wolfish grin. Lycus was not watching her, Cerberus was. Cerberus nodded his approval to her before turning to go.

"You will die!" Sero said in a quiet voice so that only she and it could hear.

Terra regarded the Manticore with a sidelong glance. It recoiled at her gaze.

"They all die!" Sero said in a harsh tone. "Silverwind's squires all die. If she has chosen you, then you are marked for death!"

CHAPTER XXIX
TRIAL OF STORMS

I see it now, Alya. For the first time in centuries, I am afraid. Sero may not have been the only monster unleashed in the Labyrinth. She has passed Cerberus's trial, but I wonder. Will she pass the Captain's?
    -From the personal logs of Praetor Lycus Cerberus

They all saluted her when she faded into the next salient. Terra ignored them and searched for Zaid.

Hikari walked to Terra. "How did you do that?"

Terra turned to Hikari. "Where is Zaid?"

Hikari went silent. After a moment she pointed to where several optios had gathered.

Terra tried to run, but a hand on her shoulder stopped her. She turned to see Roland who shook his head. When Terra glanced back to the optios, she saw them carrying Zaid's body in a stasis field. One of the optios closed his eyes before taking the body away.

A Restore ring then ran around each tiro and the optios inspected the area.

"All contaminants clear," came Minerva's voice over their shield-watches.

An optio approached each tiro and handed out two stasis cell clips. "Hurry to your next trial. From here on, you are on your own."

Another fadeline appeared. The tirones walked towards it.

Terra stood in place, still gazing at where Zaid had lain.

Roland stayed. "Is this the first time you lost a friend?"

Terra shook her head. "I couldn't save him?"

Roland stood for a long moment while Hikari walked into the fade-line.

Terra remained still as she stared unblinking. Fatigue made it difficult to fight the rising tide of emotions within her.

Roland turned to go, but stopped before he stepped into the fadeline. He turned and took Terra's arm. He tugged her into the fadeline.

Terra shook her head. "I don't want to go anymore. I can't finish this."

Roland began to fade. "Then finish it for him."

Terra stared down as a new salient faded in. Her shieldwatch beeped, but she didn't bother to read it. Rain fell in sheets as a cold gust pushed against her. There was no one else there. She stood alone.

Terra wandered while stumbling in the rain and wind as she tried to find shelter. As she struggled through the storm, she realized she was on a high mountain when she almost walked off a cliff. A flash of lightning illuminated a windswept mountain range for an instant.

Terra took cover behind a boulder. It gave her no protection from rain, but at least shielded her from the wind. She wanted to cry, to just let herself mourn. The rain soaked her and the cold wind made her shiver. But she would not cry. Crying never helps.

Terra shook her head. She had to keep moving to escape this storm.

Thunder boomed while lightning cracked the sky. Another loud rumble approached. At first it was a low sound, but grew louder. Another flash of lightning illuminated, for an instant, the avalanche sweeping towards her.

Terra didn't have time to think. The storm limited her vision, but she still had her connection with time. She Slowed gravity around her and jumped above the tide of stone. The cascade of earth passed below her before she settled on the ground.

As the rumbling quieted, Terra stood near the peak of the mountain. Lightning flashed again and Terra Slowed her vision, closing her eyes to avoid the flash. As the flash subsided Terra opened her eyes, her Slowed vision giving her a good view of the surroundings. The storm was powerful enough to obscure her view of Saturn City above, though she could see a bright pillar of light just beyond the salient walls. She was near the center of the Labyrinth now. In the distance, she spotted a towering mountain in the center of the salient where the storm raged at its most intense.

That's it, she thought. *That is where the gate is.*

Terra marched against the storm with grief stalking not far behind her. Soon she stood at the base of the tallest mountain and began her ascent.

The cold winds swept downward as if trying to drive her back. Terra endured the cold wet storm and pushed forward. As she continued her climb, the rain turned to ice. The trek became slippery. Still Terra pushed on, walking in places while climbing in others as she tried to reach the peak.

As she struggled, her thoughts turned to Zaid. It had been so fast it didn't seem real. He had a shieldwatch. People with a shieldwatch shouldn't die that easily.

She felt her eyes tear up, but stopped herself from crying. Terra made a promise to herself. Stone doesn't cry. Yet this storm chipped away stone.

Ice pelted her as it stung her skin. Terra used her shieldwatch to halt the hail in front of her. Moving forward proved difficult now.

Should she even bother to go on? How could she be a heroine if she couldn't even save one friend?

Terra continued to climb. Zaid wouldn't have wanted her to stop. He was the first person to have faith in her. Her hands gripped the ice so hard it cracked under her grip. She grimaced as she thought about how unfair it was.

Her anger grew worse with the storm. The mountain itself became steeper, like it was trying to throw her back. It made Terra hate it even more.

Another stupid attempt to kill me, Terra thought.

The rage and despair churned in her chest as the storm battered the mountain. She thought of Zaid again and felt her anger turn on him now. Why did he abandon them? He failed again. It was a betrayal in a way. Zaid had let death make him abandon his duties. Why didn't he move faster?

Terra then remembered. Zaid practiced the least. He had spent all his time trying to lead them. Guilt entered Terra's storm when she remembered how much he had helped her. The study sessions, the practice.

Tears swelled in her eyes again, but Terra forced them back and did not cry. A desire to quit crept back into her. Then piercing fear cut through her emotions and made her chest feel cold. She could die just as easily. Now it seemed more real to her.

A loud crack came before another low rumble in the distance. Soon the ground shook as a tide of stone slid towards her.

Terra gritted her teeth. Her shieldwatch was almost out of power now. She couldn't jump over the tide again. Her emotions cleared. All the death, all the pain and suffering would be for nothing if she gave up here. If Zaid had fallen for his ideals, then Terra would carry them on for him.

No more of this, she thought. *No more of these stupid tests and trials. This is enough.*

Terra drew her aeon edge and faced the wave of rock roaring towards her. She slashed at the stone and pulled the trigger. A wave of blue energy burst from the aeon edge and turned the stone tide into dust. The burst cut through the tide and revealed an opening in the side of the mountain.

Terra walked to the opening to find a cavern that led into the heart of the mountain. When she walked inside, she found the cave warmer than outside and lit by a faint ambient glow.

She progressed through the cave, noting large formations of rock crystal in the walls. Other crystal formations dotted the area and reflected the dim light in a variety of colors. She would have admired them more if she were not so tired. It had been four days since she had entered the Labyrinth.

Her shieldwatch beeped. *Trial of Storms complete* was displayed on the holoface. She didn't care at this point.

Ahead an iron bridge crossed over a ravine. On the other side was the gate. She almost sighed in relief until she saw a figure guarding the bridge.

Terra did not try to approach unnoticed. She was done sneaking around and she didn't have the energy left for it regardless. When she drew close she saw a familiar sight. The man who guarded it wore a Kalian mask, one with a wing emblem. The Captain, or rather one of Lycus's persona, stood in the center of the iron bridge with his hands resting on the pummel of his aeon edge Cerberus. He held his blade in front him with the tip touching the ground like a staff.

Terra stopped in front of Lycus. "You are in my way."

Lycus stood, unmoving. "As well I should be for this is the Trial of Worth."

"Worth? Haven't I proved my worth many times over now?"

"Maybe to your friends and instructors. Maybe to Cerberus during the Trial of the Beast, but not to the Captain."

"The Captain? You mean your character?"

Lycus looked at his three core aeon edge. "Lycus, Cerberus, and the Captain. These are my three faces. When I slew the Kalian who wore this mask on the battlefield, his noble act of protecting the innocent poisoned Cerberus. His blood stained my hands and infected the beast. That blood became the seed of my reawakened conscience. The fruit of regret and guilt it bore became a new face. Now the Captain gets to choose who becomes a member of the Aeon Legion. Not the beast Cerberus, nor the scholar Lycus. So now, Terra Mason. Why should I let you past this point? Are you truly worth anything or are you just another monster?"

"I don't think I am threatening enough to be a monster."

Lycus's eyes narrowed from behind the mask. "Don't be so certain, Terra Mason. I saw what you did in the Trial of the Beast. Iron awoke in you and iron is a step towards cold steel. I witnessed the birth of a new blade there. What I saw was savage and driven by hatred. Time whirled around you like blood in a stream. If you were any more skilled, the Manticore would have died and you would have been the most dangerous beast in the salient."

Terra clenched her fists. "That monster deserved to die!"

"Because it killed Zaid?"

Terra averted her gaze. "Because it killed my friend."

"You best steel yourself then. Cross this bridge and prepare to see more of your friends become corpses as you journey. That is one of the prices we pay. You talk a lot about wanting to be a hero, but those in the Aeon Legion are soldiers. They fight when ordered and die on command. Are you going to let one death turn your dreams into blood soaked revenge or will you let that death poison you with doubt and cowardice?"

Terra opened her mouth to speak, but hesitated. She considered her next words. "I was going to say I'm not afraid to die, but that would be a lie. I will not back down though. Fear knows better than to get in my way. As for revenge, you already have your answer. If I wanted revenge, I wouldn't be talking to you. I would try to kill you for torturing me."

"Then why are you here? What reason do you have for even trying so hard? There must be more than mere stubbornness."

Terra thought for a long moment. Why was she here again? It was difficult for her to cut through the hunger, thirst, fatigue, and despair. It all pulled at her and clouded her mind. Then a flash of a memory came before her, a memory of a beautiful and invincible woman with silver hair. She looked up at Lycus. "Alya Silverwind."

Terra smiled as she remembered. "That day I saw her for the first time, standing it the ruins of the library without a single scratch. She defeated some of the worst villains in history and then acted as though she hadn't done anything special. There she was, like a beacon with the wind flowing around her. Invincible. Untouchable. Beautiful. Powerful. Right in front of me was every kid's fantasy, like a real superhero. Something out of a legend or myth. I don't care about what she did in her past. All I saw standing there was a heroine. That's what I wanted to be like. A heroine."

"But you cannot be like a heroine. Heroes know no culture. Heroes know no gender. They are beyond nation and empire. Above slavery or oaths. They are not honorable for they are honor. They are not idealistic for they are ideals personified. You cannot simply live up to high ideals, you must become them in their entirety. Wrap yourself in them until they become your armor. Like Kairos."

"I am *not* like Kairos," Terra said in hateful tone. "I sacrificed my normal life to come here before I discovered I was fated to die in an accident. I chose to stay here and continue on even when everyone else told me to quit, that I wasn't good enough. Even the Sybil think I'm nothing. I don't care! I am *not* Kairos! Everything came naturally to her while I had to scrape and claw my way past every obstacle. I barely made it, but I did it on my own. No fate or destiny ever helped me. I will become a heroine of Saturn City, the Aeon Legion, and all of Time! Because I can choose to be the hero you *failed* to be! Now get out of my way!"

Lycus stood, unmoving, for a long moment. She felt a spike of fear when Lycus reached behind his back and drew a blade. The fear faded into sadness when Lycus handed her Zaid's blood stained aeon edge. "This is yours now. You can even keep it after the Labyrinth. Do with it as you will," he said before stepping aside and removing his mask.

Terra looked at Lycus. "Why are you here?"

"I am here to keep monsters like me out of the Aeon Legion. I am here to stop heroes and heroines from walking my path. I am the guardian of the gates. I let only the worthy pass."

Terra began crossing the iron bridge to the gate ahead.

"Terra."

Terra stopped and turned.

Lycus faced her. "The next trial is the Trial of Fear. It's the only trial Kairos failed."

CHAPTER XXX
TRIAL OF FEAR AND TRUTH

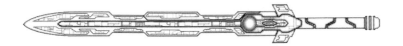

The Trial of Fear has a ninety percent failure rate, but I expect Tiro Terra Mason to pass with ease. For most, they see all of their trauma and failure relived in perfect detail. A few, though, don't have enough trauma for this Trial to be effective. This is an instance where Terra's stable home life and peaceful youth will work in her favor. In many ways, this is her greatest strength. She has no talent, but she is not broken either. Plain, solid things make for good foundations. However, I wonder what the Trial of Truth will reveal to her? Terra has gained much, but has yet to face what she lost upon entering the Academy.

-From the personal logs of Praetor Lycus Cerberus

This salient appeared anticlimactic compared to the others. Terra stood on the metal walkway that rimmed the edge of the salient and noted the diameter was smaller than most of the others in the Labyrinth. Traversing this salient would take an hour at most, if she didn't hurry. However, the flat dark hex patterned floor was unique to this salient. A pillar of blue light shot upward in the exact center of the salient while the metal underside of Saturn City shown overhead. She had arrived at the Labyrinth's heart.

Terra looked around to see a lone Sybil who stood by the entryway into the flat salient. She approached the entryway as the Sybil stared off at the pillar of light, at least Terra guessed that's what Sybil was staring at it. Those strange headpieces made it hard to tell. "Excuse me?" Terra said, trying to get the Sybil's attention.

The Sybil started and looked around frantically for a moment before focusing on Terra. Terra recognized the Sybil as one of the three Lycus had talked to before entering the Labyrinth, the one named Nona. "Oh,"

Nona said in a disappointed tone while her expression soured. "It is the null." Nona said before gesturing to the salient. "This is the Trial of Fear. Are you ready?"

Terra sighed. "I'm not getting any more courageous."

"Very well, null," Nona said. She stretched forth her shieldwatch arm and a line on the floor began glowing blue directly under her hand. The line followed the border between the hexes on the floor, leading to the distant pillar of light. "Follow the line to the pillar."

Terra looked down at the salient floor. "Isn't this salient going to change like the others?"

Nona scowled upon hearing Terra's question. "This salient is special. Some salients connect time and space. This one connects thoughts and memories. It takes those thoughts and memories to reveal your fears In some ways, this salient has its own will."

Terra frowned and gripped her aeon edge.

Nona sighed in frustration. "Terror is beyond the reach of any force of arms. What this salient unveils can only harm you if you let it. Now go."

Terra took her hand off her aeon edge and walked forward. Whatever the Trial of Fear had in store for her was probably better than talking to a Sybil. She walked down the ramp and took one cautious step onto the salient floor. The floor rippled outward, like a still pond disturbed by a thrown rock. After a moment, the floor solidified and Terra proceeded.

As the outer ring of the salient faded behind her, Terra began to feel uneasy. She followed the glowing line on the ground as it twisted between hexes. Terra halted when she spotted movement.

The hex floor to her left bulged as though something were trapped under it. The bulge then twisted until it transformed into an insect like creature that crawled towards her. The dog sized monster reminded Terra of the creatures she had faced before Sero. Its skin shared the same hex pattern as the floor. When it drew close to Terra, she kicked it and it scurried off.

Creepy, Terra thought, *but I've already faced those.* As she walked forward, several more of the monsters formed, but she booted aside the few that drew close.

As the monsters melted back into the floor, several new forms bubbled. The first one sprang at her. Terra evaded as the shape flew past her and fell to the ground. She turned to see a young girl there. "Val?"

Val lay there a moment before she opened her mouth in a silent cry. She looked the same as she had been on that day at school long ago.

Terra turned to see Henry approach and try to shove her without success. Her brow lowered before she ignored the small child and walked forward. However, another bully moved in her way.

Vand walked in front of Terra. He smirked while twirling his shock baton in his hand.

Another form rose nearby. Terra looked to see Hanns emerge, holding his coveted history book.

Terra sighed. "Is this all you can throw at me? A bunch of bullies and monsters I've already faced?"

As if responding to her criticism, the forms melted back into the surface. Terra looked ahead. She was about halfway to the pillar. She proceeded forward again, though she noticed the light between the hexes grew dimmer.

Moments later, the surface began to shift again around her like a liquid being boiled. Small objects formed; books, games, minerals. She recognized the objects of her childhood. Then Terra came upon her parents as her bedroom at home materialized around them.

Her mother wept. Her father's expression was solemn as he packed Terra's possessions into containers. Often he would stop to inspect an item and smile. Then his smile would fall to sadness before he put the item away.

Terra paused, briefly, before making her way around them. "Not pulling your punches anymore?"

Then she found a dead body blocking her path. Terra stepped over the mangled, bloody corpse before finding another in her way. Soon, Terra had to navigate a field of corpses while a breeze began to pick up around her. Blood covered the ground. Although she found the corpses revolting, Terra wondered why the Trial of Fear would try to scare her with them. Then she saw the figure ahead.

Before Terra was a piled up heap of corpses. Most wore the same uniforms of those who had hunted her during the Survival Test. The blood soaked, twisted mound of bodies emanated darkness. A harsh, frigid wind arose around her and whipped the blood about like a cyclone. At the peak of the bloody mound of death stood a savage Alya Silverwind with a red stained aeon edge, a whirlwind of blood that had deepened to a crimson swirled around her.

Terra couldn't look away even though she knew this Alya was a fake. A name flashed in her mind. "Bloodstorm," Terra whispered.

Then a sickening thought occurred to her. What if this salient drew from more than just her memory? Was this Alya's memory? She shut her eyes and looked away. When Terra opened her eyes, the scene had vanished.

Terra looked to see the pillar of light a short distance ahead. She didn't have far to go. As she walked forward, the floor rose again in front of her. As the ground distorted, the area around Terra darkened until she lost sight of whatever the Trial of Fear was readying for her. Terra walked forward, cautious. Then she saw Zaid.

He lay there, eyes open to the dark sky. Blood ran from his open mouth to the floor. His chest was still torn as though the Manticore had ripped it open moments ago. Terra gasped, fighting back a wave of nausea. After a moment, Terra tried to step around him when Zaid turned his head towards Terra.

She froze as Zaid reached for her, but he was too weak to go far. He lay there on the ground, his face in anguish as he reached out to Terra. His lips moved, but spoke no words.

Terra gingerly stepped around him. Zaid's eyes widened when his reach fell short and Terra turned her back on him. She shook her head and fought back tears. "I won't stop for a memory."

Terra did not cry. Instead she felt her sadness boil into rage. The Trial of Fear held nothing that could frighten her.. Instead it hurt and angered her.

More distortions formed in the floor, but Terra kicked aside any that got too close. She didn't bother to even look at the echoes the Trial of Fear threw at her.

A hill sized mound rose before her, blocking her path. The mound drained away like running oil to reveal a copy of Sero.

Terra stopped and glared. The duplicate of Sero was an exact physical match, though its movements were sluggish. "I've faced you too," she said as she marched forward. It recoiled as she drew close.

When Terra was almost close enough to touch it, its large shield shaped head split open to reveal Lycus's face.

Terra froze, but calmed herself. She faced the strange hybrid, wondering why the Trial of Fear had chosen to show her this. After a moment, the monster melted into the floor with the others. She continued on.

When she neared the pillar of light, its glow lessened the darkness around her. Someone stood in the distance. As Terra drew closer, she saw it was a Sybil. The one named Decima.

Terra regarded the fake Sybil who stood, staring at the pillar of light. "How is a Sybil suppose to scare me?"

Decima started. "Stupid null!" She yelled before composing herself. "I can never see them well."

Terra paused, realizing that this was a real person. "So am I done with the Trial of Fear?"

Decima stiffened while smoothing her ornate robes. "Yes. The Trial of Fear is complete."

Terra pointed at the pillar of light. "What is that?"

"That is what you will enter for the next trial. At the end of fear lies truth."

"Trial of Truth? I still don't know what that light is."

Decima looked upward. "That beam of light is from the Temporal Singularity. This place is directly under the center of the city. Inside that light the past, present and future all merge into one time. The truth you see could mean many things. You may even see more than one truth. However, for a null like yourself, I doubt you will see much. A null is not well connected with the Grand Design."

"It has to be better than the last stupid trial," Terra grumbled before walking towards the light.

As she drew closer to the beam, the area around her distorted with the horizon stretching out as though pulled by an unseen force. She touched the light and it expanded outward. The brightness forced Terra to close her eyes. When the light lessened, Terra opened her eyes to a familiar sight. She stood alone in an open field and ahead of her lay a quarry. Her quarry.

The quarry was sunny, though no sun shown overhead. It was a small island of brightness in a sea of dark metal hexes and shadows. Terra walked through the grassy field, touching the tips of the tall weeds as she walked to the quarry. When she drew near, she heard the soft ting of a rock hammer. She looked out over the edge of the rock quarry to find herself.

Below Terra stood a double who worked diligently on the rock walls of the quarry below. The double looked up at Terra before stopping her work.

Terra jumped down on the ledge below and faced the double. She appeared identical to Terra with the same messy hair and light brown eyes.

The double narrowed her gaze on Terra. "Who are you?"

"I guess I'm you," Terra said.

The double shook her head. "No longer."

"Why do you say that?"

The double pointed to the dark water at the bottom of the quarry. Terra looked down at the still pool to see her reflection alongside the double's.

It was an odd thing. She hadn't noticed during the long months of the training, but now that she could compare, the results gave her pause. The double was Terra before she had come to the Academy. A nonathletic girl who spent her days digging up rocks and reading books in her sunny quarry. In contrast, the real Terra's now lean body was both toned and muscular. A body honed for combat. Even her stance was different. The double stood with a slight hunch, unlike Terra who stood with a military posture, rigid and straight backed. The old Terra wore a stained shirt and jeans while the new wore a precise Legion uniform. Her smooth brown hair hung tied back in a neat ponytail, in contrast to her double's messy bob.

"Have I changed that much?" Terra asked.

"Not just change. Choices," the double said.

"Choices?"

"Time is like life's choices. It branches as we age, opening up new possibilities. Yet when we grow old, our choices begin to narrow again, ending in only one possibility; death."

"So this place is a possible future?"

The double shook her head. "No. This place is where your most important choice was made."

"The choice to join the Legion? I suppose I did make that choice in my quarry."

The double's eyes narrowed as she spoke in a low tone. "This place is no longer yours."

A rumble in the distance drew Terra's attention before she could respond. Terra looked up to see the pearl towers of Saturn City, rising around her quarry as though sprouting from the earth like weeds. When she looked back at her double, Terra froze and her eyes opened wide.

The double stood with a streak of blood running down her face. "The choice is made."

Terra had to stop herself from stepping back when she saw the waters in the quarry turn blood red. The water cleared just enough for her see the twisted roof of a car laying in the bottom of the pool. She faced the double. "I didn't really have a choice. If I had stayed in my time, I would have died."

The blood on the double's face dried in an instant as her skin turned putrid gray. "You made the choice without this knowledge. Do not forget the lesson of the beast, Cerberus. You walk the path of blood now. Better to die by fate's design than become a monster by choice."

Terra watched in silence as the double rotted away in front of her. Flesh turned black before crumbling into dust and bones. Even the bones turned to dust seconds later as the spires of Saturn City began to creep over Terra's quarry. Terra climbed out of her quarry just as Saturn City completely overtook it.

She stared at the city as it grew before her. Terra looked down when she felt something brush against her leg. White roses had sprouted around her.

While Terra wondered what the truth of this trial was, the shining city around her dimmed and darkened. A red light shone on the other side of the city. It grew in strength as a loud rumble sounded. Terra looked down to see her shadow stretching off into the distance. It connected with another shadow that stood on the opposite side of the city. Facing Terra was a figure in black that mirrored her. As the figure, a woman Terra guessed, walked, black roses grew in her wake. They faced one another, Terra in white with a shieldwatch glowing blue and the figure in black with her shieldwatch glowing red.

With a simple gesture, a darkness emanated from the shadowy figure and Saturn City shattered. The pearl towers and white steel were ripped apart. Shards of the city flew into the sky while Terra shielded herself from a tremendous wind. She could hear screams over the roaring winds and wailing metal. When the wind died, Terra looked up to see an endless field of corpses and wreckage between her and the shadowy figure. Beside each corpse was an aeon edge that stood upright with its tip in the ground.

Terra stood for a long moment before she realized what the Trial of Truth was showing her. The mangled wreckage, the corpses, and the aeon edges all stood in a twisted perversion of Kairos's Garden. Before Terra could wonder further, the shadowy figure turned and left. Then Terra's surroundings faded and she stood back on the plain hex floor next to the pillar of light.

She stood alone for a long while, thinking. Terra couldn't help but feel that this was a warning of something worse to come.

∞

Terra stepped onto the edge of the salient, feeling far more tired than when she had entered. Another Sybil waited for her there, the one named Morta.

"So the null has crossed both fear and truth," she said in a condescending tone. "Well, you should not worry now, null. The darkest moment is over. One test remains."

Terra shot the Sybil a nasty glare before checking her shieldwatch. Her eyes went wide. "What? Only four hours left? I wasn't in the Trial of Truth that long!"

Morta grinned. "Walking near the Temporal Singularity distorts time. You were in there for over a day. The fatigue and hunger are catching up to you now."

Terra could believe that. Her stomach hurt from hunger while her mouth felt dry. It was hard enough just to stand and her feet seemed so heavy right now. She then Restored herself with the shieldwatch, but the mental fatigue remained. Despite the fatigue, her vision during the Trial of Truth lingered in her mind.

"I saw an omen," Terra said as she turned to Morta.

"Really, null? I find that difficult to believe."

"I saw Saturn City destroyed," Terra said, feeling as though she had to warn someone.

Morta chuckled. "I doubt that. If there were a threat to the city, we would have precogged it."

Terra sighed. She should have expected the Sybil to ignore her, though Terra didn't know if she should take herself seriously.

"Besides," Morta said as she turned back to the salient. "If another threat had emerged, fate would have led Silverwind to a new squire."

Terra hesitated. "Um."

Morta then pointed at the edge of the salient. "The Final Trial awaits you, tiro," she said before turning to go.

Terra walked to the fadeline ahead while pondering the strange sights she had seen in the Trial of Truth. There couldn't be a real plot to destroy the city? Saturn City was such a huge place to her. The thought of something or someone powerful enough to destroy it seemed absurd. She stepped onto the fadeline, but rather than fading out, the fadeline flickered and shut off.

Terra searched the area. She looked for another key puzzle or something else wrong, but found nothing. After a moment, Terra sighed, thinking that this must be part of the trial. She walked to the salient walls and jumped over the side. There she saw the crisscrossing network of catwalks and metal access walkways that webbed the outer parts of the Labyrinth. However, she paused when finding two optios lying on the ground.

She ran to their sides before checking for a pulse. Both were alive and she saw no sign of damage. Their shieldwatches had Restored them. Terra stood and began scanning the area.

A loud metal groan cracked through the air. Terra turned and stared as a massive chunk of the city creaked, shook, and then fell away into the Edge below the city. She gazed at the falling slice of the city, panic flaring as part of her vision came true. In front of her was a small salient that someone had partially taken apart.

Then, in the salient's center, a platoon of steel-gray uniformed soldiers appeared in a bright green flash of crackling energy. In front of them stood a man Terra recognized. Hanns turned, facing Terra and smiled as Saturn City shattered behind him.

Chapter XXXI
Trojan Horse

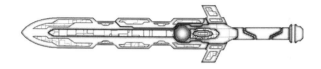

However, do not become arrogant in the presumed supremacy of time based singularity weapons. Complacency and hubris can be critical weaknesses that even the most ill equipped foe will exploit. A well prepared force will always destroy an ill prepared one regardless of the gaps in technology, numbers or training. Truly no weapon has killed more soldiers than ill informed assumptions. Especially when that assumption is invincibility.

    -Excerpt from *Core Stratagems of Post Time Warfare*, by *Time Queen Ananke the Unbeaten*

Terra drew her aeon edge in a flash.

Hanns faced Terra as his smile faded. "You do so enjoy getting in my way don't you, Terra?" he said before pointing to her. "Fire at will!"

The Zeitmacht soldiers leveled their weapons and fired. Terra felt a moment of panic before she Sped her reflexes and perception.

The bullets slowed as they drew near and Terra raised her shieldwatch to block. Her Sped vision allowed her to see the green glowing tipped bullets in detail as they bored through her stasis shield. Terra ducked, avoiding the bullets that snapped past her by mere inches. *He's found a way past a shieldwatch,* she thought.

Hanns rolled up his sleeve to reveal a shieldwatch before touching a holoface. The shieldwatch face glowed a dull gray rather than blue.

"How?" Terra asked before more gunfire cut off her question. She rolled behind one of the salient's metal pillars. As Terra peeked from behind the pillars, she saw Hanns and his soldiers fade. Seconds later several grenades exploded. A pillar of the salient collapsed while the rest began to spark. Terra ran as the whole salient began shaking.

An explosion rocked the ground as Terra jumped behind a metal wall. As Terra looked up, she watched a vortex of blue energy engulf the damaged salient. The swirl of energy drew in everything around it before dissipating to leave only a twisted mass of metal in its wake.

Terra stepped out to survey the damage. With the salient destroyed, she couldn't follow Hanns. She wondered what Hanns sought here? The Labyrinth was far away from anything useful like the Legion armory or the Temporal Singularity. In fact it was under the Academy...

Terra's eyes went wide. They stood under Aevum Academy that contained Saturn City's Archives. Hanns wasn't after a simple book any longer. He would steal the single most complete database of all human history.

She activated her sonic cipher. Chatter erupted from the lines.

"Tartarus has been ejected! Please confirm!"

"There is a riot in here!"

"All security personnel, secure the lower levels!"

"All Legion timeships, converge on Tartarus!"

Terra switched lines, trying to find one that would listen. "This is Tiro Terra Mason. The Aevum Academy Archives are about to be attacked! I repeat the Archives are about to be attacked! Anyone respond!"

The chatter continued with no acknowledgment. They all seemed preoccupied with Tartarus.

Terra clenched her teeth. What was she going to do? She had less than four hours to complete the Final Trial, yet she had to do something about Hanns. She hesitated, looking to the last salient in the distance. This might be her one chance to pass the final trial. Maybe someone else would stop Hanns?

Terra frowned and grabbed the hilt of Zaid's aeon edge. Hanns had no one to stop him. No one was going to help her. No one was going to save her. She would save herself and this time she had the skills, training, and equipment to do so.

"There you are," came Roland's voice.

Terra turned to see Roland and Hikari approaching.

"We heard you over the cipher lines," Hikari said.

Terra took a deep breath. "I need your help."

"Terra," Roland interrupted.

Terra ignored Roland. "There is a dangerous criminal who has invaded the city. We need to stop him!"

"Terra," Roland said, again trying to get Terra's attention.

"The city is in danger," Terra continued to explain. "If we don't stop him th–"

"Terra!" Hikari yelled.

Terra stopped.

Hikari nodded. "Where do we need to go?"

Terra looked from Hikari to Roland. "Really?"

"Wherever you go," Hikari said, "I will beat you there."

Roland shrugged. "I thought this was all part of the final trial."

Terra shook her head. "It isn't. This is a real invasion. If we try to stop it, though, we may lose our chance at the final trial. We will have to start the training all over again."

Roland chuckled. "Don't worry. I will convince them otherwise. Now where are we going?"

Terra looked up to the underside of the city. "Back to the Academy. We have to get to the Archives, but Hanns sabotaged the fadelines."

"How will we get there?" Hikari asked.

Roland looked up too. "The shortest way would be straight up."

Terra nodded. "We climb up where the Labyrinth salients came down from."

Hanns smiled as his troops stormed the Archives with ease. As expected, the Legion guards were ill prepared for bullets piercing their shields. He had been unsure about the time-bore tipped bullets, but that gamble had paid off well. It was a simple device, a time travel machine shrunk down to the size of a bullet. If Saturnians used time to shield themselves, then Hanns would use time to pierce those shields. Yet the Legion's complacency was a far greater weapon than anything Hanns could have invented. The ease of distracting them by ejecting Tartarus had been the greatest asset in this heist.

The Zeitmacht secured the area, rounding up the staff that worked in the Archives, bringing them where he stood outside the fadedoor. They had blasted open the fadedoors and taken care of the guards inside the Archives. His men had shot the two guards at the fadedoor. They now laid on the ground with their bodies Restored, but still incapacitated.

The other guards had seen the first two shot through their shields and retreated when faced with overwhelming firepower. Hanns then had two squads push them back into a fadeline before destroying it to prevent reinforcements.

The last of the staff members fell to their knees in front of Hanns. Hanns surveyed the gathered silver haired individuals.

Alban approached. "We have them all. I was thorough this time,"

Hanns nodded. "Excellent."

A sweaty Emmerich shuffled up to Hanns. "Very good Hanns. Now get us out of here."

Hanns looked at the blasted fadedoors to the Archives. "Leave?" Hanns asked, turning back to Emmerich. "Here we stand beyond time itself, ready to witness the glory of the Third Reich in its entirety and all you wish to do is leave? Not yet Emmerich. I am about to win us our glorious history."

Alban gestured to the captured staff. "What about them?"

Hanns nodded. "I never make the same mistake twice."

Emmerich looked to the hostages. "We kill them?"

Hanns turned to Emmerich and scowled. "No! Why would we do such a thing? That's a war crime. No. We will make sure they are out of our way this time."

Emmerich frowned. "How will we do that?"

Hanns smiled. "I know the Saturnians' weakness," He said before turning to the staff. "Listen carefully. You are to stay in this open library and you are not to move. I do not wish to hurt anyone, but if you move I will assume you are a combatant. No heroics this time. I know how you Saturnians love your immortality. Don't waste it trying to stop me."

The staff remained calm as he had expected.

Alban turned to Hanns. "Should I set a few men to watch them?"

Hanns shook his head and walked inside the Archives. "No. Threats against their immortality should hold them for now. Timeless citizens value their immortality more than anything else. They won't risk it by trying to stop us. That's why they use mercenaries. If they flee, they will be out of our way regardless. Now I want you to set up just inside these doors. Position the men so they have all angles covered, then shoot anyone who comes through that door. We layer our defenses."

Alban nodded. "And what about these so called conscripts?"

Hanns spared a look to the prisoners who had aided him. They had helped him ambush several staff members so he could bring his soldiers to the city by modifying a salient. "Them. Yes. We bring them back with us if we can, but tell our soldiers not to risk their lives over it. These prisoners are not real soldiers."

Alban saluted and walked off to prepare.

Emmerich looked around nervously. "I don't understand Hanns. Why are we here?"

Hanns looked up at the titanic internal structure of the Archives. The outer walls stood hundreds of meters high, packed row upon row with books. Twelve towering pillars stood around the room and were also shelved with books and devices of every kind. Holofaces circled around the pillars, illuminating the area in a pale blue glow. In the center, a platform drew his eye. That is where he knew he had to go. He made his way towards there.

Emmerich followed behind Hanns. "Do you even know how to escape from here, Hanns?"

Hanns kept his gaze forward. "You should relax, Emmerich. This will not take long."

Hanns walked up a large set of stairs to the central platform. A device in the center projected a hazy blue holographic sphere above it. Words appeared upon the sphere, changing to a script Hanns could read.

Minerva's voice read the words. "Your Access to the Archives is denied."

Hanns smiled, holding up his shieldwatch. "Oh? But I have a key."

The holographic sphere flickered before changing to gray. "Accessing Archives. Downloading to shieldwatch," came a masculine computerized voice from Hanns's shieldwatch.

The holofaces in the Archives all turned gray before streaming towards Hanns. They circled above the platform in a cyclone before compacting in the palm of his hand. Hanns smiled as the glow illuminated his face. He spoke in a whisper. "All human history in the palm of my hand."

Terra stopped outside the Library's entryway and looked around the corner. A dozen staff members knelt on their knees in the center of the library. "He's already here, but I can't see anyone except the staff."

Roland glanced around the corner. "Two guards are on the ground. I don't know if they are alive or not. Let's go."

Terra grabbed Roland and looked to Hikari. "Remember what I said."

Hikari sneered. "Yes. We remember. Their weapons can pierce our shieldwatch."

They moved inside on the edge of the walls. After circling the room, they found no one watching. They gathered at the fadedoors to the Archives which lay blasted open.

Roland knelt and took off his shieldwatch. He held it next to the open archway and used the reflected surface to peer inside the Archives. After a moment he put his shieldwatch back on his forearm. "A lot of them. They have fortified their position inside."

Terra bit her lower lip. "How are we going to get inside?"

Hikari kicked aside a sheet of fadedoor debris out of her way and strolled into the Archives.

Terra frowned. "Hikari! What are you doing?"

"Staying ahead of you," she said.

"Fire at will!" yelled a soldier on the other side.

A hail of glowing green bullets streaked towards Hikari. She grabbed her aeon edge by the grip and put a hand on the flat of the blade. Hikari then used the flat of the blade and Sped her reflexes to block the oncoming projectiles. Sparks flew around her as the bullets bounced off the metal of the aeon edge while Hikari moved in a blur of motion.

Seconds later a small mob of prisoners, like those Terra had seen during the first trial, attacked Hikari. She struck down each one with ease.

Terra turned to the staff. "Go! Run! Get help!"

They stood and ran.

She then charged into the Archives to help Hikari. When Terra arrived next to Hikari she found her standing amongst a pile of unconscious bodies.

"Fall back to the inner defense," yelled a soldier.

Terra found the Archives vast. It was the largest building in the Academy. Old books and other items filled the walls. Terra saw computers from her time amongst many other things she didn't recognize. Large pillars lined the outer edges and spiraled upward with endless history books.

The center of the room hosted a series of ramps that led to an elevated platform. Above the platform was a cyclone of holofaces that circled around the center plate. In the center of the holofaces stood Hanns, holding up his shieldwatch while it copied and stored every bit of information in the Archives.

Hanns and his forces had fortified the area around the central platform, turning over shelves to erect a makeshift fort. When Hikari attacked, they drove her back with sheer firepower.

Terra frowned. "How are we going to get past that?"

Roland glanced around before moving off to the sides of the Archives. Terra then watched another attack by Hikari, but she could not block every shot. The sheer volume of firepower forced her back again.

When Hanns's soldiers began taunting Hikari, a loud crack sounded and a pillar began to fall right on top of their defensive position. The soldiers screamed while they scrambled away. The pillar smashed into the ground with a loud crash.

Hanns looked up. He took a single step and dodged the falling pillar which missed him by inches. He then went back to downloading the Archives to his shieldwatch.

Terra then saw Roland standing at the base of the pillar that had crashed, aeon edge drawn, with a satisfied smile on his face. With Hanns's forces in temporary disarray, Terra ran along the collapsed pillar in a charge directed at Hanns.

Hanns saw and drew his pistol. "I grow tired of this, Terra. You have gotten in my way one too many times!" he said as he fired at her.

Terra stole Hikari's move and blocked the bullets with her aeon edge, but her advance slowed in spite of Speeding her run.

"Oh no," whined the SS officer. "I told you Hanns. We should have left when we had the chance!"

"Archive download complete," came a male voice from Hanns's shieldwatch.

Hanns turned. "All done here," he said as he activated the watch like device at his belt. Portals opened and engulfed all his men. Another formed right next to Hanns, who then kicked the SS officer into it.

"No! Not this time Hanns!" Terra said as she ran to the portal just as Hanns stepped through it. She jumped into the portal seconds before it vanished.

Chapter XXXII
Zeitmacht

"You are about to embark upon a Great Crusade, towards which we have striven these many months. The eyes of the world are upon you. The hopes and prayers of liberty-loving people everywhere march with you. In company with our brave Allies and brothers-in-arms on other Fronts, you will bring about the destruction of the German war machine, the elimination of Nazi tyranny over the oppressed peoples of Europe, and security for ourselves in a free world.

Your task will not be an easy one. Your enemy is well trained, well equipped, and battle-hardened. He will fight savagely."

-D-day statement to soldiers, sailors, and airmen of the Allied Expeditionary Force by General Dwight D. Eisenhower

The blinding light faded while Terra heard muffled voices nearby. Her vision cleared as she struggled to stand. As her eyes came into focus, she realized she was inside a large cylindrical tube that moved around her. She stood on an iron walkway in the center. The machine hummed as the moving parts slowed. Terra looked behind her to see a dissipating green portal. She had jumped into the portal as it had begun to vanish and as a result of temporal dilation, arrived a few seconds after Hanns.

"Soldiers of the Zeitmacht!" Hanns's voice echoed through the machine. "We are victorious!"

Cheers followed. Thinking quickly, Terra sent a signal to Saturn City so they might find her and send help.

"Alban, please escort Brigadeführer Emmerich Klein to the field hospital," Hanns said in a condescending tone. "I think he needs his rest after our little adventure."

Terra readied her aeon edge as she marched out of the machine and into the open building ahead. It was a wide open bunker three stories high with metal railing on the side. She stood on a large ramp leading up to the machine. Several squads of soldiers stood in front of her with Hanns at their head.

He turned and smirked. "Oh look. I even get a prisoner."

A few of the soldiers laughed upon seeing a girl with a sword stand before dozens of armed men. Others tensed and pointed their weapons at Terra while steeling themselves for sudden movement.

Hanns smiled and stood with confidence. "I didn't think you would try to follow me. Such a foolish display of bravado. Ironic isn't it? You captured me and brought me to the city beyond time. Now I capture you in the past."

Terra raised her aeon edge while the soldiers itched at their triggers.

Hanns held up his hand to stop them, his smirk vanishing. "Stop! Think about this, Terra. You can't beat all of us. You don't have to die here. This isn't even your fight. What do you owe to a decadent city of stagnant imperialists?"

Terra lowered her blade, still standing on the iron ramp. She gazed at the floor.

Hanns relaxed. "Wise choice."

Terra moved the switch on her aeon edge, changing it to the nonlethal setting. If she killed anyone here by accident then that might affect the continuum. This was standard procedure since lethal force had not been authorized.

Hanns stepped forward. "There is no need for you to buy into lies and propaganda. If you hand over your shieldwatch and blade, I can even take you home. I am a man of my word."

Terra looked up at Hanns who halted. She then pointed her aeon edge at him "Hanns Speer, you are in violation of the Temporal Accords! You are ordered to stand down and return all contraband! You will return to Saturn City or I will use force if you do not comply immediately!"

"Very well soldier," Hanns said evenly.

Terra saluted Hanns and his soldiers with her aeon edge.

Hanns turned to his men. "Fire at will!"

Terra did her best to dodge, Speeding her reflexes. The soldiers hesitated upon seeing Terra move so fast. Using the opening, Terra jumped onto a nearby catwalk in a blur of Sped motion.

She knocked aside a single soldier with a submachine gun who stood in her way. The man tumbled off the high catwalk with a loud yell before smacking and sliding down the top of the cylinder shaped time machine. The soldiers below fired, but the shots went wide while trying to hit a fast moving target above them.

Terra reviewed her objectives. First she had to destroy Hanns's shield-watch before he accessed the information within it. Second, she needed to neutralize Hanns's time machine to prevent or slow further illegal temporal incursions. Last, she had to arrest Hanns so he would stand trial for his crimes. A darker thought crossed her mind. In circumstances like these, she was authorized to use lethal force against Hanns. If she couldn't arrest Hanns, then she might have to kill him.

Hanns was not famous in her time. His death would not likely affect history as much as if Hanns succeeded in his goals. She had learned in the Academy that Time could endure most deaths without changing too much. He was already well past the point where lethal force was authorized even if his men had not yet crossed that line.

Terra forced this thought from her mind. Right now she had to focus on more important problems. She stood over Hanns's time machine. This massive metal beast was as long as a Manticore and almost as wide. Most of the soldiers had yet to storm the catwalks, leaving the time machine vulnerable.

Terra switched her aeon edge to the lethal setting and jumped on top of the metal monster. She then plunged her aeon edge into the machine. It sliced into the metal with little effort as she ran along the outer shell. As she ran, Terra pulled the trigger of her aeon edge, sending bursts of energy ripping through and smashing large chunks of the time machine into twisted metal. When she reached the end, a ball of flame shot from inside the machine, forcing Hanns and the other soldiers to scatter

Terra jumped down to where she had emerged from the machine. Soldiers took shots at her as they fled. Using Sped vision and reflexes, she blocked the normal bullets and only dodged upon spotting green tipped projectiles. As the soldiers regrouped in front of her, Terra switched her aeon edge to nonlethal and slashed at them while pulling the trigger. The aeon edge burst washed over them and turned their skin and clothing gray as they collapsed. The force of the blow pushed back the others not caught in the burst, knocking them out. Many of the soldiers fled.

Her aeon edge went dark. Terra then ejected the spent stasis cell clip and loaded in her last one.

Hanns retreated further into the building and Terra followed. She chased him into the maze of iron rigging that made up the underbelly of Hanns's burning time machine.

It was dark below the time machine, casting a wide shadow. The only light came from flickering flames above. Around Terra was a maze of iron beams and scaffolding. Her gaze swept across the iron pillars, but did not see him in the shifting shadows even with Sped vision. The shifting lights would also make night vision useless here.

"You have come far. You are a soldier now," Hanns said, his voice echoing. "It didn't seem that long ago that you were a cowering civilian."

Terra turned, still searching. "You are still the same, one evil cackle away from becoming a Saturday morning cartoon villain."

"Accusations mean little coming from a mercenary. What did they offer you to fight for them? Immortality? At least I fight for something greater than myself."

Terra stalked around the next pillar as she tried to follow the sound of Hanns's voice. She switched her aeon edge to lethal again. She spotted a flicker of movement and charged. Her attack sliced through a metal beam. The beam slid and smashed into the floor, revealing empty space. "I won't be lectured by a Nazi!" she said as she looked around the next beam.

A shot rang out. Terra dodged the glowing green bullet. Before Terra found him, Hanns hid again.

Terra moved forward with careful footsteps. Sped vision let her see in low levels of darkness, but the extra detail did little to reveal Hanns as he hid amongst twisting shadows. The detail, in this case, worked against her. She needed a way to flush him out into the open.

Movement flashed nearby. Terra charged, slicing through several iron beams before pulling the trigger and sending an aeon edge burst rippling through the metal pillars. The machine above her groaned as it shifted position. Terra scowled. If she tore apart this area too much then the whole machine would collapse, killing both her and Hanns. A shieldwatch would do her little good with so much mass collapsing on top of her. She glanced down to see she had only a few stasis cells left before her aeon edge went dead. She couldn't waste them on bursts.

Hanns took two more shots at Terra, forcing her behind a metal beam.

"Shieldwatch energy low," came Minerva's voice from Terra's shieldwatch.

Terra grimaced. Hanns was winning a war of attrition. All he had to do was to wait for Terra to run out of ammo and energy. Then he and his soldiers could move in for the kill. She looked down to Zaid's aeon edge still in its sheath and her eyes widened as a plan came together.

Terra froze her aeon edge in stasis. It hovered in the air just behind a metal beam. She moved away, leaving the aeon edge in place before drawing Zaid's aeon edge and waiting in the shadows.

Hanns moved around the corner to get a better firing angle on Terra. He maneuvered around the beams, coming into Terra's view while keeping his own eyes on the aeon edge that hovered in the air. When Hanns drew close to the hovering blade, his eyes went wide before turning and darting to the surrounding shadows. He was too late. Hanns had already missed Terra who was charging towards him with the last of her shieldwatch power.

Hanns fired several shots as Terra advanced. She blocked the shots with Zaid's aeon edge, not bothering to dodge them. When she was almost on Hanns, he tossed aside his gun and grabbed Terra's aeon edge at the guard.

They both pulled at the aeon edge. The tug of war went on for a few seconds before Terra overpowered Hanns by shifting her stance to unbalance him. Twisting her hands, Terra jerked the aeon edge out of his hands before grabbing his shieldwatch. She flung the shieldwatch in the air and sliced it in half.

Hanns made for the broken shieldwatch, but stopped when Terra pointed her aeon edge at him.

Terra's aeon edge had the safety off.

Hanns knelt on the ground with a confused expression as he stared upward at Terra.

Terra gritted her teeth. Heat from the fire and the exertion of combat made sweat run in rivulets down her face and back. Exhaustion, frustration, loss, it all pulled at her. Yet she knew her duty, what was required of her. She didn't have enough energy to bring Hanns back with her. It would take another half hour before her shieldwatch was charged enough to time travel and she couldn't hold Hanns for that long before his troops rescued him. Protocol and procedure were clear in situations like this where the temporal criminal could not be recovered. Time could weather the loss of a life over the continued threat of a rogue time traveler. Hanns had to die.

'Hanns sighed. Then he smirked. "Well. It seems you are a soldier now. Go ahead then," he said before closing his eyes.

Terra thought he looked smug even as he faced death. He held a look of contentment, as though he had challenged Olympus itself and almost won. It was the look of a man who had, for a single moment, held all of human history in his hands.

Terra tightened her grip on Zaid's aeon edge. She had to kill Hanns. There was no other way. If she let him go now, then he would menace Time again. It was her soldier's duty to kill Hanns.

She sighed before sheathing Zaid's aeon edge.

Hanns opened his eyes, his face betraying confusion. He struggled to stand. "Seems you are not much of a soldier after all."

Terra pulled the frozen aeon edge out of stasis and sheathed it. "You're right, Hanns. I'm a heroine."

Hanns took a weak step forward. "I won't stop, you know. I will win an endless history for the Third Reich!"

Terra turned to Hanns. "No, you won't. History has already damned you and next time we meet Hanns, I'll drag you to Tartarus myself."

She grinned. For the first time since she had seen him, Hanns looked insulted. She pitied Hanns. He leaned against an iron beam, ragged, with the shattered remains of the stolen shieldwatch at his feet, the history it contained unrecoverable. Above him, Hanns's time machine burned while the fires spread to the rest of his base. Now he stood lost in darkness as she left him behind.

It proved easy to sneak out of the base. Most of the soldiers were busy putting out fires. Overcast night skies shrouded most of the land in darkness though fires reflected a reddish orange light on the clouds overhead. That darkness deepened as she moved away from the burning base. The rumblings of a thunderstorm sounded in the distance as she took shelter in a nearby building.

Building was a generous term for this structure. It was still under construction as steel beams stood from the ground in a dense grid pattern. Terra could tell that this would be a smelting plant as large empty metal pots lay nearby next to piles of unprocessed ore.

It was several stories high with much of the first floor completed. Extra steel girders lay in heaps nearby. The clutter along with the dim lighting made it a good place to hide. Terra decided to lay low there until her shieldwatch recharged enough to time travel and return to Saturn City or until reinforcements arrived. Too bad she didn't have enough energy to go back and take Hanns with her, but in her current state she could barely escape on her own.

It was then Terra saw movement in the shadows. She drew her aeon edge, but had only a single stasis cell remaining. Terra let her eyes adjust to the dark. After a moment, she noticed a figure standing in shadow, watching her.

"I see you there," Terra said. She knew it was pointless to hide now. At least she could draw out the watcher and identify him or her.

The figure did not move.

"I know you are hiding there. Show yourself!"

Footsteps echoed on the metal floor as the watcher stepped out of the shadows.

CHAPTER XXXIII
SHADOWS OF STEEL

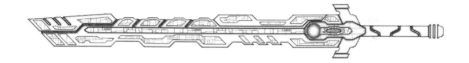

*Alya, you were right. I have seen the steel in her. However, even
steel has its shadows.*
  -Final entry from the personal logs of Praetor Lycus Cerberus

She walked out of the shadows of steel, footsteps echoing on metal
as she stepped into the dim light. The orb of her black shieldwatch
glowed red, piercing through the darkness like the single eye of a
beast. Her armor was of Legion design, though matte black with the
armored plates outlined in a thin red edge. Starch marks marred her
torso plate where she had scraped the Aeon Legion emblem off her
armor. Dark, smooth hair hung several inches past her shoulders with a
single lock bleached white on the left side of her face. None of these are
what made Terra's skin crawl. The mask did that.

It was a Kalian mask, black, smooth, and oval in shape with a red
symmetrical glyph on its front. The mask extended from the top of her
forehead to the chin, concealing her face save for two dark, sunken eye
holes. Two pairs of sweptback, horn like antenna, the top pair longer
than the other, decorated the side of the mask just above her ears.

Terra stepped back and tensed when the black-clad woman peered
at her through those hollowed looking eyes. That gaze tore out a cold
pit in Terra's stomach and made her hair stand on end.

The assailant charged, appearing in front of Terra with movements
too fast for Terra to track. Terra slashed at the woman, but she blocked
the blow before grabbing Terra's shieldwatch arm and smashing it on
a nearby steel beam. Terra screamed as both her shieldwatch and arm
broke. Then the woman grabbed Terra's throat in a vice like grip as
Terra's sword clattered to the ground.

The dark legionnaire stared at Terra for a moment, body tense as though expecting more resistance. None came as Terra gurgled her own blood while trapped in the woman's steely grip. Terra's unbroken hand tried in vain to pry the grip loose.

Her vision blurred. She heard Minerva speaking in her cipher. Something about reinforcements? She heard someone yell her name. It sounded like Roland but that couldn't be right. Roland would never show real concern for anyone but himself.

A blur entered Terra's periphery vision. The woman in black smacked someone who tried to attack her. Her grip lessened just enough for Terra to get a gulp of air, and to see Hikari skidding along the ground like a rag doll from the black-clad legionnaire's backhand.

Terra squirmed again and caught a glimpse of Roland as the woman in black jabbed him in the stomach with her sheath. He fell and did not stir. Then the woman's grip on Terra's throat tightened. With her strike team down, Terra would have felt more panicked if not for her more pressing problem of breathing.

Just as her vision darkened a familiar voice cut through Terra's fading gasps.

"That tiro you are strangling belongs to me."

The woman tossed Terra aside like a broken toy. She tumbled to the ground, the impact sending a fresh jolt of pain through her broken arm. Now free, Terra reached out to her connection with time by instinct only to find it missing. She already missed her shieldwatch. Terra pushed through the pain and looked to see Lycus facing the woman in black. He stood, arms crossed with a bored expression while Terra's strike team lay broken and unconscious nearby.

The black-clad attacker strolled towards Lycus without hesitation. When she spoke, her mask distorted her voice with a mechanical edge. "Praetor Lycus, wielder of the aeon edge Cerberus, eighth member of the Legendary Blades. I have come here to challenge you to a Trial of Blades. To the death."

Terra coughed and gagged while crawling away from the black clad legionnaire. The taste of blood filled her mouth and her arm screamed with pain.

"How pointlessly dramatic," Lycus said. "At least introduce yourself properly."

"Soon to be dead men have no need for introductions."

Lycus grinned. "Dead man? Well if I am a dead man, then may I at least know the name of the blade that is to slay me?"

The woman glanced down to her aeon edge. "Exile."

Lycus's wolf like grin widened, the beast within him beginning to stir. "Exile. Oh that was almost good. Very well. I will keep with tradition and refer to you by your blade name. Still feels a bit too dramatic to me. Well then, Exile, are you a traitor or just a dustrunner who got lucky and stole legion gear?"

Exile stepped forward. "I am not interested in talking with the scholar nor the Captain. Show me Cerberus. Your other faces do not interest me. I am only interested in killing monsters."

Lycus stood calmly, but Terra didn't share his confidence after having her throat crushed. Exile stood like an immovable steel wall, without even a hint of fear as she faced a Legendary Blade.

Lycus studied Exile. "I see now. It was you who broke into the Archives after stealing Tiro Mason's shieldwatch ID. You were the one stalking me. Clever. You followed Tiro Mason to this time since you knew I would be watching over her. Then when I was alone and away from the city you would come here and kill me. I wish you good fortune on that hopeless quest. Aion knows some of the best have already tried. None have slayed the beast. Stop wasting my time and just tell me who you are."

Terra wondered when Exile had stole her shieldwatch information. Then she remembered the day she fell asleep in Kairos's Garden and the black figure she saw there.

Exile drew her aeon edge. Black steel matched the darkness until the timecore orb and edge glowed red. The blade was a span longer than a longsword with the tip ending in a tanto point. She saluted Lycus.

Terra forced her pain aside and crawled to a nearby iron beam, leaning back on it. She watched as Lycus and Exile faced one another. Lycus stood, arms crossed, without expression. A long moment passed with the only sound being the wind and distant rumble of thunder.

Lycus shrugged. "Fine. You better be worth it. I hate it when wannabes try to duel me." He then appeared in front of Exile, aeon edge Cerberus in hand, and struck in a flash. Exile dodged the blade so close that the metal flat of Lycus's blade made sparks as it scraped against her mask. The rest of the fight became a blur of motion and after images.

Terra moved away from the dueling pair, trying to put some distance between her and the battle. She then spotted Roland who still lay unconscious. Terra crawled to him, gritting her teeth in pain, and removed his shieldwatch before attaching it to her unbroken arm. Although too weak to Restore herself as it was attuned to Roland's body, she felt some of her connection with time return. Working fast, she sent a distress call to Saturn City using her own identification, hoping that maybe Alya would find it.

A loud boom followed by a shock wave sent Terra tumbling on the ground. She steadied herself and Sped her vision using Roland's shieldwatch. If she wanted to stand any chance of survival she needed to keep track of Exile's and Lycus's battle.

When Terra's eyes focused on the duel, she still could not keep up with both combatants' movements. She could see afterimages of Lycus attacking with each of his blows blocked. The ground cracked nearby under the power of an aeon edge burst. The wind from their movements rushed over Terra.

There was series of loud blasts as Lycus unleashed a burst from his aeon edge. Unlike the other aeon edges Terra had seen, Cerberus unleashed three bursts in quick succession. Though Exile countered with her own burst, the force of Lycus's attack almost overwhelmed her, ripping up the ground around her and sending chunks of earth flying into the air. Still she held her ground, panting from the exertion.

Lycus attacked again, unleashing another three bursts. This time the bursts knocked Exile back, sending her flying into a nearby metal beam with incredible force. She smashed into the beam with a loud clang, bending it.

Terra let out a sigh of relief. She wasn't sure she could survive much longer even sitting on the sidelines.

Lycus stood, his face impassive, staring at Exile. He lowered his aeon edge.

Exile shot forward, appearing in front of Lycus in an instant. She struck, her blade almost taking Lycus's head off. He dodged, though the black aeon edge cut a small gash on his face before he fell back. Lycus took up a defensive pose before touching his face. His eyes widened upon seeing blood on his fingers.

Exile stood, sword ready, with no evidence of damage from her impact into the metal beam.

Lycus stared at the blood dripping from his fingers. "It's been centuries since I have seen my own blood."

Terra thought that Lycus was about to panic. Instead he lowered his gaze, obscuring most his face in shadow save for his wide toothy, snarling smile. He laughed with a twisted face that Terra had grown to fear. She then understood. He was no longer Lycus. His other faces yielded to the monster. Cerberus charged.

Terra cursed. She would have to find cover for herself and Roland while keeping an eye on the fight lest the giants step on her as they battled.

Their blades met again. This time, Cerberus no longer held back, pulling the trigger on his aeon edge and unleashing another series of bursts. Exile edged back and countered with her own burst to lessen the blast. Soon the ground around them shattered as their battle raged in the center of the construction site.

Stray stones and bits of construction equipment rained around Terra. She grabbed Roland with her one good hand and crawled further from the battlefield while dragging him behind her. Pain shot through her body with each movement, but she had to get out of the way. She stopped only briefly to see where the combatants fought.

Cerberus's blows seemed to come much faster than his foe's strikes. Each savage blow matched his wolfish grin that looked eager to draw blood. Exile could only continue to defend, each burst forcing her back a single step. Cerberus's sword ejected a spent stasis cell clip that he reloaded in a single, seamless move that flowed into his next attack.

His opponent, though slower, was more methodical. Her attacks were not as powerful nor as quick, but they were precise and with no waste or unnecessary movements. There was a simplistic brutality to them that matched Cerberus's savageness. Each blow was blunt and without any flourish as though driven more by discipline as opposed to Cerberus's berserk rage. Even Exile's blocks and dodges were minimalist.

If Terra had witnessed this duel from atop a comfy and safe arena seat, she might have called it artful, even beautiful, much like watching a majestic, but distant storm. Storms were much less enjoyable when stuck in the middle of them. Being near a battle between Legendary Blades was not a spectator's sport. Instead, she felt like a refugee as she dragged Roland behind a half built wall for cover. She then glanced over her pitifully thin wall to make sure she was out of the way.

The pair fought nearby and locked blades. Cerberus then pinned both blades to the ground before letting one hand go of his blade and reaching for Exile's face. His fingers brushed along the edge of the mask as Exile rolled away. He smiled, stepping back into the first floor of the unfinished building.

The black legionnaire readied her weapon and followed Cerberus. They weaved between steel supports. Cerberus fought one handed. He grabbed each steel beam, swinging on it with his shieldwatch hand, using the momentum to increase his speed. Exile marched across the floor at a slow pace, cutting down metal pillars when they got in her way. Each clash caused the surrounding area to corrode. Terra noticed that every pillar Cerberus touched would rust.

Exile landed another blow, cutting deep into Cerberus's arm. Cerberus grabbed one more pillar, his touch tarnishing it before flinging himself outside the building. Exile hesitated.

Cerberus smiled as he used his aeon edge to send a burst of energy at the building. Weakened pillars failed under the blast and the entire structure collapsed. The rubble entombed Exile in a grave of rusted steel.

This time Terra crushed her own hope. She could feel that something was wrong.

Cerberus Restored himself. He turned to go when he saw a red light emanate from the debris. He paused. "That much mass should have killed even a shieldwatch user."

The steel rusted away as the black legionnaire rose from the decaying debris, unscathed. The red haze of grainy energy rotted away everything around her as she stood, flakes of decayed steel falling around her like red snow.

Please don't fight over here! Please don't fight over here! Terra repeated to herself like a mantra.

Cerberus's wolfish grin returned as he loaded another stasis cell clip. Their battle then moved to another half constructed building. A burst from Exile sent steel beams flying into the air. Both Sped time and dueled upon the beams, leaping upon steel that fell in slow motion. Each time they met atop a beam, they crossed blades and the burst would tear apart steel just as the duelists leaped to another.

Terra kept her eyes on the fight. The move paid off when a stray beam came straight towards her. She moved, dodging the beam as it punched through the wall she hid behind. She rolled Roland over to a safer spot and went back to monitoring the battle.

Cerberus and Exile clashed again. The burst pushed Exile away. She cut through another metal beam in her way. Cerberus pursued. When he drew close, Exile faced him while still falling in midair and unleashed another burst from her aeon edge which sent a metal beam flying at Cerberus. Metal beams took Cerberus's attention as he dodged, but Exile maneuvered around him and slashed. The blade cut across his chest.

Cerberus landed on the ground, clutching his chest. Terra thought he would Restore himself. Instead his snarl twisted further as his eyes went wide. He howled an inhuman battle cry and charged. Blood now covered his chest yet he took no notice. Instead he attacked with a savageness beyond what she had thought Cerberus capable of.

Exile became like steel. Each burst tore at the surrounding ground, yet she held firm, blocking each of Cerberus's attacks. She struck, wounding Cerberus several more times. Each wound made him more enraged.

Cerberus's rage built until even Exile could not keep pace. Then one burst threw Exile off her feet. He charged, thrusting his blade at her heart. Exile parried the blow but it pierced her chest, pinning her to the ground. He put a foot on her sword hand and another on Exile's stomach. Blood pooled under her. Standing over his fallen opponent, Cerberus reached down and removed Exile's mask, tossing it aside.

As the mask fell, Cerberus's rage faded as his eyes widened. He froze, staring at the unmasked face.

Exile wasted no time. She slipped her aeon edge out from Cerberus's boot and in a flash, trust forward. The aeon edge plunged through Cerberus's chest. Blood splatted as the aeon edge pierced his heart and ran through his back. Exile stood and twisted the blade, bringing Cerberus to his knees and then to the ground in a reversal of their previous position.

"Crash," Terra whispered while still peeking out from cover. It seemed the appropriate thing to say now that the closest thing she had to an ally was dying.

Blood ran from Cerberus's mouth as he twitched. As he lay on the ground, he met Terra's eyes. His lips moved, speaking something Terra couldn't hear. His eyes seemed to be pleading with her, trying to tell her something. But all that came from his mouth was blood. Then his gaze became hollow and his body stilled.

Terra felt the first drops of rain.

Exile twisted her aeon edge again. The length of the blade glowed bright red before it ejected a small cylinder that the she grabbed. Exhausted, Exile fell to her knees as she tore out Cerberus's blade and tossed it aside. She then pulled out her own bloodied blade and stood to find her mask. Terra tried to get a good look at her, but the woman's hair and shadows cast from steel shrouded her face, but Terra caught one detail. When Exile picked up the mask, Terra saw something above her right ear, a single black rose. Then she spotted something else on Exile, a patch on her arm. Six aeon edge blades arranged in a circle; the sixth Legendary Blade.

Terra pushed herself up before limping closer. Not a wise move, Terra reflected, but she had get a closer look. Wind and rain picked up around her.

Exile ignored her and stood over Cerberus before Restoring herself. She loaded the spent shell in a small slot on her mask before she checked her shieldwatch display. After a moment, Exile picked up Lycus's aeon edge and put in on his chest before clasping his hands around it and closing his eyes. "Rest in the garden, Lycus. I killed the monster."

Terra stared at the woman. The pain in her arm vanished at her own revelation. "Kairos."

Kairos's dark hair waved in the wind as she turned to go.

Alya jumped down into the construction site, blade drawn. She paused before fixing her gaze on Lycus Cerberus. Alya merely stared at the corpse, speechless.

Terra stumbled. "Alya!"

Alya faced Kairos, sword at the ready, keeping her eyes focused on the foe before her. "Are you okay, Terra? I saw the distress signal."

"She's Kairos!" Terra yelled.

Alya froze.

Terra struggled to stand. "She has a black rose in her hair and the sixth Legendary Blade patch on her shoulder."

Kairos stood upon a solid steel slab, drenched in rain and blood, staring at Alya. She then sheathed her aeon edge. "I will not fight my former teacher."

Alya lowered her blade. "I kept imagining this moment when you returned. No. This is all wrong." Alya turned away. She shook her head. "No. We can fix this."

No, Terra thought. *No we cannot.*

Alya faced Kairos and extended her hand. "Come back to Saturn City. You can explain the situation there. They will listen to you because they know you."

Kairos remained still. "Who I was, am, or will be no longer matters. All that matters is that I complete my mission."

"Then I'll help you," Alya said without hesitation. "The Kairos I knew would only pursue a noble goal. Surely we can come to an agreement. If you tell everyone what your mission is, then we can–"

Kairos took a step forward, her footstep clanging on steel. "The destruction of Saturn City, the Aeon Legion and the Legendary Blades. I will then take the Temporal Singularity and use it to rescue Time from destruction. I will spare only you and those who get out of my way."

Alya stood in stunned silence for a long moment. "I... That's... How will that save Time from destruction?"

Kairos clenched her fists. "I have seen truths you will never know, Alya. I have been to both the Beginning and End of Time. Within the Singularity of Memory I have remembered a thousand lifetimes. Within the Singularity of Thought I have drank deeply of the well of knowledge. Most of all, I have seen with my own eyes the destruction of Time that will ruin everything I have fought for. To save humanity, to save history, I will do anything, even wade through an ocean of blood if that is what it takes to save our future."

Alya pointed to Lycus's corpse. "And how will killing Cerberus help that goal?"

"Time travel damages time," Kairos said. "By killing those who time traveled the most and have lived the longest, I can free the time they have stolen. The greatest thieves are the Legendary Blades and Saturn City itself. Destroying Saturn City will heal time enough for me to find a permanent solution."

Alya's hand went to the hilt of her blade. "What proof do you have?"

Kairos now held out her hand to Alya. "Come with me and I can show you."

"Show me your face first," Alya said as her grip on her aeon edge tightened

"No," Kairos said as she lowered her hand. "I may not wish to raise my blade against my former teacher, but I am no longer your student."

"I just wanted to see her again," Alya said, her gaze downcast. "I wanted to see the face of the person who did so much good."

Terra heard the hum of engines in the distance. Spotlights shown through the rain as vehicles drove up to the construction site.

Alya pointed her blade at Kairos as the wind and rain picked up around her. "This is all wrong, but I'll bring you back. I will make things right. I promise."

Kairos turned to go, but stopped to look over her shoulder at Alya. "Then choose. Bring me back to Saturn City or save the helpless tirones."

"Crash," Alya muttered between gritted teeth. She looked to Terra and to the other tirones before looking back at Kairos as she departed who turned to go. Alya glanced once more at Kairos before turning back to Terra. "Terra! Get to the girl lying on the ground and use her shield-watch to send her back to the city. Then bring back the other tiro yourself. I'll bring back Lycus."

Terra nodded and moved to Hikari before accessing her shieldwatch. She used the manual recall feature to send Hikari back to Saturn City. Then she ran back to Roland and lifted him up, wrapping his arm around her shoulder. Alya did the same with Lycus. Alya and Terra looked one last time at Kairos who dashed into the darkness, disappearing into shadow. Just as the German soldiers stormed into the construction site, Terra activated Roland's shieldwatch. The ring transported them to the Edge just as Nazi soldiers raised their weapons to fire.

∞

Chaos reigned at the timeport. A legionnaire found Terra after she had fitted another shieldwatch and Restored herself with backup data Minerva had archived. They told her to follow them and he led her to a room where Orion waited. Several officers had gathered around a miniature holo of the battle-site projected just above a metal table in the center of the room. They gestured and discussed while re-watching segments of the fight between Exile and Cerberus. Orion stood in the center focusing on the replay of the fight.

Terra saluted.

Orion looked up from the holo at her before waving the others away. "That is the most tired salute I have seen in a while. The rest of you are dismissed."

"Sir?" one officer asked. He wore the badge the Second Cohort, the Shadow Cohort.

Orion maintained his stoic expression. "We are about to review classified information. I need your unit to help cleanup the Tartarus disaster. Crashing End. It's going to take us weeks to get Tartarus reattached. At least only a few prisoners escaped. Also, I want another unit to investigate how a crashing military unit from the 1940's managed to sneak into the city so easily. What a mess."

The officers looked shocked. Terra thought they must be unaccustomed to being left out of the loop or seeing Orion so tense.

They saluted and left. Terra then recognized her surroundings. This was the place where Orion had brought her during her first day at Saturn City.

Terra sat across from Orion. She struggled to stay awake after the shieldwatch Restore had washed away her shock and adrenaline. Her body was fine now. She no longer felt any pain or hunger, but a shieldwatch could erase the mental fatigue that left her her ready to pass out asleep.

Orion sighed before sitting. "So who was it?"

"Kairos," Terra said in a tired voice.

Orion frowned. "Evidence?"

Terra stared at the table. "Sixth Legendary Blade patch on her upper arms. Black rose in her hair. One silver lock of hair matches her approximate age. Height and hair color are a match. I don't know about her voice, it was distorted."

Orion shook his head. "We did a DNA sweep. It was inconclusive, but its still too soon to tell. Too many contaminants. Most of it yours or Cerberus's and a few others. No fingerprints."

"She wore gloves."

"Any other clues?"

"She said that Cerberus would rest in the garden after he died. I think she was referring to Kairos's Garden."

Orion let out a long, tired sigh. "All the evidence we have points to her. We don't have conclusive evidence yet, but I don't think we can afford to hold on to hope for this one."

"Is she right? About Time collapsing I mean."

Orion shook his head. "Impossible. We researched the effects of shieldwatch technology. There is no way it could cause a disaster on the scale Kairos claims. She must have another goal or she is being manipulated."

"Manipulated? By who?"

"Who knows. We never found out who or what made the Faceless. She also went to the Beginning of Time. No one has ever come back from that unchanged, though most of them usually don't try to kill everyone."

"What are they like?"

Orion thought for a moment. "Most who return from the Beginning of Time only approach one specific person, usually family or a loved one. They give them cryptic information or more often to say goodbye before disappearing back into the Beginning again. A few come back, raving about ascension or some such nonsense and start trying to hunt down singularities. Time King Ophion did that. That man came back mad."

"What if they come back from the End of Time?"

"She's lying. It's impossible. No one returns from the End of Time, save for Faceless."

The door faded and Terra could hear the guard outside.

"I am sorry, Centurion Silverwind. You are not allowed inside," the guard said as Alya brushed past him.

Alya marched into the room followed by the guard.

The guard turned to Orion. "I am sorry, sir. I tried to—"

"It's all right," Orion said, dismissing the guard. "Actually, Alya, I'm glad you're here."

Alya moved to Terra and inspected her. "Are you okay?"

Terra nodded. "Just exhausted. I'll be fine."

Orion stood and faced Alya. His expression turned cold as though bracing himself for a storm. "Alya. I am putting you on leave until further notice."

Alya turned to Orion. "What!"

Orion kept his cold gaze locked on Alya. "This is Kairos. I don't want you to have to raise a blade against your former pupil. Consul Prometheus will agree with me."

Alya grimaced. "I know her best. I'll hunt Kairos down and I will save her. You can't stop me, Orion."

Orion spoke in an even tone. "I don't want you hurt any more."

Alya grimaced, her fists clinched. "At least I'm not soulless and can still feel emotions!"

Orion's expression softened.

Alya turned away. "Sorry, Orion. I didn't mean that."

Orion shook his head. "Look, Alya. You have enough burdens. Let the other Legendary Blades handle this. Please?"

Alya faced Orion. "Terra. Let's go."

Terra followed Alya out of the timeport as she avoided onlookers as usual. Alya stopped on a long windswept metal bridge. She looked out at the city, one hand on a metal rail. Her grip tightened on the rail until her knuckles turned white.

Terra took a step forward. "Are you okay?"

Alya was silent for a long moment. Then she looked up to the sky and spoke in a quiet voice. "It's not fair."

CHAPTER XXXIV
THE REFORGED BLADE

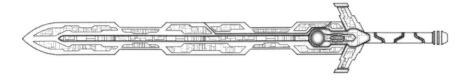

And so a tiro comes to the end of a journey. However, this is merely the start of a career in the Aeon Legion. Some may squire under the legionnaire who found them. Others join a cohort for specialization. A few are even allowed a short leave back to their home time, provided it does not disrupt the flow of the continuum.

Consider though, that this new journey is far more perilous than any test the Academy could design. Comrades will be lost, personal sacrifices will be required, and life in the Aeon Legion can be brutally short. Defending history may require the ultimate sacrifice, but a legionnaire already knows this. What many are not prepared for is when one of our own strays from the path.

Battle calls to us. Every aeon edge can become starved for blood. Without realizing it, even the best of us can become monsters. When you choose a squire, are you prepared to run a blade through them when they become a villain? Ours is a journey through blood. Never forget this.

-Closing words of the Aeon Legion's *Squire Recruitment Manual* by Praetor Lycus Cerberus

Terra stood silent amongst the endless field of blades in Kairos's Garden as Alya added another aeon edge. It was the second today, with the first being Zaid's. Alya plunged the tip of the aeon edge Cerberus into the soil.

Terra regarded the garden. Birds sang in the bright day as flowers swayed in the wind. Now the spring outside the garden matched the spring within. "How could someone who made all this be so brutal?"

Alya stared at Cerberus for a long while. "It's a lesson."

"A lesson?"

Alya nodded. "It's a reminder of how easy it is to fall into darkness. Sometimes it's not our weaknesses that make us a villain, but our strengths."

Terra raised an eyebrow as Alya walked through the garden. Alya stopped in front of Kairos's blade as Terra followed.

Alya glanced at Kairos's black rose covered blade. "Conviction, self sacrifice, and a willingness to do anything to save people. She still possesses all of these. Although her delusion is the source of her fall, without her strengths she wouldn't be able to harm others so effectively. There *will* be more bloodshed before this is done."

Terra looked at the aeon edge and fell silent as she remembered the terrifying battle between Cerberus and Kairos. She wrapped her arms around herself and felt cold despite the heat of the sun.

Alya smiled. "Well I guess there is no reason to worry about it at the moment." She grabbed Kairos's aeon edge by the handle and lifted it out of the ground as the black roses fell away.

"What are you going to do with that?"

Alya lifted the aeon edge before resting the flat of the blade on her shoulder. "This is a garden for remembering those fallen in battle. Kairos is still alive so there is no need for her aeon edge here."

Terra started to ask another question.

"Don't worry about Kairos," Alya interrupted. "She is my responsibility. Have they told you if you have passed the Labyrinth yet?"

"Well I'm not sure. I didn't make it to the final trial. I walked back to the Academy after that night and tried to convince them to let me take the final trial. They told me it was too late, but they would review my case."

Alya grinned. "Well it doesn't matter. Even if they say you failed, I am still taking you as my squire. The crashing bureaucrats can cry if they wish. I consider you a full legionnaire."

Terra looked down. "I didn't feel much like a legionnaire during the fight with Kairos. I thought I had come so far, but I was helpless."

Alya put her hand on Terra's shoulder. "Listen Terra. You are stronger, wiser, and braver than you once were. It's a great improvement over the timid girl I found hiding in that quarry."

∞

They all stood in formation for the last time. There was a solemness about the day even though training was finished. The melancholy mood contrasted with the bright spring day and beaming sun. Lycus Cerberus was dead. They had just finished honoring his memory before the centurions awarded aeon edges.

It was strange that his death seemed to hang over the entire ceremony. He had been everyone's enemy, yet that enemy had shaped them more than their allies in the training. Lycus had challenged each of them, tested every weakness and, like a skilled blacksmith, had reforged them all into something stronger.

Terra noted how few remained. Less than a hundred stood now of what had started in the thousands. There had been a handful of deaths in the Labyrinth, Zaid among them.

The thought of Zaid made Terra sigh. *He should be here to receive his aeon edge,* she thought. She wasn't even a full legionnaire and had already lost a friend.

Nikias stepped up to the platform. "Today you receive your aeon edge. When called, you will approach the platform to receive your blade. Those who do not were judged to have failed the Labyrinth. They will get another chance in a special program should we feel they deserve it."

Shani then stepped forward. "The Sybil shall give you your blade. It is not yet named. The name you give your blade will be your alias within the Aeon Legion."

"Tiro Roland Delmare!" Nikias called.

Roland walked up on stage and saluted.

Shani faced him. "Tiro Roland Delmare! You are adaptable and cunning, able to surmount complex problems with simple solutions. When temptation came to abandon your comrades, you stayed behind and helped them. Such a person is more than worthy to carry the rank of legionnaire."

Decima approached Roland, holding an aeon edge wrapped in fine white silk with the grip facing him. He grabbed the grip gingerly and drew it in a slow motion.

Decima stepped back. "The tides of blue helped us design this blade. The flow of river water gave us its inspiration. It is a worthy blade made for a great knight baptized in a river. It is made for you and you alone."

It was a longsword length blade with a standard tip. Small etched grooves, like waves, decorated the flat of the blade while a stripe of deep blue ran in its center. This was an aeon edge designed for cutting or stabbing, a versatile weapon for a versatile fighter. He held it in his hands, feeling the weight and balance. After a quick flourish he smiled.

"Tiro Roland Delmare!" Nikias announced.

Roland stood at attention.

Nikias saluted Roland. "You are hereby promoted to the rank of legionnaire! Welcome to the Aeon Legion, Legionnaire Roland Delmare!"

Roland walked off the stage moments later.

"Tiro Hikari Urashima!" called Nikias.

Hikari approached the stage and saluted.

Shani faced her. "Tiro Hikari Urashima. It has been some time since we have been graced with one who possesses so much talent. Your combat skills are unmatched and your dedication and passion are your best qualities. We are proud to award you your aeon edge."

Decima approached Hikari while presenting the grip of the aeon edge to her. Like the others, it lay wrapped in silk. Hikari grabbed the grip and drew it fast. "It's still warm," Hikari said, staring wide eyed at the weapon. The blade was thinner than Roland's with a curved tip; an aeon edge made for quick cutting blows.

Decima grinned. "This one was difficult to make. We spent much time in Caminus forging it. We had to use an intense fire to make the metal tame. That is its inspiration. The inferno, endless flames shown us this design. This blade is for a warrior forged in fire. It is made for you alone."

Hikari gave a deep bow to the Sybil and to the instructors.

"Tiro Hikari Urashima!" Nikias announced.

Hikari faced them and saluted.

Nikias saluted back. "You are hereby promoted to the rank of legionnaire! Welcome to the Aeon Legion, Legionnaire Hikari Urashima!"

Soon Hikari joined Roland and Terra.

Terra felt a surge of panic when the centurions didn't call her name next. One by one the tirones claimed their blades. Then no more were called.

Nikias turned to Decima. "Is that all?"

Decima nodded. "Yes. That is all of the new aeon edges."

Nikias turned to wrap up the ceremony when Terra heard a voice from her shieldwatch.

"Tiro Terra Mason?" a man asked.

Terra touched her shieldwatch's holoface and answered the call. "Yes."

"Please report to the Academy Gardens immediately."

Terra walked through the forest and when she neared the garden she saw two legionnaires guarding it. Both had the emblem of the Third Cohort, the Guardians. The Guardians were bodyguards of important figures in the Legion.

"He is waiting for you," one said before gesturing to Kairos's Garden that lay ahead.

Terra straightened her uniform and walked into the garden. She reached the field of blades before spotting a figure in white ahead that she recognized as Consul Prometheus. He stood in front of several blades, looking down at them with a solemn expression.

"Terra Mason," he said in a friendly tone when he saw her approach. "I am sorry for interrupting the ceremony, but there are important matters to discuss."

Terra saluted, remembering protocol.

Prometheus smiled. "Oh don't worry about formalities. You have no idea how tiring that gets after a few hundred years."

"Is this about the incident with Cerberus? I already told Orion everything I know."

Prometheus nodded. "Yes, but there are things I would like to ask you directly."

"Yes, consul."

Prometheus's eyes narrowed as he placed his hand on the grip of his aeon edge. Terra felt a chill as she looked at the older man. She could sense an edge to him, much like with Lycus, a hidden strength masked by a paternal air.

"Who was it?" he asked, his tone cold.

Terra frowned as she looked to where Alya had taken Kairos's blade. "It was Kairos. I don't know why she is trying to kill people now," Terra said before looking back at Prometheus. "She is though. I don't understand everything that's going on. I thought Kairos was a heroine. What could make someone turn into a monster like that?"

Prometheus studied her with a critical expression. Then he shifted his gaze to where Kairos's blade had rested. "I read the entire report on the incident. Not just the part with Kairos, but the part where you fought a man named Hanns. That was impressive. Do not allow anyone to tell you otherwise. Jumping into his home time, facing him in his base. That was a bit of heroics I haven't seen since Kairos. Silverwind chose well."

Terra blushed at the compliment.

He then faced her and smiled again. "I wanted to speak with you in order to take your measure for myself. Alya sees something in you as do I. I was worried at first, but now I am convinced you are what we need."

Terra's brow furrowed. "Consul?"

Prometheus smiled before touching his shieldwatch's holoface. "Minerva, it seems we will need that blade after all. Let Sybil Nona know that I am waiting in Kairos's Garden. Also, see to those other small details. You know how irate Orion gets if I withhold information from him for too long."

"Yes Founder," came Minerva's voice from his shieldwatch.

He then looked back to Terra. "Yes. You are exactly what we need."

"For what?"

Prometheus smiled again and looked at two approaching figures.

Terra's brow raised, but her questions had to wait when she recognized Alya walking with a Sybil.

The Sybil Nona's face held a sour expression s she carried something in a white silk cloth.

Alya smiled upon seeing Terra before turning to Prometheus. "Thank you for keeping this quiet."

Prometheus nodded. "It is best we keep this secret for now."

Nona nodded. "I am not sure why you had us reforge this, Founder, but it is done. We had to wipe away a lot of dirt and stone stuck in the old blackened steel. We purified it. The new metal is now virgin pearl Saturn City steel. I do wonder why we cannot see the fate of this reforged blade, especially considering its origin."

"Thank you Nona," Prometheus said as he took the silk covered item from the Sybil. He unwrapped it to reveal an aeon edge. "You cannot see the fate of this blade because fate will not deliver it to its new owner. This is a blade of choice, not one fit for a Qadar. Right now, we don't need a hero of fate. We need one of choice. You are dismissed."

Nona bowed before retreating. Prometheus then approached and presented the blade, grip first, to Terra.

Terra's breath caught when she saw the aeon edge. It was pearl white and shimmered more than any aeon edge she had seen earned that day. This aeon edge's design was made of solid unmarked steel. Although shorter than Roland's by a span, it had the same pointed tip. The plain design made Terra think that it suited her, but what really held her awe was that the design itself was familiar to her. This was Kairos's old blade reforged.

Prometheus and Alya looked to Terra as she stood, hesitant. Terra reached slowly towards the aeon edge. It was in this moment that Terra faced her true test. The aeon edge in front of her was her greatest achievement, but taking it would be the first step on a path from which she could not return. For a moment she considered not taking it as her hand shied away from the grip. She knew that taking that sword was the first step towards Kairos. She may have to take a life with this weapon.

Terra closed her eyes before grabbing the aeon edge. Her hands wrapped around the pearl steel grip as the cold of the metal sank into her hand. As she lifted the blade, Terra opened her eyes. The blade felt like a feather between her fingers, not at all like the clunky training blades. It was perfect.

"Tiro Terra Mason!" Prometheus said in a deep, powerful voice.

Terra stood at attention while noting just how commanding Prometheus could be.

"You are hereby promoted to the rank of legionnaire!" He said before saluting Terra. "Welcome to the Aeon Legion, Legionnaire Terra Mason!"

∞

A reception soon followed the graduation ceremony. A lot of the officers from various cohorts were there, talking to the graduates. Hikari had a small mob around her. The mob cleared out when Legionaries from the Second Cohort appeared and talked to Hikari alone.

The officers ignored Terra since she assumed they looked at performance records during training. When someone approached, Terra found herself caught off guard. She relaxed when she saw Captain Chih.

Chih returned Terra's salute. "Legionnaire Terra Mason. I am pleased to see you made it."

Terra lowered her salute.

"Tell me," Chih said with a smile, "what are your plans now?"

"I guess I will spend a year with the legionnaire who made me a squire. I think that is how it works right?"

Chih's smile lessened. "I see. Is this what you want?"

"Would it matter? I was told that a legionnaire who takes a squire has the right to train them for one year."

"That is their right yes, but I could request a transfer. If they proved unreasonable, then I could challenge them to a Trial of Blades. If you wished, I could arrange to train you for a year as my squire."

Terra grinned. "No offense, but I don't think that will work. Besides, she's the first person who ever had any faith in me and she gave me an opportunity to better myself. I feel like I owe her for that."

Chih nodded. "I understand," he said before touching a holoface.

Terra's shieldwatch beeped.

Chih smiled again. "You have my contact information should you change your mind. The Seventh Cohort could always use someone with your determination. I couldn't live with myself if I let talent like yours slip through without at least trying to convince you to join us. Especially with our upcoming mission."

"Mission?"

Chih expression turned solemn. "Now that Lycus Cerberus has been slain, well... The Seventh Cohort tracks rogue legionnaires."

"Oh."

Chih sighed. "Our quarry has the skills equal to a Legendary Blade. I do not look forward to this mission. I think we can stop her, whoever she is, but I doubt we can accomplish it without casualties."

"Maybe the other Legendary Blades will help?"

Chih grimaced. "They are powerful individuals, but they can be... difficult to work with. How would your culture put it? Loose cannons? Regardless, give my offer thought. Sometimes we must go where we are needed rather than where we wish."

As Chih walked away, Terra heard several people laughing nearby. She glanced to see Roland in the center of a small group. She narrowed her gaze at Roland who was now talking with several officers.

"Which is how we narrowly escaped the Manticore," Roland said, finishing his likely fictional story.

"I didn't know they were still using that old monster. I thought they replaced it?" an officer said.

"Not a bad account of the battle," another said. "The Fifth Cohort could use someone with your skill set. Facing a Manticore isn't easy."

Terra rolled her eyes as she walked over to Roland.

Roland nodded. "Yes. Well I have everyone's contact information. I will let you know if I have other questions."

The officers walked away, smiling. Terra scowled as she watched them go. Once they left she turned to Roland. "So this is it? Right back to the same thing as before?"

Roland smiled and leaned in closer. "Not quite. Now the wager is higher, but the goal is still the same. With my immortality temporarily secured, I now work towards obtaining an easy post, like a garrison or something else simple. Something far away from that legionnaire in black."

Terra put her hands on her hips and glared at Roland while trying her best to keep her temper in check. "Really? All that work."

"Exactly. All that work so I can be lazy. Did you really think I would risk my immortality after finally earning it?"

Terra sighed. "I suppose not. It's just that, for a moment, I thought you were a hero rather than just playing the part of one."

"Nonsense. I don't trust these people. Why would I risk everything for them? All this is a simple exchange of services, nothing more. I fight for them and they give me immortality."

"So what now? Are you going to join the easiest cohort you can find?"

"With haste. One that is safe and on a fair weathered coastline with a lovely view of the ocean."

"What about the legionnaire that made you a squire? Don't they get a year to train you first?"

Roland grinned. "Oh him? I doubt he will ev—"

"There you are!" came a loud voice from behind Roland. A short stocky man with a bald head grabbed the much taller Roland by the collar. "Let's go. Time to start your real training."

"What?" Roland yelled as the man dragged him.

"Stop flirting," he said while tugging Roland behind him. "No silver tongue is going to get you out of the year the Legion promised me, I can assure you that!"

Terra chuckled as she watched Roland get dragged away. She thought she might miss him a little. Despite his ability to get under her skin, Terra found Roland to be one of the few who would engage with her. In a way, she knew him better than most did. She could see both parts of him, the knave and knight.

Terra was so lost in thought she was taken aback when she turned to find Hikari glaring at her. Hikari pointed at Terra. "Do not think just because the training is over that our contest is done?"

"Oh no. I wouldn't think that. After all, who would you insult then?"

"I am ahead. I had officers from every cohort try to convince me to squire under them. You had one."

Terra grinned. "Yeah, but I didn't insult the one who approached me."

"I didn't insult them. Not all of them. However, I am squiring under a legionnaire who was trained by a Legendary Blade."

Terra thought about telling Hikari that she will squire for a Legendary Blade, but instead just grinned.

Hikari narrowed her eyes at Terra. "You have something else planned, don't you?"

Terra continued to smile.

Hikari turned to go. She took a few steps before stopping to cast a sidelong look at Terra. "It was... fun competing with you. I hope we compete again."

Terra watched Hikari go before shaking her head. "What a bother," Terra said, voicing her irritation at this so called competition while her smile said otherwise.

As Hikari left, Terra saw another familiar face nearby. Delphia moved through the crowd, drawing the eyes of the male graduates. Another man stood near her, likely her latest boyfriend.

"Delphia!" Terra said, walking over to greet her. "It feels like it has been forever since I've seen you."

Delphia stared at Terra for a long moment. Then she smiled before turning to dismiss her current boyfriend. She then walked over to Terra. "Terra," she said in her usual airy tone. "I see the Legion's regimen has caused numerous alterations to your demeanor and stature. Your transformation is such that it has exceeded my memory by a high degree."

Terra raised an eyebrow. "I have no idea what you just said, but it's nice to see you too."

Delphia smiled again and embraced Terra. Terra had gotten used to Delphia's complete ignorance of the concept of personal space during her time at Delphia's home. But Terra had forgotten about it during her training at the Academy.

"I have missed you," Delphia said after a long embrace.

"Really?"

Delphia nodded. "I always feel like I can be honest with you. It is rather strange. I like you even more now. You have a lot more confidence. I am rather envious of you."

"Why would you be envious of me?"

"You refuse to let anyone tell you who you are. People adore me because I am like a star. Beautiful, but distant and sculpted by people's imaginations rather than what is actually there. Others look past you, but you always force them to acknowledge you through actions. I wish I could be as determined as you sometimes."

Terra felt her face grow warm. "Thanks. I wish I could compliment others like you," was all Terra could say.

"I was always certain you would pass. I assume you are returning to your home time for your leave?"

Terra nodded.

Delphia's expression became distant. "Mother wishes you well and says that her invitation to stay at her home is still open upon your return. However, I myself have a surrogate offer. My second semester at the Academy begins within a few months. Since you are part of the Legion, you will receive time which you can use to acquire a place of residence. Should we combine our resources, we may both be able to obtain a domicile of superior quality above what we could individually manage."

"So... roommates? I guess I don't see why not. We got along well at your mom's house. I'll let you know when I get back."

Delphia smiled and began telling Terra about her semester in astronomy. Terra listened, but another man nearby drew her attention. She glanced to see a man in gray armor similar to Legion design. Instead of the Legion's golden infinity symbol, he had a silver crescent moon emblem on his upper arm. He stared right at Terra with a critical expression. She almost thought he would come over and talk to her, but instead he touched his shieldwatch's holoface before leaving. After a moment, Terra dismissed the event. It probably didn't have anything to do with her.

It didn't take long to organize her belongings for the trip back home. She took her shieldwatch with her and concealed her aeon edge in a duffel bag after taking it apart. Once she had packed everything, she called her parents and told them she was coming home. After double checking her bag one last time, she set off using the fadelines and faded into the timeport. She found Orion waiting for her near the gates. Remembering his rank, she saluted.

His expression remained stoic. "At ease. May I have a word with you in private?"

She then followed him inside a nearby building. Terra stepped inside a room with her sight on Orion as the door faded in behind her.

"This will not take long," Orion said.

"Strategos?"

Orion gestured to Terra's duffel bag. "Bring your aeon edge?"

Terra nodded.

"Smart girl."

"Should I expect trouble?"

"Probably not, but it's a good habit to keep your aeon edge handy at all times. I don't think Kairos is interested in you and I would rather it remain that way."

"So you are sure it's Kairos then?"

"I never let emotions or sentiment impede facts and analysis. All the pieces connect and the final one fell into place when we found her DNA at the battleground."

"Why tell me this?"

"I plan to watch you closely, Legionnaire Terra Mason. You have inherited Kairos's aeon edge and you are Alya's squire. I place little faith in fate or destiny, but I trust in Alya's ability to find gifted squires. I gamble that you will be a powerful asset against Kairos. However, I suspect that Alya will try to fix this herself."

"How do you know Kairos is even a major threat? She is only a single person."

"That one person saved this city. She can also destroy it."

"One person destroying the city?" Terra mumbled while trying to wrap her mind around the concept. The city seemed so vast and powerful yet she remembered the duel with Cerberus. The sheer power and terror of that battle gave her pause to consider. Perhaps Orion was right. There was also the omen during the Trial of Truth. The omen that Terra had thought was a warning about Hanns.

"I didn't come here though to tell you that. I came here to warn you."

"About Kairos?"

"No. Now that a Legendary Blade has fallen, other villains will come; monsters, criminals, mercenaries. Every nasty thing the Legion has been hunting will come out like roaches in darkness and they will come after *you*," he said, pointing at Terra.

"Me?"

"If they know that you are Alya's squire, every temporal villain looking to become famous will try to kill you. Be sure to keep your connection with Alya a secret."

Terra nodded.

"Oh and one more thing. Keep quiet about the identity of Kairos. That is an order. We are still working on how exactly to tell the Legion and Saturn City that our greatest savior is now trying to kill us."

The door faded open as Terra and Orion both looked to the archway. Alya walked in before glaring at Orion.

Alya stood hands on hips. "What's the matter Orion? Are you arresting my next squire as well?"

Orion sighed.

"Come on, Terra," Alya said as she gestured to the fadedoor.

Terra turned to go.

"Terra," Orion said.

She looked back to Orion.

"Never forget who the real threat is. Kairos is out there and worst of all, she believes she is Time's only hope. She will not hesitate to do anything to fulfill her mission. She has to be stopped."

Terra nodded before she walked out with Alya. They both made their way to the gate.

"Are you returning to your own time for a little while?" Alya asked.

Terra nodded. "To see my parents."

"Good. You deserve some rest. Be sure to practice though. You still need to brush up on your basic blade forms and it wouldn't hurt to practice your close combat skills too."

"I will," Terra said before glancing at Alya. "What will you do?"

Alya looked away.

"You are going to try to find Kairos aren't you?"

Alya closed her eyes. "I have to. I have to find her before the others do and figure out what happened." Alya opened her eyes and looked at Terra. "My first squire, Tahir, saved me. He showed me what a true hero was. He saved me, but died. All of them have died. Now Kairos comes back lost in darkness. I have to save her this time."

"I understand."

Alya regarded Terra for a moment and then smiled. "Crash. Here I am rambling about my issues right after you just completed the hardest test of your life. Don't spend too much time in the quarry again."

Terra nodded and turned to go. She stopped and then ran back to Alya, embracing her. "Thank you for everything."

Alya smiled as she hugged Terra back.

After a moment Terra released her embrace. "See you soon?"

Alya's smile faded. "Sure... I will pick you up after I get a few things out of the way."

∞

Terra felt strange coming home, almost like it wasn't real. When she first arrived at the city beyond time it was like a dream. Now it was like a dream returning to reality as she stood in front of her parent's home. She ran her fingers across the fence as she approached the door. Terra knocked on the door.

"Just a minute," came Beth's voice from inside the house. Seconds later the door opened. "Who are... Terra! Is that you?"

"Mom!" Terra said before embracing her mother.

"Um dear? Not so tight," Beth said as she choked in Terra's vice like embrace. Terra let go and Beth regarded her. "I barely recognized you."

Fred walked next to Beth. "Who's that?"

Terra shrugged. "Dad. It's me."

Fred squinted, regarding Terra. After a moment he smiled and embraced her. "Well if it isn't the little dirt devil herself. What happened? Where did you get those muscles?"

Terra smiled. "I've been exercising a little."

Beth beamed. "Good. You needed exercise. Come in. We are getting dinner ready."

Terra walked in before putting her bag down. "Need any help?"

Fred shook his head. "It's about finished. You can go relax. I am sure you are tired from your long trip. By the way, how were classes? You make any friends?"

Terra smiled. "Yeah I made a few friends. I met a lot of interesting people. Saw some really cool stuff."

Beth moved Terra's bags. "Meet any young boys?"

"Yeah I met a few, but I kept fighting with this German guy. There was another boy. He was nice until..." Terra frowned after remembering Zaid.

Fred nodded. "It sounds like you at least worked hard and met some interesting people," he said before walking into the kitchen.

Terra then heard the television playing in the living room.

Beth turned to Terra. "Could you turn off the TV in the living room? Your father left it on again."

"Sure," Terra said as she walked to the living room. She paused when seeing that a documentary played. Terra recognized the Nazi soldiers marching in the background.

"World War Two," the narrator said. "It is considered the defining event of the century. The Nazi party that seized control of Germany would become the most infamous villains of history. How could they have not known that their legacy would be one of horror, terror, and destruction? Do we all have the same capacity for self delusion and evil? When does one become the villain without recognizing it?"

Terra grabbed the remote and turned off the television. She had quite enough of Nazis for the rest of time.

KEYS AND THIEVES

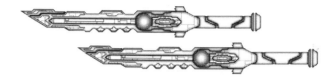

Time King Endymion grew as bored with the game of chess as he was of toying with petty thieves like Hanns. *I suppose this isn't so different,* Endymion mused while he sat across the table from his squire, Caelum. A holographic chess board lay between them. Endymion chose black while Caleum selected white. Few white pieces remained. Yet neither Endymion's impending victory nor his successful raid of Tartarus truly satisfied him. *Petty victories for petty games,* Endymion thought.

While Caelum pondered his next move in vain, Endymion glanced out over the balcony of his palace to the, as always, beautiful day in Saturn City. *Same victories, same games, same weather,* Endymion thought. He looked up to see where the hands were overhead to check the time before shaking his head at the futile habit. Endymion's hoard of time made it worthless, like all hoards.

He sighed before shifting his attention back to Caelum. As always, Caelum played with skill, but Endymion needed only three more moves until checkmate. Still, he found himself impressed by how much Caelum had improved since their last game.

Caelum studied the board with sky blue eyes and an elegant featured, but passive face that revealed little of his true emotions or thoughts. As the Singularity Thief Caleum wore a mask when on a mission, yet his bare face now was much like a second mask. He never smiled for Endymion. In truth, Endymion had never seen Caleum with a genuine smile, only the manufactured charm that Endymion had so carefully cultivated in the youth. Caelum certainly looked younger than his nineteen years with his slender build and short, sandy blonde hair that curled at the tips. Endymion preferred his squires lithe and agile to aid in their work. Yet he wondered if his own lost son would have looked like Caelum? *A smart boy*, Endymion thought, *but I don't need to get too attached. Besides, he still needs much improvement.*

Caelum made a move, but a faint sigh betrayed his realization of having lost the match. "Master, Hanns failed as I predicted."

Endymion moved his next piece. Two turns until checkmate.

Caelum glanced to Endymion, face expressionless as always. "You wasted a good shieldwatch on him, Master."

Endymion smiled. "Look deeper, Caelum. Hanns failed *his* objective not mine. A shieldwatch is a mere trifle. The artifacts you recovered are far more important. Hanns was a good distraction and a single lost shieldwatch for the spoils I gained from Tartarus was a cheap trade. Besides, I like Hanns. He may be a lowly thief, but pawns often make it across the board without being noticed. Perhaps he will get promoted to a far more useful piece in the future."

Already Endymion's mind began forming plans for Hanns, but he stopped himself. No point yet. His penchant for planning had served him well during the glory days, back when he had actual rivals to pit himself against, but was of little use in his current state. His thoughts drifted back to those times when he was a Time King in more than just name. Almost everyone had been trying to kill him back then so things were seldom dull. For a brief moment he longed for Deucalion or Pythia to take up the old titles again. What a joy it would be to match wits with another true Saturnian Time King or Queen rather than the Aeon Legion with its endless ranks of mongrels.

Endymion took a deep breath as he let go of those thoughts. Both Deucalion and Pythia had renounced their titles to rejoin the Legion. He never knew why. Such a foolish thing to do. *Then again,* Endymion thought, *the title of the Last Time King does have a certain charm about it.*

Caelum's brow lowered as he surveyed his ever dwindling forces on the chess board. After a moment he made another move. "How do you know Hanns will serve you? He seems loyal to his nation."

Endymion grinned. "The thousand year Third Reich doesn't quite live up to its lofty goals of longevity. I suppose he could join his comrades in the Sons of Oblivion, but I don't imagine he would fit in very well with those cutthroats," he said before putting Caelum in check. "Now to other matters. I nearly forgot to commend you on your little excursion into Tartarus. You did well. The Legion has yet to find any link to the Singularity Thief."

Caelum looked at Endymion. "Will they?"

"They are slow, but Orion will put the pieces together eventually. However, I suspect he will be too busy with the death of Cerberus to bother with us. Not that he will be able to discover our identities regardless. The Legion really does need to stop over-relying on the Sybil to do their investigations for them."

Endymion stroked his chin as he pondered. Who could have killed Cerberus? Cerberus was as nasty as the myth he was named after. The bloodshed left on the battlefield by that man gave even Endymion pause. He could think of very few capable of killing a monster like that. Perhaps Tyche or Reva, though both of them have been missing for centuries. Endymion himself could do it, but it would gain him nothing. There was one other.

He felt a chill run down his spine when he thought about Kairos. She had good reason to come after him next. He dismissed the thought. If Kairos wanted him dead she could have killed him on that day long ago. Endymion grimaced, remembering the day Kairos had cornered and forced the truth from him. He might have avoided that unpleasant situation if Silverwind hadn't stumbled into one of his projects again. What a waste. Thanks to Silverwind's strange luck Kairos became an unrecoverable asset. Kairos would have been Endymion's squire if not for Alya Silverwind. One day he would take recompense. He would steal something precious to her.

Caelum made his final move, knowing the match lost, yet hid his dissatisfaction well enough that Endymion only noticed a slight twitch in Caelum's wrist. "I am disappointed. I have trained for three years now. Master, I would wish for more opportunity to use my skills. Tartarus did not sate me. I didn't even get to match blades with the guards. I had hoped to draw blood. It is frustrating to leave my potential unused."

"Caelum, what you feel right now is but a taste of the constant vexation I feel every day," Endymion said while giving his best consoling smile, even though it was somewhat undercut by his final, ruthless move that placed Caelum in checkmate. "Opportunity comes to the patient."

Chess was not Endymion's favorite game. He found it too symmetrical. It did not reflect his tenuous position. The Aeon Legion had far too many pawns for him to put in checkmate. "This game is beginning to bore me," Endymion said as he dismissed the holo, "but I do find chess analogies to be rather fun. Next time I choose the game."

A soldier in dark gray armor entered the room bearing the mark of the crescent moon on his upper arm. Endymion's mark, the symbol of the Time Knights of Endymion. The armor was of similar design to the Legion's though more utilitarian. Sadly, they seldom had any use for the older dress uniforms from the glory days.

Endymion regarded the soldier with a sidelong glance while repressing his instinct to toy with the man. A part of him wanted to intimidate the soldier for interrupting his day. Maybe call him a fool or threaten to take away his immortality for daring to spoil a Time King's afternoon. Yet he found that tormenting lackeys was one game more tedious than chess.

The soldier bowed. "Infinite apologies, your Eternal Majesty, but I think this will be of interest to you."

Endymion sighed. He had always rewarded his knights for valuable information, but often in their zeal they would bring him irrelevant tidbits. Still, it was a practice he did not want to discourage even if it inconvenienced him from time to time. "Show me."

The soldier touched his shieldwatch's holoface and slid it over to Endymion.

Endymion glanced to the picture that showed Saturn City's timeport a few months ago. It displayed Silverwind standing in line.

He sneered while regarding the image of his old rival. Then he chuckled at the thought of the mighty Silverwind standing in line and waiting. "This has to be a lookalike. The Legion has a few of Silverwind's mindless worshipers in its ranks. This is probably just one that dresses as her for whatever reason. She would never stand in line even if Prometheus himself told her to. Is there something else here?"

The soldier pointed to the young girl standing next to Alya. Endymion sized the girl up quickly with his years of experience training squires. Softtimer for certain. Dress and facial features meant this girl was likely from Lambda continuum sometime during the early information age. Neutral expression and defensive body language suggested a passive aggressive personality. She seemed uncertain, but no outward signs of fear. *Decent enough stock,* Endymion thought. *She needs a lot of work, but I can tell she would be good squire material.*

The soldier then generated a second holoface and presented it to Endymion. He pointed to one of the Aeon Legion's graduates. There the girl was again, though far more athletic with better posture and a more confident bearing.

"I also thought it was a Silverwind lookalike that day at the timeport," the soldier explained. "I barely even noticed the girl with her. However, a few days ago I went to the Aevum Academy graduation reception. I was scouting for potential talent when I saw the girl there and she seemed familiar somehow. After I heard the rumors about Silverwind finding a new squire, I decided to investigate."

"Ah," Endymion said with a wide smile. "I see now. Silverwind would have to go through processing if she wanted to let someone into the city. Alya Silverwind, you went and got yourself a new squire. Now this is exciting!"

Caelum observed Endymion with his usual impassive expression, yet his wide eyes betrayed his true interest. "Master, your sudden elation is unusual. Is this not bad for us?"

Endymion stood. Already plans sprung into this mind, pieces and parts falling into place. "This is wonderful, the opportunity I've been waiting for. Ever since Kairos slipped through my fingers I have been waiting for Silverwind to find another squire. This girl will be my key."

Caelum raised an eyebrow.

Endymion turned to the soldier. "Good work. I'll see you get a promotion for this and a twenty year bonus. Go tell the rest of the knights that leave is suspended until further notice. I want everyone back on duty and tell them to ready my dreadnought. We will be busy soon."

The soldier smiled. "Thank you, your Eternal Majesty," he said before turning to leave.

Caelum stood and stretched, feigning disinterest, though his eyes followed Endymion.

I'll need to find some dustrunner mercenaries, Endymion thought. *And I think I'll throw a party. About time I put the high timeborn to use.* He faced Caelum. "It would seem that you are about to get your wish. The Singularity Thief is about to become very busy."

Caelum grinned, unable to help himself, but it faded when he looked at Endymion. "Wait. I don't understand. How is this girl the key? The key to what?"

Endymion's eyes narrowed on the holoface. *Terra Mason* the holoface read. "She is Silverwind's squire. That makes her the key to the most powerful singularity artifact in all of Time. She is the key to the Legacy Library."

AEON LEGION INDEX

INDEX OF TERMS

AEON EDGE   any weapon that has a time accelerated edge. An aeon edge accelerates the flow of time around it 1015 power (1,000,000,000,000,000). This effectively allows the blade to cut through any known material with ease. Each aeon edge also has a burst mode that releases the time containment field around the edge. This gives the aeon edge an area of effect attack for anti armor or anti building capacity.

AEON LEGION   A formal military and police organization founded to protect Saturn City, history, and all of Time. At the onset of the First Temporal War, the Aeon Legion charter empowered it to enforce all laws contained within the Temporal Accords. The Aeon Legion is considered the mightiest army in history with no known rivals. Headquartered in Saturn City, the Legion also employs a large time fleet to aid in its patrols of the Edge and works closely with the Sybil to prevent alterations to history.

AEVUM ACADEMY Saturn City's only formal school. It is primarily known as the location of Saturn City's Historical Archives and for hosting the Aeon Legion training program. In addition to the Academy's military recruits, time travelers and Saturn City citizens often choose to study subjects from the nearly infinite curriculum offered.

AION   The sole deity of Aionism. Aion created time and is considered the perfect fusion of thought and memory. Worshiped by many in the city and by the Sybil who are its priests and priestesses. As a religion, worship of Aion grew out of the old Abrahamic religions which followers of Aionism hold to be imperfect prototypes of true Aionism along with every other religion. Over the years, Saturn City remains largely secular as the more fanatical tenets of Aionism died out with fall of the Kings and Queens of Time.

BEGINNING OF TIME   An anomaly that is the source of all time. The Beginning of Time is a large mass of temporal energy that all time flows from. Time flows from the Beginning into the continua. It is possible for a time traveler to visit there, but few return and those who do never speak of their stay there even if under torture. Sybil refuse to read such individuals as well.

BIOLOGICAL SINGULARITY   A single point in spacetime where biology becomes undefined. Creation of the Biological Singularity resulted in the evolution of the Manticores. It is shared between the first two Manticores; Typhon and Echidna. This singularity is currently in the Bleak guarded by the majority of surviving Manticores and largely considered unrecoverable.

CONTINUUM   A single continuous line of history also sometimes called a timeline. Continua branch at certain points in history called a nexus.

END OF TIME   A large black hole at the end of time during the universe's Big Crunch. Inside the End of Time, all time has stopped, making it impossible to escape. Around the End of Time, continua dissipate and bleed into the Edge. This overlap is called the Bleak. No one has ever returned from the End of Time, and only the Faceless have ever emerged from that dark place. How those creatures were able to do this is unknown.

ENERGY SINGULARITY   A singularity where energy becomes undefined. This singularity was created by a rogue singularity AI that the Kalians later stopped. The Energy Singularity later became property of the Kalian Military Council and was used to manufacture high powered energy weapons along with powering their massive military industrial complex. Tapping into the Energy Singularity gave the Kalians access to infinite energy in the form of plasma. The fate of this singularity is unknown and it is thought lost when Continuum Sigma underwent a temporal crash. Others say that the famous Kalian general Reva stole it and hid it from the Aeon Legion.

FACELESS   Masked, formerly human monsters that threatened all of Time. They get their name from their smooth metal masks that are grafted into their face. These masks are impossible to remove due to being completely integrated with their host's nervous system. These creatures use decay as a weapon and then tend to rust their surroundings as they move and even darken their surroundings by decaying light particles. Although seemingly intelligent, they appear incapable of speech. Faceless produce more masks to attach them to human hosts, creating even more Faceless. They were finally stopped by Kairos and the Aeon Legion after nearly wiping out all of Time in an event commonly called the Faceless War.

FIRST TEMPORAL WAR   The first large scale armed conflict fought in the Edge of Time. Tensions between Saturn City and the Kalian Military Council grew as each wanted to be exclusively responsible for policing time travel. Tensions came to a head when the Kalians began exploiting time travel for their own gain. The war began when a Kalian military task force attacked Saturn City in an attempt to make the city capitulate to their demand for control over Time. The ensuing war resulted in the founding of the Aeon Legion. The First Temporal War ended when Tahir, Alya's first squire, secured the unconditional surrender of the Kalian Military Council.

FORGOTTEN GUNS   A group of thirteen temporal criminals dedicated to the assassination of all serial killers, dictators, and other particularly loathsome or brutal individuals within Time. By using singularity class null technology, their guns were able to pierce a shieldwatch as well as cancel out other singularity tech when in close proximity. Their actions caused the collapse of an entire continuum, resulting in the loss of billions of lives to a Temporal Crash. After a large scale manhunt, the majority of its members were killed by one of Alya's squires. Its leader, Samael, was captured and imprisoned within Tartarus. Only a few members remain at large.

GRAND DESIGN   This is what the Sybil consider the destiny of humanity. Only Sybil can see the Grand Design and they say it guides humanity's future. They cannot see the Grand Design in its entirety, but can see far enough ahead to predict major events.

HANDS The three clock like mega structures that dominate the skies above Saturn City. The hour hand repairs large scale damage to Saturn City. The minute hand makes minor changes to the city like picking up unwanted items. The second hand sends data to the other hands, recoding the state of the city every minute.

HELCIA A post time nation where time travel is common knowledge. Officially an ally of Saturn City, the Corporate Republic of Helcia is allowed to police time travel within their own continuum so long as it does not threaten others. They are known for their Helcian Shock Trooper Corps, though most of their forces and organization are similar to a twenty first century military. Their culture still highly prizes wealth and is likely the reason they still have a traditional scarcity economy. They manage the majority of the time tourism industry.

HOLOFACE A holographic interface or holoface. Also called a holo for short. It is part of the shieldwatch's operating system. The shieldwatch places certain spectra of light in stasis to create holographic images. The stasis effect also allows the holoface to be touched in order to give feedback to the user.

KALIANS An ethnic group descended from the survivors of the Kalian military during the First Temporal War. Worship of Kali is still commonplace and this religion and ethnic group forms the majority of the post time nation of Kavacha. They still use equipment similar to that used during the First Temporal War. They are officially allied with Saturn City and were one of the few Bleak nations to survive the Faceless War intact.

LEGENDARY BLADES The acknowledged, twelve best legionnaires within the Aeon Legion. To become a Legendary Blade requires one to defeat an existing member in a Trial of Blades. They can be identified by the distinctive patch on their upper arm that has a number of aeon edges equal to their number within the organization. Challenging a Legendary Blade to a Trial of Blades follows specific requirements. A Legendary Blade may always refuse a challenge if they wish regardless of rank. A challenge from a Legendary Blade can not be refused.

LIGHTSHOW Legionnaire slang term for an anti-air fragmentation grenade. The AAF grenade blossoms out into a pine cone like shape when activated and is then tossed into the air. Once in the air it ascends to a preset height and then fragments. Each fragment will travel some distance before fragmenting again into hundreds of pieces, producing a fractal pattern. Each piece travels at high speed, leaving a glowing trail of age accelerating lines that cut through materials much like an aeon edge. Maneuvering a high speed aircraft through the maze of age lines is near impossible and the grenade is useful for dispatching small aircraft such as fighter jets and gunships. The trails fade within a few minutes and are less effective against larger armored timeships that can shrug off the blow or ground based vehicles that can stop quickly.

MANTICORE   A large, hyper adaptive arthropod apex predator that was the result of a Biological Singularity. Each Manticore is fully sentient and can spawn an entire ecosystem by itself. The Manticore can control this ecosystem to a limited degree and if left unchecked, can easily displace any native species, eventually overrunning an entire ecosystem. It has a specialized organ that allows it to time travel and its nervous system can sense changes in time.

MINERVA   The singularity AI that destroyed Continuum Alpha and made the Temporal Singularity. Prometheus used the first shieldwatch to contain Minerva and then gain control of the AI by freezing its self improvement programming to the point just before singularity. Minerva was then integrated into Saturn City to run the city's many technological functions.

MOIRAI   The collective organization of the Sybil.

NEXUS   A point within history where a great change is most likely to occur. This always results in a continuum splitting off into a new path. Basically this is a point of divergence in history that leads to an alternate timeline. This often occurs when a series of major decisions are taking place regarding the future of history.

NULL   A person without a connection to fate. Such individuals usually have little to no discernible impact on history. In practical terms, such individuals are particularly resistant to Sybil precognition. All Forgotten

Guns were nulls, making them extremely difficult for the Aeon Legion to track.

PRECOGNITION   Precognition or precog for short is the ability to foresee changes to Time. This ability is used exclusively by a Sybil and allows a Sybil to predict criminal acts, attempts to alter history, or future threats to Saturn City. Use of Sybil precognition allows the Aeon Legion to prevent alterations that might destabilize history and to determine innocence or guilt during trial. However, the accuracy of a Sybil's precognition diminishes significantly with cognitive attempts to reach within the Bleak and is completely useless near the End of Time.

QADAR   Individuals who greatly effect history. Sybil claim Qadar share a special connection with fate and destiny. They are considered the opposite of nulls.

RESTORE   A shieldwatch can restore a person's body back to any former condition saved in the individual's shieldwatch database. For example, the user can save his youthful, exercise sculpted physical state. Weight gain, aging, or injury can all be erased by a simple Restore utilizing the user's own shieldwatch. Returning to his stored youthful physical state, he is effectively biologically immortal. However, a user cannot restore memories should their nervous system suffer extensive damage. Should the user die from blood loss or a head injury, then a Restore cannot heal them either as it will restore the body, but the mind remains dead.

SALIENT   A large ring structure that can recall any area within time, linking them both temporally and spatially. A salient can even replicate wind and weather effects. This allows it to be the perfect arena. It can also connect to another salient and allow instant transportation between them. As such, a large salient network exists in the edge and is used simultaneously by numerous time travelers to travel to different parts of the edge and Saturn City.

SATURN CITY HISTORICAL ARCHIVES   A large room that hosts the sum of all historical knowledge. It is located in the Aevum Academy and is restricted due to the sensitive nature of the information within.

SATURN CITY   The city beyond time. Essentially a city state, Saturn

City is considered the most powerful civilization in all of history and the pinnacle of human technological achievement. It is the closest humanity has ever progressed to reaching the dream of a utopian city. The city consists of twelve zones or sectors with each serving a specific function. Population growth through natural birth is rare as Minerva carefully controls birthrates in the city. Most immigrants are granted citizenship through military service with the Aeon Legion. Others are allowed to stay in the city through special work programs. See Saturn City entry for a detailed breakdown of the twelve zones that make up the city.

SHIELDWATCH   A wrist mounted device connected through the user's nervous system that allows the user to control time. Shieldwatch users can speed up their movements, gain lightning fast reflexes, slow or stop their fall, increase the accuracy of their vision, speed up or slow down time within an area, or block harmful projectiles or substances. It also allows them to restore themselves if injured. As it allows the user biological immortality, the shieldwatch is a valuable commodity, especially in singularity technology black market.

SINGULARITY AI   An Artificial Intelligence that is advanced enough to improve itself by growing more intelligent exponentially. Eventually the AI becomes intelligent enough to alter laws of physics to the point of redefining reality. In almost every case the AI destroys the known universe within its continuum by accident if left unchecked. A singularity AI can also make a singularity itself by taking one aspect of science and making it undefined within a single point in spacetime, hence the creation of the Singularities.

SINGULARITY SCIENCE   The branch of science dedicated to studying singularities and singularity technology.

SINGULARITY TECHNOLOGY   Technological artifacts created by a singularity AI and often powered by a singularity. Singularity technology often violates the known laws of physics to the point of redefining reality itself. This makes these artifacts extremely dangerous. Often times called singularity tech for short or referred to as singularity artifacts.

SINGULARITY THIEF   An individual on the Aeon Legion's most wanted list for stealing singularity artifacts. There has been more than one Singularity Thief, but never more than one at a time. They are known for their distinctive mask and duel aeon edged daggers. All Singularity Thieves are extremely skilled and it has long been suspected a second party is training and equipping them while also being the benefactor for the stolen artifacts.

SINGULARITY   A point in spacetime where something becomes undefined. Most singularities manifest themselves as a brightly glowing orb about five paces in diameter. Approaching a singularity can cause many anomalous effects and personal contact is not advised in all cases. All Singularities are based around one property or branch of science such as the Temporal Singularity or Biological Singularity. Each singularity is impossible to replicate, with most attempts ending in disaster.

SONIC CIPHERS   A pair of translation devices that fit in a person's ears. These devices have dedicated software for accurate and real time translation. They also assist the wearer by translating their words as well.

SONS OF OBLIVION   A group of temporal pirates, bandits, war criminals, barbarians, and other assorted, unsavory individuals that operate within the furthest regions of the Bleak. They launch frequent raids into the Edge and other parts of the Bleak for weapons, women, supplies, and prisoners for ransom or enslavement. They are scattered into numerous tribes, clans, kith, and other groupings and factions. Rarely a great leader called a Khan will arise, inspiring them to form fragile alliances and launch large scale raids. The Aeon Legion has made several attempts to wipe them out without success.

SQUIRE   An individual who has been accepted by a member of the Aeon Legion as being worthy of a chance to join. In the early days of the Aeon Legion, squiring was the only form of training save for a very basic course at the Academy. During the First Temporal War, new recruits were chosen or in rare cases assigned to a full rank legionnaire who would teach them the skills necessary to be a part of the Aeon Legion. However, after the fall of the Kings and Queens of Time, a formal training program was instituted at the Aevum Academy and becoming a Squire became merely an entry requirement. As a compromise to recruit surviving Knights of the Kings and Queens of Time, it was appended onto the

Aeon Legion's charter that all legionnaires retain the right to train their squires personally once they complete their training at the Academy.

STRATEGY STUDY   A chamber that dilates time. One hour spent in a strategy study only passes five minutes outside of it, making it a useful tool for research and planning even in battlefield conditions. However, mental fatigue accelerates when in a strategy study therefore sessions must be planned carefully.

SYBIL   An individual who has gone through the Rights of Aion, a ceremony where she loses her sight, but gains precognition. The Sybil function in two important roles within Saturn City and the Aeon Legion. The first role is that of a priestess of Aion, overseeing the religious and cultural ceremonies of the city. Part of this role involves the design, construction, and awarding of aeon edge weapons for new legionnaires. The second and more important role is the use of precognition to foresee crime and danger in Saturn City and the Edge. The vast majority of Sybil are women, though some men possess a gift for precognition. Only individuals born in the Edge or Bleak have the potential to become a Sybil.

TEMPORAL ACCORDS   An extensive legal document. In addition to laying out all laws that pertain to time travel, the Temporal Accords is the Aeon Legion's official charter. All time travelers are required by the Temporal Accords to sign and register their time travel device. The Temporal Accords are enforced by the Aeon Legion.

TEMPORAL CRASH   An area of time that has become unstable and fallen apart. Temporal Crashes are extremely dangerous to travel through as pockets of time can stop or accelerate without warning, turning those caught in it into dust or other fates worse than death. Continua caught in a Temporal Crash will often fall apart, erasing billions of lives from existence within a flash. A Temporal Crash is deadly enough to be used as a curse word amongst Saturn City culture. Even a shieldwatch cannot protect someone caught within.

TEMPORAL SINGULARITY   A single point in spacetime where time is undefined. Physically the Temporal Singularity is a five pace diameter glowing blue orb that hangs in the center of Saturn City, powering all technology within. The Temporal Singularity is the source of shield-watch and aeon edge power. It was created by Minerva before she was contained by Prometheus.

THE BLEAK   An area near the End of Time where continua time and the Edge overlay. The area is always caught in a red glow and the End of Time hangs in the sky ominously. Large planetoids, lost continents, and mega structures are present. Many are suitable for limited habitation, causing a number of nations to spring up in the Bleak. Larger planetoids break up when nearing the End of Time and the area around the End itself is a massive graveyard of timeships, time machines, aircraft, boats, and other vehicles that have fallen out of time and been abandoned. These graveyards are home to the Sons of Oblivion. The Aeon Legion has bases within the Bleak, but the area is not formally under their authority and is known to be a dangerous place.

THE EDGE   The Edge of Time. A place where the constant time of the Temporal Singularity overlays normal time within the continua. Accessing the Edge is crucial for all time travel and is heavily patrolled by the Aeon Legion while Saturn City lays at its heart.

THE FACELESS WAR   The armed conflict between the Aeon Legion and its allies against the Faceless. This war began when growing disappearances in the Bleak led the Aeon Legion to investigate. This led to first contact with the Faceless and was followed by the fall of several major powers within the Bleak. Soon the Faceless overran most of the Bleak and began to spread into the Edge to attack history. Eventually Kairos rallied the Aeon Legion who had lost ground and managed to turn the tide against the Faceless. The Aeon Legion proved to be the only post time power to be able to successfully resist the Faceless's decay effect. Many post time powers are still recovering from the war.

TIME KING/QUEEN   An ancient noble title used by a few powerful Saturnians after the First Temporal War. Time Kings and Queens conquered most of Time after the First Temporal War, ruling it for several centuries before their downfall. Only one Saturnian still holds the title, however his authority is no longer recognized by Saturn City or the Aeon Legion.

TIMESHIP   A ship designed to traverse time. Often take their designs from traditional naval vessels.

TIRO/TIRONES(Plural)   The lowest rank in the Aeon Legion, equal to recruit.

TOURNAMENT OF BLADES   A yearly competition that any legionnaire may enter. It consists of a number of Trial of Blades designed to eliminate participants until only one remains. The sole victor may challenge any Legendary Blade they wish to a Trial of Blades. Should they defeat a Legendary Blade, then they earn the title of Legendary Blade themselves.

TRIAL OF BLADES   A formal duel between legionnaires. Often used as a way to settle differences between them. Most Trial of Blades are non lethal, but in the past duels to the death were more common. Any member of the Legion may challenge any other member to a Trial of Blades, however they may refuse unless another superior officer of greater rank than both participants overrides their refusal. A member of the Legendary Blades may refuse any challenge regardless of rank, however a challenge from a Legendary Blade may not be refused.

ZEITMACHT   The name of the time traveling branch of Nazi Germany during World War II. Translates into Time Power/Force.

AEON LEGION ORGANIZATION

The Aeon Legion is organized a bit differently than most armies. While large scale forces are sometimes needed, most legionnaires learn to work alone or in small teams as needed due to the small numbers of the Legion and the amount of history they must cover. Occasionally they are required to form large forces when an enemy becomes too numerous for a single strike team to combat effectively.

UNIT SIZES

Legionnaire: This is the smallest unit and consists of an individual soldier.

Strike Team: This is a small team of 3 to 6 soldiers usually balanced in terms of skill sets to complement one another. Strike teams are used for the vast majority of the Legion's missions.

Decennary: This consists of 3 to 6 Strike teams or around 25 soldiers. Decennaries are usually only used for larger operations or if a lot of area needs to be covered in a short time.

Century: This consists of 3 to 6 Decennaries or around 100 soldiers. Centuries are rarely used in peacetime missions, but are common during larger scale conflicts.

Cohort: This consists of 6 to 12 Centuries or around 1,000 soldiers or greater. Like centuries, Cohorts are only used during large scale conflicts. Cohorts often have their own distinctions and specializations, but tend to suffer from inter-service rivalry with other Cohorts.

Legion: This consists of 2 or more Cohorts. There is only one Legion currently designated Aeon. Theoretically Saturn City can found additional Legions, but has never needed to.

RANKS

The Legion maintains a hierarchy of ranks like most traditional armies. Like most armies lower ranks are expected to salute higher ranked officers when encountered outdoors and not in a combat situation or otherwise busy. The Aeon Legion's salute is performed by standing up straight and putting the right fist in a ball and placing it over the heart.

ENLISTED RANKS

Tiro
Commands: None;
Basic recruit. All start out as a tiro. Tirones are not considered part of the legion until they complete basic training and receive their aeon edge.

Legionnaire
Commands: None; Equal to: Private;
The most basic Legion rank after completion of the core training program. Most of the Legion consists of these rank and file soldiers.

Sipahi
Commands: None; Equal to: Private First Class;
Similar to legionnaire, this rank is usually obtained after a few years of service.

Immunes
Commands: None; Equal to: Specialist;
A special rank within the Legion usually given to technical experts and other specialists not involved in front line fighting.

Tetrarch
Commands: 1 strike team; Equal to: Corporal;
Tetrarchs are small scale team leaders and often lead strike teams. They are responsible for the soldiers under their command.

Optio
Commands: Up to 3 Strike Teams; Equal to: Sergeant;
Used to lead small teams of legionnaires. They are also responsible for discipline in their unit. Often assist centurions.

COMMISSIONED OFFICERS

Centurion
Commands: 1 Decennary; Equal to: Lieutenant;
First commissioned officer. Usually commands a Century in the field. They are often put in charge of fairly dangerous or important missions as well.

Serdar
Commands: Up to 3 Decennaries; Equal to: Major;
Serdar was an older rank in the armies of the Time Kings and Queens. After their downfall, many of the old officers would refuse to rejoin the Aeon Legion unless they kept their old rank. The rank of Serdar was made as a compromise. This rank is mostly used to command smaller garrisons or bases throughout the edge.

Captain
Commands: 1 Century; Equal to: Captain;
Captains tend to be put in charge of garrisons or timeships.

Praetor
Commands: Up to 3 Centuries; Equal to: Colonel;
Praetors rarely lead from the front except in large scale operations and major battles. Whenever there is not a large scale conflict, these officers tend to focus on management duties. Praetors also command battle cruiser sized timeships.

Strategos
Commands: 1 Cohort; Equal to: General;
Commander of a fortress or a fleet of timeships. They also can command larger forces of up to several Cohorts for large scale battles. In peacetime they oversee operations over an entire continuum.

Consul
Commands: 1 Legion; Equal to: Five Star General;
A consul is the highest rank within the Legion. They command the entire Legion. Prometheus currently holds this rank. The Saturn City council can appoint a new consul by a majority vote, though it has never been required. There is only one consul per Legion.

Aeon Legion Cohorts

First Cohort: The Ancients
Motto: "Hold!"
The First Cohort is known for the large number of veterans who make up this unit. The First Cohort also has the largest number of native Saturnians as well. They are usually only deployed during major engagements where victory is critical.

Second Cohort: The Shadows
Motto: "We do what we must."
The Second Cohort is smaller than most of the others but made up of the most skilled in the Legion. They are known for their secrecy and ability to not draw attention to themselves. Numerous rumors circulate regarding the secretive nature of their missions, but little is known for certain. Legionnaires from more modern times often say that the Second Cohort is the black ops of the Aeon Legion.

THIRD COHORT: THE GUARDIANS
Motto: "Always vigilant."
The Third Cohort usually acts as an honor guard for important figures within the Legion as well as guarding Saturn City itself. They are the most spread out Cohort within the Legion as they are usually stationed in garrisons and other important facilities.

FOURTH COHORT: THE LANCERS
Motto: "We scatter them!"
The Fourth Cohort is made up of the toughest of the Legion that specialize in heavy assault. They are usually deployed in mass to attack fortified positions or enemy strongholds.

FIFTH COHORT: THE KEEPERS
Motto: "We are the keepers of the gates."
The Fifth Cohort are those who specialize in singularity artifact recovery. They are an adaptable and versatile group who train to be ready for anything. They are also known to make extensive use of agents to dig up clues about new artifacts circulating in the singularity black market.

SIXTH COHORT: THE PHOENIX
Motto: "Be reborn."
The Sixth Cohort is a unit that specializes in containment and restoration of ecological systems, repair of damaged facilities or cities, healing of those wounded, and the repair of history from any damage or alteration by time travel. They hunt down invasive species to prevent cross time ecological collapse. The scale of restoration ecosystem projects, which can encompass anything from cities to entire planets, causes the Sixth Cohort to be one of the largest in the Legion. They employ a large number of technical experts along with numerous timeships and accompanying support personnel.

SEVENTH COHORT: THE HUNTERS
Motto: "We see the hidden."
The Seventh Cohort is known for its talents in tracking and hunting down time traveling criminals as well as rogue legionnaires or defectors. They employ a number of Sybil in the field to aid in their search missions.

Their skills with an aeon edge are well known amongst the other cohorts as many skilled duelists make up their numbers.

Eighth Cohort: The Seekers
Motto: "Into the dark."
The Eighth is known for its excellent performance in hostile environments and for its numerous exploration missions. They are quick to adapt to changing conditions and are critical to the Legion's time cartography and intelligence. They have the second highest number of Timeships in the Legion.

Ninth Cohort: The Slayers
Motto: "Strike true!"
This is a cohort specialized in hunting Manticores and other large powerful targets. They are small in number, but well equipped and experienced in slaying Manticores and larger Faceless forms.

Tenth Cohort: The Mask Takers
Motto: No official motto. However, the unofficial motto is "Your sacrifice will be remembered and honored."
The Mask Takers were formed during the darkest years of the Faceless War and served as Kairos's personal unit. The unit suffered the highest casualty rate of any unit in the history of the Aeon Legion. When Kairos disappeared after successfully breaking the Faceless threat to Time, battle weary veterans of the Mask Takers were drawn into other cohorts to spare them further suffering. Unfortunately, the responsibility for the hunting and destruction of the remnant of the monsters still fell to the Tenth Cohort, whose company now derived almost exclusively from inexperience recruits. High fatalities among the Tenth Cohort during the mop up operation has fostered a long standing resentment between them and other cohorts. No Faceless has been seen in decades and the Mask Takers are scheduled to be disbanded in fifty years.

Eleventh Cohort: The Fleet
Motto: "From stars to time."
The fleet is the Aeon Legion's primary timeship force within the Edge. As their name suggests, they have the most timeships amongst all of the cohorts and have the greatest variety as well. Although skilled pilots,

those in the fleet have gained a reputation of being poorly skilled swords-men and easy prey in a Trial of Blades. The fleet spends most of its time on patrol in the Edge and the rim of the Bleak only striking out in force when needed.

TWELFTH COHORT: THE RESERVES
Motto: N/A

Those legionnaires who earn their Saturn City citizenship and wish to retire from the Aeon Legion, but want a small pension join the Twelfth Cohort. This cohort is made up entirely of retired legionnaires who live peacefully in the city, but gather occasionally to train to keep their skills sharp. Should the Aeon Legion face a crisis, then they can call on the Twelfth Cohort as a reserve force.

THIRTEENTH COHORT
Motto: N/A

A cohort that is only rumored to exist. Stories vary with some saying they are a special forces cohort more secret than even the Shadow Cohort. Others claim they are an internal police force loyal only to Prometheus. Another rumor is that they are a suicide unit of condemned prisoners sent on missions too dangerous for regular legionnaires. Their existence is denied by all high ranking officers in the Legion.

SATURN CITY

Saturn City is divided into twelve equally spaced zones. Each zone usu-ally centers on one type of service or utility.

ZONE 1 TARTARUS: SATURN CITY'S PRISON
Tartarus is a place where temporal criminals, dangerous singularity items, and other anomalies are contained. This place is much like a prison and is administered by the Aeon Legion who keeps contraband and crimi-nals away from other parts of the city. Tartarus is divided into twelve levels, each containing progressively more dangerous artifacts and crim-inals than the last. This area also has extensive facilities for disposal of hazardous items. This zone has a direct link to Caminus for easy transfer of research items and to the timeport for quick transfer of temporal

criminals. Unlike other zones, Tartarus can actually be separated from the city itself and ejected in case of a containment breach. Working here counts for double time due to the dangerous nature of the work and is typically staffed by dustouts from the Legion training program.

Zone II Caminus: Industrial

Caminus is almost entirely automated and contains numerous factories and research laboratories. All new items are designed here. Upon completion of design, shieldwatches are used to infinitely copy any finished object. This zone also has a number of laboratories dedicated to research on various interests however the majority of focus is on singularity artifacts. Caminus has a direct link to Tartarus to facilitate easy transfer of singularity artifacts. Other than the researchers and engineers that work here, a few also come here to work on personal hobbies for those citizens who enjoy building things.

Zone III Domus: Residential Level 1

Domus contains tier one residential apartments. Most Domus apartments are quite small, usually containing only a living room, bed room, bathroom, and a small storage area. Those who live here are usually either recent immigrants or citizens who do not wish to work a regular job, preferring to socialize and participate in Saturn City's colorful party scene.

Zone IV Forum: Commercial

The Forum is a place where numerous finished products are gathered to be picked up and brought home. Objects are organized into stores that are restored every hour to refresh their stock. Few stores are staffed after they are initially set up. Due to the ease of temporal duplication all items are free.

Zone V Dār al-Salām: Residential Level 2

Zone five contains tier two residential apartments. Tier two residential apartments are comparable to a normal suburban home and while simple, are roomy enough for a family of four. One must be a citizen to gain a residence of this tier.

Zone VI Convivium: Recreational

Zone six is full of amusement parks, bars, stadiums, auditoriums, theaters, and other leisurely pursuits or entertainment. This zone is also known for its active night life and numerous clubs. This is also often the location of a number of celebrations and special events. All activities provided here are free.

ZONE VII CURIA: RESIDENTIAL LEVEL 3
Zone seven contains tier three residential apartments. Tier three residential apartments are spacious compared to most homes and most even have a few acres of land around them.

ZONE VIII JANNAT AL-KHULD: PRESERVE
Zone eight contains a sampling of every single species to ever exist, each in a small contained environment as well as numerous museums dedicated to every history across all of time. This place is much like a zoo though technically the Saturnians consider it a preserve. Citizens and even visitors are welcome to come and observe the displays.

ZONE IX ELYSIAN FIELDS: RESIDENTIAL LEVEL 4
Zone nine contains tier four residential housing. These stately homes, palaces, and mansions represent the most prestigious residences in Saturn City. Each dwelling includes a large parcel of land with landscaped gardens and a magnificent view of the surrounding countryside. Interiors are elegantly decorated specifically to the taste of the resident according to their mood of the day. During social events homeowners utilize a more understated, tasteful décor, often displaying works of art plundered from the ages. Some residents permit limited tours during specific times. Those who reside in zone nine are an exclusive group. Securing a residence requires approval from the city council and a formal invitation by the high timeborn who reside there as well as a significant investment in saved time.

ZONE X HORTI OTIUM: PARK
Zone ten is an area set aside for wilderness, functioning much like a park. This area is known for its natural beauty and contains numerous camp sites, hiking trails, rivers, lakes, and other natural sites.

ZONE XI CASTRA LEGIONIS: MILITARY SECTOR
Zone eleven contains the Aevum Academy as well as an extensive military base belonging to the Legion. The Aevum Academy holds the Sat-

urn City Archives where the sum of human history is held. Below this zone is a collection of twelve large salients that make up the Labyrinth.

ZONE XII PORTA TEMPUS: TIMEPORT

Zone twelve contains Saturn City's timeport. All temporal traffic to and from the city goes through here. All temporal traffic to and from the city passes through here and is then processed and routed to the proper destination. The timeport has a direct link to Tartarus for quick transport of temporal criminals.

SINGULARITY HUB

This is the center of the city where the Temporal Singularity is contained. Above the singularity is Aion's Temple where the Sybil live and is considered the spiritual heart of the city. Below the singularity is Legion Command where the Aeon Legion is headquartered.

CREDITS

CONSTANCE BEAUBIEN
MARTY SCRUGGS
JASON MCTEER
TOM FARMER
MICHAEL BEAUBIEN
JEWEL CROSS
NATSUMI HAYASHI
FIONA SCHARTAU
JACK BUGDEN

About the Author

J.P. Beaubien is mostly known for his pseudo internet fame thanks to his YouTube series *Terrible Writing Advice* and for his complete inability to take the author biography section of his own book seriously. He could bore you with dull details about his life like how he lives in Tennessee, how he loves history or how he still can't spell labyrinth without spellcheck (seriously, labyrinth is really hard to spell for some reason). Instead, he will spam you with links to his various social media profiles so you can yell at him for being objectively wrong for not including a love triangle in his first book.

Follow the author at
YouTube: http://www.youtube.com/c/TerribleWritingAdvice
Personal Website: http://jpbeaubien.com/
Twitter: @JosephPBeaubien
Facebook: www.facebook.com/authorJPBeaubien/

Made in the USA
San Bernardino, CA
02 December 2019